**A Breathtaking Saga of Pageantry and
Strife. A Quest for Spirit, Passion and
Enlightenment. A Samurai Who Had the
Power to Change His Land!**

Tokugawa Hidetada: When he inherited the office
of Shōgun from his father, he began building a
new city—while the western lords prepared for
war and a band of traitors plotted against his
life . . .

Otsū: The fires of suffering and love had made
her pure. When she meets Musashi once again,
he tells her, "Laugh for me, Otsū. A samurai's
wife must not weep . . ."

Gudō: The strange Zen priest had helped Musashi before. But when Musashi begs him for one
word of guidance, the priest draws a circle in the
dirt—and points the way to wisdom . . .

Sasaki Kojirō: Somehow, the dignity of his sword
had changed his brash and arrogant personality—but his bitterness toward Musashi could
only be washed away in blood . . .

Miyamoto Musashi: While his opponent waits for
their great bout, he paints a heron beneath a
willow tree. Is he a cowardly artist or a master
swordsman? A brutal killer or a man of enlightenment? Now Musashi will meet Kojirō's challenge to fight by the sea—and the whole world
will know his name!

Books in the Musashi Saga by Eiji Yoshikawa

Published by POCKET BOOKS

MUSASHI

BOOK V:
THE
WAY OF LIFE
AND
DEATH

EIJI YOSHIKAWA

Translated from the Japanese by Charles S. Terry
Foreword by Edwin O. Reischauer

POCKET BOOKS

New York   London   Toronto   Sydney   Tokyo

Map design by Ray Lundgren Graphics, Ltd.
Map research by Jim Moser

POCKET BOOKS, a division of Simon & Schuster Inc.
1230 Avenue of the Americas, New York, NY 10020

Published by arrangement with Kodansha International
Library of Congress Catalog Card Number: 80-8791

ISBN: 0-671-67723-3

First Pocket Books printing September 1989

10 9 8 7 6 5 4 3 2 1

POCKET and colophon are trademarks of
Simon & Schuster Inc.

Printed in the U.S.A.

CONTENTS

Contents

PLOT SUMMARY
Book I: *The Way of the Samurai*

Wounded in the great battle of Sekigahara, Takezō (later Musashi) and Matahachi were taken in by a beautiful girl, Akemi, and her lascivious mother, Okō. After a violent confrontation with local bandits, in which he slew the leader, Takezō left his friend with the two women and traveled back to his home province of Mimasaka. There, he was accused of having murdered Matahachi. A wild and undisciplined youth, Takezō was hunted by his own townspeople, and reacted with bitter rage—until the Buddhist town monk, Takuan Sōhō, was able to capture him without a single blow. Takuan tied Takezō up in the branches of a tall tree, but Matahachi's beloved, Otsū, took pity on him and freed him. Begging him to run away with her, she forsook Matahachi forever, but the eccentric Takuan had an even greater power over Takezō—and led him to Himeji Castle. There, by the light of a single lamp in a windowless room, Takezō began to study Suntzu's *The Art of War*, the Books of Zen, and the history of Japan. Weeks stretched into months, and gradually Takezō was transformed. When the day came for him to leave, he took the name Miyamoto Musashi, and set off for Kyoto—and his first tests as a man of the sword . . .

PLOT SUMMARY
Book IV: *The Bushido Code*

After his stunning victory over the House of Yoshioka, Musashi travels east and takes up farming with a young orphan boy named Iori. While Musashi struggles to gain a new understanding of life, his chief rival, Kojirō, is creating a stir in the new capital city of Edo (modern-day Tokyo), challenging the established warriors and spreading a trail of blood and self-aggrandizement through the city. Edo is a swirl of power struggles and politics, and Kojirō quickly becomes popular. Musashi has no interest in that kind of life, but when he single-handedly defeats a band of highwaymen he receives an invitation to visit a royal house in the city. There he is reunited with Takuan, the Yagyūs and Osugi, who has stepped up her campaign to smear his name. Meanwhile, Jōtarō has fallen in with a band of criminals, and Otsū has come to live in the house of Yagyū Hyōgo, a grandson of the famous sword-master, Sekishūsai. As Musashi and Kojirō are slowly drawn toward their fated duel, Musashi is reaching a turning point in his life: He must choose between following his own difficult path toward enlightenment, or take up the role of a samurai for hire.

FOREWORD[1]
by Edwin O. Reischauer[2]

Musashi might well be called the *Gone with the Wind* of
Japan. Written by Eiji Yoshikawa (1892–1962), one of
Japan's most prolific and best-loved popular writers, it is
a long historical novel, which first appeared in serialized
form between 1935 and 1939 in the *Asahi Shimbun,*
Japan's largest and most prestigious newspaper. It has
been published in book form no less than fourteen times,
most recently in four volumes of the 53-volume complete
works of Yoshikawa issued by Kodansha. It has been
produced as a film some seven times, has been repeatedly
presented on the stage, and has often been made into
television mini-series on at least three nationwide net-
works.

Miyamoto Musashi was an actual historical person,
but through Yoshikawa's novel he and the other main
characters of the book have become part of Japan's living
folklore. They are so familiar to the public that people
will frequently be compared to them as personalities
everyone knows. This gives the novel an added interest

---

[1]This Foreword has been taken in its entirety from the original
single-volume American hardcover edition of *Musashi: An Epic
Novel of the Samurai Era.*
[2]Edwin O. Reischauer was born in Japan in 1910. He has been a
professor at Harvard University since 1946, and is now Professor
Emeritus. He left the university temporarily to be the United States
Ambassador to Japan from 1961 to 1966, and is one of the best-
known authorities on the country. Among his numerous works are
Japan: The Story of a Nation and *The Japanese.*

to the foreign reader. It not only provides a romanticized slice of Japanese history, but gives a view of how the Japanese see their past and themselves. But basically the novel will be enjoyed as a dashing tale of swashbuckling adventure and a subdued story of love, Japanese style.

Comparisons with James Clavell's *Shōgun* seem inevitable, because for most Americans today *Shōgun,* as a book and a television mini-series, vies with samurai movies as their chief source of knowledge about Japan's past. The two novels concern the same period of history. *Shōgun,* which takes place in the year 1600, ends with Lord Toranaga, who is the historical Tokugawa Ieyasu, soon to be the Shōgun, or military dictator of Japan, setting off for the fateful battle of Sekigahara. Yoshikawa's story begins with the youthful Takezō, later to be renamed Miyamoto Musashi, lying wounded among the corpses of the defeated army on that battlefield.

With the exception of Blackthorne, the historical Will Adams, *Shōgun* deals largely with the great lords and ladies of Japan, who appear in thin disguise under names Clavell has devised for them. *Musashi,* while mentioning many great historical figures under their true names, tells about a broader range of Japanese and particularly about the rather extensive group who lived on the ill-defined borderline between the hereditary military aristocracy and the commoners—the peasants, tradesmen and artisans. Clavell freely distorts historical fact to fit his tale and inserts a Western-type love story that not only flagrantly flouts history but is quite unimaginable in the Japan of that time. Yoshikawa remains true to history or at least to historical tradition, and his love story, which runs as a background theme in minor scale throughout the book, is very authentically Japanese.

Yoshikawa, of course, has enriched his account with much imaginative detail. There are enough strange coincidences and deeds of derring-do to delight the heart of any lover of adventure stories. But he sticks faithfully to such facts of history as are known. Not only Musashi

himself but many of the other people who figure prominently in the story are real historical individuals. For
example, Takuan, who serves as a guiding light and
mentor to the youthful Musashi, was a famous Zen monk,
calligrapher, painter, poet and tea-master of the time,
who became the youngest abbot of the Daitokuji in Kyoto
in 1609 and later founded a major monastery in Edo, but
is best remembered today for having left his name to a
popular Japanese pickle.

The historical Miyamoto Musashi, who may have
been born in 1584 and died in 1645, was like his father a
master swordsman and became known for his use of two
swords. He was an ardent cultivator of self-discipline as
the key to martial skills and the author of a famous work
on swordsmanship, the *Gorin no sho*. He probably took
part as a youth in the battle of Sekigahara, and his clashes
with the Yoshioka school of swordsmanship in Kyoto,
the warrior monks of the Hōzōin in Nara and the famed
swordsman Sasaki Kojirō, all of which figure prominently
in this book, actually did take place. Yoshikawa's account
of him ends in 1612, when he was still a young man of
about 28, but subsequently he may have fought on the
losing side at the siege of Osaka castle in 1614 and
participated in 1637–38 in the annihilation of the Christian
peasantry of Shimabara in the western island of Kyushu,
an event which marked the extirpation of that religion
from Japan for the next two centuries and helped seal
Japan off from the rest of the world.

Ironically, Musashi in 1640 became a retainer of the
Hosokawa lords of Kumamoto, who, when they had been
the lords of Kumamoto, had been the patrons of his chief
rival, Sasaki Kojirō. The Hosokawas bring us back to
Shōgun, because it was the older Hosokawa, Tadaoki,
who figures quite unjustifiably as one of the main villains
of that novel, and it was Tadaoki's exemplary Christian
wife, Gracia, who is pictured without a shred of plausibil-
ity as Blackthorne's great love, Mariko.

The time of Musashi's life was a period of great

transition in Japan. After a century of incessant warfare among petty daimyō, or feudal lords, three successive leaders had finally reunified the country through conquest. Oda Nobunaga had started the process but, before completing it, had been killed by a treacherous vassal in 1582. His ablest general, Hideyoshi, risen from the rank of common foot soldier, completed the unification of the nation but died in 1598 before he could consolidate control in behalf of his infant heir. Hideyoshi's strongest vassal, Tokugawa Ieyasu, a great daimyō who ruled much of eastern Japan from his castle at Edo, the modern Tokyo, then won supremacy by defeating a coalition of western daimyō at Sekigahara in 1600. Three years later he took the traditional title of Shōgun, signifying his military dictatorship over the whole land, theoretically in behalf of the ancient but impotent imperial line in Kyoto. Ieyasu in 1605 transferred the position of Shōgun to his son, Hidetada, but remained in actual control himself until he had destroyed the supporters of Hideyoshi's heir in sieges of Osaka castle in 1614 and 1615.

The first three Tokugawa rulers established such firm control over Japan that their rule was to last more than two and a half centuries, until it finally collapsed in 1868 in the tumultuous aftermath of the reopening of Japan to contact with the West a decade and a half earlier. The Tokugawa ruled through semi-autonomous hereditary daimyō, who numbered around 265 at the end of the period, and the daimyō in turn controlled their fiefs through their hereditary samurai retainers. The transition from constant warfare to a closely regulated peace brought the drawing of sharp class lines between the samurai, who had the privilege of wearing two swords and bearing family names, and the commoners, who though including well-to-do merchants and land owners, were in theory denied all arms and the honor of using family names.

During the years of which Yoshikawa writes, however, these class divisions were not yet sharply defined.

All localities had their residue of peasant fighting men, and the country was overrun by rōnin, or masterless samurai, who were largely the remnants of the armies of the daimyō who had lost their domains as the result of the battle of Sekigahara or in earlier wars. It took a generation or two before society was fully sorted out into the strict class divisions of the Tokugawa system, and in the meantime there was considerable social ferment and mobility.

Another great transition in early seventeenth century Japan was in the nature of leadership. With peace restored and major warfare at an end, the dominant warrior class found that military prowess was less essential to successful rule than administrative talents. The samurai class started a slow transformation from being warriors of the gun and sword to being bureaucrats of the writing brush and paper. Disciplined self-control and education in a society at peace was becoming more important than skill in warfare. The Western reader may be surprised to see how widespread literacy already was at the beginning of the seventeenth century and at the constant references the Japanese made to Chinese history and literature, much as Northern Europeans of the same time continually referred to the traditions of ancient Greece and Rome.

A third major transition in the Japan of Musashi's time was in weaponry. In the second half of the sixteenth century matchlock muskets, recently introduced by the Portuguese, had become the decisive weapons of the battlefield, but in a land at peace the samurai could turn their backs on distasteful firearms and resume their traditional love affair with the sword. Schools of swordsmanship flourished. However, as the chance to use swords in actual combat diminished, martial skills were gradually becoming martial arts, and these increasingly came to emphasize the importance of inner self-control and the character-building qualities of swordsmanship rather than its untested military efficacy. A whole mystique of the sword grew up, which was more akin to philosophy than to warfare.

Yoshikawa's account of Musashi's early life illustrates all these changes going on in Japan. He was himself a typical rōnin from a mountain village and became a settled samurai retainer only late in life. He was the founder of a school of swordsmanship. Most important, he gradually transformed himself from an instinctive fighter into a man who frantically pursued the goals of Zen-like self-discipline, complete inner mastery over oneself, and a sense of oneness with surrounding nature. Although in his early years lethal contests, reminiscent of the tournaments of medieval Europe, were still possible, Yoshikawa portrays Musashi as consciously turning his martial skills from service in warfare to a means of character building for a time of peace. Martial skills, spiritual self-discipline and aesthetic sensitivity became merged into a single indistinguishable whole. This picture of Musashi may not be far from the historical truth. Musashi is known to have been a skilled painter and an accomplished sculptor as well as a swordsman.

The Japan of the early seventeenth century which Musashi typified has lived on strongly in the Japanese consciousness. The long and relatively static rule of the Tokugawa preserved much of its forms and spirit, though in somewhat ossified form, until the middle of the nineteenth century, not much more than a century ago. Yoshikawa himself was a son of a former samurai who failed like most members of his class to make a successful economic transition to the new age. Though the samurai themselves largely sank into obscurity in the new Japan, most of the new leaders were drawn from this feudal class, and its ethos was popularized through the new compulsory educational system to become the spiritual background and ethics of the whole Japanese nation. Novels like *Musashi* and the films and plays derived from them aided in the process.

The time of Musashi is as close and real to the

modern Japanese as is the Civil War to Americans. Thus the comparison to *Gone with the Wind* is by no means far-fetched. The age of the samurai is still very much alive in Japanese minds. Contrary to the picture of the modern Japanese as merely group oriented "economic animals," many Japanese prefer to see themselves as fiercely individualistic, high-principled, self-disciplined and aesthetically sensitive modern-day Musashis. Both pictures have some validity, illustrating the complexity of the Japanese soul behind the seemingly bland and uniform exterior.

Musashi is very different from the highly psychological and often neurotic novels that have been the mainstay of translations of modern Japanese literature into English. But it is nevertheless fully in the mainstream of traditional Japanese fiction and popular Japanese thought. Its episodic presentation is not merely the result of its original appearance as a newspaper serial but is a favorite technique dating back to the beginnings of Japanese storytelling. Its romanticized view of the noble swordsman is a stereotype of the feudal past enshrined in hundreds of other stories and samurai movies. Its emphasis on the cultivation of self-control and inner personal strength through austere Zen-like self-discipline is a major feature of Japanese personality today. So also is the pervading love of nature and sense of closeness to it. *Musashi* is not just a great adventure story. Beyond that, it gives both a glimpse into Japanese history and a view into the idealized self-image of the contemporary Japanese.

January 1981

17th Century
JAPAN

HOKKAIDO

SEA OF JAPAN

HONSHU

PACIFIC OCEAN

Edo (Tokyo)

Chichibu

Mt. Fuji

Kamakura

Okazaki

Nagoya

Nara

Kyoto

Sakai

Himeji

Mikazuki

Funashima

Shimonoseki

SHIKOKU

KYUSHU

Funashima

Shimonoseki

Moji

Buzen

17th Century
JAPAN

The Travels of Miyamoto Musashi

HOKKAIDO

SEA OF JAPAN

HONSHU

PACIFIC OCEAN

Edo
(Tokyo)

Hōtengahara

Mt. Fuji

Sekigahara

Kuwana

Kyoto

Eagle Mt.

Miyamoto

Himeji

Nara

SHIKOKU

Funashima

KYUSHU

THE
WAY OF LIFE
AND
DEATH

1

The Locust Tree

Matahachi opened his eyes and looked around, got up and poked his head out the back door.

"Akemi!" he called.

There was no answer.

Something prompted him to open the closet. She had recently finished making a new kimono. It was gone.

Going next door first, to Umpei's, he then walked through the alley toward the street, anxiously asking everyone he met if they'd seen her.

"I saw her this morning," said the charcoal vendor's wife.

"You did? Where?"

"She was all dressed up. I asked her where she was off to, and she said to see relatives in Shinagawa."

"Shinagawa?"

"Doesn't she have relatives there?" she asked skeptically.

He started to say no, but caught himself. "Uh, yes, of course. That's where she's gone."

Run after her? In truth, his attachment to her was not particularly strong, and he was more annoyed than anything else. Her disappearance left a bittersweet taste.

He spat and gave vent to an oath or two, then strolled down to the beach, just on the other side of the Shibaura highroad. A little back from the water stood a scattering

1

of fishermen's houses. It was his habit to come here every morning while Akemi was cooking rice and look for fish. Usually at least five or six had fallen from the nets, and he would return just in time to have them cooked for breakfast. Today he ignored the fish.

"What's the matter, Matahachi?" The pawnbroker from the main street tapped him on the shoulder.

"Good morning," said Matahachi.

"It's nice to be out early, isn't it? I'm glad to see you come out for a walk every morning. Great for your health!"

"You're joking, I suppose. Maybe if I was rich like you, I'd be walking for my health. For me, walking's work."

"You don't look too well. Something happen?"

Matahachi picked up a handful of sand and cast it bit by bit into the wind. Both he and Akemi were well acquainted with the pawnbroker, who had tided them over several emergencies.

Undaunted, the man continued: "You know, there's something I've been meaning to talk to you about, but I never seem to have the chance. Are you going out to work today?"

"Why bother? It's not much of a living, selling watermelons."

"Come fishing with me."

Matahachi scratched his head and looked apologetic. "Thanks, but I really don't like to fish."

"Well, you don't have to fish if you don't want to. But come along anyway. It'll make you feel better. That's my boat over there. You can scull a boat, can't you?"

"I guess so."

"Come along. I'm going to tell you how to make a lot of money—maybe a thousand pieces of gold. How would you like that?"

Suddenly Matahachi had a great interest in going fishing.

About a thousand yards offshore, the water was still

shallow enough to touch bottom with the scull. Letting the boat drift, Matahachi asked, "Just how do I go about making this money?"

"I'll tell you soon enough." The pawnbroker readjusted his bulky frame on the seat at the waist of the boat. "I'd appreciate it if you'd hold a fishing pole out over the water."

"Why?"

"It's better if people think we're fishing. Two people rowing out this far just to talk would look suspicious."

"How's this?"

"Fine." He took out a pipe with a ceramic bowl, packed it with expensive tobacco and lit it. "Before I tell you what I have in mind, let me ask you a question. What do your neighbors say about me?"

"About you?"

"Yes, about Daizō of Narai."

"Well, pawnbrokers are supposed to be skinflints, but everybody says you're very good about lending money. They say you're a man who understands life."

"I don't mean my business practices. I want to know their opinion of me personally."

"They think you're a good man, a man with a heart. I'm not just flattering you. That's really what they say."

"Don't they ever comment on what a religious man I am?"

"Oh, yes, of course. Everybody's amazed at how charitable you are."

"Have men from the magistrate's office ever come around inquiring about me?"

"No. Why should they?"

Daizō gave a little laugh. "I suppose you think my questions are foolish, but the truth of the matter is that I'm not really a pawnbroker."

"What?"

"Matahachi, you may never have another chance to make so much money all at once."

"You're probably right."

3

"Do you want to catch hold?"

"Of what?"

"The money vine."

"Wh-what do I have to do?"

"Make a promise to me and carry it out."

"That's all?"

"That's all, but if you change your mind later, you're as good as dead. I know the money interests you, but think hard before you give your final answer."

"Just what do I have to do?" Matahachi asked suspiciously.

"You have to become a well digger. There's nothing to it."

"At Edo Castle?"

Daizō gazed out over the bay. Cargo boats loaded with building materials and bearing the flags of several great clans—Tōdō, Arima, Katō, Date, Hosokawa—were lined up almost prow to stern.

"You catch on quick, Matahachi." The pawnbroker refilled his pipe. "Edo Castle is precisely what I have in mind. If I'm not mistaken, Umpei's been trying to persuade you to dig wells for him. It'd be perfectly natural for you to decide to take him up on the offer."

"That's all I have to do? . . . How is becoming a well digger going to bring me that much money?"

"Be patient. I'll tell you all about it."

When they returned to shore, Matahachi was euphoric. They parted with a promise. That evening he was to slip away unobserved and go to Daizō's house to receive an advance payment of thirty pieces of gold.

He went home, took a nap and awoke a few hours later with the image of the vast sum that would soon be his dancing before his eyes.

Money, a fantastic amount, enough to compensate for all the bad luck he had had up till then. Enough to last him for the rest of his life. Even more exciting was the prospect of being able to show people that they were wrong, that he had what it took after all.

With the money fever upon him, he could not calm down. His mouth still felt dry, even a little numb. Going outside, he stood in the deserted alleyway facing the bamboo grove behind the house and thought: "Who is he, anyway? Just what is he up to?" Then he began to go over the conversation with Daizō.

The well diggers were presently working at the Go-shinjō, the new castle in the western encirclement. Daizō had told him, "You're to bide your time until the chance presents itself, and then you're to shoot the new shōgun with a musket." The gun and ammunition would be on the castle grounds, under a huge, centuries-old locust tree near the back gate at the bottom of Momiji Hill.

Needless to say, the laborers were under close surveillance, but Hidetada liked going around with his attendants to inspect the work. It would be simple enough to accomplish the objective. In the ensuing uproar, Matahachi could escape by jumping into the outer moat, from which Daizō's accomplices would rescue him—"without fail," he had said.

Back in his room, Matahachi stared at the ceiling. He seemed to hear Daizō's voice whispering certain words over and over and recalled how his own lips had trembled when he'd said, "Yes, I'll do it." His skin covered with goose pimples, he jumped to his feet. "This is awful! I'm going over there right now and tell him I don't want any part of it."

Then he remembered something else Daizō had said: "Now that I've told you all this, you're committed. I'd hate to see anything happen to you, but if you try to back out, my friends will have your head within—oh, three days at the outside." Daizō's piercing stare as he had said this flashed before Matahachi's eyes.

Matahachi walked the short distance down Nishi-kubo Lane to the corner of the Takanawa highroad, where the pawnshop stood. The bay, cloaked in darkness, was at the end of a side street. He entered the alley alongside the familiar storehouse, went to the inconspicuous back door of the shop and knocked softly.

"It's not locked," came the immediate response.

"Daizō?"

"Yes. Glad you came. Let's go into the storehouse."

A rain shutter had been left open. Matahachi went into the outer corridor and followed the pawnbroker.

"Sit down," said Daizō, placing a candle on a long wooden clothes chest. Sitting down himself and crossing his arms, he asked, "Did you see Umpei?"

"Yes."

"When will he take you to the castle?"

' The day after tomorrow, when he has to bring ten new laborers. He said he'd include me."

"Then everything's set?"

"Well, we still have to get the district headman and the five-man neighborhood association to put their seals on the documents."

"No problem. It so happens I'm a member of the association."

"Really? You?"

"What's so surprising about that? I'm one of the more influential businessmen in the neighborhood. Last spring, the headman insisted I join."

"Oh, I wasn't surprised. I . . . I just didn't know, that's all."

"Ha, ha. I know exactly what you thought. You thought it was scandalous for a man like me to be on the committee that looks after neighborhood affairs. Well, let me tell you, if you have money, everybody'll say you're a fine man. You can't avoid becoming a local leader even if you try. Think, Matahachi. Before long you're going to have lots of money too."

"Y-y-yes," stammered Matahachi, unable to suppress a shiver. "W-w-will you give me the advance now?"

"Wait a minute."

Picking up the candle, he went to the rear of the storehouse. From a casket on the shelf, he counted out thirty pieces of gold. He came back and said, "Do you have anything to wrap them in?"

"No."

"Use this." He snatched a cotton rag from the floor and threw it to Matahachi. "You'd better put it in your stomach wrapper and make sure it's done up tight."

"Should I give you a receipt?"

"Receipt?" echoed Daizō with an involuntary laugh. "My, aren't you the honest one! But no, I don't need one. If you make a mistake, I'll confiscate your head."

Matahachi blinked and said, "I suppose I'd better be going now."

"Not so fast. Some obligations go with that money. Do you remember everything I told you this morning?"

"Yes. Well, there is one thing. You said the musket would be under the locust tree. Who's going to put it there?" Considering how difficult it was for ordinary workers to enter the castle grounds, he wondered how anyone could possibly manage to sneak in a musket and ammunition. And how could anyone without supernatural powers bury them so they'd be ready and waiting half a month from now?

"That doesn't concern you. You just do what you've agreed to do. You're nervous now because you're not used to the idea. After you've been there a couple of weeks, you'll be all right."

"I hope so."

"First you have to make up your mind you're going through with it. Then you have to be on the lookout for the right moment."

"I understand."

"Now, I don't want any slipups. Hide that money where no one can find it. And leave it there until after you've carried out your mission. When projects like this fall through, it's always because of money."

"Don't worry. I've thought about that already. But

7

let me ask you this: How can I be sure that after I've done my job you won't refuse to pay me the rest?''

"Hmph! It may seem like bragging, but money's the least of my worries. Feast your eyes on those boxes." He held the candle up so Matahachi could see better. All over the room were boxes—for lacquered trays, for armor, for many other purposes. "Every one of them contains a thousand pieces of gold."

Without looking very closely, Matahachi said apologetically, "I don't doubt your word, of course."

The secret conversation went on for another hour or so. Matahachi, feeling somewhat more confident, left by the back way.

Daizō went to a nearby room and looked in. "Akemi, are you there?" he called. "I think he'll go straight from here to hide the money. You'd better follow him."

After a few visits to the pawnshop, Akemi, enthralled with Daizō's personality, had unburdened herself, complaining about her present circumstances and expressing her desire to move on to something better. A couple of days earlier, Daizō had remarked that he was in need of a woman to run his house. Akemi had shown up at his door very early this morning. When he'd let her in, he'd told her not to worry, he'd "take care of" Matahachi.

The prospective assassin, serenely unaware he was being followed, returned home. Hoe in hand, he then climbed through the dark grove behind the house to the top of Nishikubo Hill and buried his treasure.

Having observed all this, Akemi reported to Daizō, who immediately set out for Nishikubo Hill. It was almost dawn when he returned to the storehouse and counted the gold pieces he had dug up. He counted them a second time, and a third, but there was no mistake. Only twenty-eight.

Daizō cocked his head and frowned. He profoundly disliked people who stole his money.

2

Tadaaki's Madness

Osugi was not one to be driven to despair by the sorrows and bitter disappointments of unrequited maternal devotion, but here, with the insects singing amid the lespedeza and eulalia plants, with the great river flowing slowly by, she was not unmoved by feelings of nostalgia and the impermanence of life.

"Are you home?" The rough voice sounded harsh in the still evening air.

"Who is it?" she called.

"I'm from Hangawara's. A lot of fresh vegetables came in from Katsushika. The boss told me to bring you some."

"Yajibei's always so thoughtful."

She was seated at a low table, candle beside her and writing brush in hand, copying the *Sutra on the Great Love of Parents*. She had moved into a small rented house in the sparsely populated district of Hamachō and was making a reasonably comfortable living treating other people's aches and pains with moxa. She had no physical complaints to speak of. Since the beginning of autumn, she had felt quite young again.

"Say, Granny, did a young man come to see you earlier this evening?"

"For a moxa treatment, you mean?"

"Unh-unh. He came to Yajibei's, seemed to have

9

something important on his mind. He asked where you were living now, and we told him.''

"How old was he?"

"Twenty-seven or -eight, I guess."

"What did he look like?"

"Sort of round-faced. Not very tall."

"Mm, I wonder. . . ."

"He had an accent like yours. I thought maybe he came from the same place. Well, I'll be going. Good night."

As the footsteps faded, the voices of the insects rose again like the sound of drizzling rain. Putting down her brush, Osugi gazed at the candle, thinking of the days when she was young and people had read portents in the halo of the candlelight. Those left behind had no way of knowing how husbands, sons and brothers who'd gone off to war were faring, or what fate might lie in their own uncertain futures. A bright halo was taken as a sign of good fortune, purplish shadows as an indication that someone had died. When the flame crackled like pine needles, a person they were expecting was sure to come.

Osugi had forgotten how to interpret the omens, but tonight the cheerful halo, as colorfully beautiful as a rainbow, suggested something splendid in the offing.

Could it have been Matahachi? Her hand reached toward the brush once but drew back. As though entranced, she forgot herself and her surroundings and for the next hour or two thought only of her son's face, which seemed to float about in the darkness of the room.

A rustling noise at the back entrance brought her out of her reverie. Wondering if a weasel was playing havoc with her kitchen, she took the candle and went to investigate.

The sack of vegetables was by the sink; on top of the sack was a white object. Picking it up, she found it was heavy—as heavy as two pieces of gold. On the white paper in which they were wrapped, Matahachi had written: "I still don't have the heart to face you. Please

10

forgive me if I neglect you for another six months. I'll just leave this note, without coming in."

A samurai with murder in his eyes was crashing through the tall grass to reach two men standing on the riverbank. Gasping for breath, he called, "Hamada, was it him?"

"No," groaned Hamada. "Wrong man." But his eyes sparkled as he continued to survey the surroundings.

"I'm sure it was."

"It wasn't. It was a boatman."

"Are you sure?"

"When I ran after him, he climbed into that boat over there."

"That doesn't make him a boatman."

"I checked."

"I must say, he's fast on his feet."

Turning away from the river, they started back through the fields of Hamachō.

"Matahachi . . . Matahachi!"

At first, the sound barely rose above the murmuring of the river, but as it was repeated and became unmistakable, they stopped and looked at one another in astonishment.

"Somebody's calling him! How could that be?"

"Sounds like an old woman."

With Hamada in the lead, they quickly traced the sound to its source, and when Osugi heard their footsteps, she ran toward them.

"Matahachi? Is one of you—"

They surrounded her and pinioned her arms behind her.

"What are you doing to me?" Puffing up like an enraged blowfish, she shouted, "Who are you anyway?"

"We're students of the Ono School."

"I don't know anybody named Ono."

11

"You never heard of Ono Tadaaki, tutor to the shō-gun?"

"Never."

"Why, you old—"

"Wait. Let's see what she knows about Matahachi."

"I'm his mother."

"You're the mother of Matahachi, the melon ven-dor?"

"What do you mean, you pig! Melon vendor! Mata-hachi is a descendant of the House of Hon'iden, and that's an important family in the province of Mimasaka. I'll have you know the Hon'idens are high-ranking re-tainers of Shimmen Munetsura, lord of Takeyama Castle in Yoshino."

"Enough of this," said one man.

"What should we do?"

"Pick her up and carry her."

"Hostage? Do you think it'll work?"

"If she's his mother, he'll have to come for her."

Osugi pulled her scrawny body together and fought like a cornered tigress, but to no avail.

Bored and dissatisfied these past several weeks, Ko-jirō had fallen into the habit of sleeping a lot, in the daytime as well as at night. At the moment, he was lying on his back, grumbling to himself, hugging his sword to his chest.

"It's enough to make my Drying Pole weep. A sword like this, a swordsman like myself—rotting away in an-other man's house!"

There was a loud click and a metallic flash.

"Stupid fool!"

Striking in a great arc above him, the weapon slith-ered back into its scabbard like a living creature.

"Splendid!" cried a servant from the edge of the veranda. "Are you practicing a technique for striking from a supine position?"

"Don't be silly," sniffed Kojirō. He turned over onto

12

his stomach, picked up two specks and flicked them toward the veranda. "It was making a nuisance of itself."

The servant's eyes widened. The insect, resembling a moth, had had both its soft wings and tiny body sliced neatly in two.

"Are you here to lay out my bedding?" asked Kojirō.

"Oh, no! Sorry! There's a letter for you."

Kojirō unhurriedly unfolded the letter and began to read. As he read, a touch of excitement came to his face. According to Yajibei, Osugi had been missing since the night before. Kojirō was requested to come at once and confer on a course of action.

The letter explained in some detail how they had learned where she was. Yajibei had had all his men out searching for her all day long, but the crux of the matter was the message Kojirō had left at the Donjiki. It had been crossed out and beside it was written: "To Sasaki Kojirō: The person holding Matahachi's mother in custody is Hamada Toranosuke of the House of Ono."

"Finally," said Kojirō, the words coming from deep in his throat. At the time he'd rescued Matahachi, he'd suspected that the two samurai he cut down had some connection with the Ono School.

He chuckled and said, "Just what I was waiting for." Standing on the veranda, he glanced up at the night sky. There were clouds, but it didn't look like rain.

Very shortly afterward, he was seen riding up the Takanawa highroad on a rented packhorse. It was late when he reached the Hangawara house. After questioning Yajibei in detail, he made up his mind to spend the night there and move into action the next morning.

Ono Tadaaki had received his new name not long after the Battle of Sekigahara. It was as Mikogami Tenzen that he'd been summoned to Hidetada's encampment to lecture on swordsmanship, which he did with distinction. Along with bestowal of the name came his appointment

13

as a direct vassal of the Tokugawas and the granting of a new residence on Kanda Hill in Edo.

Since the hill afforded an excellent view of Mount Fuji, the shogunate designated it as a residential district for retainers from Suruga, the province in which Fuji was situated.

"I was told the house is on Saikachi Slope," said Kojirō.

He and one of Hangawara's men were at the top of the hill. In the deep valley below them, they could see Ochanomizu, a section of river from which water for the shōgun's tea was said to be drawn.

"Wait here," said Kojirō's guide. "I'll see where it is." He returned shortly with the information that they had already passed it.

"I don't remember any place that looked as though it might belong to the shōgun's tutor."

"Neither did I. I thought he'd have a big mansion, like Yagyū Munenori. But his house is that old one we saw on the right. I've heard it used to belong to the shōgun's stable keeper."

"I suppose it's nothing to be surprised about. Ono's only worth fifteen hundred bushels. Most of Munenori's income was earned by his ancestors."

"This is it," said the guide, pointing.

Kojirō stopped to inspect the general layout of the buildings. The old earthen wall extended back from the middle section of the slope to a thicket on a hill beyond. The compound appeared to be quite large. From the doorless gate he could see, beyond the main house, a building he took to be the dōjō and an annex, apparently of more recent construction.

"You can go back now," said Kojirō. "And tell Yajibei if I don't return with the old lady by evening, he can assume I've been killed."

"Yes, sir." The man ran swiftly down Saikachi Slope, stopping several times to look back.

Kojirō hadn't wasted any time trying to get near

Yagyū Munenori. There was no way to defeat him and thereby take for himself the other man's glory, for the Yagyū Style was the one actually employed by the Tokugawas. That in itself was sufficient excuse for Munenori to refuse to take on ambitious rōnin. Tadaaki was inclined to take on all comers.

Compared with the Yagyū Style, Ono's was more practical, the aim being not to make a great display of skill but to actually kill. Kojirō had heard of no one who had succeeded in attacking the House of Ono and putting it to shame. While Munenori was in general the more highly respected, Tadaaki was considered the stronger.

Ever since coming to Edo and learning of this situation, Kojirō had told himself that one of these days he would be knocking on the Ono gate.

Numata Kajūrō glanced out the window of the dōjō's dressing room. He did a double take and his eyes swept the room, looking for Toranosuke. Spotting him in the middle of the room, giving a lesson to a younger student, he ran to his side and, in a low voice, sputtered, "He's here! Out there, in the front yard!"

Toranosuke, his wooden sword poised in front of him, shouted to the student, "On guard." Then he pressed forward, his footsteps resounding sharply on the floor. Just as the two reached the north corner, the student did a somersault and his wooden sword went sailing through the air.

Toranosuke turned and said, "Who are you talking about? Kojirō?"

"Yes, he's just inside the gate. He'll be here any minute."

"Much sooner than I expected. Taking the old lady hostage was a good idea."

"What do you plan to do now? Who's going to greet him? It should be someone who's prepared for anything. If he has the nerve to come here alone, he may try a surprise move."

15

"Have him brought to the dōjō. I'll greet him myself. The rest of you stay in the background and keep quiet."

"At least there're plenty of us here," said Kajūrō. Looking around, he was encouraged to see the faces of stalwarts like Kamei Hyōsuke, Negoro Hachikurō and Itō Magobei. There were also about twenty others; they had no idea of Kojirō's way of thinking, but they all knew why Toranosuke wanted him here.

One of the two men Kojirō had killed near the Donjiki was Toranosuke's elder brother. Though he was a good-for-nothing, not well thought of at school, his death nevertheless had to be avenged because of the blood relationship.

Despite his youth and his modest income, Toranosuke was a samurai to be reckoned with in Edo. Like the Tokugawas, he came originally from Mikawa Province, and his family was numbered among the oldest of the shōgun's hereditary vassals. He was also one of the "four generals of Saikachi Slope," the others being Kamei, Negoro and Itō.

When Toranosuke had come home the night before with Osugi, the consensus was that he had scored a noteworthy coup. Now it would be difficult for Kojirō not to show his face. The men vowed that if he did appear, they would beat him within an inch of his life, cut off his nose and hang him on a tree by the Kanda River for all to see. But they were by no means certain he'd show up; in fact, they had placed wagers on it, the majority betting that he wouldn't.

Assembling in the main room of the dōjō, they left the floor space open in the middle and waited anxiously.

After a time, one man asked Kajūrō, "Are you sure it was Kojirō you saw?"

"Absolutely sure."

They sat in formidable array. Their faces, woodenly stiff at first, were now showing signs of strain. Some feared that if this kept up much longer, they would fall victim to their own tenseness. Just as the breaking point seemed near, the rapid patter of sandals came to a halt outside the dressing room, and the face of another student, standing on tiptoe, appeared in the window.

"Listen! There's no sense in waiting here. Kojirō's not coming."

"What do you mean? Kajūrō just saw him."

"Yes, but he went straight to the house. How he got admitted, I don't know, but he's in the guest room talking with the master."

"The master?" echoed the group with a collective gasp.

"Are you telling the truth?" demanded Toranosuke, the look on his face close to consternation. He strongly suspected that if the circumstances of his brother's death were investigated, it would turn out that he'd been up to no good, but he'd glossed over this in relating the incident to Tadaaki. And if his master knew he'd abducted Osugi, it wasn't because he himself had told him.

"If you don't believe me, go look."

"What a mess!" groaned Toranosuke.

Far from sympathizing with him, his fellow students were annoyed by his lack of decisiveness.

Advising the others to keep cool while they went to see what the situation was, Kamei and Negoro were just stepping into their zōri when an attractive, light-complexioned girl came running out of the house. Recognizing Omitsu, they stopped where they were and the others rushed to the doorway.

"All of you," she cried in an excited, shrill voice. "Come right away! Uncle and the guest have drawn swords. In the garden. They're fighting!"

Though Omitsu was officially regarded as Tadaaki's niece, it had been whispered about that she was really the daughter of Itō Ittōsai by a mistress. Rumor had it that since Ittōsai was Tadaaki's teacher, Tadaaki must have agreed to rear the girl.

The look of fear in her eyes was most unusual. "I heard Uncle and the guest talking—their voices got louder and louder—and the next thing I knew . . . I don't suppose Uncle's in danger, but—"

The four generals emitted a collective yelp and lit out for the garden, which was set off from the outer compound by a shrub fence. The others caught up with them at the woven-bamboo gate.

"The gate's locked."

"Can't you force it?"

This proved unnecessary. The gate gave way under the weight of the samurai pressing against it. As it fell, a spacious area backed by a hill came into view. Tadaaki, his faithful Yukihira sword held at eye level, stood in the middle. Beyond him, at a fair distance, was Kojirō, the great Drying Pole rising above his head, fire shooting from his eyes.

The charged atmosphere seemed to create an invisible barrier. For men raised in the strict tradition of the samurai class, the awe-inspiring solemnity surrounding the combatants, the dignity of the deadly unsheathed swords, was inviolable. Despite their agitation, the spectacle momentarily deprived the students both of their mobility and of their emotions.

But then two or three of them started toward Kojirō's rear.

"Stay back!" cried Tadaaki angrily. His voice, harsh and chilling, not at all the fatherly voice they were accustomed to, arrested all movement on the part of his students.

People were apt to guess Tadaaki's age to be as much as ten years less than his fifty-four or -five years and take his height for average, whereas actually it was somewhat less than that. His hair was still black, his body small but solidly built. There was nothing stiff or awkward in the movements of his long limbs.

Kojirō had not yet made one strike—had not, in fact, been able to.

Yet Tadaaki had had to face one fact instantly: he

was up against a terrific swordsman. "He's another
Zenki!" he thought with an imperceptible shudder.

Zenki was the last fighter he had encountered to have
such scope and driving ambition. And that had been long
ago, in his youth, when he traveled with Ittōsai, living
the life of a *shugyōsha*. Zenki, the son of a boatman in
Kuwana Province, had been Ittōsai's senior disciple. As
Ittōsai aged, Zenki began to look down on him, even
proclaiming that the Ittō Style was his own invention.

Zenki had caused Ittōsai much grief, for the more
adept he became with the sword, the more harm he
caused other people. "Zenki," Ittōsai had lamented, "is
the greatest mistake in my life. When I look at him, I see
a monster embodying all the bad qualities I ever had. It
makes me hate myself to watch him."

Ironically, Zenki served the youthful Tadaaki well—
as a bad example—spurring him to higher achievements
than might otherwise have been possible. Eventually,
Tadaaki clashed with the evil prodigy at Koganegahara in
Shimōsa and killed him, whereupon Ittōsai awarded him
his certificate in the Ittō Style and gave him the book of
secret instructions.

Zenki's one flaw had been that his technical capabil-
ity was marred by a lack of breeding. Not so Kojirō. His
intelligence and education were evident in his swordsmanship.

"I can't win this fight," thought Tadaaki, who felt
himself in no way inferior to Munenori. In fact, his
assessment of Munenori's skill was not very high.

While he stared at his awesome opponent, another
truth came home to rest. "Time appears to have passed
me by," he thought ruefully.

They stood motionless; not the slightest change was
evident. But both Tadaaki and Kojirō were expending
vital energy at a fearful rate. The physiological toll took
the form of sweat pouring copiously from their foreheads,
air rushing through flaring nostrils, skin turning white,

then bluish. Though a move seemed imminent, the swords remained poised and unwavering.

"I give up," said Tadaaki, abruptly dropping back several paces. They had agreed it was not to be a fight to the finish. Either man could withdraw by acknowledging defeat.

Springing like a beast of prey, Kojirō brought the Drying Pole into action with a downward stroke of whirl-wind force and speed. Though Tadaaki ducked just in time, his topknot flew up and was lopped off. Tadaaki himself, while dodging, executed a brilliant reprisal, slic-ing off some six inches of Kojirō's sleeve.

"Coward!" rose the cry from the students, whose faces burned with rage. By seizing on his opponent's capitulation as the opening for an attack, Kojirō had violated the samurai's code of ethics.

Every one of the students started for Kojirō.

He responded by flying with the speed of a cormo-rant to a large jujube tree at one end of the garden and half hiding himself behind the trunk. His eyes shifted with intimidating rapidity.

"Did you see it?" he shouted. "Did you see who won?"

"They saw it," said Tadaaki. "Hold off!" he told his men, sheathing his sword and returning to the veranda of his study.

Summoning Omitsu, he told her to tie up his hair. While she was doing this, he caught his breath. His chest glistened with rivulets of sweat.

An old saying came back to his mind: it is easy to surpass a predecessor, but difficult to avoid being sur-passed by a successor. He'd been enjoying the fruits of hard training in his youth, complacent in the knowledge that his Ittō Style was no less flourishing than the Yagyū Style. Meanwhile society was giving birth to new ge-niuses like Kojirō. The realization came as a bitter shock, but he was not the sort of man to ignore it.

When Omitsu was finished, he said, "Give our young

guest some water to rinse his mouth out with and show him back to the guest room.''

The faces of the students around him were white with shock. Some were forcing back tears; others stared resentfully at their master.

"We'll assemble in the dōjō," he said. "Now." He himself led the way.

Tadaaki took his place on the raised seat in front and silently contemplated the three rows of his followers sitting facing him.

At length he lowered his eyes and said quietly, "I fear that I, too, have become old. As I look back, it seems to me my best days as a swordsman were when I defeated that devil Zenki. By the time this school was opened and people began talking about the Ono group on Saikachi Slope, calling the Ittō Style unbeatable, I'd already passed my peak as a swordsman."

The meaning of the words was so alien to their customary way of thinking that the students could not believe their ears.

His voice became firmer, and he looked directly at their doubting, discontented faces. "In my opinion, this is something that happens to all men. Age creeps up on us while we're not looking. Times change. The followers surpass their leaders. A younger generation opens up a new way. . . . This is the way it ought to be, for the world advances only through change. Yet this is inadmissible in the field of swordsmanship. The Way of the Sword must be a way that does not permit a man to age.

"Ittōsai . . . I don't know if he's still alive. I've had no word from my master for years. After Koganegahara, he took the tonsure and retreated to the mountains. His aim, he said, was to study the sword, to practice Zen, to search for the Way of Life and Death, to climb the great peak of perfect enlightenment.

"Now it's my turn. After today, I could no longer hold my head up before my master. . . . I regret I haven't lived a better life."

21

"M-m-master!" broke in Negoro Hachikurō. "You say you lost, but we don't believe you'd lose to a man like Kojirō under normal circumstances, even if he is young. There must have been something wrong today."

"Something wrong?" Tadaaki shook his head and chuckled. "Nothing wrong. Kojirō's young. But that's not why I lost. I lost because the times have changed."

"What does that mean?"

"Listen and see." He looked from Hachikurō to the other silent faces. "I'll try to make it brief, because Kojirō is waiting for me. I want you to listen carefully to my thoughts and my hopes for the future."

He then informed them that as of this day, he was retiring from the dōjō. His intention was not to retire in the ordinary sense but to follow in the footsteps of Ittōsai and go out in search of great enlightenment.

"That is my first great hope," he told them.

Next, he requested Itō Magobei, his nephew, to take charge of his only son, Tadanari. Magobei was also enjoined to report the day's happenings to the shogunate and explain that Tadaaki had decided to become a Buddhist priest.

Then he said, "I have no deep regrets over my defeat by a younger man. What does trouble and shame me is this: new fighters like Sasaki are appearing in other quarters, but not a single swordsman of his caliber has come out of the Ono School. I think I know why. A lot of you are hereditary vassals of the shōgun. You've let your status go to your heads. After a bit of training, you begin congratulating yourselves on being masters of the 'invincible Ittō Style.' You're too self-satisfied."

"Wait, sir," Hyōsuke protested in a trembling voice. "That's not fair. Not all of us are lazy and arrogant. We don't all neglect our studies."

"Shut up!" Tadaaki glared at him fiercely. "Laxness on the part of students is a reflection of laxness on the part of the teacher. I'm confessing my own shame now, passing judgment on myself.

22

"The task ahead of you is to eliminate laxness, to make the Ono School a center where youthful talent can develop correctly. It must become a training ground for the future. Unless it does, my leaving and making way for a reform will accomplish nothing."

At last, the sincerity of his statement began to take effect. His students hung their heads, pondering his words, each reflecting on his own shortcomings.

"Hamada," said Tadaaki.

Toranosuke replied, "Yes, sir," but he was obviously taken by surprise. Under Tadaaki's cold stare, his own eyes dropped to the floor.

"Stand up."

"Yes, sir," he said, without rising.

"Stand up! This instant."

Toranosuke rose to his feet. The others looked on mutely.

"I'm expelling you from the school." He paused to let this sink in. "But in doing so, I hope there will come a day when you'll have mended your ways, learned discipline and grasped the meaning of the Art of War. Perhaps at that time we can be together again as teacher and student. Now get out!"

"M-master, why? I don't remember doing anything to deserve this."

"You don't remember because you don't understand the Art of War. If you think about it long and carefully, you'll see."

"Tell me, please. I can't leave until you do." The veins stood out on his forehead.

"All right. Cowardice is the most shameful weakness a samurai can be accused of. The Art of War admonishes strictly against it. It is an ironclad rule at this school that any man guilty of a cowardly act must be expelled.

"Nevertheless, you, Hamada Toranosuke, let several weeks pass after your brother's death before challenging Sasaki Kojirō. In the meantime, you ran around trying to take revenge on some insignificant melon vendor. And yesterday you took this man's aged mother captive and brought her here. Do you call that conduct becoming a samurai?"

"But, sir, you don't understand. I did it to draw Kojirō out." He was about to launch into a spirited defense, but Tadaaki cut him short.

"That's precisely what I mean by cowardice. If you wanted to fight Kojirō, why didn't you go directly to his house? Why didn't you send him a message challenging him? Why didn't you declare your name and your purpose?"

"W-w-well, I did consider those things, but—"

"Consider? There was nothing to stop you from doing that. But you adopted the cowardly ruse of getting others to help you lure Kojirō here so you could attack him en masse. By comparison, Kojirō's attitude was admirable." Tadaaki paused. "He came alone, to see me personally. Refusing to have anything to do with a coward, he challenged me, on the grounds that a student's misconduct is his teacher's misconduct.

"The result of the confrontation between his sword and mine revealed a shameful crime. I now humbly confess that crime."

The room was deathly quiet.

"Now, Toranosuke, upon reflection, do you still believe yourself to be a samurai without shame?"

"Forgive me."

"Get out."

Eyes downcast, Toranosuke walked backward ten paces and knelt on the floor with his arms before him, preparatory to bowing.

"I wish you the best of health, sir. . . . And the same to the rest of you." His voice was dark.

He rose and walked sadly from the dōjō.

Tadaaki stood up. "I, too, must take my leave of the world." Suppressed sobs were audible. His final words were stern, yet full of affection. "Why mourn? Your day has come. It's up to you to see that this school advances

24

into a new age with honor. Beginning now, be humble, work hard and try with all your might to cultivate your spirit."

Returning to the guest room, Tadaaki appeared quite unperturbed as he quietly took a seat and addressed Kojirō.

After apologizing for keeping him waiting, he said, "I've just expelled Hamada. I advised him to change his ways, to try to understand the real meaning of the samurai's discipline. I intend, of course, to release the old woman. Would you like to take her back with you, or should I arrange for her to go later?"

"I'm satisfied with what you've done. She can go with me." Kojirō moved as though to rise. The bout had completely drained him, and the subsequent wait had seemed very, very long.

"Don't go yet," said Tadaaki. "Now that it's all over, let's have a cup together and let bygones be bygones." Clapping his hands, he called, "Omitsu! Bring some sake."

"Thank you," said Kojirō. "It's kind of you to ask me." He smiled and said hypocritically, "I know now why Ono Tadaaki and the Ittō Style are so famous." He had no respect whatsoever for Tadaaki.

"If his natural talents are developed in the right way," thought Tadaaki, "the world will bow at his feet. But if he takes the wrong turn, there's another Zenki in the making."

"If you were my student—" The words were on the tip of Tadaaki's tongue. Instead of saying them, he laughed and replied modestly to Kojirō's flattery.

In the course of their conversation, Musashi's name came up and Kojirō learned he was under consideration to become one of the select group of men who gave lessons to the shōgun.

Kojirō merely said, "Oh?" But his expression betrayed his displeasure. Turning his eyes quickly toward the setting sun, he insisted it was time for him to go.

Not many days after that, Tadaaki vanished from Edo. He had the reputation of being a simple, straightforward warrior, the embodiment of honesty and selflessness, but a man who lacked Munenori's knack for politics. Not understanding why a man who could apparently accomplish anything he set his mind to would flee the world, people were consumed with curiosity and read all sorts of meanings into his disappearance.

As a result of his failure, Tadaaki, it was said, had lost his mind.

3

The Poignancy of Things

Musashi said it was the worst storm he'd ever seen.

Iori gazed wistfully at the sodden, tattered book pages scattered hither and yon, and thought sadly: "No more studying."

Two days of autumn—the two hundred tenth and two hundred twentieth days of the year—were especially dreaded by farmers. It was on these two days that typhoons were most likely to destroy the rice crop. Iori, more attuned to the dangers than his master, had taken the precaution of tying down the roof and weighting it with rocks. Nevertheless, during the night, the wind had ripped the roof off, and when it was light enough to inspect the damage, it was evident that the cabin was beyond any hope of repair.

With his experience at Hōtengahara in mind, Musashi set off shortly after dawn. Watching him go, Iori thought: "What good will it do him to look at the neighbors' paddies? Of course they're flooded. Doesn't his own house mean anything to him?"

He built a fire, using bits and pieces of the walls and floor, and roasted some chestnuts and dead birds for breakfast. The smoke stung his eyes.

Musashi came back a little after noon. About an hour later, a group of farmers wearing thick straw rain capes arrived to offer their thanks—for assistance to a sick person, for help in draining off the flood water, for a number of other services. As one old man admitted, "We always get into quarrels at times like these, what with everybody in a hurry to take care of his own problems first. But today we followed your advice and worked together."

They also brought gifts of food—sweets, pickles and, to Iori's delight, rice cakes. As he thought about it, Iori decided that that day he'd learned a lesson: if one forgot about oneself and worked for the group, food would naturally be forthcoming.

"We'll build you a new house," one farmer promised. "One that won't be blown down." For the present, he invited them to stay at his house, the oldest in the village. When they got there, the man's wife hung their clothes out to dry, and when they were ready to go to bed, they were shown to separate rooms.

Before he fell asleep, Iori became aware of a sound that stirred his interest. Turning over to face Musashi's room, he whispered through the shoji, "Do you hear that, sir?"

"Umm?"

"Listen. You can just hear them—drums from the shrine dances. Strange, isn't it, having religious dances the night after a typhoon?"

The only reply was the sound of deep breathing.

The next morning, Iori got up early and asked the farmer about the drums. Coming back to Musashi's room, he said brightly, "Mitsumine Shrine in Chichibu isn't so far from here, is it?"

"I shouldn't think so."

"I wish you'd take me there. To pay my respects."

Puzzled, Musashi asked why the sudden interest and was told that the drummers had been musicians in a neighboring village, practicing for the Asagaya Sacred Dance, which their household had specialized in since the distant past. They went every month to perform at the Mitsumine Shrine Festival.

The beauty of music and the dance was known to Iori only through these Shinto dances. He was inordinately fond of them, and having heard that the Mitsumine dances were one of the three great types in this tradition, he had his heart set on seeing them.

"Won't you take me?" he pleaded. "It'll be five or six days, at least, before our house is ready."

Iori's fervency reminded Musashi of Jōtarō, who had often made a nuisance of himself—whining, pouting, purring—to get what he wanted. Iori, so grown up and self-sufficient for his age, rarely resorted to such tactics. Musashi wasn't thinking about it particularly, but an observer might have noticed the effects of his influence. One thing he had deliberately taught Iori was to make a strict distinction between himself and his teacher.

At first he replied noncommittally, but after a little thought, he said, "All right, I'll take you."

Iori jumped in the air, exclaiming, "The weather's good too." Within five minutes, he'd reported his good fortune to their host, requested box lunches and procured new straw sandals. Then he was in front of his teacher again, asking, "Shouldn't we get started?"

The farmer saw them off with the promise that their house would be finished by the time they returned.

They passed places where the typhoon had left ponds, small lakes almost, in its wake, but otherwise it was difficult to believe the heavens had unleashed their fury only two days earlier. Shrikes flew low in the clear blue sky.

The first night, they chose a cheap inn in the village of Tanashi and went to bed early. The next day, their road led them farther into the great Mushashino Plain.

Their journey was interrupted for several hours at the Iruma River, which was swollen to three times its normal size. Only a short section of the dirt bridge stood, uselessly, in the middle of the stream.

While Musashi watched a group of farmers carrying new piling out from both sides to make a temporary crossing, Iori noticed some old arrowheads and remarked on them, adding, "There's tops of helmets too. There must have been a battle here." He amused himself along the riverbank, digging up arrowheads, rusted fragments of broken swords and miscellaneous pieces of old, unidentifiable metal.

Suddenly he snatched his hand away from a white object he'd been about to pick up.

"It's a human bone," he cried.

"Bring it over here," said Musashi.

Iori had no stomach for touching it again. "What are you going to do with it?"

"Bury it where it won't be walked on."

"It's not just a couple of bones. There're lots of them."

"Good. It'll give us something to do. Bring all you can find." Turning his back to the river, he said, "You can bury them over there, where those gentians are blooming."

"I don't have a spade."

"You can use a broken sword."

When the hole was deep enough, Iori put the bones in it, then gathered up his collection of arrowheads and bits of metal and buried them with the bones. "Is that all right?" he asked.

"Put some rocks over it. Make it into a proper memorial."

"When was there a battle here?"

"Have you forgotten? You must have read about it. The *Taiheiki* tells about two fierce battles, in 1333 and 1352, in a place called Kotesashigahara. That's about where we are now. On one side was the Nitta family, supporting the Southern Court, and on the other a huge army led by Ashikaga Takauji."

"Oh, the battles of Kotesashigahara. I remember now."

At Musashi's urging, Iori continued. "The book tells us Prince Munenaga lived in the eastern region for a long time and studied the Way of the Samurai, but was astonished when the Emperor appointed him shōgun.''

"What was the poem he composed on that occasion?" Musashi asked.

Iori glanced up at a bird soaring through the azure sky and recited:

> "How could I have known
> I'd ever be master of
> The catalpa bow?
> Had I not passed through life
> Without touching it?"

"And the poem in the chapter telling how he crossed into Musashi Province and fought at Kotesashigahara?"

The boy hesitated, biting his lip, then began, in phrasing largely of his own making:

> "Why, then, should I cling
> To a life that is fulfilled
> When nobly given
> For the sake of our great lord,
> For the sake of the people?"

"And the meaning?"

"I understand that."

"Are you sure?"

"Anyone who can't understand without having it explained to him isn't really Japanese, even if he is a samurai. Isn't that true?"

"Yes. But tell me, Iori, if that's the case, why are you behaving as though handling those bones made your hands dirty?"

"Would it make you feel good to handle the bones of dead people?"

"The men who died here were soldiers. They'd fought and perished for the sentiments expressed in Prince Munenaga's poem. The number of samurai like that is uncountable; their bones, buried in the earth, are the foundation on which this country is built. Were it not for them, we'd still have neither peace nor the prospect of prosperity.

"Wars, like the typhoon we had, pass. The land as a whole is unchanged, but we must never forget the debt we owe to the white bones under the ground."

Iori nodded at almost every word. "I understand now. Shall I make an offering of flowers and bow before the bones I buried?"

Musashi laughed. "Bowing's not really necessary, if you keep the memory alive in your heart."

"But . . ." Not quite satisfied, the boy picked some flowers and placed them before the pile of stones. He was about to clasp his hands together in obeisance when another troubling thought came to him. "Sir, it's all well and good if these bones really belonged to samurai who were loyal to the Emperor. But what if they're the remains of Ashikaga Takauji's men? I wouldn't want to pay respect to them."

Iori stared at him, waiting for his answer. Musashi fixed his eyes on the thin sliver of daylight moon. But no satisfactory reply came to mind.

At length, he said, "In Buddhism there is salvation even for those guilty of the ten evils and the five deadly sins. The heart itself is enlightenment. The Buddha forgives the wicked if only they'll open their eyes to his wisdom."

"Does that mean loyal warriors and evil rebels are the same after they die?"

"No!" Musashi said emphatically. "A samurai holds his name to be sacred. If he sullies it, there's no redress throughout all generations."

"Then why does the Buddha treat bad people and loyal servants alike?"

"Because people are all fundamentally the same. There are those who are so blinded by self-interest and desire that they become rebels or brigands. The Buddha

32

is willing to overlook this. He urges all to accept enlightenment, to open their eyes to true wisdom. This is the message of a thousand scriptures. Of course, when one dies, all becomes void.''

"I see," said Iori, without really seeing. He pondered the matter for a few minutes and then asked, "But that's not true of samurai, is it? Not *everything* becomes void when a samurai dies.''

"Why do you say that?"

"His name lives on, doesn't it?"

"That's true."

"If it's a bad name, it stays bad. If it's a good name, it stays good, even when the samurai is reduced to bones. Isn't that the way it is?"

"Yes, but it isn't really quite so simple," said Musashi, wondering if he could successfully guide his pupil's curiosity. "In the case of a samurai, there is such a thing as an appreciation of the poignancy of things. A warrior lacking this sensitivity is like a shrub in a desert. To be a strong fighter and nothing more is to be like a typhoon. It's the same with swordsmen who think of nothing but swords, swords, swords. A real samurai, a genuine swordsman, has a compassionate heart. He understands the poignancy of life.''

Silently, Iori rearranged the flowers and clasped his hands.

4

Two Drumsticks

Halfway up the mountain, antlike human figures, climbing in continual procession, were swallowed up by a thick ring of clouds. Emerging near the summit, where Mitsumine Shrine was situated, they were greeted by a cloudless sky.

The mountain's three peaks, Kumotori, Shiraiwa and Myōhōgatake, straddled four eastern provinces. Within the Shinto complex there were Buddhist temples, pagodas, various other buildings and gates. Outside was a flourishing little town, with teahouses and souvenir shops, the offices of the high priests and the houses of some seventy farmers whose produce was reserved for the shrine's use.

"Listen! They've started playing the big drums," Iori said excitedly, gobbling down his rice and red beans. Musashi sat opposite, enjoying his repast at a leisurely pace.

Iori threw down his chopsticks. "The music's started," he said. "Let's go and watch."

"I had enough last night. You go alone."

"But they only did two dances last night. Don't you want to see the others?"

"Not if it means hurrying."

Seeing his master's wooden bowl was still half full,

Iori said in a calmer tone, "Thousands of people have arrived since yesterday. It'd be a shame if it rained."

"Oh?"

When Musashi finally said, "Shall we go now?" Iori bounded for the front door like a dog unleashed, borrowed some straw sandals, and set them in place on the doorstep for his master.

In front of the Kannon'in, the subtemple where they were staying, and on both sides of the shrine's main gate, great bonfires blazed. Every house had a lighted torch in front of it, and the whole area, several thousand feet above sea level, was as bright as day. Overhead, in a sky the color of a deep lake, the River of Heaven glittered like magic smoke, while in the street swarms of men and women, oblivious of the chill in the mountain air, surged toward the stage where the sacred dances were performed. Flutes and great drums echoed on the mountain breeze. The stage itself was empty, except for the gently fluttering banners that would soon serve as a backdrop.

Jostled by the mob, Iori got separated from Musashi but quickly pushed his way through the crowd until he spied him standing near a building, staring up at a list of donors. Iori called his name, ran up to him, tugged at his sleeve, but Musashi's attention was riveted on one plaque, larger than the others. It stood out from all the rest because of the size of the contribution made by "Daizō of Narai, Shibaura Village, Province of Musashi."

The booming of the drums built to a crescendo.

"They've started the dance," squealed Iori, his heart flying to the sacred dance pavilion. "*Sensei,* what are you looking at?"

Musashi, stirred from his reverie, said, "Oh, nothing special. . . . I just remembered something I have to do. You go watch the dances. I'll be along later."

Musashi sought out the office of the Shinto priests, where he was greeted by an old man.

"I'd like to inquire about a donor," said Musashi.

"Sorry, we don't have anything to do with that here. You'll have to go to the residence of the chief Buddhist priest. I'll show you where it is."

Though Mitsumine Shrine was Shinto, general supervision of the whole establishment was in the hands of a Buddhist prelate. The plaque over the gate read: "Office of the High Priest in Charge," in suitably large characters.

At the entrance hall, the old man talked at some length with the priest on duty. When they were finished, the priest invited Musashi inside and very politely led him to an inner room. Tea was served, along with a tray of splendid cakes. Next came a second tray, followed shortly by a handsome young acolyte bearing sake. Presently no less a personage than a provisional bishop appeared.

"Welcome to our mountain," he said. "I fear we have only simple country fare to offer you. I trust you'll forgive us. Please make yourself comfortable."

Musashi was at a loss to understand the solicitous treatment. Without touching the sake, he said, "I came to make an inquiry about one of your donors."

"What?" The benign countenance of the priest, a rotund man of about fifty, underwent a subtle alteration. "An inquiry?" he asked suspiciously.

In rapid succession, Musashi asked when Daizō had come to the temple, whether he came there often, whether he ever brought anyone with him, and if so, what sort of person.

With every question the priest's displeasure grew, until finally he said, "Then you're not here to make a contribution but merely to ask questions about someone who did?" His face was a study in exasperation.

"The old man must have misunderstood me. I never intended to make a donation. I only wanted to ask about Daizō."

36

"You could have made that perfectly clear at the entrance," the priest said haughtily. "From all I can see, you're a rōnin. I don't know who you are or where you come from. You must understand that I can't give out information about our donors to just anyone."

"I assure you nothing will happen."

"Well, you'll have to see the priest in charge of such matters." Looking as though he felt he'd been robbed, he dismissed Musashi.

The register of contributors turned out to be no more helpful, for it recorded only that Daizō had been there several times. Musashi thanked the priest and left.

Near the dance pavilion, he looked around for Iori without seeing him. If he'd looked up, he would have. The boy was almost directly over his head, having climbed a tree to get a better view.

Watching the scene unfolding on the stage, Musashi was transported back to his childhood, to the night festivals at the Sanumo Shrine in Miyamoto. He saw phantom images of the crowds, of Otsū's white face in their midst. Of Matahachi, always chewing food, of Uncle Gon, walking about importantly. Vaguely he sensed the face of his mother, worried about his being out so late, coming to look for him.

The musicians, clad in unusual costumes intended to simulate the elegance of the imperial guards of old, took their places on the stage. In the light of the fire, their tawdry finery, glittering with patches of gold brocade, was suggestive of the mythical robes of the age of the gods. The beating of the slightly slack drumheads reverberated through the forest of cryptomeria, then the flutes and well-seasoned boards, clapped rhythmically with small blocks, sounded the prelude. The master of the dance came forward, wearing the mask of an ancient man. This unearthly face, from whose cheeks and chin much of the lacquer had peeled, moved slowly as he sang the words of *Kamiasobi*, the dance of the gods.

"On sacred Mount Mimuro
With its godly fence,
Before the great deity,
The leaves of the sakaki tree
Grow in profuse abundance,
Grow in profuse abundance."

The tempo of the drums picked up and other instruments joined in. Soon song and dance melded in a lively, syncopated rhythm.

"Whence came this spear?
It is the spear of the sacred dwelling
Of the Princess Toyooka who is in Heaven—
The spear of the sacred dwelling."

Musashi knew some of the songs. As a child, he had sung them and donned a mask and taken part in the dancing at Sanumo Shrine.

"The sword that protects the people,
The people of all lands.
Let's hang it festively before the deity,
Hang it festively before the deity."

The revelation struck like lightning. Musashi had been watching the hands of one of the drummers, wielding two short, club-shaped drumsticks. He sucked in his breath and fairly shouted, "That's it! Two swords!"

Startled by the voice, Iori took his eyes away from the stage just long enough to look down and say, "Oh, there you are."

Musashi didn't even glance up. He stared straight ahead, not in dreamy rapture like the others but with a look of almost frightening penetration.

"Two swords," he repeated. "It's the same principle. Two drumsticks, but only one sound." He folded his arms more tightly and scrutinized the drummer's every movement.

From one point of view, it was simplicity itself. People were born with two hands; why not use both of them? As it was, swordsmen fought with only one sword, and often one hand. This made sense, so long as everybody followed the same practice. But if one combatant were to employ two swords at once, what chance would an opponent using only one have of winning?

Against the Yoshioka School at Ichijōji, Musashi had discovered his long sword in his right hand, his short sword in his left. He had grasped both weapons instinctively, unconsciously, each arm involved to the utmost in protecting him. In a life-and-death struggle, he had reacted in an unorthodox fashion. Now, all of a sudden, the rationale seemed natural, if not inevitable.

If two armies were facing each other in battle, it would be unthinkable under the rules of the Art of War for either to make use of one flank while allowing the other to stand idle. Was there not a principle here that the lone swordsman could not afford to ignore? Ever since Ichijōji, it had seemed to Musashi that to use both hands and both swords was the normal, human way. Only custom, followed unquestioningly over the centuries, had made it seem abnormal. He felt he had arrived at an undeniable truth: custom had made the unnatural appear natural, and vice versa.

While custom was bred by daily experience, being on the boundary between life and death was something that occurred only a few times during a lifetime. Yet the ultimate aim of the Way of the Sword was to be able to stand on the brink of death at any time: facing death squarely, unflinchingly, should be as familiar as all other daily experiences. And the process had to be a conscious one, though movement should be as free as if it were purely reflexive.

The two-sword style had to be of this nature—conscious but at the same time as automatic as a reflex, completely free of the restrictions inherent in conscious action. Musashi had been trying for some time to unite in a valid principle what he knew instinctively with what he had learned by intellectual means. Now he was close to formulating it in words, and it would make him famous throughout the country for generations to come.

Two drumsticks, one sound. The drummer was conscious of left and right, right and left, but at the same time unconscious of them. Here, before his eyes, was the Buddhist sphere of free interpenetration. Musashi felt enlightened, fulfilled.

The five sacred dances, having begun with the song of the master of the dance, continued with performances by the dancers. There was the broad, sweeping Dance of Iwato, then the Dance of Ara Mikoto no Hoko. The melodies of the flutes quickened; bells rang in lively rhythm.

Musashi looked up at Iori and said, "Aren't you ready to leave?"

"Not yet," came the absentminded reply. Iori's spirit had become part of the dance; he felt himself to be one of the performers.

"Come back before it gets too late. Tomorrow we're going to climb the peak to the inner shrine."

5

The Demon's Attendant

The dogs of Mitsumine were a feral breed, said to result from the crossing of dogs brought by immigrants from Korea more than a thousand years earlier with the wild dogs of the Chichibu Mountains. Only a step removed from the wild stage, they roamed the mountainside and fed like wolves on the other wildlife in the region. But since they were regarded as messengers of the deity and were spoken of as his "attendants," worshipers often took home printed or sculptured images of them as good-luck charms.

The black dog with the man following Musashi was the size of a calf.

As Musashi entered the Kannon'in, the man turned, said, "This way," and beckoned with his free hand.

The dog growled, tugged at his leash—a piece of thick rope—and began sniffing.

Flicking the leash across the dog's back, the man said, "Shh, Kuro, be quiet."

The man was about fifty, solidly but supplely built, and like his dog, he seemed not quite tame. But he was well dressed. With his kimono, which looked like a priest's robe or a samurai's formal wear, he wore a narrow, flat obi and a hemp *hakama*. His straw sandals, of the sort men wore at festivals, were fitted with new thongs.

"Baiken?" The woman held back, to keep away from the dog.

"Down," commanded Baiken, rapping the animal sharply on the head. "I'm glad you spotted him, Okō."

"Then it was him?"

"No doubt about it."

For a moment, they stood silently looking through a break in the clouds at the stars, hearing but not really listening to the sacred dance music.

"What'll we do?" she asked.

"I'll think of something."

"We can't let this chance go to waste."

Okō stared expectantly at Baiken.

"Is Tōji at home?" he asked.

"Yes; he got drunk on the festival sake and fell asleep."

"Get him up."

"What about you?"

"I've got work to do. After I make my rounds, I'll come to your place."

Outside the main shrine gate, Okō broke into a trot. Most of the twenty or thirty houses were souvenir shops or teahouses. There were also a few small eating establishments, from which emanated the cheerful voices of revelers. From the eaves of the shack Okō entered hung a sign saying "Rest House." On one of the stools in the dirt-floored front room sat a young servant enjoying a catnap.

"Still sleeping?" asked Okō.

The girl, expecting a scolding, shook her head vigorously.

"I don't mean you—my husband."

"Oh, yes, he's still asleep."

With a disapproving click of her tongue, Okō grumbled, "A festival's going on, and he's sleeping. This is the only shop that isn't full of customers."

Near the door, a man and an old woman were steaming rice and beans in an earthen oven. The flames struck the only cheerful note in the otherwise gloomy interior.

Okō walked over to where a man was sleeping on a bench by the wall, tapped him on the shoulder and said, "Get up, you! Open your eyes for a change."

"Huh?" he mumbled, raising himself slightly.

"Oh, my," she exclaimed, as she backed away. Then she laughed and said, "I'm sorry. I thought you were my husband."

A piece of matting had slipped to the ground. The man, a round-faced youth with large, questioning eyes, picked it up, pulled it over his face and stretched out again. His head rested on a wooden pillow and his sandals were spattered with mud. On the table next to him were a tray and an empty rice bowl; by the wall, a travel pack, a basket hat and a staff.

Turning back to the girl, Okō said, "I suppose he's a customer?"

"Yes. He said he's planning to go up to the inner shrine early in the morning and asked if it was all right to take a nap here."

"Where's Tōji?"

"I'm over here, stupid." His voice came from behind a torn shoji. Reclining in the next room, with one foot hanging out into the shop, he said sullenly, "And why carry on about me taking a little snooze? Where've you been all this time, when you should have been tending to business?"

In many ways, the years had been even less kind to Okō than they had to Tōji. Not only was the charm of her earlier years no longer evident, but running the Oinu Teahouse required her to do a man's work to make up for her shiftless spouse, since Tōji made a pittance hunting in the winter but did little else. After Musashi burned down their hideout with its trick room at Wada Pass, their henchmen had all deserted them.

Tōji's bleary red eyes gradually focused on a barrel

43

of water. Pulling himself to his feet, he went over to it and gulped down a dipperful.

Okō leaned on a bench and looked over her shoulder at him. "I don't care if there is a festival going on. It's about time you learned when to stop. You're lucky you didn't get run through by a sword while you were out."

"Huh?"

"I'm telling you you'd better be more careful."

"I don't know what you're talking about."

"Did you know Musashi's here at the festival?"

"Musashi? Miyamoto . . . Musashi?" Jolted into wakefulness, he said, "Are you serious? Look, you'd better go hide in the back."

"Is that all you can think of—hiding?"

"I don't want what happened at Wada Pass to happen again."

"Coward. Aren't you eager to get even with him, not only for that but for what he did to the Yoshioka School? I am, and I'm only a woman."

"Yeah, but don't forget, we had lots of men to help us then. Now there's just the two of us." Tōji hadn't been at Ichijōji, but he had heard how Musashi had fought and had no illusions about who would end up dead if the two of them ran into each other again.

Sidling up to her husband, Okō said, "That's where you're wrong. There's another man here, isn't there? A man who hates Musashi as much as you do."

Tōji knew she was referring to Baiken, whom they had become acquainted with when their wanderings brought them to Mitsumine.

Since there were no more battles, being a freebooter was no longer profitable, so Baiken had opened a smithy in Iga, only to be driven out when Lord Tōdō tightened his rule over the province. Intending to seek his fortune in Edo, he had disbanded his gang, but then, through the introduction of a friend, had become the watchman at the temple's treasure house.

Even now, the mountains between the provinces of

Musashi and Kai were infested with bandits. In hiring Baiken to guard the treasure house, with its religious treasures and donated cash, the temple elders were fighting fire with fire. He had the advantage of being intimately familiar with the ways of bandits, and he was also an acknowledged expert with the chain-ball-sickle. As the originator of the Yaegaki Style, he might possibly have attracted the attention of a daimyō, had it not been for the fact that his brother was Tsujikaze Temma. In years long past, the two of them had terrorized the region between Mount Ibuki and the Yasugawa district. Changing times meant nothing to Baiken. To his way of thinking, Temma's death at the hands of Takezō had been the ultimate cause of all his subsequent difficulties.

Okō had long since told Baiken about their grievance against Musashi, exaggerating her rancor in order to cement her friendship with him. He had responded by scowling and saying, "One of these days . . ."

Okō had just finished telling Tōji how she had caught sight of Musashi from the teahouse, then lost him in the crowd. Later, on a hunch, she had gone to the Kannon'in, arriving just as Musashi and Iori were leaving for the outer shrine. This information she had promptly imparted to Baiken.

"So that's the way it is," said Tōji, taking courage from the knowledge that a dependable ally had already been lined up. He knew Baiken, using his favorite weapon, had beaten every swordsman at the recent shrine tournament. If he attacked Musashi, there was a good chance of winning. "What did he say when you told him?"

"He'll come as soon as he finishes his rounds."

"Musashi's no fool. If we're not careful—" Tōji shuddered and uttered a gruff, unintelligible sound. Okō followed his eyes to the man sleeping on the bench.

"Who's that?" asked Tōji.

"Just a customer," answered Okō.

"Wake him up and get him out of here."

45

Okō delegated this task to the girl servant, who went to the far corner and shook the man until he sat up.

"Get out," she said bluntly. "We're closing up now."

He stood up, stretched and said, "That was a nice nap." Smiling to himself and blinking his large eyes, he moved quickly but smoothly, wrapping the matting around his shoulders, donning his basket hat and adjusting his pack. He placed his staff under his arms, said, "Thanks a lot," with a bow and walked quickly out the door.

Okō judged from his clothing and accent that he was not one of the local farmers, but he seemed harmless enough. "Funny-looking man," she said. "I wonder if he paid his bill."

Okō and Tōji were still rolling up blinds and straightening up the shop when Baiken came in with Kuro.

"Good to see you," said Tōji. "Let's go to the back room."

Baiken silently removed his sandals and followed them, while the dog nosed around for scraps of food. The back room was only a broken-down lean-to with a first coat of rough plaster on the walls. It was out of earshot of anyone in the shop.

When a lamp had been lit, Baiken said, "This evening in front of the dance stage, I overheard Musashi tell the boy they'd go up to the inner shrine tomorrow morning. Later I went to the Kannon'in and checked it out."

Both Okō and Tōji swallowed and looked out the window; the peak on which the inner shrine stood was dimly outlined against the starry sky.

Knowing whom he was up against, Baiken had made a plan of attack and mobilized reinforcements. Two priests, guards at the treasure house, had already agreed to help and had gone on ahead with their lances. There was also a man from the Yoshioka School, who ran a small dōjō at the shrine. Baiken calculated he could mobilize perhaps ten freebooters, men he'd known in Iga who were now working in the vicinity. Tōji would carry a musket, while Baiken would have his chain-ball-sickle.

"You've done all this already?" asked Tōji in disbelief.

Baiken grinned but said nothing more.

A diminutive sliver of moon hung high above the valley, hidden from view by a thick fog. The great peak was still sleeping, with only the gurgling and roaring of the river to accentuate the silence. A group of dark figures huddled on the bridge at Kosaruzawa.

"Tōji?" Baiken whispered hoarsely.

"Here."

"Be sure to keep your fuse dry."

Conspicuous among the motley crew were the two lancer priests, who had the skirts of their robes tucked up ready for action. The others were dressed in a variety of outfits, but all were shod so as to be able to move nimbly.

"Is this everybody?"

"Yes."

"How many altogether?"

They counted heads: thirteen.

"Good," said Baiken. He went over their instructions again. They listened in silence, nodding occasionally. Then, at a signal, they scurried into the fog to take up positions along the road. At the end of the bridge, they passed a milestone saying: "Six Thousand Yards to the Inner Shrine."

When the bridge was empty again, a great company of monkeys emerged from hiding, jumping from limbs, climbing vines, converging on the road. They ran out onto the bridge, crawled under it, threw stones into the ravine. The fog toyed with them, as if encouraging their frolic. Had a Taoist Immortal appeared and beckoned, perhaps they would have been transformed into clouds and flown off with him to heaven.

The barking of a dog echoed through the mountains.

The monkeys vanished, like sumac leaves before an autumn wind.

Kuro came up the road, dragging Okō along with him. He'd somehow broken loose, and though Okō had eventually got hold of the leash, she hadn't been able to make him go back. She knew Tōji didn't want the dog around to make noise, so she thought maybe she could get him out of the way by letting him go up to the inner shrine.

As the restlessly shifting fog began to settle in the valleys like snow, the three peaks of Mitsumine and the lesser mountains between Musashino and Kai rose against the sky in all their grandeur. The winding road stood out white, and birds began to ruffle their feathers and chirp a greeting to the dawn.

Iori said, half to himself, "Why is that, I wonder?"

"Why is what?" asked Musashi.

"It's getting light, but I can't see the sun."

"For one thing, you're looking toward the west."

"Oh." Iori gave the moon, sinking behind the distant peaks, a cursory glance.

"Iori, a lot of your friends seem to live here in the mountains."

"Where?"

"Over there." Musashi laughed and pointed to some monkeys clustered around their mother.

"I wish I was one of them."

"Why?"

"At least they have a mother."

They climbed a steep part of the road in silence and came to a relatively flat stretch. Musashi noticed the grass had been trampled by a large number of feet.

After winding around the mountain for a while more, they reached a level area where they were facing east.

"Look," cried Iori, looking over his shoulder at Musashi. "The sun's coming up."

"So it is."

48

From the sea of clouds beneath them, the mountains of Kai and Kōzuke jutted up like islands. Iori stopped and stood stock still, feet together, arms at his sides, lips tightly set. He stared in rapt fascination at the great golden sphere, imagining himself to be a child of the sun. All at once he exclaimed in a very loud voice, "It's Amaterasu Ōmikami! Isn't it?" He looked to Musashi for confirmation.

"That's right."

Raising his arms high above his head, the boy filtered the brilliant light through his fingers. "My blood!" he cried. "It's the same color as the sun's blood." Clapping his hands, as he would at a shrine to summon the deity, he bowed his head in silent obeisance, thinking: "The monkeys have a mother. I have none. But I have this goddess. They have none."

The revelation filled him with joy, and as he burst into tears, he seemed to hear from beyond the clouds the music of the shrine dances. The drums boomed in his ears, while the counterpoint of the flutes hovered around the melody of the Dance of Iwato. His feet caught the rhythm; his arms swayed gracefully. From his lips came the words he had memorized only the night before:

> "The catalpa bow—
>   With each coming of spring,
>   I hope to see the dancing
>   Of the myriad of gods,
>   Oh, how I hope to see their dancing—"

Suddenly realizing Musashi had gone on ahead, he abandoned his dance and ran to catch up.

The morning light barely penetrated the forest they now entered. Here, in the approach to the inner shrine, the cryptomerias were of enormous circumference and all about the same height. Tiny white flowers grew in the thick patches of moss clinging to the trees. Suspecting the trees were ancient—five hundred years old, perhaps even a thousand—Iori had an urge to bow to them. Here and there, bright red vine maple caught his eye. Low striped bamboo encroaching on the road narrowed it to a path.

Without warning, the earth seemed to tremble under their feet. Close upon the thunderous report came an unnerving scream and a cascade of sharp echoes. Iori covered his ears with his hands and dived into the bamboo.

"Iori! Stay down!" Musashi commanded from the shadow of a large tree. "Don't move even if they trample on you!"

The gloomy half light seemed infested with lances and swords. Because of the scream, the attackers thought at first the bullet had found its mark, but there was no body in sight. Uncertain as to what had happened, they froze.

Iori was at the center of a circle of eyes and unsheathed blades. In the deathly silence that followed, curiosity got the better of him. He slowly raised his head above the bamboo. Only a few feet away, a sword blade, extending from behind a tree, caught a flash of sunlight.

Losing all control, Iori screamed at the top of his lungs, *"Sensei!* Somebody's hiding there!" As he shouted, he jumped to his feet and made a dash for safety.

The sword leapt from the shadows and hung like a demon above his head. But only for an instant. Musashi's dagger flew straight to the swordsman's head and lodged in the temple.

"Ya-a-h!"

One of the priests charged at Musashi with his lance. Musashi caught the lance and held it tightly with one hand.

Another death cry sounded, as if the man's mouth were full of rocks. Wondering if his attackers could be fighting among themselves, Musashi strained his eyes to see. The other priest took careful aim with his lance and hurtled toward him. Musashi caught this lance too and held it securely under his right arm.

"Jump him now!" screamed one of the priests, realizing that Musashi had his hands full.

His voice stentorian, Musashi shouted, "Who are you? Identify yourselves, or I'll assume you're all enemies. It's a shame to spill blood on this holy ground, but I may have no choice."

Whirling the lances around and sending the two priests off on different tangents, Musashi whipped out his sword and finished off one of them before he had stopped tumbling. Spinning around, he found himself confronting three more blades, lined up across the narrow path. Without pausing, he moved toward them threateningly, one step at a time. Two more men came out and took their places shoulder to shoulder beside the first three.

As Musashi advanced and his opponents retreated, he caught a glimpse of the other lancer priest, who had recovered his weapon and was chasing Iori. "Stop, you cutthroat!" But the moment Musashi turned to go to Iori's rescue, the five men let out a howl and charged. Musashi rushed head on to meet them. It was like the collision of two raging waves, but the spray was blood, not brine. Musashi kept whirling from opponent to opponent with the speed of a typhoon. Two bloodcurdling cries, then a third. They fell like dead trees, each sliced through the middle of the torso. In Musashi's right hand was his long sword, in his left the short one.

With cries of terror, the last two turned and ran, Musashi close behind them.

"Where do you think you're going?" he shouted, splitting one man's head open with the short sword. The black spurt of blood caught Musashi in the eye. Reflexively, he raised his left hand to his face and, in that instant, heard a strange metallic sound behind him.

He swung his long sword to deflect the object, but the effect of the action was very different from the intention. Seeing the ball and chain wrapped around the blade near the sword guard, he was seized with alarm. Musashi had been taken off guard.

"Musashi!" shouted Baiken. He pulled the chain taut. "Have you forgotten me?"

Musashi stared for a moment before exclaiming, "Shishido Baiken, from Mount Suzuka!"

"That's right. My brother Temma's calling you from the valley of hell. I'll see that you get there quick!"

Musashi could not free his sword. By slow degrees, Baiken was taking in the chain and moving closer, to make use of the razor-sharp sickle. As Musashi looked for an opening for his short sword, he realized with a start that if he had been fighting with only his long sword, he would be utterly defenseless now.

Baiken's neck was so swollen it was nearly as thick as his head. With a strained cry, he jerked powerfully on the chain.

Musashi had blundered; he knew that. The ball-chain-sickle was an unusual weapon, but not unfamiliar to him. Years earlier, he had been struck by admiration when he had first seen the hellish device in the hands of Baiken's wife. But it was one thing to have seen it, something else to know how to counter it.

Baiken gloated, a broad, evil grin spreading over his face. Musashi knew there was only one course open to him: he had to let go of his long sword. He looked for the right moment.

With a ferocious howl, Baiken leapt and swept the sickle toward Musashi's head, missing by only a hair's breadth. Musashi released the sword with a loud grunt. No sooner had the sickle been withdrawn than the ball came whirring through the air. Then the sickle, the ball, the sickle . . .

Dodging the sickle put Musashi right in the path of the ball. Unable to get close enough to strike, he wondered frantically how long he could keep it up. "Is this it?" he asked. The question was conscious, but as the tension increased, his body became difficult to control and his responses purely physiological. Not only his muscles but his very skin was struggling instinctively; concentration became so intense the flow of oily sweat stopped. Every hair on his body stood on end.

It was too late to get behind a tree. If he made a dash for it now, he'd probably run into another foe.

He heard a clear, plaintive cry, and thought: "Uh-oh. Iori?" He wanted to look but in his heart gave the boy up for lost.

"Die! You son of a bitch!" The cry came from behind Musashi, then: "Musashi, why're you taking so much time? I'm taking care of the vermin behind you."

Musashi didn't recognize the voice but decided he could focus his attention on Baiken alone.

To Baiken, the most important factor was his distance from his opponent; his effectiveness depended on manipulating the length of the chain. If Musashi could move a foot beyond the reach of the chain or approach a foot nearer, Baiken would be in trouble. He had to make sure that Musashi did neither.

Musashi marveled at the man's secret technique, and as he marveled, it suddenly struck him that here was the principle of the two swords. The chain was a single length, the ball functioned as the right sword, the sickle as the left.

"Of course!" he cried triumphantly. "That's it—that's the Yaegaki Style." Now confident of victory, he leapt back, putting five feet between the two of them. He transferred his sword to his right hand and hurled it straight as an arrow.

Baiken twisted his body, and the sword glanced off, burying itself in the root of a nearby tree. But as he twisted, the chain wrapped itself around his torso. Before he could even cry out, Musashi slammed his full weight into him. Baiken got his hand as far as the hilt of his sword, but Musashi broke his hold with a sharp chop to the wrist. In a continuation of the same motion, he drew the weapon and split Baiken open, like lightning splitting

53

a tree. As he pulled the blade down, he twisted ever so slightly.

"What a pity," thought Musashi. As the story was later told, he even uttered a sigh of compassion as the originator of the Yaegaki Style breathed his last.

"The *karatake* slice," exclaimed an admiring voice. "Straight down the trunk. No different from splitting bamboo. It's the first time I've ever seen it."

Musashi turned and said, "Why, if it isn't . . . Gonnosuke from Kiso. What are you doing here?"

"It's been a long time, hasn't it? The god of Mitsu-mine must have arranged it, perhaps with the aid of my mother, who taught me so much before she died."

They fell to chatting, but Musashi suddenly stopped and cried, "Iori!"

"He's all right. I rescued him from that pig of a priest and had him climb a tree."

Iori, watching them from a high branch, started to speak but instead shaded his eyes and looked toward a small flat area beyond the edge of the forest. Kuro, tied to a tree, had caught Okō's kimono sleeve with his teeth. She yanked desperately at the sleeve. In a trice, it tore off, and she ran away.

The lone survivor, the other priest, was hobbling along, leaning heavily on his lance, blood flowing from a head wound. The dog, perhaps crazed by the smell of blood, started making a terrible racket. The noise echoed and re-echoed for a time, but then the rope gave way, and the dog went after Okō. When he reached him, the priest lifted his lance and aimed for the dog's head. Wounded in the neck, the beast ran into the woods.

"That woman's getting away," cried Iori.

"Never mind. You can come down now."

"There's an injured priest over there. Shouldn't you catch him?"

"Forget it. He doesn't matter anymore."

"The woman's probably the one from the Oinu Tea-house," said Gonnosuke. He explained his presence, the heaven-sent coincidence that had enabled him to come to Musashi's assistance.

Deeply grateful, Musashi said, "You killed the man who fired the gun?"

"No." Gonnosuke smiled. "Not me; my staff. I knew ordinarily you could take care of men like that, but if they were going to use a gun, I decided I'd better do something. So I came here ahead of them and slipped up behind the man while it was still dark."

They checked the corpses. Seven had been killed with the staff, only five with the sword.

Musashi said, "I haven't done anything except defend myself, but this area belongs to the shrine. I feel I should explain things to the government official in charge. Then he can ask his questions and get the incident cleared up."

On their way down the mountain, they ran into a contingent of armed officials at the bridge at Kosaruzawa. Musashi told his story. The captain in charge listened, seemingly puzzled, but nevertheless ordered Musashi tied up.

Shocked, Musashi wanted to know why, since he was on his way to report to them in the first place.

"Get moving," ordered the captain.

Angry as Musashi was about being treated as an ordinary criminal, there was still another surprise coming. There were more officials farther down the mountain. By the time they arrived in the town, his guard numbered no fewer than a hundred.

6

Brother Disciples

"Come now, no more tears." Gonnosuke hugged Iori to his chest. "You're a man, aren't you?"

"It's because I'm a man . . . that I'm crying." He lifted his head, opened his mouth wide and bawled at the sky.

"They didn't arrest Musashi. He gave himself up." Gonnosuke's mild words masked his own deep concern. "Come on, let's go now."

"No! Not until they bring him back."

"They'll let him go soon. They'll have to. Do you want me to leave you here by yourself?" Gonnosuke walked a few paces away.

Iori didn't move. Just then, Baiken's dog came charging out of the woods, his muzzle a dull, bloody red.

"Help!" screamed Iori, running to Gonnosuke's side.

"You're worn out, aren't you? Look, would you like me to carry you piggyback?"

Iori, pleased, mumbled his thanks, climbed on the proffered back and wrapped his arms around the broad shoulders.

With the festival over the night before, the visitors had departed. A gentle breeze wafted bits of bamboo wrapping and scraps of paper along the deserted streets.

Passing the Oinu Teahouse, Gonnosuke glanced inside, intending to go by unnoticed.

But Iori piped out, "There's the woman who ran away!"

"I imagine that's where she'd be." He stopped and wondered aloud, "If the officials dragged in Musashi, why didn't they arrest her too?"

When Okō saw Gonnosuke, her eyes blazed with anger.

Seeing she seemed to be hurriedly gathering her belongings together, Gonnosuke laughed. "Going on a trip?" he asked.

"None of your business. Don't think I don't know you, you meddling scoundrel. You killed my husband!"

"You brought it on yourselves."

"I'll get even one of these days."

"She-demon!" Iori shouted over Gonnosuke's head.

Retreating into the back room, Okō laughed scornfully. "You're fine ones to be saying bad things about me when you're the thieves who broke into the treasure house."

"What's this?" Gonnosuke let Iori slide to the ground and went into the teahouse. "Who are you calling thieves?"

"You can't fool me."

"Say that again, and—"

"*Thieves!*"

As Gonnosuke grabbed her arm, she turned and stabbed at him with a dagger. Not bothering with his staff, he wrested the dagger from her hand and sent her sprawling through the front door.

Okō jumped up and screamed, "Help! Thieves! I'm being attacked."

Gonnosuke took aim and hurled the dagger. It entered her back and the point came out in front. Okō pitched forward onto her face.

From nowhere, Kuro bounded forth and was at the

body, first slurping blood hungrily, then lifting his head to howl at the sky.

"Look at those eyes!" exclaimed Iori in horror.

Okō's cry of "Thieves!" had caught the ears of the excited villagers. Sometime before dawn, someone had broken into the temple treasure house. It was clearly the work of outsiders, for the religious treasures—old swords, mirrors and the like—had been left untouched, but a fortune in gold dust, bullion and cash, accumulated over a period of many years, was missing. The news had leaked out slowly and was still unconfirmed. The effect of Okō's scream, the most tangible proof so far, was electric.

"There they are!"

"Inside the Oinu!"

The cries attracted a still larger mob, armed with bamboo spears, boar guns, sticks and rocks. In no time it seemed that the whole village was surrounding the teahouse, thirsty for blood.

Gonnosuke and Iori ducked out the back and for the next several hours were driven from hiding place to hiding place. But now they had an explanation: Musashi had been arrested not for the "crime" he was about to confess but as a thief. It was not until they reached Shōmaru Pass that they shook off the last of the search parties.

"You can see Musashino Plain from here," said Iori. "I wonder if my teacher's all right."

"Hmm. I imagine he's in prison by now and being questioned."

"Isn't there any way to save him?"

"There must be."

"Please do something. Please."

"You don't have to beg. He's like a teacher to me too. But, Iori, there's not much you can do here. Can you make it back home by yourself?"

"I suppose so, if I have to."

"Good."

"What about you?"

"I'm going back to Chichibu. If they refuse to release Musashi, I'll get him out some way. Even if I have
to tear the prison down." For emphasis, he thumped the
ground once with his staff. Iori, who had seen the power
of this weapon, quickly nodded his agreement. "That's a
boy. You go back and watch over things until I bring
Musashi home safe and sound." Placing his staff under
his arm, he turned back toward Chichibu.

Iori didn't feel lonely or afraid, nor did he worry
about getting lost. But he was dreadfully sleepy, and as
he walked along under the warm sun, he could hardly
keep his eyes open. At Sakamoto, he saw a stone Buddha
by the wayside and lay down in its shadow.

The evening light was fading when he awoke and
heard soft voices on the other side of the statue. Feeling
rather guilty about eavesdropping, he pretended he was
still asleep.

There were two of them, one sitting on a tree stump,
the other on a rock. Tied to a tree a little distance away
were two horses with lacquered boxes suspended from
both sides of their saddles. A wooden tag attached to one
of the boxes said: "From Shimotsuke Province. For use
in the construction of the west encirclement. Lacquerware Supplier to the Shōgun."

To Iori, who now peeked around the statue, they did
not look like the normal run of well-fed castle officials.
Their eyes were too sharp, their bodies too muscular.
The older one was a vigorous-looking man of more than
fifty. The last rays of the sun reflected strongly from his
bonnetlike hat, which came down over both ears and
projected out in front, concealing his features.

His companion was a slender, wiry youth wearing a
forelock that suited his boyish face. His head was covered
with a Suō-dyed hand towel, tied beneath his chin.

"How about the lacquerware boxes?" the younger
one asked. "That was pretty good, wasn't it?"

"Yes, that was clever, making people think we're

59

connected with the work going on at the castle. I wouldn't have thought of that myself.''

"I'll have to teach you these things little by little.''

"Careful now. Don't start making fun of your elders. But who knows? Maybe in four or five years, old Daizō will be taking orders from you.''

"Well, young people do grow up. Old people just get older, no matter how hard they work at staying young.''

"Do you think that's what I'm doing?''

"It's obvious, isn't it? You're always thinking of your age, and that's what makes you so devoted to seeing your mission accomplished.''

"You know me pretty well, I guess.''

"Shouldn't we be going?''

"Yes; night's catching up with us.''

"I don't like the idea of being caught up with.''

"Ha, ha. If you scare easily, you can't have much confidence in what you're doing.''

"I haven't been at this business very long. Even the sound of the wind makes me nervous sometimes.''

"That's because you still think of yourself as an ordinary thief. If you keep in mind that you're doing it for the good of the country, you'll be all right.''

"You always say that. I believe you, but something keeps telling me I'm not doing the right thing.''

"You have to have the courage of your convictions.'' But the admonition sounded slightly unconvincing, as though Daizō was reassuring himself.

The youth jumped lightly into the saddle and rode on ahead. "Keep your eye on me,'' he called back over his shoulder. "If I see anything, I'll signal.''

The road made a long descent to the south. Iori watched from behind the stone Buddha for a minute, then decided to follow them. Somehow the idea had formed in his mind that these were the treasure house thieves.

Once or twice they looked back cautiously. Apparently finding nothing to warrant alarm, they seemed to forget about him after a time. Before long, the evening glow was gone, and it was too dark to see more than a few yards ahead.

The two riders were almost at the edge of Musashino Plain when the youth pointed and said, "There, Chief, you can see the lights of Ōgimachiya." The road was flattening out. A short distance ahead, the Iruma River, twisting like a discarded obi, shone silvery in the moonlight.

Iori was now being careful to remain inconspicuous. His idea that these men were the thieves had become a conviction, and he knew all about bandits from his days in Hōtengahara. Bandits were vicious men who would commit mayhem over a single egg or a handful of red beans. Unprovoked murder was nothing to them.

By and by, they entered the town of Ōgimachiya. Daizō lifted his arm and said, "Jōta, we'll stop here and have a bite to eat. The horses have to be fed, and I'd like a smoke."

They tied the horses in front of a dimly lit shop and went inside. Jōta stationed himself by the door, keeping his eyes on the boxes the whole time he was eating. When he was finished, he went out and fed the horses.

Iori went into a food shop across the street, and when the two men rode off, he grabbed the last handful of his rice and ate it as he walked.

They rode side by side now; the road was dark but level.

"Jōta, did you send a courier to Kiso?"

"Yes, I took care of that."

"What time did you tell them?"

"Midnight. We should be there on schedule."

In the still night, Iori caught enough of their conversation to know that Daizō called his companion by a boy's name, while Jōta addressed the older man as "Chief." This might mean nothing more than that he was the head of a gang, but somehow Iori got the impression they were father and son. This made them not mere bandits but hereditary bandits, very dangerous men he would never be able to capture by himself. But if he could stick with them long enough, he could report their where-abouts to the officials.

The town of Kawagoe was fast asleep, as soundless as a swamp in the dead of night. Having passed rows of darkened houses, the two riders turned off the highway and began climbing a hill. A stone marker at the bottom said: "Forest of the Head-burying Mound—Above."

Climbing up through the bushes alongside the path, Iori reached the top first. There was a lone pine tree of great size, to which a horse was tied. Squatting at the base were three men dressed like rōnin, arms folded on their knees, looking expectantly toward the path.

Iori had hardly ensconced himself in a hiding place before one of the men stood up and said, "It's Daizō, all right." All three ran forward and exchanged jovial salu-tations. Daizō and his confederates had not met for nearly four years.

Before long, they got down to work. Under Daizō's direction, they rolled a huge stone aside and began dig-ging. Dirt was piled to one side, a great store of gold and silver to the other. Jōta unloaded the boxes from the horses and dumped out their contents, which, as Iori had suspected, consisted of the missing treasure from Mi-tsumine Shrine. Added to the previous cache, the total booty must have had a value of many tens of thousands of ryō.

The precious metals were poured into plain straw sacks and loaded on three horses. The empty lacquered boxes, along with other objects that had served their purpose, were dumped into the hole. After the ground had been smoothed over, the stone was restored to its original position.

"That should do it," said Daizō. "Time for a smoke." He sat down by the pine tree and took out his pipe. The others brushed off their clothes and joined him.

During the four years of his so-called pilgrimage, Daizō had covered the Kantō Plain very thoroughly.

There were few temples or shrines without a plaque attesting to his generosity, the extent of which was no secret. Strangely, though, no one had thought to ask how he had come by all this money.

Daizō, Jōtarō and the three men from Kiso sat in a circle for about an hour, discussing future plans. That it was now risky for Daizō to return to Edo was not in doubt, but one of them had to go. There was gold in the storehouse at Shibaura to be recovered and documents to be burned. And something had to be done about Akemi.

Just before sunup, Daizō and the three men began the journey down the Kōshū highroad to Kiso. Jōtarō, on foot, set off in the opposite direction.

The stars Iori was gazing at offered no answer to his question: "Who to follow?"

Under the transparently blue autumn sky, the strong rays of the afternoon sun seemed to sink right into Jōtarō's skin. His head filled with thoughts of his role in the coming age, he was strolling across the Musashino Plain as though he owned it.

Casting a somewhat apprehensive glance behind him, he thought: "He's still there." Thinking the boy might want to talk to him, he'd already stopped a couple of times, but the boy had made no attempt to catch up with him.

Deciding to find out what was going on, Jōtarō chose a clump of eulalia and hid in it.

When Iori reached the stretch of road where he'd last seen Jōtarō, he began looking around worriedly.

Abruptly Jōtarō stood up and called out, "You there, runt!"

Iori gasped but recovered quickly. Knowing he couldn't get away, he walked on past and asked nonchalantly, "What do you want?"

"You've been following me, haven't you?"

"Unh-unh." Iori shook his head innocently. "I'm on my way to Jūnisō Nakano."

"You're lying! You were following me."

"I don't know what you're talking about." Iori started to break and run, but Jōtarō caught him by the back of his kimono.

"Out with it!"

"But . . . I . . . I don't know anything."

"Liar!" said Jōtarō, tightening his grip. "Somebody sent you after me. You're a spy!"

"And you—you're a lousy thief!"

"What?" Jōtarō shouted, his face almost touching Iori's.

Iori bent nearly to the ground, broke loose and took off.

Jōtarō hesitated a minute, then set off after him.

Off to one side, Iori could see thatched roofs scattered about like wasp nests. He ran through a field of reddish autumn grass, kicking apart several dusty molehills.

"Help! Help! Thief!" cried Iori.

The small village he was entering was inhabited by families charged with fighting fires on the plain. Iori could hear a blacksmith's hammer and anvil. People came running out of dark stables and houses where persimmons had been hung to dry. Waving his arms, Iori panted, "The man with the bandanna . . . chasing me . . . is a thief. Capture him. Please! . . . Oh, oh! Here he comes."

The villagers stared in bewilderment, some looking fearfully at the two youths, but to Iori's dismay they made no move to capture Jōtarō.

"He's a thief! He stole from the temple!"

He stopped halfway through the village, conscious that the only thing disturbing the peaceful atmosphere was his own shouting. Then he took to his heels again and found a place to hide and catch his breath.

Jōtarō cautiously slowed down to a dignified walk. The villagers watched in silence. He certainly didn't look like either a robber or a rōnin up to no good; in fact, he seemed like a clean-cut youth incapable of committing any kind of crime.

Disgusted that the villagers—grownups!—wouldn't stand up to a thief, Iori made up his mind to hurry back to Nakano, where he could at least present his case to people he knew.

He left the road and struck out across the plain. When he could see the cryptomeria grove behind the house, there was only a mile to go. Filled with relief, he changed his pace, from a trot to a full run.

Suddenly he saw that his way was blocked by a man with both arms outstretched.

He didn't have time to figure out how Jōtarō had got ahead of him, but he was on home ground now. He jumped back and drew his sword.

"You bastard," he screamed.

Jōtarō rushed forward empty-handed and caught Iori's collar, but the boy pulled free and jumped ten feet to the side.

"Son of a bitch," muttered Jōtarō, feeling warm blood running down his right arm from a two-inch cut.

Iori took a stance and fixed his mind on the lesson Musashi had drummed into him. Eyes . . . Eyes . . . Eyes . . . His strength concentrated in his bright pupils, his whole being seemed to be channeled into a pair of fiery eyes.

Outstared, Jōtarō whipped out his own sword. "I'll have to kill you," he snarled.

Iori, taking fresh courage from the strike he had scored, charged, his attack the one he always employed against Musashi.

Jōtarō was having second thoughts. He hadn't believed Iori could use a sword; now he put his full strength into the fight. For the sake of his comrades, he had to get this meddling child out of the way. Seemingly ignoring Iori's attack, he pressed forward and swung viciously, but unsuccessfully.

After two or three parries, Iori turned around, ran, stopped, and charged again. When Jōtarō countered, he retreated again, encouraged to see that his strategy was working. He was drawing the opponent into his own territory.

Pausing to catch his breath, Jōtarō looked around the dark grove and shouted, "Where are you, you stupid little bastard?" The answer was a shower of bark and leaves. Jōtarō raised his head and shouted, "I see you," though all he could actually see through the foliage was a couple of stars.

Jōtarō started climbing toward the rustling sound Iori made as he moved out on a limb. From there, unfortunately, there was nowhere to go.

"I've got you now. Unless you can grow wings, you'd better give up. Otherwise you're dead."

Iori moved silently back to the fork of two limbs. Jōtarō climbed slowly and carefully. When Jōtarō reached out to grab him, Iori again moved out on one of the limbs. With a grunt, Jōtarō caught hold of a branch with both hands and started to pull himself up, giving Iori the chance he'd been waiting for. With a resounding whack, his sword connected with the branch Jōtarō was on. It broke, and Jōtarō plummeted to the ground.

"How do you like that, thief!" gloated Iori.

His fall broken by lower branches, Jōtarō wasn't seriously injured, except for his pride. He cursed and started back up the tree, this time with the speed of a leopard. When he was under Iori's feet again, Iori slashed back and forth with his sword to keep him from getting any nearer.

While they were locked in stalemate, the plaintive tones of a *shakuhachi* came to their ears. For a moment, they both stopped and listened.

Then Jōtarō decided to try reasoning with his adversary. "All right," he said, "you put up a better fight than I expected. I admire you for that. If you'll tell me who asked you to follow me, I'll let you go."

"Admit you're licked!"

"Are you crazy?"

"I may not be very big, but I'm Misawa Iori, the only disciple of Miyamoto Musashi. Begging mercy would be an insult to my master's reputation. Give up!"

"Wh-what?" said Jōtarō incredulously. "S-say that once more." His voice was shrill and unsteady.

"Listen carefully," Iori said proudly. "I am Misawa Iori, the only pupil of Miyamoto Musashi. Does that surprise you?"

Jōtarō was ready to admit defeat. With a mixture of doubt and curiosity, he asked, "How is my teacher? Is he well? Where is he?"

Astonished, but keeping a safe distance from Jōtarō, who was moving closer, Iori said, "Ha! *Sensei* would never have a thief for a disciple."

"Don't call me that. Didn't Musashi ever mention Jōtarō?"

"Jōtarō?"

"If you're really Musashi's pupil, you must've heard him mention my name sometime or other. I was about your age then."

"That's a lie."

"No it isn't. It's the truth."

Overcome with nostalgia, Jōtarō reached out to Iori and tried to explain that they should be friends because they were disciples of the same teacher. Still wary, Iori took a swipe at his ribs.

Squeezed precariously between two limbs, Jōtarō barely succeeded in clasping his hand around Iori's wrist. For some reason, Iori let go of the branch he was holding on to. When they fell, they fell together, one landing on top of the other, both knocked senseless.

The light in Musashi's new house was visible from all directions, since, though the roof was in place, the walls hadn't been built yet.

Takuan, arriving the day before for an after-the-storm call, had decided to wait for Musashi's return. Today, just after nightfall, his enjoyment of his solitary surroundings had been interrupted by a mendicant priest asking for hot water to go with his supper.

After his meager meal of rice balls, the aged priest had taken it upon himself to play his *shakuhachi* for Takuan, fingering his instrument in a halting, amateurish fashion. Yet as Takuan listened, the music struck him as having genuine feeling, albeit of the artless sort often expressed in poems by non-poets. He thought, too, that he could recognize the emotion the player was attempting to wring from his instrument. It was remorse, from the first off-key note to the last—a wailing cry of repentance.

It seemed to be the story of the man's life, but then, Takuan reflected, that couldn't have been too different from his own. Whether people were great or not, there was not much variety in their inner life experience. Any difference lay merely in how they dealt with common human weaknesses. To Takuan, both he and the other man were basically a bundle of illusions wrapped in human skin.

"I do believe I've seen you before somewhere," Takuan murmured thoughtfully.

The priest blinked his almost sightless eyes and said, "Now that you mention it, I thought I recognized your voice. Aren't you Takuan Sōhō from Tajima?"

Takuan's memory cleared. Moving the lamp closer to the man's face, he said, "You're Aoki Tanzaemon, aren't you?"

"Then you *are* Takuan. Oh, I wish I could crawl into a hole and hide this miserable flesh of mine!"

"How strange we should meet in a place like this. It's been nearly ten years since that time at the Shippōji, hasn't it?"

"Thinking of those days gives me a chill." Then he said stiffly, "Now that I'm reduced to wandering about in darkness, this wretched sack of bones is sustained only by thoughts of my son."

"Do you have a son?"

"I've been told he's with that man who was tied up in the old cryptomeria tree. Takezō, was it? I hear he's called Miyamoto Musashi now. The two of them are said to have come east."

"You mean your son is Musashi's disciple?"

"That's what they say. I was so ashamed. I couldn't face Musashi, so I resolved to put the boy out of my mind. But now . . . he's seventeen this year. If only I could have one look at him and see what kind of a man he's growing up to be, I'd be ready and willing to die."

"So Jōtarō's your son. I didn't know that," said Takuan.

Tanzaemon nodded. There was no hint in his shriveled form of the proud captain filled with lust for Otsū. Takuan gazed at him with pity, pained to see Tanzaemon so tormented by guilt.

Seeing that despite his priestly garb he lacked even the comfort of religious faith, Takuan decided the first thing he should do was bring him face to face with the Buddha Amida, whose infinite mercy saves even those guilty of the ten evils and the five deadly sins. There would be time enough after he'd recovered from his despair to look for Jōtarō.

Takuan gave him the name of a Zen temple in Edo. "If you tell them I sent you, they'll let you stay as long as you wish. As soon as I have time, I'll come and we'll have a long talk. I have an idea where your son might be. I'll do everything I can to make sure you see him in the not too distant future. In the meantime, give up brooding. Even after a man's fifty or sixty, he can still know happiness, even do useful work. You may live for many more years. Talk it over with the priests when you get to the temple."

Takuan shooed Tanzaemon out the door, unceremoniously and without showing any sympathy, but Tanzaemon seemed to appreciate the unsentimental attitude.

After numerous bows of gratitude, he picked up his reed hat and *shakuhachi* and left.

For fear of slipping, Tanzaemon chose to go through the woods, where the path sloped more gently. Presently his cane struck an obstacle. Feeling around with his hands, he was surprised to find two bodies lying motionless on the damp ground.

He hurried back to the cabin. "Takuan! Can you help me? I came across two unconscious boys in the woods." Takuan roused himself and came outside. Tanzaemon continued: "I don't have any medicine with me, and I can't see well enough to get water for them."

Takuan slipped on his sandals and shouted toward the bottom of the hill. His voice carried easily. A farmer answered, asking him what he wanted. Takuan told him to bring a torch, some men and some water. While he waited, he suggested to Tanzaemon that the road was the better way to go, described it in detail and sent him on his way. Halfway down the hill, Tanzaemon passed the men coming up.

When Takuan arrived with the farmers, Jōtarō had come to and was sitting underneath the tree, looking dazed. One hand resting on Iori's arm, he was debating whether to revive him and find out what he wanted to know or to get away from there. He reacted to the torch like a nocturnal animal, tensing his muscles, ready to run.

"What's going on here?" asked Takuan. As he looked more closely, inquisitive interest turned to surprise, a surprise matched by Jōtarō's. The young man was much taller than the boy Takuan had known, and his face had changed quite a bit.

"You're Jōtarō, aren't you?"

The youth placed both hands on the ground and bowed. "Yes, I am," he replied haltingly, almost fearfully. He'd recognized Takuan instantly.

"Well, I must say, you've grown up to be a fine

young man." Turning his attention to Iori, he put his arm around him and ascertained that he was still alive.

Iori revived, and after looking around curiously for a few seconds, burst into tears.

"What's the matter?" Takuan asked soothingly. "Are you hurt?"

Iori shook his head and blubbered, "I'm not hurt. But they took my teacher away. He's in the prison in Chichibu." With Iori bawling the way he was, Takuan had trouble understanding him, but soon the basic facts of the story became clear. Takuan, realizing the seriousness of the situation, was nearly as grieved as Iori.

Jōtarō, too, was deeply agitated. In a shaky voice, he said abruptly, "Takuan, I have something to tell you. Could we go somewhere where we can talk?"

"He's one of the thieves," said Iori. "You can't trust him. Anything he says will be a lie." He pointed accusingly at Jōtarō, and they glared at each other.

"Shut up, both of you. Let me decide who's right and who's wrong." Takuan led them back to the house and ordered them to build a fire outside.

Seating himself by the fire, Takuan commanded them to do likewise. Iori hesitated, his expression saying very plainly he had no intention of being friendly with a thief. But seeing Takuan and Jōtarō talking amiably over old times, he felt a pang of jealousy and grudgingly took a seat near them.

Jōtarō lowered his voice, and like a woman confessing her sins before the Buddha, became very earnest.

"For four years now, I've been receiving training from a man named Daizō. He comes from Narai in Kiso. I've learned about his aspirations and what he wants to do for the world. I'd be willing to die for him, if necessary. And that's why I've tried to help him with his work. . . . Well, it does hurt to be called a thief. But I'm still Musashi's disciple. Even though I'm separated from him, I've never been apart from him in spirit, not even for a day."

He hurried on, not waiting to be asked questions. "Daizō and I have sworn by the gods of heaven and earth not to tell anyone what our aim in life is. I can't even tell you. Still, I can't stand by when Musashi's been thrown in prison. I'll go to Chichibu tomorrow and confess."

Takuan said, "Then it was you and Daizō who robbed the treasure house."

"Yes," Jōtarō replied without the slightest sign of contrition.

"So you *are* a thief," said Takuan.

Jōtarō lowered his head to avoid Takuan's eyes. "No . . . no," he murmured lamely. "We're not just common burglars."

"I was not aware that thieves came in different varieties."

"Well, what I'm trying to say is we don't do these things for our own gain. We do them for the people. It's a matter of moving public property for the good of the public."

"I don't understand reasoning like that. Are you telling me your robberies are righteous crimes? Are you saying you're like the bandit heroes in Chinese novels? If so, it's a poor imitation."

"I can't answer that without revealing my secret agreement with Daizō."

"Ha, ha. You aren't going to let yourself be taken in, are you?"

"I don't care what you say. I'll confess only to save Musashi. I hope you'll put in a good word for me with him later."

"I wouldn't be able to think of a good word to put in. Musashi's innocent. Whether you confess or not, he'll be freed eventually. It seems to me it's far more important for you to take yourself to the Buddha. Use me as an intermediary and confess everything to him."

"Buddha?"

"That's what I said. To hear you tell it, you're doing

72

something grand for the sake of other people. In fact, you're putting yourself before others. Has it not occurred to you that you leave quite a number of people unhappy?"

"One can't consider himself when one is working on behalf of society."

"Stupid fool!" He struck Jōtarō soundly on the cheek with his fist. "One's self is the basis of everything. Every action is a manifestation of the self. A person who doesn't know himself can do nothing for others."

"What I meant—I wasn't acting to satisfy my own desires."

"Shut up! Don't you see you're barely grown? There's nothing more frightening than a half-baked do-gooder who knows nothing of the world but takes it upon himself to tell the world what's good for it. You needn't say any more about what you and Daizō are doing; I have a very good idea already. . . . What are you crying about? Blow your nose."

Ordered to bed, Jōtarō lay down obediently but couldn't get to sleep for thinking of Musashi. He clasped his hands together over his chest and silently begged forgiveness. Tears dribbled into his ears. He turned on his side and began thinking about Otsū. His cheek hurt; Otsū's tears would hurt worse. Still, revealing his secret promise to Daizō was inconceivable, even if Takuan tried to get it out of him in the morning, as he was sure to do.

He got up without making a sound, went outside and looked up at the stars. He would have to hurry; the night was nearly gone.

"Stop!" The voice froze Jōtarō where he was. Behind him, Takuan was a huge shadow.

The priest came to his side and put his arm around him. "Are you determined to go and confess?"

Jōtarō nodded.

"That's not very intelligent," said Takuan sympathetically. "You'll die a dog's death. You seem to think that if you give yourself up, Musashi will be set free, but

73

it isn't that simple. The officials will keep Musashi in prison until you tell them everything you've been refusing to tell me. And you—you'll be tortured until you talk, whether it takes a year, two years or more."

Jōtarō hung his head.

"Is that what you want, to die a dog's death? But you have no choice now: either you confess everything under torture or you tell me everything. As a disciple of the Buddha, I'll not sit in judgment. I'll relay it to Amida."

Jōtarō said nothing.

"There is one other way. By the sheerest chance, I happened to meet your father last night. He now wears the robes of a mendicant priest. Of course, I never dreamed you were here too. I sent him to a temple in Edo. If you've made up your mind to die, it'd be good for you to see him first. And when you see him, you can ask him if I'm not right.

"Jōtarō, there're three paths open to you. You must decide for yourself which one to follow." He turned away and started back into the house.

Jōtarō realized that the *shakuhachi* he had heard the night before must have belonged to his father. Without being told, he could imagine how his father must look and feel as he wandered around from place to place.

"Takuan, wait! I'll talk. I'll tell everything to the Buddha, including my promise to Daizō." He caught hold of the priest's sleeve, and the two went into the grove.

Jōtarō confessed in a long monologue, omitting nothing. Takuan neither moved a muscle nor spoke.

"That's all," said Jōtarō.

"Everything?"

"Every single thing."

"Good."

Takuan remained silent for fully an hour. Dawn came. Crows began cawing; dew glistened everywhere.

Takuan sat on the root of a cryptomeria. Jōtarō leaned against another tree, head bowed, waiting for the tongue-lashing he knew was coming.

When Takuan finally spoke, he appeared to have no more doubts. "I must say, you got mixed up with quite a crowd. Heaven help them. They don't understand which way the world is turning. It's a good thing you told me before matters got worse." Reaching into his kimono, he produced, surprisingly enough, two gold coins and handed them to Jōtarō. "You'd better get away as fast as you can. The slightest delay may bring disaster not only to you but to your father and your teacher. Get as far away as possible but don't go near the Kōshū highroad or the Nakasendō. By noon today, they'll be carrying out a rigid check on all travelers."

"What'll happen to *Sensei?* I can't go away and leave him where he is."

"Leave that to me. After a year or two, when things have quieted down, you can go to see him and make your apologies. *Then* I'll put in a good word for you."

"Good-bye."

"Just a minute."

"Yes?"

"Go to Edo first. In Azabu there's a Zen temple called Shōjuan. Your father should be there by now. Take this seal I received from the Daitokuji. They'll know it's mine. Get them to give you and your father priests' hats and robes, as well as the necessary credentials. Then you can travel in disguise."

"Why do I have to pretend to be a priest?"

"Is there no end to your naiveté? You, my silly young friend, are an agent of a group planning to kill the shōgun, set fire to Ieyasu's castle in Suruga, throw the whole Kantō district into confusion and take over the government. In short, you're a traitor. If you're caught, the mandatory punishment is death by hanging."

Jōtarō's mouth fell open.

"Now go."

"May I ask one question? Why should men who want to overthrow the Tokugawas be considered traitors? Why aren't the ones who overthrew the Toyotomis and seized control of the country traitors?"

"Don't ask me," Takuan answered with a cold stare.

7

The Pomegranate

Takuan and Iori arrived at Lord Hōjō Ujikatsu's mansion in Ushigome later the same day. A young retainer stationed at the gate went to announce Takuan, and a few minutes later Shinzō came out.

"My father is at Edo Castle," said Shinzō. "Won't you come in and wait?"

"At the castle?" said Takuan. "I'll go on then, since that's where I was headed anyway. Would you mind if I left Iori here with you?"

"Not at all," replied Shinzō with a smile and a quick glance at Iori. "May I order a palanquin for you?"

"If you would."

The lacquered palanquin was barely out of sight before Iori was at the stables, inspecting Lord Ujikatsu's well-fed chestnut browns and dappled grays one by one. He particularly admired their faces, which he thought much more aristocratic than those of workhorses of his acquaintance. There was a mystery here, though: how could the warrior class afford to keep large numbers of horses standing idle, instead of having them out working the fields?

He was just beginning to imagine cavalrymen riding into battle when Shinzō's loud voice distracted him. He looked toward the house, expecting a scolding, but saw

77

that the object of Shinzō's wrath was a thin old woman with a staff and a stubbornly set face.

"Pretending to be out!" shouted Shinzō. "Why would my father have to pretend to an old hag he doesn't even know?"

"My, aren't you angry?" Osugi said sarcastically. "I gather you're his lordship's son. Do you know how many times I've come here trying to see your father? Not a few, I'll tell you, and every time I've been told he's out."

A little rattled, Shinzō said, "It doesn't have anything to do with how many times you come. My father doesn't like to receive people. If he doesn't want to see you, why do you keep coming back?"

Undaunted, Osugi cackled, "Doesn't like to see people! Why does he live among them, then?" She bared her teeth.

The idea of calling her a dirty name and letting her hear the click of his sword being released crossed Shinzō's mind, but he didn't want to make an unseemly show of temper, nor was he sure it would work.

"My father is not here," he said in an ordinary tone of voice. "Why don't you sit down and tell me what this is all about?"

"Well, I think I'll accept your kind offer. It's been a long walk and my legs are tired." She sat down on the edge of the step and began rubbing her knees. "When you speak softly to me, young man, I feel ashamed for raising my voice. Now, I want you to convey what I say to your father when he comes home."

"I'll be glad to do that."

"I came to tell him about Miyamoto Musashi."

Puzzled, Shinzō asked, "Has something happened to Musashi?"

"No, I want your father to know what kind of man he is. When Musashi was seventeen, he went to Sekigahara and fought against the Tokugawas. *Against* the Tokugawas, do you hear? What's more, he's done so many evil deeds in Mimasaka that no one there has anything good to say about him. He killed any number of people, and he's been running away from me for years because I've been trying to take my rightful revenge on him. Musashi's a useless vagabond, and he's dangerous!"

"Now, wait—"

"No, just listen! Musashi started playing around with the woman my son was engaged to. He actually stole her and made off with her."

"Hold on now," said Shinzō, raising his hand in protest. "Why tell such stories about Musashi?"

"I'm doing it for the sake of the country," Osugi said smugly.

"What good will it do the country to slander Musashi?"

Osugi rearranged herself and said, "I hear that slick-tongued rogue is soon to be appointed an instructor in the shōgun's house."

"Where did you hear that?"

"A man who was at the Ono dōjō. I heard it with my own ears."

"Did you, now?"

"A swine like Musashi shouldn't even be allowed in the shōgun's presence, let alone be appointed tutor. A teacher to the House of Tokugawa is a teacher to the nation. It makes me sick just to think of it. I'm here to warn Lord Hōjō, because I hear he recommended Musashi. Do you understand now?" She sucked in the saliva at the corners of her mouth and went on: "I'm sure it's to the country's benefit to warn your father. And let me warn you too. Be careful you don't get taken in by Musashi's smooth talk."

Fearing she might go on in this vein for hours, Shinzō summoned his last ounce of patience, swallowed hard and said, "Thank you. I understand what you've said. I'll pass it on to my father."

"Please do!"

With the air of someone who has finally achieved a

cherished goal, Osugi got up and walked toward the gate, her sandals flopping noisily on the path.

"Filthy old hag!" cried a boyish voice.

Startled, Osugi barked, "What? . . . What?" and looked around until she spotted Iori among the trees, showing his teeth like a horse.

"Eat that!" he shouted, and flung a pomegranate at her. It struck so hard it broke.

"Ow-w-w!" screamed Osugi, clutching at her chest

She bent to pick up something to throw at him, bu he ran out of sight. She ran to the stable and was lookin; inside when a large, soft lump of horse manure struck he; squarely in the face.

Sputtering and spitting, Osugi wiped the mess from her face with her fingers, and the tears began to flow. To think that traveling about the country on her son's behalf had led to this sort of thing!

Iori watched at a safe distance from behind a tree. Seeing her weeping like an infant, he was suddenly very ashamed of himself. He half wanted to go and apologize to her before she got out the gate, but his fury at hearing her malign Musashi had not subsided. Caught between pity and hatred, he stood there for a time biting his fingernails.

"Come up here, Iori. You can see the red Fuji." Shinzō's voice came from a room high up on the hill.

With a great sense of relief, Iori ran off. "Mount Fuji?" The vision of the peak dyed crimson in the evening light emptied his mind of all other thoughts.

Shinzō, too, seemed to have forgotten his conversation with Osugi.

8

Land of Dreams

Ieyasu turned the office of shōgun over to Hidetada in 1605 but continued to govern from his castle in Suruga. Now that the work of laying the foundations for the new regime was largely completed, he was beginning to let Hidetada take over his rightful duties.

When he yielded his authority, Ieyasu had asked his son what he intended to do.

Hidetada's reply, "I'm going to build," was said to please the old shōgun immensely.

In contrast to Edo, Osaka was still preoccupied with preparations for the final battle. Illustrious generals laid secret plots, couriers carried messages to certain fiefs, displaced military leaders and rōnin were provided with solace and compensation. Ammunition was stockpiled, lances polished, moats deepened.

And more and more townsmen deserted the western cities for the booming city in the east, frequently changing loyalties, for the fear lingered that a Toyotomi victory might mean a reversion to chronic strife.

To the daimyō and higher-ranking vassals who had yet to decide whether to entrust the fate of their children and grandchildren to Edo or Osaka, the impressive construction program in Edo was an argument in favor of the Tokugawas.

Today, as on many other days, Hidetada was engaged in one of his favorite pastimes. Dressed as though for a country outing, he left the main encirclement and went to the hill at Fukiage to inspect the construction work.

At about the time the shōgun and his retinue of ministers, personal attendants and Buddhist priests stopped for a rest, a commotion broke out at the bottom of Momiji Hill.

"Stop the son of a bitch!"

"Catch him!"

A well digger was running around in circles, trying to shake off the carpenters who were chasing him. He darted like a hare between stacks of lumber and hid briefly behind a plasterers' hut. Then he made a dash for the scaffolding on the outer wall and began climbing.

Cursing loudly, a couple of the carpenters climbed after him and caught hold of his feet. The well digger, arms waving frantically, fell back into a pile of shavings.

The carpenters fell on him, kicking and beating him from all sides. For some strange reason, he neither cried out nor attempted to resist, but clung as tightly as he could to the ground, as if that was his only hope.

The samurai in charge of the carpenters and the inspector of workmen came running up.

"What's going on here?" asked the samurai.

"He stepped on my square, the filthy pig!" one carpenter whined. "A square is a carpenter's soul!"

"Get hold of yourself."

"What would you do if he walked on your sword?" demanded the carpenter.

"All right, that's enough. The shōgun is resting up there on the hill."

Hearing the shōgun mentioned, the first carpenter quieted down, but another man said, "He's got to go wash. Then he's got to bow to the square and apologize!"

"We'll take care of the punishment," said the inspector. "You men go back to work."

He seized the prostrate man by the collar and said, "Lift your face."

"Yes, sir."

"You're one of the well diggers, aren't you?"

"Yes, sir."

"What are you doing down here? This isn't where you work."

"He was around here yesterday too," said the carpenter.

"Was he?" said the inspector, staring at Matahachi's pale face and noticing that for a well digger he was a little too delicate, a little too refined.

He conferred with the samurai for a minute, then led Matahachi away.

Matahachi was locked in a woodshed behind the Office of the Inspector of Workmen and for the next several days had nothing to look at but some firewood, a sack or two of charcoal and barrels for making pickles. Fearing the plot would be discovered, he was soon in a state of terror.

Once inside the castle, he'd reconsidered and decided that if it meant being a well digger the rest of his life, he wasn't going to become an assassin. He'd seen the shōgun and his entourage several times and done nothing.

What took him to the foot of Momiji Hill whenever he could manage it during his rest periods was an unforeseen complication. A library was to be built, and when it was, the locust tree would be moved. Matahachi guiltily supposed the musket would be uncovered and this would link him directly to the plot. But he hadn't been able to find a time when no one was around to dig up the musket and throw it away.

Even when sleeping, he'd break out in a sweat. Once he dreamed he was in the land of the dead, and wherever he looked there were locust trees. A few nights after his confinement in the woodshed, in a vision as clear as day, he dreamed of his mother. Instead of taking pity on him,

83

Osugi shouted angrily and threw a basketful of cocoons at him. When the cocoons rained down on his head, he tried to run away. She pursued him, her hair mysteriously transformed into white cocoons. He ran and ran, but she was always behind him. Bathed in sweat, he jumped off a cliff and began falling through the darkness of hell, falling endlessly through blackness.

"Mother! Forgive me," he cried out like a hurt child, and the sound of his own voice awakened him. The reality he woke to—the prospect of death—was more terrifying than the dream.

He tried the door, which was locked, as he already knew. In desperation he climbed up a pickle barrel, broke a small window near the roof and squeezed through. Using piles of lumber and rock and small hills of excavated dirt for cover, he made his way stealthily to the vicinity of the western rear gate. The locust tree was still there. He sighed with relief.

He found a hoe and started digging as if he expected to discover his own life. Unnerved by the noise he was making, he stopped and looked all around him. Seeing no one, he began again.

The fear that someone had already found the musket made him swing the hoe frantically. His breathing became rapid and uneven. Sweat and grime mixed, making him look as if he'd just come from a mud bath. He was beginning to get dizzy, but he could not stop.

The blade struck something long. Casting the hoe aside, he reached down to pull it out, thinking: "I've got it."

His relief was short-lived. The object wasn't wrapped in oil paper, there was no box, and it wasn't cool like metal. He took hold, held it up and dropped it. It was a slender white wristbone or shinbone.

Matahachi did not have the heart to pick up the hoe again. It seemed like another nightmare. But he knew he was awake; he could count every leaf of the locust tree.

"What would Daizō have to gain by lying?" he

wondered, as he walked around the tree, kicking at the dirt.

He was still circling the tree when a figure walked quietly up behind him and slapped him lightly on the back. With a loud laugh, right beside Matahachi's ear, he said, "You won't find it."

Matahachi's whole body went limp. He almost fell into the hole. Turning his head toward the voice, he stared blankly for several minutes before uttering a little croak of astonishment.

"Come with me," said Takuan, taking him by the hand.

Matahachi could not move. His fingers went numb, and he clawed at the priest's hand. A chill of abject horror spread from his heels upward.

"Didn't you hear? Come with me," said Takuan, scolding with his eyes.

Matahachi's tongue was almost as useless as a mute's. "Th-this . . . fix . . . dirt . . . I—"

In a pitiless tone, Takuan said, "Leave it. It's a waste of time. The things people do on this earth, good or bad, are like ink on porous paper. They cannot be erased, not in a thousand years. You imagine that kicking a little dirt around will undo what you've done. It's because you think like that that your life is so untidy. Now come with me. You're a criminal, your crime heinous. I'm going to cut off your head with a bamboo saw and cast you into the Pool of Blood in hell." He seized Matahachi's earlobe and pulled him along.

Takuan rapped on the door of the shed where the kitchen helpers slept.

"One of you boys come out here," he said.

A boy came out, rubbing the sleep from his eyes. When he recognized the priest he'd seen talking with the shōgun, he came awake and said, "Yes, sir. Can I do something for you?"

"I want you to open that woodshed."

"There's a well digger locked up in there."

85

"He isn't in there. He's right here. There's no point in putting him back in through the window, so open the door."

The boy hastened to fetch the inspector, who rushed out, apologizing and begging Takuan not to report the matter.

Takuan shoved Matahachi into the shed, went inside and closed the door. A few minutes later, he poked his head out and said, "You must have a razor somewhere. Sharpen it and bring it here."

The inspector and the kitchen helper looked at each other, neither daring to ask the priest why he wanted the razor. Then they honed the razor and handed it over to him.

"Thanks," said Takuan. "Now you can go back to bed."

The inside of the shed was pitch black, only a glimpse of starlight being visible through the broken window. Takuan seated himself on a pile of kindling. Matahachi slumped down on a reed mat, hanging his head in shame. For a long time there was silence. Unable to see the razor, Matahachi wondered nervously whether Takuan was holding it in his hand.

At last Takuan spoke. "Matahachi, what did you dig up under the locust tree?"

Silence.

"I could show you how to dig up something. It would mean extracting something from nothingness, recovering the real world from a land of dreams."

"Yes, sir."

"You haven't the least idea what the reality I'm talking about is. No doubt you are still in your world of fantasy. Well, since you're as naive as an infant, I suppose I'll have to chew your intellectual food for you. . . . How old are you?"

"Twenty-eight."

"The same age as Musashi."

Matahachi put his hands to his face and wept.

Takuan did not speak until he had cried himself out. Then he said, "Isn't it frightening to think that the locust tree nearly became the grave marker of a fool? You were digging your own grave, actually on the verge of putting yourself into it."

Matahachi flung his arms around Takuan's legs and pleaded, "Save me. Please save me. My eyes . . . my eyes are open now. I was taken in by Daizō of Narai."

"No, your eyes are not open. Nor did Daizō deceive you. He simply tried to make use of the biggest fool on earth—a greedy, unsophisticated, petty-minded dolt who nevertheless had the temerity to take on a task any sensible man would shrink from."

"Yes . . . yes . . . I was a fool."

"Just who did you think this Daizō was?"

"I don't know."

"His real name is Mizoguchi Shinano. He was a retainer of Ōtani Yoshitsugu, who's a close friend of Ishida Mitsunari. Mitsunari, you will remember, was one of the losers at Sekigahara."

"N-no," gasped Matahachi. "He's one of the warriors the shogunate is trying to track down?"

"What else would a man out to assassinate the shōgun be? Your stupidity is appalling."

"He didn't tell me that. He just said he hated the Tokugawas. He thought it'd be better for the country if the Toyotomis were in power. He was talking about working for the sake of everybody."

"You didn't bother to ask yourself who he really was, did you? Without once using your head, you went boldly about the business of digging your own grave. Your kind of courage is frightening, Matahachi."

"What am I to do?"

"Do?"

"Please, Takuan, please, help me!"

"Let go of me."

"But . . . but I didn't actually use the gun. I didn't even find it!"

"Of course you didn't. It didn't arrive on time. If Jōtarō, whom Daizō duped into becoming a part of this dreadful plot, had reached Edo as planned, the musket might very well have been buried under the tree."

"Jōtarō? You mean the boy—"

"Never mind. That doesn't concern you. What does concern you is the crime of treason, which you have committed and which cannot be pardoned. Nor can it be condoned by the gods and the Buddha. You may as well stop thinking about being saved."

"Isn't there any way . . . ?"

"Certainly not!"

"Have mercy," sobbed Matahachi, clinging to Takuan's knees.

Takuan stood up and kicked him away. "Idiot!" he shouted in a voice that threatened to lift the roof off the shed. The ferocity of his glare was beyond description— a Buddha refusing to be clung to, a terrifying Buddha unwilling to save even the penitent.

For a second or two, Matahachi met the look resentfully. Then his head dropped in resignation, and his body was racked with sobs.

Takuan took the razor from the top of the woodpile and touched Matahachi's head with it lightly.

"As long as you're going to die, you may as well die looking like a disciple of the Buddha. Out of friendship, I'll help you do that. Close your eyes and sit quietly with your legs crossed. The line between life and death is not thicker than an eyelid. There is nothing frightening about death, nothing to cry over. Don't weep, child, don't weep. Takuan will prepare you for the end."

The room where the shōgun's Council of Elders met to discuss matters of state was isolated from other parts of Edo Castle. This secret chamber was completely enclosed by other rooms and hallways. Whenever it was necessary to receive a decision from the shōgun, the ministers would either go to his audience chamber or send a petition in a lacquered box. Notes and replies had been going back and forth with unusual frequency, and Takuan and Lord Hōjō had been admitted to the room several times, often remaining there for day-long deliberations.

On this particular day, in another room, less isolated but no less well guarded, the ministers had heard the report of the envoy sent to Kiso.

He said that though there had been no delay in acting on the order for Daizō's arrest, Daizō had escaped after closing up his establishment in Narai, taking his entire household with him. A search had brought to light a substantial supply of arms and ammunition, together with a few documents that had escaped destruction. The papers included letters to and from Toyotomi supporters in Osaka. The envoy had arranged for shipment of the evidence to the shōgun's capital and then rushed back to Edo by fast horse.

The ministers felt like fishermen who had cast a big net and not caught so much as a single minnow.

The very next day, a retainer of Lord Sakai, who was a member of the Council of Elders, made a report of a different sort: "In accordance with your lordship's instructions, Miyamoto Musashi has been released from prison. He was handed over to a man named Musō Gonnosuke, to whom we explained in detail how the misunderstanding came about."

Lord Sakai promptly informed Takuan, who said lightly, "Very good of you."

"Please ask your friend Musashi not to think too badly of us," said Lord Sakai apologetically, uncomfortably aware of the error made in the territory under his jurisdiction.

One of the problems solved most quickly was that of Daizō's base of operations in Edo. Officials under the Commissioner of Edo descended on the pawnshop in Shibaura and in one swift move confiscated everything, both property and secret documents. In the process, the unlucky Akemi was taken into custody, though she was completely in the dark regarding her patron's treacherous plans.

Received in audience by the shōgun one evening, Takuan related events as he knew them and told him how everything had turned out. He ended by saying, "Please do not forget for a moment that there are many more Daizōs of Narai in this world."

Hidetada accepted the warning with a vigorous nod.

"If you attempt to search out all such men and bring them to justice," Takuan continued, "all your time and effort will be consumed in coping with insurgents. You won't be able to carry out the great work expected of you as your father's successor."

The shōgun perceived the truth of Takuan's words and took them to heart. "Let the punishments be light," he directed. "Since you reported the conspiracy, I leave it to you to decide the penalties."

After expressing his heartfelt thanks, Takuan said, "Quite without intending to, I see I've been here at the castle for more than a month. It's time to leave now. I'll go to Koyagyū in Yamato to visit Lord Sekishūsai. Then I'll return to the Daitokuji, traveling by way of the Senshū district."

Mention of Sekishūsai seemed to evoke a pleasant memory for Hidetada. "How is old Yagyū's health?" he asked.

"Unfortunately, I'm told that Lord Munenori thinks the end is near."

Hidetada recalled a time when he had been at the Shōkokuji encampment and Sekishūsai had been received by Ieyasu. Hidetada had been a child at the time, and Sekishūsai's manly bearing had made a deep impression on him.

Takuan broke the silence. "There is one other matter," he said. "In consultation with the Council of Elders and with their permission, Lord Hōjō of Awa and I have recommended a samurai by the name of Miyamoto Musashi to be a tutor in your excellency's household. I hope that you will look favorably upon this recommendation.''

"I've been informed of that. It's said that the House of Hosokawa is interested in him, which is very much to his favor. I have decided it would be all right to appoint one more tutor.''

It was a day or two before Takuan left the castle, and in the time he acquired a new disciple. Going to the woodshed behind the inspector's office, he had one of the kitchen helpers open the door for him, letting the light fall on a freshly shaven head.

Temporarily blinded, the novice, who thought himself a condemned man, slowly lifted his downcast eyes and said, "Ah!"

"Come," said Takuan.

Wearing the priest's robe Takuan had sent him, Matahachi stood up unsteadily on legs that felt as if they had begun to decay. Takuan gently put his arm around him and helped him out of the shed.

The day of retribution had arrived. Behind his eyelids, closed in resignation, Matahachi could see the reed mat on which he would be forced to kneel before the executioner raised his sword. Apparently he had forgotten that traitors faced an ignominious death by hanging. Tears trickled down his clean-shaven cheeks.

"Can you walk?" asked Takuan.

Matahachi thought he was replying; in fact, no sound came out. He was barely conscious of going through the castle gates and crossing the bridges spanning the inner and outer moats. Trudging along dolefully beside Takuan, he was the perfect image of the proverbial sheep being led to slaughter. "Hail to the Buddha Amida, hail to the Buddha Amida. . . ." Silently he repeated the invocation to the Buddha of Eternal Light.

Matahachi squinted and looked beyond the outer moat at stately diamyō mansions. Farther to the east lay

91

Hibiya Village; beyond, the streets of the downtown district were visible.

The floating world called out to him anew, and along with his yearning for it, fresh tears came to his eyes. He closed them and rapidly repeated, "Hail to the Buddha Amida, hail to the Buddha Amida. . . ." The supplication became first audible, then louder and louder, faster and faster.

"Hurry up," Takuan said sternly.

From the moat, they turned toward Ōtemachi and cut diagonally across a large vacant lot. Matahachi felt he had walked a thousand miles already. Would the road simply go on like this all the way to hell, daylight gradually giving way to utter darkness?

"Wait here," commanded Takuan. They were in the middle of a flat open area; to the left, muddy water came down the moat from Tokiwa Bridge.

Directly across the street was an earthen wall, only recently covered with white plaster. Beyond this was the stockade of the new prison and a group of black buildings, which looked like ordinary town houses but was actually the official residence of the Commissioner of Edo.

His legs quaking, Matahachi could no longer support himself. He plopped down on the ground. Somewhere in the grass, the cry of a quail suggested the pathway to the land of the dead.

Run for it? His feet were not bound, nor were his hands. But no, he thought, he couldn't get away with it. If the shōgun decided he was worth finding, there would not be a leaf, a blade of grass, to hide behind.

In his heart, he cried out to his mother, who at this moment seemed very dear to him. If only he had never left her side, he wouldn't be here now. He recalled other women too: Okō, Akemi, Otsū, others he had been fond of or dallied with. But his mother was the only woman he genuinely longed to see. If only he were given the opportunity to go on living, he was certain he would never again go against her will, never again be an unfilial son.

He felt a damp chill on the back of his neck. He looked up at three wild geese winging their way toward the bay and envied them.

The urge to take flight was like an itch. And why not? He had nothing to lose. If he were caught, he would be no worse off than he was now. With a desperate look in his eyes, he glanced toward the gate across the street. No sign of Takuan.

He jumped up and started to run.

"Stop!"

The loud voice alone was enough to break his spirit. He looked around and saw one of the commissioner's executioners. The man stepped forward and brought his long staff down on Matahachi's shoulder, felling him with one blow, then pinned him down with the staff, as a child might pin down a frog with a stick.

When Takuan came out of the commissioner's residence, he was accompanied by several guards, including a captain. They led out another prisoner, who was tied up with a rope.

The captain selected the place where the punishment would be carried out, and two freshly woven reed mats were spread on the ground.

"Shall we get on with it?" he asked Takuan, who nodded his assent.

As captain and priest sat down on stools to watch, the executioner shouted, "Stand up!" and lifted his staff. Matahachi dragged himself to his feet but was too weak to walk. The executioner seized him angrily by the back of his robe and half dragged him to one of the mats.

He sat. His head dropped. He could no longer hear the quail. Though he was conscious of voices, they sounded indistinct, as though separated from him by a wall.

Hearing his name whispered, he looked up in surprise.

"Akemi!" he gasped. "What are you doing here?"

She was kneeling on the other mat.

"No talking!" Two of the guards made use of their staffs to separate them.

The captain stood up and began reading the official judgments and sentences in stern, dignified tones. Akemi held back her tears, but Matahachi wept shamelessly. The captain finished, sat down and shouted, "Strike."

Two low-ranking guards carrying long switches of split bamboo pranced into position and began systematically lashing the prisoners across the back.

"One. Two. Three," they counted.

Matahachi moaned. Akemi, head bowed and face ashen, clamped her teeth together with all her might in an effort to bear the pain.

"Seven. Eight. Nine." The switches frayed; smoke seemed to rise from their tips.

A few passersby stopped at the edge of the lot to watch.

"What's going on?"

"Two prisoners being punished, it looks like."

"A hundred lashes, probably."

"They're not even to fifty yet."

"Must hurt."

A guard approached and startled them by thumping the ground sharply with his staff. "Off with you. You're not allowed to stand here."

The gawkers moved to a safer distance and, looking back, saw that the punishment was over. The guards discarded their switches, which were now only bundles of flabby strands, and wiped the sweat off their faces.

Takuan stood up. The captain was already on his feet. They exchanged amenities, and the captain led his men back toward the commissioner's compound. Takuan stood still for several minutes, looking at the bowed figures on the mats. He said nothing before walking away.

The shōgun had bestowed a number of gifts on him; these he had donated to various Zen temples in the city.

Yet the gossips of Edo were soon at it again. According to which rumor one heard, he was an ambitious priest who meddled in politics. Or one the Tokugawas had persuaded to spy on the Osaka faction. Or a "black-robed" conspirator.

The rumors meant nothing to Takuan. Though he cared very much about the welfare of the nation, it made little difference to him whether the gaudy flowers of the time—the castles at Edo and Osaka—blossomed or fell.

A few thin rays of sunlight filtered through the clouds; the voice of the quail was audible again. Neither of the forms moved for quite some time, though neither had completely lost consciousness.

Finally Akemi mumbled, "Matahachi, look—water." Before them were two wooden pails of water, each with a dipper, placed there as evidence that the Office of the Commissioner was not entirely heartless.

After gulping down several mouthfuls, Akemi offered the dipper to Matahachi. When he failed to respond, she asked, "What's the matter? Don't you want any?"

Slowly he reached out and took the dipper. Once it touched his lips, he drank ravenously.

"Matahachi, have you become a priest?"

"Huh? . . . Is that all?"

"Is what all?"

"Is the punishment over? They haven't cut off our heads yet."

"They weren't supposed to. Didn't you hear the man read the sentences?"

"What did he say?"

"He said we were to be banished from Edo."

"I'm alive!" he shrieked. Almost insane with joy, he jumped up and walked away without so much as a backward glance at Akemi.

She put her hands to her head and began to fuss with her hair. Then she adjusted her kimono and tightened her obi. "Shameless," she muttered through crooked lips. Matahachi was only a speck on the horizon.

9

The Challenge

Iori was bored after only a few days at the Hōjō residence. There was nothing to do but play.

"When's Takuan coming back?" he asked Shinzō one morning, really wanting to know what had happened to Musashi.

"My father is still at the castle, so I suppose Takuan is too," said Shinzō. "They'll be back sooner or later. Why don't you amuse yourself with the horses?"

Iori raced to the stable and threw a lacquer and mother-of-pearl saddle on his favorite steed. He had ridden the horse both the day before and the day before that without telling Shinzō. Receiving permission made him feel proud. He mounted and tore out the back gate at full gallop.

The houses of daimyō, the paths through the fields, the rice paddies, the forests—the sights came at him in rapid succession and were left behind just as rapidly. Bright red snake gourds and russet grass proclaimed that autumn was at its height. The Chichibu Range rose beyond Musashino Plain. "He's in those mountains somewhere," thought Iori. He envisioned his beloved master in jail, and the tears on his cheeks made the wind feel soothingly cool.

Why not go see Musashi? Without giving the matter further thought, he whipped the horse, and horse and rider surged through the silvery sea of fluffy eulalia.

After covering a mile at breakneck speed, he reined in the horse, thinking: "Maybe he's gone back to the house."

He found the new house finished but unlived in. At the nearest paddy, he called out to the farmers harvesting their rice, "Has anyone seen my teacher?" They shook their heads sadly in reply.

Then it had to be Chichibu. On horseback, he could make the journey in a day.

After a time he came to the village of Nobidome. The entrance to the village was virtually blocked by samurai's mounts, packhorses, traveling chests, palanquins and between forty and fifty samurai having their lunch. He turned around to look for a way around the village.

Three or four samurai's attendants came running after him.

"Hey, you rascal, wait!"

"What're you calling me?" Iori asked angrily.

"Off the horse!" They were on either side of him now.

"Why? I don't even know you."

"Just keep your mouth shut and get off."

"No! You can't make me!"

Before he knew what was happening, one of the men lifted Iori's right leg high in the air, tumbling him off the other side of the horse.

"Someone wants to see you. Come along with me." He took hold of Iori's collar and pulled him toward a roadside teahouse.

Osugi stood outside, a cane in one hand. With a wave of her other hand, she dismissed the attendants. She was dressed for traveling and in the company of all those samurai. Iori didn't know what to make of it, nor did he have time to give it much thought.

"Brat!" said Osugi, then she whacked him across the shoulder with her cane. He went through the motions of taking a stance, though he knew he was hopelessly outnumbered. "Musashi has only the best of disciples. Ha! I hear you're one of them."

"I . . . I wouldn't say things like that if I were you."

"Oh, wouldn't you now?"

"I . . . I don't have any business with you."

"Oh, yes you do. You're going to tell us a few things. Who sent you to follow us?"

"Follow you?" Iori asked with a snort of disdain.

"How dare you talk that way!" the old woman screeched. "Hasn't Musashi taught you any manners?"

"I don't need any lessons from you. I'm leaving."

"No you aren't!" cried Osugi as she caught him on the shin with her cane.

"O-w-w!" Iori collapsed to the ground.

Attendants grabbed the boy and marched him over to the miller's shop by the village gate, where sat a samurai of obviously high rank. He had finished eating and was sipping hot water. Seeing Iori's predicament, he broke into a grin.

"Dangerous," thought the boy, as his eyes met Kojirō's.

With a look of triumph, Osugi thrust out her chin and said, "See! Just as I thought—it was Iori. What's Musashi got up his sleeve now? Who else could have sent him to follow us?"

"Umm," mumbled Kojirō, nodding and dismissing his attendants, one of whom asked if he wanted the boy tied up.

Kojirō smiled and shook his head. Held by Kojirō's eyes, Iori was unable to stand straight, let alone run away.

Kojirō said, "You heard what she said. Is it true?"

"No; I just came out for a ride. I wasn't following you or anybody else."

"Hmm, could be. If Musashi's any kind of a samurai, he wouldn't resort to cheap tricks." Then he began thinking out loud. "On the other hand, if he heard we'd suddenly left on a trip with a contingent of Hosokawa samurai, he might get suspicious and send someone to check on our movements. It would only be natural."

The change in Kojirō's circumstances was striking. Instead of the forelock, his head was shaved in proper samurai fashion. And in place of the loud clothing he used to wear, he had on a solid black kimono, which together with his rustic *hakama* made a most conservative impression. The Drying Pole he now carried at his side. His hope of becoming a vassal in the House of Hosokawa had been realized—not for the five thousand bushels he had wanted but for a stipend about half that large.

The present entourage, under the command of Kakubei, was an advance party on the way to Buzen to make things ready for Hosokawa Tadatoshi's return. With his father's age foremost in his mind, he had submitted his request to the shogunate quite some time earlier. Permission had finally been granted, an indication that the shogunate had no qualms about the Hosokawas' loyalty.

Osugi had asked to come along because she felt it imperative to return home. She had not relinquished her position as head of the family, yet she had been absent for nearly ten years. Uncle Gon might have looked after things for her if he were still alive. As it was, she suspected there were a number of family matters awaiting her attention.

They would be going through Osaka, where she had left Uncle Gon's ashes. She would be able to carry them to Mimasaka and hold a memorial service. It had been a long time, too, since she'd held a service for her neglected ancestors. She could return to her quest after she had straightened out affairs at home.

Recently she'd felt pleased with herself, believing she had struck a strong blow against Musashi. On first hearing of his recommendation from Kojirō, she had fallen into a state of extreme depression. If Musashi were to receive the appointment, he would be that much farther from her reach.

She'd taken it upon herself to prevent this disaster to the shogunate and the nation from happening. She hadn't seen Takuan, but she visited the House of Yagyū as well as the House of Hōjō, denouncing Musashi, claiming that it would be a dangerous folly to raise him to a high station. Not content with that, she reiterated her calumnies at the house of every government minister whose servants allowed her through the gate.

Kojirō, of course, made no effort to stop her, but he offered no special encouragement either, knowing that she wouldn't rest until she had done a thorough job. And thorough it was: she even wrote malicious letters about Musashi's past and threw them into the compounds of the Commissioner of Edo and the members of the Council of Elders. Before she was done, even Kojirō wondered if she hadn't gone too far.

Kojirō encouraged Osugi to make the journey, believing it would be better for him if she was back in the country where she could do a minimum of harm. If Osugi had any regret, it was only that Matahachi was not going with her, for she was still convinced that someday he would see the light and return to her.

Iori had no way of knowing the circumstances. Unable to flee, loath to cry for fear it would discredit Musashi, he felt trapped among enemies.

Deliberately, Kojirō stared directly into the boy's eyes and to his surprise found his stare returned. Not once did Iori's eyes waver.

"Do you have brush and ink?" Kojirō asked Osugi.

"Yes, but the ink's all dried up. Why?"

"I want to write a letter. The signs Yajibei's men put up didn't draw Musashi out, and I don't know where he is. Iori is the best messenger one could ask for. I think I should send Musashi a note on the occasion of my departure from Edo."

"What are you going to write?"

"Nothing elaborate. I'll tell him to practice his swordsmanship and visit me in Buzen one of these days. I'll let him know I'm willing to wait the rest of my life. He can come whenever he has the necessary confidence."

Osugi threw up her hands in horror. "How can you talk like that? The rest of your life, indeed! I haven't got that much time to wait. I must see Musashi dead within the next two or three years at most."

"Leave it to me. I'll take care of your problem at the same time I take care of mine."

"Can't you see I'm getting old? It has to be done while I'm still alive."

"If you look after yourself, you'll be around when my invincible sword does its work."

Kojirō took the writing kit and walked to a nearby stream, where he wet his finger to moisten the ink stick. Still standing, he took some paper from his kimono. He wrote quickly, but both his calligraphy and his composition were those of an expert.

"You can use this for paste," said Osugi, taking a few grains of cooked rice and placing them on a leaf. Kojirō mashed them between his fingers, spread the stuff along the edge of the letter and sealed it. On the back, he wrote: "From Sasaki Ganryū, Retainer to the House of Hosokawa."

"Come here, you. I'm not going to hurt you. I want you to take this letter to Musashi. Make sure he gets it, because it's important."

Iori hung back a minute but then grunted his assent and snatched the letter from Kojirō's hand. "What's written in it?"

"Just what I told the old lady."

"May I look at it?"

"You aren't to break the seal."

"If you wrote something insulting, I won't take it."

"There's nothing rude in it. I asked him to remember our promise for the future and told him I look forward to

101

seeing him again, perhaps in Buzen, if he should happen to come there.''

''What do you mean by 'seeing him again'?''

''I mean meeting him on the boundary between life and death.'' Kojirō's cheeks reddened slightly.

Stuffing the letter into his kimono, Iori said, ''All right, I'll deliver it,'' and ran off. About thirty yards away, he stopped, turned and stuck out his tongue at Osugi. ''Crazy old witch!'' he shouted.

''Wh-what?'' She was ready to go after him, but Kojirō took her arm and held her back.

''Let it pass,'' he said with a rueful smile. ''He's only a child.'' Then to Iori he shouted, ''Don't you have anything better to say?''

''No . . .'' Tears of anger rose from his chest. ''You'll be sorry, though. There isn't any way Musashi could lose to the likes of you.''

''Just like him, aren't you? Never say die. But I like the way you stick up for him. If he ever dies, come to me. I'll put you to work sweeping the garden or something.''

Not knowing Kojirō was only teasing, Iori was insulted to the marrow. He picked up a rock. When he raised his arm to throw it, Kojirō fixed his eyes on him.

''Don't do that,'' he said in a calm but forceful voice.

Iori, feeling the eyes had hit him like two bullets, dropped the stone and ran. He ran on and on until, completely exhausted, he collapsed in the middle of Musashino Plain.

He sat there for two hours thinking about the man he looked up to as his teacher. Though he knew Musashi had many enemies, he thought of him as a great man and wanted to become a great man himself. Believing he had to do something to fulfill his obligations to his master and ensure his safety, he resolved to develop his own strength as quickly as possible.

Then the memory of the terrifying light in Kojirō's

eyes came back to haunt him. Wondering whether Musashi could defeat a man that strong, he pessimistically decided even his master would have to study and practice harder. He got to his feet.

The white mist rolling down from the mountains spread over the plain. Deciding he should go on to Chichibu and deliver Kojirō's letter, he suddenly remembered the horse. Fearing bandits might have got hold of it, he searched frantically, calling and whistling at every other step.

He seemed to hear the sound of hooves coming from the direction of what he took to be a pond. He ran toward it. But there was no horse, no pond. The shimmering mist receded into the distance.

Seeing a moving black object, he approached it. A wild boar stopped rooting for food and charged dangerously close to him. The boar was swallowed up in the reeds and in its wake the mist formed a white line, looking as if it had been spread by a magician's wand. As he gazed at it, he became conscious of gurgling water. Going closer, he saw the reflection of the moon in a rocky brook.

He had always been sensitive to the mysteries of the open plain. He firmly believed that the tiniest ladybird possessed the spiritual power of the gods. In his eyes, nothing was without a soul, neither fluttering leaves nor beckoning water nor driving wind. Surrounded now by nature, he experienced the tremulous loneliness of autumn nearly gone, the sad wistfulness that must be felt by grasses and insects and water.

He sobbed so hard his shoulders shook—sweet tears, not bitter ones. If some being other than a human— a star perhaps, or the spirit of the plain—had asked him why he was weeping, he wouldn't have been able to say. If the inquiring spirit had persisted, soothing and coaxing him, he might finally have said, "I often cry when I'm out in the open. I always have the feeling the house in Hōtengahara is somewhere near."

Crying was refreshment for his soul. After he had cried to his heart's content, heaven and earth would comfort him. When the tears were dry, his spirit would come forth from the clouds clean and fresh.

"That's Iori, isn't it?"

"I believe it is."

Iori turned toward the voices and the two human figures standing out blackly against the evening sky.

"Sensei!" cried Iori, stumbling as he ran toward the man on horseback. "It's you!" Beside himself with joy, he clung to the stirrup and looked up to make sure he wasn't dreaming.

"What happened?" asked Musashi. "What are you doing out here alone?" Musashi's face seemed to be very thin—was it the moonlight?—but the warmth of the voice was what Iori had hungered for weeks to hear.

"I thought I'd go to Chichibu—" The saddle caught Iori's eye. "Why, this is the horse I was riding!"

Gonnosuke, laughing, said, "Is it yours?"

"Yes."

"We didn't know who it belonged to. It was wandering around near the Iruma River, so I regarded it as a gift from heaven to Musashi."

"The god of the plain must have sent the horse to meet you," said Iori with perfect sincerity.

"Your horse, you say? That saddle couldn't belong to a samurai getting less than five thousand bushels."

"Well, it's really Shinzō's."

Dismounting, Musashi asked, "You've been staying at his house, then?"

"Yes. Takuan took me there."

"What about our new house?"

"It's finished."

"Good. We can go back there."

"Sensei . . ."

"Yes."

"You're so thin. Why's that?"

"I've spent quite a bit of time meditating."

"How did you get out of prison?"

"You can hear about it from Gonnosuke later. For now, let's say the gods were on my side."

"You don't have to worry anymore, Iori," said Gonnosuke. "No one has any doubts about his innocence."

Relieved, Iori became quite talkative, telling them about his meeting with Jōtarō and Jōtarō's going to Edo. When he came to the "repulsive old woman" who had showed up at the Hōjō mansion, he remembered Kojirō's letter.

"Oh, I forgot something important," he exclaimed, and handed the letter to Musashi.

"A letter from Kojirō?" Surprised, he held it in his hand for a moment as though it were a missive from a long-lost friend. "Where did you see him?" he asked.

"At the village of Nobidome. That mean old woman was with him. He said he was going to Buzen."

"Oh?"

"He was with a lot of Hosokawa samurai. . . . Sensei, you better be on your toes and not take any chances."

Musashi stuffed the unopened letter into his kimono and nodded.

Not certain his meaning had got through, Iori said, "That Kojirō's very strong, isn't he? Has he got something against you?" He related to Musashi every detail of his encounter with the enemy.

When they reached the cabin, Iori went down to the bottom of the hill to get food, and Gonnosuke gathered wood and fetched water.

They sat down around the fire burning brightly in the hearth, and savored the pleasure of seeing each other safe and sound again. It was then that Iori noticed the fresh scars and bruises on Musashi's arms and neck.

"How did you get all those marks?" he asked. "You're covered with them."

"It's nothing important. Did you feed the horse?"

"Yes, sir."

"Tomorrow you must return it."

Early the next morning, Iori mounted the horse and galloped off for a short ride before breakfast. When the sun was above the horizon, he brought the horse to a halt and gaped in awe.

Racing back to the cabin, he yelled, "*Sensei,* get up. Quick! It's like when we saw it from the mountain in Chichibu. The sun—it's huge, and it looks like it's going to roll over the plain. Get up, Gonnosuke."

"Good morning," said Musashi from the grove, where he was taking a stroll.

Too excited to think about breakfast, Iori said, "I'm going now," and rode off.

Musashi watched as boy and horse took on the semblance of a crow at the very center of the sun. The black spot grew smaller and smaller, until at last it was absorbed by the great flaming orb.

10

The Gateway to Glory

Before sitting down to breakfast, the gateman raked the garden, set fire to the leaves and opened the gate. Shinzō had been up for some time too. He started his day as he always did, by reading a selection from the Chinese classics. This was followed by sword practice.

From the well, where he'd gone to wash, he walked to the stable to have a look at the horses.

"Groom," he called.

"Yes, sir."

"Isn't the chestnut roan back yet?"

"No, but it isn't the horse I'm worried about so much as the boy."

"Don't worry about Iori. He grew up in the country. He can take care of himself."

The elderly gateman came up to Shinzō and informed him that some men had come to see him and were waiting in the garden.

Walking toward the house, Shinzō waved, and as he came up to them, one man said, "It's been a long time."

"It's good to see you all together again," said Shinzō.

"How's your health?"

"Splendid, as you can see."

"We heard you'd been wounded."

"It didn't amount to much. What brings you here at this early hour?"

"There's a little matter we'd like to talk over with you."

The five former students of Obata Kagenori, all handsome sons of banner guards or Confucian scholars, exchanged significant glances.

"Let's go over there," said Shinzō, indicating a maple-covered hillock in one corner of the garden.

Coming to the gateman's fire, they stopped and stood around it.

Shinzō put his hand to his neck, then noticing the others were looking at him, said, "When it's cold, it does ache a little." They took turns examining the scar.

"I heard that was the work of Sasaki Kojirō."

There was a short, tense silence.

"As it happens, our purpose in coming today was to talk about Kojirō. Yesterday we learned he was the man who killed Yogorō."

"I suspected that. Do you have any proof?"

"Circumstantial, but convincing. Yogorō's body was found at the bottom of Isarago Hill, behind the temple. Kakubei's house is halfway up the hill. Kojirō was living there."

"Hmm. I wouldn't be surprised if Yogorō went alone to see Kojirō."

"We're pretty sure that's what happened. Three or four nights before the body was found, a florist saw a man answering to Yogorō's description climbing the hill. Kojirō must've killed him and carried the body down the hill."

The six men stared solemnly at each other, their eyes reflecting their silent anger.

Shinzō, his face reddened by the fire, asked, "Is that all?"

"No. We wanted to talk about the future of the House of Obata and how we're going to take care of Kojirō."

Shinzō stood lost in thought. The man who had spoken first said, "You may have heard this already. Kojirō's become a vassal of Lord Hosokawa Tadatoshi. He's on his way to Buzen now, and he hasn't paid for what he did—ruin our master's reputation, kill his only son and heir and slaughter our comrades."

"Shinzō," urged a third man, "as disciples of Obata Kagenori, we have to do something."

Bits of white ash drifted up from the fire. One man caught a whiff of smoke and coughed.

After listening to them for a few minutes, as they expressed their bitter indignation, Shinzō said, "I'm one of the victims, of course, and I have a plan of my own. But tell me just what you have in mind."

"We're thinking of lodging a protest with Lord Hosokawa. We'll tell him the whole story and ask that Kojirō be turned over to us."

"Then what?"

"We'll see his head up on a pike in front of the graves of our teacher and his son."

"You might be able to do that if he were turned over to you tied up. But the Hosokawas aren't likely to do that. Even though he's only recently been engaged, he is their vassal, and it's his skill they're interested in. Your complaint would only be taken as further proof of his ability. What daimyō is going to turn over one of his vassals to anyone without compelling reasons?"

"Then we'll have to take extreme measures."

"Such as?"

"The group he's traveling with is fairly large. We could easily catch up with them. With you as our leader, the six of us and other loyal disciples—"

"Are you suggesting attacking him?"

"Yes. Go with us, Shinzō."

"I don't like it."

"Aren't you the one who's been chosen to carry on the Obata name?"

"Admitting an enemy is better than we are is difficult,'' Shinzō said thoughtfully. ''Still, objectively, Koji-rō's the better swordsman. Even with dozens of men, I'm afraid we'd only end up adding to our shame.''

''You're going to stand by and do nothing?'' asked one man indignantly.

''No, I resent Kojirō's getting away with what he's done as much as any of you. But I'm willing to wait until the time is right.''

''You're awfully patient,'' one man said sarcasti-cally.

''Aren't you evading your responsibility?'' asked another.

When Shinzō made no reply, the five men decided further talk was useless and departed in haste.

On the way they passed Iori, who had dismounted at the gate and was leading the horse to the stable. After tying the animal up, he saw Shinzō by the fire and went to join him.

''Oh, so you're back,'' said Shinzō.

''Yes,'' said Iori. ''Say, did you have a quarrel?''

''Why do you ask?''

''When I came in just now, I passed some samurai. They seemed angry. They were saying strange things, like 'I overestimated him,' and 'He's a weakling.' ''

''That doesn't mean anything,'' said Shinzō with a little laugh. ''Come closer and warm yourself.''

''Who needs a fire? I rode all the way from Musa-shino without stopping.''

''You seem in good spirits. Where did you stay last night?''

''At the house. *Sensei*'s back!''

''I heard he was or soon would be.''

''You already knew?''

''Takuan told me. Iori, have you heard the news?''

''What news?''

''Your teacher's going to be a great man. It's a wonderful stroke of luck for him. He's going to be one of the shōgun's teachers. He'll be the founder of his own school of swordsmanship."

"Do you mean that?"

"Does it make you happy?"

"Of course—happier than anything. Can I borrow the horse?"

"Now? You just came back."

"I'll go and tell him."

"You don't have to do that. Before the day's out, the Council of Elders will issue a formal summons. As soon as we receive word, I'll go myself and tell Musashi."

"Will he come here?"

"Yes," Shinzō assured him. With a last look at the dying fire, he started toward the house, cheered a bit by Iori but worried about the fate of his angry friends.

The summons was not long in coming. A messenger arrived about two hours later with a letter for Takuan and an order for Musashi to appear the following day at the Reception Pavilion just outside Wadakura Gate. After his appointment was confirmed, he would be received in audience by the shōgun.

When Shinzō, with an attendant, reached the house on Musashino Plain, he found Musashi sitting in the sun with a kitten on his lap, talking with Gonnosuke.

Words were few. Shinzō said only, "I've come for you."

"Thanks," said Musashi. "I was about to call you to thank you for looking after Iori."

Without further ado, he mounted the horse Shinzō had brought along for him and they returned to Ushigome.

That evening, as he sat with Takuan and Lord Ujikatsu, he felt immensely fortunate to be able to regard these men, as well as Shinzō, as true friends.

In the morning, Musashi awoke to find clothes suitable to the occasion already laid out for him, together with such things as a fan and tissue paper. And at breakfast, Lord Ujikatsu said to him, "It's a great day. You should rejoice." The meal included rice with red beans, a whole sea bream for each person and other dishes served only on festive occasions. The menu was very much as it would have been for a coming-of-age ceremony in the Hōjō family.

Musashi wanted to refuse the appointment. In Chichibu, he had reconsidered his two years in Hōtengahara and his ambition to put his swordsmanship to work in the interest of good government. Now the belief that Edo, not to speak of the rest of the country, was ready for the type of ideal government he envisioned seemed less tenable. The sanctity of the Way and the application of the principles of swordsmanship for the sake of peace seemed no more than lofty ideals, at least until either Edo or Osaka succeeded in consolidating its rule over the whole country. And he hadn't made up his mind on another point: if the final battle were to come tomorrow, should he support the Eastern Army or the Western Army? Or should he leave the world behind and survive on mountain grasses until peace was restored?

Even on this morning, he could not escape the feeling that if he contented himself with a high position, his pursuit of the Way would be aborted.

But he couldn't refuse. What finally swayed him was the trust in him shown by his supporters. There was no way to say no; he could not break faith with Takuan, his old friend and stern mentor, and Lord Ujikatsu, now a valued acquaintance.

Dressed in formal attire and riding a splendid horse with a beautiful saddle, he set forth on a brilliantly sunlit road for the castle, each step supposedly carrying him closer to the gateway to glory.

In front of the Reception Pavilion was a graveled courtyard and, on a high post, a sign saying: "Dismount." As Musashi got off the horse, an official and one of the stablemen came forward.

"My name is Miyamoto Musashi," he announced in

a formal tone of voice. "I have come in response to a summons issued yesterday by the Council of Elders. May I request that you show me to the official in charge of the waiting room?" He had come alone, as was expected of him. Another official came and escorted him to the waiting room, where he was advised to stay "until there is word from within."

It was a large room, more than twenty mats in size, known as the "Orchid Room," after the paintings of birds and spring orchids on the walls and door panels. Before long, a servant came with tea and cakes, but that was Musashi's only contact with human beings for nearly half a day. The little birds in the pictures did not sing, the orchids gave off no fragrance. Musashi began to yawn.

He assumed that the ruddy-faced, white-haired man who eventually appeared was one of the ministers. Perhaps in his prime he had been a distinguished warrior.

"You're Musashi, are you?" Lord Sakai Tadakatsu said lightly as he sat down. "Forgive us for making you wait so long." Though Lord of Kawagoe and a well-known daimyō, in the shōgun's castle he was merely another official, attended by only one samurai. His manner suggested he cared little about pomp or protocol.

Musashi bowed to the floor and remained in this position as he announced in stiffly formal language: "My name is Miyamoto Musashi. I am a rōnin from Mimasaka, the son of Munisai, who was descended from the Shimmen family. I have come to the castle gate in compliance with the shōgun's will, as stated in the summons sent to me."

Tadakatsu nodded several times, causing his double chin to shake. "Many thanks for your trouble," he said, but then went on in an apologetic vein: "With regard to your appointment to official position, for which you were recommended by the priest Takuan and Lord Hōjō of Awa, there was, last evening, a sudden change in the shōgun's plans. As a result, you will not be engaged. Since several of us were not satisfied with this decision, the Council of Elders reviewed this matter today. In fact, we have been discussing it until just now. We took the question to the shōgun again. I am sorry to say that we were unable to alter this latest decision."

There was sympathy in his eyes, and he seemed for a moment to be searching for words of consolation. "In our fleeting world," he went on, "this sort of thing happens all the time. You mustn't let yourself be annoyed by what people say about you. In matters having to do with official appointments, it is often difficult to tell whether one has been fortunate or unfortunate."

Musashi, still bowing, said, "Yes, sir."

Tadakatsu's words were music to his ears. Gratitude swelled from the bottom of his heart, filling his whole body.

"I understand the decision, sir. I am grateful to you." The words came out naturally. Musashi was not concerned with face, nor was he being ironic. He felt that a being greater than the shōgun had just bestowed on him an appointment much higher than that of official tutor. The word of the gods had been vouchsafed to him.

"He took it well," thought Tadakatsu, gazing rather pointedly at Musashi. Aloud he said, "Perhaps it is presumptuous of me, but I've been told you have artistic interests unusual in a samurai. I would like to show an example of your work to the shōgun. Replying to the malicious gossip of ordinary people is unimportant. I think it would be more befitting a noble samurai to rise above the babble of the crowd and leave behind a word-less testimony to the purity of his heart. A work of art would be appropriate, don't you think?"

While Musashi was still pondering the meaning of this, Tadakatsu said, "I hope I will see you again," and left the room.

Musashi raised his head and sat up straight. It was a couple of minutes before he grasped the meaning of Tadakatsu's words—that is, there was no need to answer malicious gossip, but he had to give evidence of his character. If he could do this, his honor would be unsullied, and the men who had recommended him would suffer no loss of face.

Musashi's eye fell on a six-panel screen in one corner of the room. It was invitingly blank. Summoning a young samurai from the guard room, he explained that Lord Sakai had asked him to draw a picture and requested materials with which to comply—brushes, ink of good quality, some aged cinnabar and a bit of blue pigment.

It occurred to Musashi what an odd fact it was that most children could draw—and sing, for that matter—but that they forgot how to as they grew older. Perhaps the little bit of wisdom they acquired inhibited them. He himself was no exception. As a child he had often drawn pictures, this having been one of his favorite ways of overcoming loneliness. But from the age of thirteen or fourteen until he was past twenty, he gave up drawing almost entirely.

In the course of his travels he had often stopped over at temples or the houses of the wealthy, where he had the opportunity to see good paintings—murals, or scrolls hanging in alcoves—and this had given him a lively interest in art.

The aristocratic simplicity and subtle profundity of Liang-k'ai's painting of chestnuts had made an especially deep impression. After seeing that work at Kōetsu's house, he had availed himself of every opportunity to view rare Chinese paintings of the Sung dynasty, the works of the fifteenth-century Japanese Zen masters and the paintings of contemporary masters of the Kanō School, particularly Kanō Sanraku and Kaihō Yūshō. Naturally, he had his likes and dislikes. Liang-k'ai's bold, virile brushwork, as seen by a swordsman's eye, struck him as revealing the prodigious strength of a giant. Kaihō Yūshō, possibly because he was of samurai origin, had in his old age achieved such a high degree of purity that Musashi considered him a worthy man to take as a model. He was also attracted by the light impromptu effects in the works of the hermit priest and aesthete Shōkadō Shōjō, whom he liked all the more because he was reputed to be a close friend of Takuan.

Painting, which seemed far removed from the path he had chosen, was hardly an art for a person who rarely spent a full month in any one place. Yet he did paint from time to time.

As in the case of other adults who have forgotten how to draw, his mind would work, but not his spirit. Intent upon drawing skillfully, he was unable to express himself naturally. Many had been the times he'd become discouraged and quit. Then, sooner or later, some impulse invariably moved him to pick up the brush again—in secret. Being ashamed of his paintings, he never showed them to others, though he allowed people to inspect his sculpture.

Until now, that is. To commemorate this fateful day, he resolved to paint a picture fit for the shōgun, or anyone else, to see.

He worked rapidly and without interruption until it was finished. Then he quietly put the brush in a jar of water and left, without a single backward glance at his work.

In the courtyard, he did turn around for one last look at the imposing gate, one question filling his mind: Did glory lie inside or outside the gate?

Sakai Tadakatsu returned to the waiting room and sat for some time gazing at the still damp painting. The picture was of Musashino Plain. In the middle, appearing very large, was the rising sun. This, symbolizing Musashi's confidence in his own integrity, was vermilion. The rest of the work was executed in ink to capture the feeling of autumn on the plain.

Tadakatsu said to himself, "We've lost a tiger to the wilds."

11

The Sound of Heaven

"Back already?" asked Gonnosuke, blinking his eyes at the sight of Musashi in stiffly starched formal dress.

Musashi went inside the house and sat down. Gonnosuke knelt at the edge of the reed matting and bowed. "Congratulations," he said warmly. "Will you have to go to work right away?"

"The appointment was canceled," Musashi said with a laugh.

"Canceled? Are you joking?"

"No. And I consider it a good thing, too."

"I don't understand. Do you know what went wrong?"

"I saw no reason to ask. I'm grateful to heaven for the way it turned out."

"But it seems a pity."

"Are even you of the opinion I can find glory only within the walls of Edo Castle?"

Gonnosuke did not answer.

"For a time, I had such an ambition. I dreamed of applying my understanding of the sword to the problem of providing peace and happiness for the people, making the Way of the Sword the Way of Government. I thought being an official would give me a chance to test my idea."

"Somebody slandered you. Is that it?"

"Perhaps, but don't give it another thought. And

117

don't misunderstand me. My ideas, I've learned, particularly today, are little more than dreams."

"That's not true. I've had the same idea; the Way of the Sword and the spirit of good government ought to be one and the same."

"I'm glad we agree. But in fact, the truth of the scholar, alone in his study, does not always accord with what the world at large considers to be true."

"Then you think the truth you and I are searching for is of no use in the real world."

"No, it's not that," said Musashi impatiently. "As long as this country exists, no matter how things change, the brave man's Way of the Spirit will never cease to be useful. . . . If you give the matter some thought, you'll see that the Way of Government is not concerned with the Art of War alone. A flawless political system must be based on a perfect blending of military and literary arts. To cause the world to live in peace is the ultimate Way of the Sword. That's why I've come to the conclusion that my thoughts are only dreams, childish dreams at that. I must learn to be a humble servant of two gods, one of the sword, one of the pen. Before I attempt to govern the nation, I must learn what the nation has to teach." He concluded with a laugh but abruptly stopped and asked Gonnosuke if he had an ink box or a writing kit.

When he finished writing, he folded up his letter and said to Gonnosuke, "I'm sorry to trouble you, but I'd like to ask you to deliver this for me."

"To the Hōjō residence?"

"Yes. I've written fully about my feelings. Give Takuan and Lord Ujikatsu my warmest greetings. . . . Oh, there's one more thing. I've been keeping something of Iori's. Please give it to him." He pulled out the pouch Iori's father had left him and placed it beside the letter.

With an anxious look on his face, Gonnosuke moved forward on his knees and said, "Why are you returning this to Iori now?"

"I'm going to the mountains."

"Mountains or city, wherever you go, Iori and I want to be with you as your disciples."

"I won't be away forever. While I am, I'd like you to take care of Iori, say for the next two or three years."

"What? Are you going into retirement?"

Musashi laughed, uncrossed his legs and leaned back on his arms. "I'm much too young for that. I'm not giving up my great hope. Everything's still ahead of me: desire, illusion, everything. . . . There's a song. I don't know who wrote it, but it goes like this:

> "While yearning to gain
> The depths of the mountains,
> I'm drawn against my will
> To the places
> Where people reside."

Gonnosuke lowered his head as he listened. Then he stood up and put the letter and pouch in his kimono. "I'd better go now," he said quietly. "It's getting dark."

"All right. Please return the horse, and tell Lord Ujikatsu that since the clothes are soiled from travel, I'll keep them."

"Yes, of course."

"I don't think it would be discreet for me to go back to Lord Ujikatsu's house. The cancellation of the appointment must mean that the shogunate regards me as unreliable or suspicious. It might cause Lord Ujikatsu trouble to be associated any more closely with me. I didn't write that in the letter, so I want you to explain it to him. Tell him I hope he's not offended."

"I understand. I'll be back before morning."

The sun was rapidly setting. Gonnosuke took the horse's bit and led the animal down the path. Since it had been lent to Musashi, the idea of riding it never crossed his mind.

It was about two hours later when he reached Ushigome. The men were sitting around, wondering what had become of Musashi. Gonnosuke joined them and gave the letter to Takuan.

An official had already been there to inform them of unfavorable reports on Musashi's character and past activities. Of all the points against him, the most damaging was that he had an enemy who had sworn vengeance. According to the rumors, Musashi was in the wrong.

After the official left, Shinzō had told his father and Takuan about Osugi's visit. "She even tried to sell her wares here," was the way he put it.

What was left unexplained was why people accepted so unquestioningly what they were told. Not just ordinary people—women gossiping around the well or laborers drinking in cheap sake shops—but men who had the intelligence to sift fact from fabrication. The shōgun's ministers had discussed the matter for many long hours, but even they had ended up giving credence to Osugi's calumnies.

Takuan and the others half expected Musashi's letter to express his discontent, but in fact it said little beyond giving his reason for going away. He began by saying that he had asked Gonnosuke to tell them how he felt. Then came the song he had sung for Gonnosuke. The short letter ended: "Indulging my chronic wanderlust, I am setting out on another aimless journey. On this occasion, I offer the following poem, which may amuse you:

"If the universe
Is indeed my garden,
When I look at it,
I stand at the exit of
The house called the Floating World."

Though Ujikatsu and Shinzō were deeply touched by Musashi's consideration, Ujikatsu said, "He's too self-effacing. I'd like to see him once more before he goes away. Takuan, I doubt that he'd come if we sent for him, so let's go to him." He got to his feet, ready to leave immediately.

"Could you wait a moment, sir?" asked Gonnosuke. "I'd like to go with you, but Musashi asked me to give something to Iori. Could you have him brought here?"

When Iori came in, he asked, "Did you want me?" His eyes went immediately to the pouch in Gonnosuke's hand.

"Musashi said you were to take good care of this," said Gonnosuke, "since it's the only keepsake you have from your father." He then explained that the two of them would be together until Musashi's return.

Iori couldn't hide his disappointment, but not wanting to appear weak, he nodded halfheartedly.

In answer to Takuan's inquiries, Iori told all he knew about his parents. When there were no more questions, he said, "One thing I've never known is what became of my sister. My father didn't say much about her, and my mother died without telling me anything I can remember. I don't know where she lives, or whether she's alive or dead."

Takuan placed the pouch on his knee and took out a crumpled piece of paper. As he read the cryptic message Iori's father had written, his eyebrows shot up in surprise. Staring hard at Iori, he said, "This tells us something about your sister."

"I thought maybe it did, but I didn't understand it and neither did the priest at the Tokuganji."

Skipping over the first part, Takuan read aloud:
" 'Since I had resolved to die of starvation before serving a second lord, my wife and I wandered around for many years, living in the humblest circumstances. One year we had to abandon our daughter at a temple in the central provinces. We put 'one sound of heaven' in her baby clothes and entrusted her future to the threshold of compassion. Then we went on to another province.

" 'Later, I acquired my thatched house in the fields of Shimōsa. I thought back to that earlier time, but the place was far away and we had had no word, so I feared it might not be in the girl's interest to try to find her. I consequently left matters as they were.

" 'How cruel parents can be! I am reproved by the words of Minamoto no Sanetomo:

" 'Even the animals,
    Which cannot speak their feelings,
    Are not bereft of
    The tender generous love
    Of parents for their offspring.

" 'May my ancestors take pity on me for refusing to sully my honor as a samurai by taking a second lord. You are my son. No matter how much you crave success, do not eat dishonorable millet!' "

As he placed the paper back in the pouch, Takuan said, "You'll be able to see your sister. I've known her since I was a young man. Musashi knows her too. Come with us, Iori." He gave no hint as to why he said this, nor did he mention Otsū or the "sound of heaven," which he recognized to be her flute.

They all left together and hurried to the cabin, arriving shortly after the first rays of the rising sun touched it. It stood empty. On the edge of the plain was one white cloud.

12

The Runaway Ox

The shadow of the plum branch cast on the white plaster wall by the pallid sun was beautiful in a restrained way evocative of monochrome ink painting. It was early spring in Koyagyū, and quiet, the branches of the plum trees seemingly beckoning southward to the nightingales that would soon flock to the valley.

Unlike the birds, the *shugyōsha* who presented themselves at the castle gate knew no season. They came in a constant stream, seeking either to receive instruction from Sekishūsai or to try their hand against him. The litany varied little: "Please, just one bout"; "I beg you, let me see him"; "I'm the only true disciple of so-and-so, who teaches at such-and-such a place." For the past ten years, the guards had been giving the same reply: because of their master's advanced age, he was unable to receive anyone. Few swordsmen, or would-be swordsmen, would let it go at that. Some launched diatribes on the meaning of the true Way and how there should be no discrimination between young and old, rich and poor, beginner and expert. Others simply pleaded, while still others rashly tried to offer bribes. Many went away muttering angry imprecations.

Had the truth been generally known, namely that Sekishūsai had passed away late the previous year, matters might have been greatly simplified. But it had been decided that since Munenori couldn't get away from Edo until the fourth month, the death should be kept secret until the funeral service had been held. One of the handful of people outside the castle who knew the circumstances now sat in a guest room asking rather insistently to see Hyōgo.

It was Inshun, the elderly abbot of the Hōzōin, who throughout In'ei's dotage and after his death had upheld the temple's reputation as a martial arts center. Many even believed he had improved it. He had done everything possible to maintain the close ties between the temple and Koyagyū that had existed since the days of In'ei and Sekishūsai. He wanted to see Hyōgo, he said, because he wanted to have a talk about the martial arts. Sukekurō knew what he really wanted—to have a bout with the man whom his grandfather had privately regarded as a better swordsman than either himself or Munenori. Hyōgo, of course, would have no part in such a match, since he thought it would benefit neither side and was therefore senseless.

Sukekurō assured Inshun that word had been sent. "I'm sure Hyōgo would come to greet you if he were feeling better."

"So you mean to say he still has a cold?"

"Yes; he can't seem to get rid of it."

"I didn't know his health was so frail."

"Oh, it isn't really, but he's been in Edo for some time, you know, and he can't quite get used to these cold mountain winters."

While the two men chatted, a servant boy was calling Otsū's name in the garden of the innermost encirclement. A shoji opened, and she emerged from one of the houses, trailing a wisp of incense smoke. She was still in mourning more than a hundred days since Sekishūsai's passing, and her face looked as white as a pear blossom.

"Where've you been? I've been looking everywhere," asked the boy.

"I've been in the Buddhist chapel."

"Hyōgo's asking for you."

When she entered Hyōgo's room, he said, "Ah, Otsū, thank you for coming. I'd like you to greet a visitor for me."

"Yes, of course."

"He's been here quite a while. Sukekurō went to keep him company, but listening to him go on and on about the Art of War must have Sukekurō pretty exhausted by now."

"The abbot of the Hōzōin?"

"Um."

Otsū smiled faintly, bowed and left the room.

Meanwhile, Inshun was not too subtly feeling Sukekurō out regarding Hyōgo's past and character.

"I'm told that when Katō Kiyomasa offered him a position, Sekishūsai refused to consent unless Kiyomasa agreed to an unusual condition."

"Really? I don't recall ever hearing of any such thing."

"According to In'ei, Sekishūsai told Kiyomasa that since Hyōgo was extremely quick-tempered, his lordship would have to promise in advance that if Hyōgo committed any capital offenses, he would pardon the first three. Sekishūsai was never known to condone impetuosity. He must have had rather a special feeling about Hyōgo."

This came as such a surprise that Sukekurō was still at a loss for words when Otsū entered. She smiled at the abbot and said, "How good to see you again. Unfortunately, Hyōgo is tied up preparing a report which must be sent to Edo immediately, but he asked me to convey his apologies at not being able to see you this time." She busied herself serving tea and cakes to Inshun and the two young priests attending him.

The abbot looked disappointed, though he politely ignored the discrepancy between Sukekurō's excuse and Otsū's. "I'm sorry to hear that. I had some important information for him."

"I'll be happy to pass it on," said Sukekurō, "and you can rest assured Hyōgo's ears alone will hear it."

"Oh, I'm sure of that," said the old priest. "I just wanted to warn Hyōgo in person."

Inshun then repeated a rumor he'd heard about some samurai from Ueno Castle in Iga Province. The dividing line between Koyagyū and the castle lay in a sparsely inhabited area about two miles to the east, and ever since Ieyasu had confiscated it from the Christian daimyō Tsutsui Sadatsugu and reassigned it to Tōdō Takatora, many changes had been taking place. Takatora had, since taking up residence the previous year, repaired the castle, revised the tax system, improved the irrigation facilities and carried out other measures to consolidate his holdings. All this was common knowledge. What Inshun had got wind of was that Takatora was in the process of trying to expand his lands by pushing back the boundary line.

According to the reports, Takatora had dispatched a number of samurai to Tsukigase, where they were building houses, cutting down plum trees, waylaying travelers and openly trespassing on Lord Yagyū's property.

"It could be," observed Inshun, "Lord Takatora is taking advantage of your being in mourning. You may think I'm an alarmist, but it looks as though he's planning to push the boundary back in this direction and put up a new fence. If he is, it'd be a lot easier to attend to things now than after he's finished. If you sit back and do nothing, you'll regret it later, I'm afraid."

Speaking as one of the senior retainers, Sukekurō thanked Inshun for the information. "I'll have the situation investigated, and lodge a complaint if one is warranted." Expressing thanks on behalf of Hyōgo, Sukekurō bowed as the abbot took his leave.

When Sukekurō went to inform Hyōgo of the rumors, Hyōgo just laughed. "Let it be," he said. "When my uncle gets back, he can look into it."

Sukekurō, who knew the importance of guarding every foot of land, wasn't quite satisfied with Hyōgo's attitude. He conferred with the other ranking samurai and together they agreed that, though discretion was called for, something should be done. Tōdō Takatora was one of the most powerful daimyō in the country.

The following morning, as Sukekurō was leaving the dōjō above the Shinkagedō after sword practice, he ran into a boy of thirteen or fourteen.

The lad bowed to Sukekurō, who said jovially, "Hello there, Ushinosuke. Peeking into the dōjō again? Did you bring me a present? Let's see . . . wild potatoes?" He was only half teasing, since Ushinosuke's potatoes were always better than anyone else's. The boy lived with his mother in the isolated mountain village of Araki and often came to the castle to sell charcoal, boar meat and other things.

"No potatoes today, but I brought this for Otsū." He held up a package wrapped in straw.

"What's that, now—rhubarb?"

"No, it's alive! In Tsukigase, I sometimes hear nightingales singing. I caught one!"

"Hmm, you always come by way of Tsukigase, don't you?"

"That's right. That's the only road."

"Let me ask you a question. Have you seen a lot of samurai in that area lately?"

"Some."

"What are they doing there?"

"Building cabins . . ."

"Have you seen them putting up fences, anything like that?"

"No."

"Have they been cutting down plum trees?"

"Well, besides the cabins, they've been fixing bridges, so they've been cutting down all kinds of trees. For firewood too."

"Are they stopping people on the road?"

"I don't think so. I haven't seen them do that."

Sukekurō cocked his head. "I've heard those samurai are from Lord Tōdō's fief, but I don't know what they're doing in Tsukigase. What do people in your village say?"

"They say they're rōnin chased out of Nara and Uji. They didn't have anyplace to live, so they came to the mountains."

Despite what Inshun had said, Sukekurō thought this a not unreasonable explanation. Ōkubo Nagayasu, the magistrate of Nara, had not relaxed his efforts to keep his jurisdiction free of indigent rōnin.

"Where's Otsū?" asked Ushinosuke. "I want to give her her present." He always looked forward to seeing her, but not just because she gave him sweets and said nice things to him. There was something about her beauty that was mysterious, otherwordly. At times, he couldn't decide whether she was human or a goddess.

"She's in the castle, I imagine," said Sukekurō. Then, looking toward the garden, he said, "Oh, you seem to be in luck. Isn't that her over there?"

"Otsū!" Ushinosuke called loudly.

She turned and smiled. Running breathlessly to her side, he held up his package.

"Look! I caught a nightingale. It's for you."

"A nightingale?" Frowning, she kept her hands close to her sides.

Ushinosuke looked disappointed. "It has a beautiful voice," he said. "Wouldn't you like to hear it?"

"I would, but only if it's free to fly wherever it wants to. Then it'll sing pretty songs for us."

"I guess you're right," he said with a little pout. "Do you want me to turn it loose?"

"I appreciate your wanting to give me a present, but yes, that'd make me happier than keeping it."

Silently, Ushinosuke split open the straw package, and like an arrow the bird flew away over the castle wall.

"There, you see how glad it is to be free?" said Otsū.

"They call nightingales harbingers of spring, don't they? Maybe somebody'll bring you good news."

"A messenger bringing news as welcome as the coming of spring? It's true there's something I'm longing to hear."

As Otsū started walking toward the woods and bamboo grove in back of the castle, Ushinosuke fell in at her side.

"Where are you going?" he asked.

"I've been inside a lot lately. I thought I'd go up the hill and look at the plum blossoms for a change."

"Plum blossoms? Those up there aren't much to look at. You should go to Tsukigase."

"That might be nice. Is it far?"

"A couple of miles or so. Why don't you go? I brought firewood today, so I have the ox with me."

Having scarcely been outside the castle all winter, Otsū made up her mind quickly. Without telling anyone where she was going, the two of them strolled down to the back gate, which was used by tradesmen and others having business at the castle. It was guarded by a samurai armed with a lance. He nodded and smiled at Otsū. Ushinosuke, too, was a familiar figure, and he let them out the gate without checking the boy's written permission to be in the castle grounds.

People in the fields and on the road spoke a friendly greeting to Otsū, whether they knew her or not. When the dwellings became sparser, she looked back at the white castle nestled on the skirt of the mountain and said, "Can I get back home while it's still light?"

"Sure, but I'll come back with you anyway."

"Araki Village is beyond Tsukigase, isn't it?"

"It doesn't matter."

Chatting about various things, they passed a salt shop, where a man was bartering some boar meat for a sack of salt. He finished his transaction, came out and walked along the road behind them. With the snow melting, the road grew worse and worse. There were few travelers.

"Ushinosuke," said Otsū, "you always come to Koyagyū, don't you?"

"Yes."

"Isn't Ueno Castle closer to Araki Village?"

"It is, but there's no great swordsman like Lord Yagyū at Ueno Castle."

"Do you like swords?"

"Uh-huh."

He stopped the ox, let go of the rope and ran down to the edge of the stream. There was a bridge from which a log had fallen. He put it back in place and waited for the man behind them to cross first.

The man looked like a rōnin. As he walked by Otsū, he eyed her brazenly, then glanced back several times from the bridge and from the other side, before disappearing into a fold of the mountain.

"Who do you suppose that is?" asked Otsū nervously.

"Did he frighten you?"

"No, but . . ."

"There're lots of rōnin in the mountains around here."

"Are there?" she said uneasily.

Over his shoulder, Ushinosuke said, "Otsū, I wonder if you'd help me. Do you think you could ask Master Kimura to hire me? I mean, you know, I could sweep the garden, draw water—do things like that."

It was only recently that the boy had received special permission from Sukekurō to enter the dōjō and watch the men at practice, but already he had only one ambition. His ancestors bore the surname Kikumura; the head of the family for several generations had used the given name Mataemon. Ushinosuke had decided that when he became a samurai he would take the name Mataemon, but none of the Kikumuras had done anything of particular note. He'd change his surname to that of his village, and if his dream came true, become famous far and wide as Araki Mataemon.

As Otsū listened, she thought of Jōtarō and was seized by a sense of loneliness. She was twenty-five now; he must be nineteen or twenty. Looking around at the plum blossoms—not yet in full bloom—she couldn't help but feel that spring had already passed for her.

"Let's go back, Ushinosuke," she said suddenly.

He gave her a questioning look but obediently turned the ox around.

"Stop!" shouted a loud male voice.

Two other rōnin had joined the one from the salt shop. All three came and stood around the ox with their arms folded.

"What do you want?" asked Ushinosuke.

The men kept their eyes fixed on Otsū.

"I see what you mean," said one.

"She's a beauty, isn't she?"

"I've seen her somewhere before," said the third man. "In Kyoto, I think."

"She must be from Kyoto, certainly not from any of the villages around here."

"I don't remember whether it was at the Yoshioka School or somewhere else, but I know I've seen her."

"Were you at the Yoshioka School?"

"For three years, after Sekigahara."

"If you've got any business with us, say what it is!" Ushinosuke said angrily. "We want to get back before dark."

One of the rōnin glared at him, as if noticing him for the first time. "You're from Araki, aren't you? One of the charcoal-makers?"

"Yes. So what?"

"We don't need you. Run along home."

"That's just what I'm going to do."

He pulled the rope taut, and one man gave him a look that would have had most boys trembling with fright.

"Get out of the way," said Ushinosuke.

"This lady's going with us."

"Going where?"

"What difference does it make to you? Give me that rope."

"No!"

"Say, he doesn't think I mean it."

The other two men, squaring their shoulders and glowering, moved in on Ushinosuke. One presented a fist as hard as a pine knot in front of his chin.

Otsū clutched the ox's back. The tilt of Ushinosuke's eyebrows said very clearly something was going to happen.

"Oh, no, stop!" she cried, hoping to keep the boy from doing anything rash.

But the plaintive note in her voice just spurred him to action. He lashed out swiftly with one leg, caught the man in front of him, sending him staggering backward. No sooner was Ushinosuke's foot in contact with the ground again than he rammed his head into the gut of the man on his left. Simultaneously he got a grip on the man's sword and pulled it from its scabbard. Then he began swinging.

He moved with lightning quickness. He whirled and seemed to be attacking in every direction at the same time, all three opponents at once, with equal force. Whether he was acting brilliantly out of instinct or out of childish recklessness, his unorthodox tactics took the rōnin by surprise.

The reverse swing of the sword drove forcefully into the chest of one man. Otsū cried out, but her voice was drowned by the scream of the wounded man. He fell toward the ox, a geyser of blood spurting into the animal's face. Terrified, the ox let out an indescribable shriek. Just then, Ushinosuke's sword cut deeply into its rump. With another shriek, the ox set off at a near gallop.

The other two rōnin rushed at Ushinosuke, who was leaping nimbly from rock to rock in the stream bed. "I didn't do anything wrong! It was you!" he shouted.

132

Realizing he was out of their reach, the two rōnin started after the ox.

Ushinosuke jumped back onto the road and took after them, shouting, "Running away? You running away?"

One man stopped and half turned.

"You little bastard!"

"Leave him till later!" shouted the other man.

The ox, blind with fear, left the valley road and ran up a low hill, traveled a short distance along the crest and plunged down the other side. In a very short time, it covered a considerable distance, reaching a point not far from the Yagyū fief.

Otsū, her eyes shut in resignation, managed to keep from being thrown by clinging to the packsaddle. She could hear the voices of the people they were passing but was too stunned to utter a cry for help. Not that it would have done any good. None of the people commenting on the spectacle had the courage to stop the demented beast.

When they were almost to Hannya Plain, a man came from a side road into the middle of the main road, which, though very narrow, was the Kasagi highroad. He had a letter case slung from his shoulder and appeared to be a servant of some sort.

People were shouting, "Watch out! Get out of the way!" but he walked on, right in the path of the ox.

Then there was a terrible cracking sound.

"He's been gored!"

"The idiot!"

But it wasn't as the bystanders first thought. The sound they'd heard was not that of the ox striking the man but of the man landing a stunning blow on the side of the animal's head. The ox lifted its heavy neck sideways, turned halfway around and started back the other way. It hadn't gone ten feet before it came to a dead halt, saliva streaming from its mouth, its whole body shaking.

"Get down quick," the man said to Otsū.

Onlookers crowded around excitedly, staring at the man's foot, which was firmly planted on the rope.

Once she was safely on the ground, Otsū bowed to her rescuer, though she was still too dazed to know where she was or what she was doing.

"Why should a gentle animal like this go mad?" asked the man, as he led the ox to the side of the road and tied it to a tree. Catching sight of the blood on the animal's legs, he said, "What's this, now. Why, it's been cut—with a sword!"

While he was examining the wound and muttering to himself, Kimura Sukekurō pushed through the ring of people and sent them on their way.

"Aren't you Abbot Inshun's attendant?" he asked, even before he'd had a chance to catch his breath.

"How fortunate to meet you here, sir. I have a letter for you from the abbot. If you don't mind, I'd like to ask you to read it immediately." He took the letter from the case and handed it to Sukekurō.

"For me?" Sukekurō asked with surprise. Having ascertained there was no mistake, he opened it and read: "Regarding the samurai at Tsukigase, I have, since our conversation yesterday, verified that they are not Lord Tōdō's men. They are riffraff, rōnin expelled from the cities, who have holed up there for the winter. I hasten to inform you of this unfortunate error on my part."

"Thank you," said Sukekurō. "This agrees with what I've learned from another source. Tell the abbot I am much relieved and trust that he is too."

"Forgive me for delivering the letter in the middle of the road. I'll convey your message to the abbot. Good-bye."

"Wait a minute. How long have you been at the Hōzōin?"

"Not long."

"What's you name?"

"I'm called Torazō."

"I wonder," mumbled Sukekurō, scrutinizing the

man's face. "Are you by any chance Hamada Torano-suke?"

"No."

"I've never met Hamada, but there's a man at the castle who insists Hamada's now serving as Inshun's attendant."

"Yes, sir."

"Is it a case of mistaken identity?"

Torazō, red in the face, lowered his voice. "Actually, I am Hamada. I've come to the Hōzōin for reasons of my own. To avoid further disgrace to my teacher and greater shame to myself, I'd like to keep my identity secret. If you don't mind . . ."

"Don't worry. I had no intention of prying into your affairs."

"I'm sure you've heard about Tadaaki. His abandoning his school and retiring to the mountains was due to a mistake of mine. I've given up my status. Doing menial tasks at the temple will be good discipline. I didn't give the priests my real name. It's all very embarrassing."

"The outcome of Tadaaki's fight with Kojirō is no secret. Kojirō told everyone he met between Edo and Buzen. I take it you've resolved to clear your teacher's name."

"One of these days . . . I'll see you again, sir." Torazō took his leave swiftly, as though unable to endure another moment.

13

Hemp Seed

Hyōgo was growing concerned. After going to Otsū's room with a letter from Takuan in his hand, he'd searched for her all over the castle grounds, more and more urgently as the hours passed.

The letter, dated the tenth month of the previous year but inexplicably delayed, told of Musashi's pending appointment as an instructor to the shōgun. Takuan had asked that Otsū come to the capital as soon as possible, since Musashi would soon need a house as well as "someone to look after it." Hyōgo couldn't wait to see her face light up.

Not finding her, he finally went to question the guard at the gate and was told men were out looking for her. Hyōgo took a deep breath, thinking how unlike Otsū it was to cause people to worry, how unlike her not to leave word. She rarely acted impulsively, even in the smallest matters.

Before he began to imagine the worst, however, news came that they were back, Otsū with Sukekurō, and Ushinosuke with the men sent to Tsukigase. The boy, apologizing to everyone for no one knew what, was obviously in a hurry to be on his way.

"Where do you think you're going?" asked one of the attendants.

"I've got to get back to Araki. My mother will worry if I don't."

"If you try to go back now," said Sukekurō, "those rōnin will get you, and it's not likely they'd let you go alive. You can stay here tonight and go home in the morning."

Ushinosuke mumbled something vaguely acquiescent and was told to go to a wood storehouse in the outer encirclement, where the apprentice samurai slept.

Beckoning to Otsū, Hyōgo took her aside and told her what Takuan had written. He wasn't surprised when she said, "I'll leave in the morning," a deep blush revealing her feelings.

Hyōgo then reminded her of Munenori's coming visit and suggested she return to Edo with him, though he knew quite well what her answer would be. She was in no mood to wait two more days, much less two more months. He made another attempt, saying that if she waited until after the funeral service, she could travel with him as far as Nagoya, since he'd been invited to become a vassal of Lord Tokugawa of Owari. When she again demurred, he told her how much the idea of her making the long journey alone displeased him. In every town and inn along the way she would encounter inconveniences, if not actual danger.

She smiled. "You seem to forget. I'm used to traveling. There's nothing for you to worry about."

That evening, at a modest farewell party, everyone expressed his affection for Otsū, and the next morning, which was bright and clear, family and servants gathered at the front gate to see her off.

Sukekurō sent a man to fetch Ushinosuke, thinking that Otsū could ride his ox as far as Uji. When the man returned and reported the boy had gone home the night before after all, Sukekurō ordered a horse to be brought.

Otsū, feeling she was of too low a status to be so favored, refused the offer, but Hyōgo insisted. The horse, a dapple gray, was led by an apprentice samurai down the gentle slope to the outer gate.

Hyōgo went partway, then stopped. He couldn't deny it. At times he envied Musashi, as he would have envied any man whom Otsū loved. That her heart belonged to another did not diminish his affection for her. She'd been a delightful companion on the trip down from Edo, and in the subsequent weeks and months he had marveled at the devotion with which she had cared for his grandfather. Though deeper than ever, his love for her was selfless. Sekishūsai had instructed him to deliver her to Musashi safely; Hyōgo intended to do just that. It wasn't his nature to covet another man's good fortune nor to think of depriving him of it. He could not think of any act as being apart from the Way of the Samurai; carrying out his grandfather's wish would in itself have been an expression of his love.

He was lost in reverie when Otsū turned and bowed her thanks to her well-wishers. As she set off, she brushed against some plum blossoms. Unconsciously watching the petals fall, Hyōgo could almost smell the fragrance. He felt he was seeing her for the last time and took comfort in a silent prayer for her future life. He stood and stared as she disappeared from sight.

"Sir."

Hyōgo turned around and a smile came slowly to his face. "Ushinosuke. Well, well. I hear you went home last night after I told you not to."

"Yes, sir; my mother . . ." He was still at an age when mention of separation from his mother brought him to the verge of tears.

"That's all right. It's good for a boy to take care of his mother. But how did you get by those rōnin at Tsukigase?"

"Oh, that was easy."

"Was it, now?"

The boy smiled. "They weren't there. They heard Otsū was from the castle, so they were afraid of being attacked. I guess they must've gone to the other side of the mountain.''

"Ha, ha. We don't have to worry about them anymore, do we? Have you had breakfast?''

"No," said Ushinosuke, slightly embarrassed. "I got up early to dig some wild potatoes for Master Kimura. If you like them, I'll bring you some too.''

"Thank you.''

"Do you know where Otsū is?''

"She just left for Edo.''

"Edo? . . .'' Hesitantly he said, "I wonder if she asked you or Master Kimura what I wanted her to.''

"And what was that?''

"I've been hoping you'd let me become a samurai's attendant.''

"You're still a little too young for that. Maybe when you're older.''

"But I want to learn swordsmanship. Won't you teach me, please. I have to learn while my mother's still alive.''

"Have you been studying under someone?''

"No, but I've practiced using my wooden sword on trees and animals.''

"That's a good way to start. When you get a little older, you can come and join me in Nagoya. I'm going there to live soon.''

"That's way off in Owari, isn't it? I can't go so far away, not while my mother's still alive.''

Hyōgo, not unmoved, said, "Come with me.'' Ushinosuke followed along silently. "We'll go to the dōjō. I'll see if you have the natural ability to become a swordsman.''

"The dōjō?'' Ushinosuke wondered if he was dreaming. Since early childhood, he'd regarded the ancient Yagyū dōjō as symbolizing everything he aspired to in the world. Though Sukekurō had said he could enter, he had not done so yet. But now, to be invited inside by a member of the family!

"Rinse your feet."

"Yes, sir." Ushinosuke went to a small pond near the entrance and very carefully washed his feet, taking care to remove the dirt from under his toenails.

Once inside, he felt small and insignificant. The beams and rafters were old and massive, the floor polished to a sheen he could see his reflection in. Even Hyōgo's voice when he said, "Get a sword," sounded different.

Ushinosuke selected a black-oak sword from among the weapons hanging on one wall. Hyōgo took one too, and with the point directed toward the floor, walked to the middle of the room.

"Are you ready?" he asked coldly.

"Yes," said Ushinosuke, raising his weapon to chest level.

Hyōgo opened his stance slightly on the diagonal. Ushinosuke was puffed up like a hedgehog. His eyebrows were raised, his face was set in a fierce frown, and his blood raced. When Hyōgo signaled with his eyes that he was about to attack, Ushinosuke grunted loudly. Feet pounding the floor, Hyōgo advanced rapidly and struck laterally at Ushinosuke's waist.

"Not yet!" shouted the boy. As though kicking the floor away from him, he leaped high in the air, clearing Hyōgo's shoulder. Hyōgo reached out with his left hand and lightly pushed the boy's feet upward. Ushinosuke did a somersault and landed behind Hyōgo. He was up in a split second, running to retrieve his sword.

"That's enough," said Hyōgo.

"No; once more!"

Grabbing his sword, Ushinosuke held it high over his head with both hands and flew like an eagle toward Hyōgo. Hyōgo's weapon, aimed straight at him, stopped him dead in his tracks. He saw the look in Hyōgo's eyes and his own filled with tears.

"This boy has spirit," thought Hyōgo, but he pre-

tended to be angry. "You're fighting dirty," he shouted.
"You jumped over my shoulder."

Ushinosuke did not know what to say to that.

"You don't understand your status—taking liberties
with your betters! Sit down, right there." The boy knelt
and put his hands out in front of him to bow in apology.
As he came toward him, Hyōgo dropped the wooden
sword and drew his own weapon. "I'll kill you now.
Don't bother to scream."

"K-k-kill me?"

"Stick out your neck. For a samurai, *nothing* is more
important than abiding by the rules of proper conduct.
Even if you are only a farm boy, what you did is unforgiv-
able."

"You're going to kill me just for doing something
rude?"

"That's right."

After looking up at the samurai for a moment, Ushinosuke, resignation in his eyes, lifted his hands in the
direction of his village and said, "Mother, I'm going to
become part of the soil here at the castle. I know how
sad you'll feel. Forgive me for not being a good son."
Then he obediently extended his neck.

Hyōgo laughed and put his sword back in its scabbard. Patting Ushinosuke on the back, he said, "You
don't think I'd really kill a boy like you, do you?"

"You weren't serious?"

"No."

"You said proper conduct is important. Is it all right
for a samurai to play jokes like that?"

"It wasn't a joke. If you're going to train to become
a samurai, I have to know what you're made of."

"I thought you meant it," said Ushinosuke, his
breathing returning to normal.

"You told me you hadn't had lessons," said Hyōgo.
"But when I forced you to the edge of the room, you
jumped over my shoulder. Not many students, even with
three or four years of training, could execute that ploy."

"I never studied with anyone, though."

"It's nothing to hide. You must have had a teacher, and a good one. Who was he?"

The boy thought for a moment, then said, "Oh, I remember how I learned that."

"Who taught you?"

"It wasn't a human being."

"A goblin maybe?"

"No, a hemp seed."

"What?"

"A hemp seed."

"How could you learn from a hemp seed?"

"Well, way up in the mountains there are some of those fighters—you know, the ones who seem to disappear right in front of your eyes. I watched them train a couple of times."

"You mean the *ninja,* don't you? It must have been the Iga group you saw. But what does that have to do with a hemp seed?"

"Well, after hemp's planted in the spring, it doesn't take long before a little sprout comes up."

"Yes?"

"You jump over it. Every day you practice jumping back and forth. When it gets warmer, the sprout grows fast—nothing else grows as fast—so you have to jump higher every day. If you don't practice every day, it's not long before the hemp is so high you can't jump over it."

"I see."

"I did it last year, and the year before that. From spring till fall."

Sukekurō came into the dōjō just then and said, "Hyōgo, here's another letter from Edo."

After Hyōgo read it, he said, "Otsū couldn't have gone very far, could she?"

"Not more than five miles, probably. Has something come up?"

"Yes. Takuan says Musashi's appointment has been canceled. They seem to have doubts about his character.

142

I don't think we should let Otsū go on to Edo without telling her."

"I'll go."

"No. I'll go myself."

With a nod to Ushinosuke, Hyōgo left the dōjō and went directly to the stable.

He was halfway to Uji when he began to have second thoughts. Musashi's not receiving the appointment would make no difference to Otsū; she was thinking of the man himself, not his status. Even if Hyōgo managed to persuade her to stay a while longer in Koyagyū, she would no doubt want to go on to Edo. Why spoil her journey by telling her the bad news?

He turned back toward Koyagyū and slowed down to a trot. Though he appeared to be at peace with the world, a fierce battle raged in his heart. If only he could see Otsū once more! While he had to admit to himself this was the real reason for going after her, he would not have admitted it to anyone else.

Hyōgo tried to rein in his emotions. Warriors had weak moments, foolish moments, like everybody else. Still, his duty, that of every samurai, was clear: to persevere until he reached a state of stoic balance. Once he had crossed the barrier of illusion, his soul would be light and free, his eyes open to the green willows around him, to every blade of grass. Love was not the only emotion capable of firing a samurai's heart. His was another world. In an age hungry for young men of talent, this was no time to be distracted by a flower along the wayside. What was important, as Hyōgo saw it, was to be in the right place to ride the wave of the times.

"Quite a crowd, isn't it?" Hyōgo remarked light-heartedly.

"Yes; Nara doesn't have many days as fine as this," replied Sukekurō.

"It's like an outing."

Following a few steps behind them was Ushinosuke,

for whom Hyōgo was developing quite a fondness. The boy came to the castle more frequently now and was on his way to becoming a regular attendant. He carried their lunches on his back and had an extra pair of sandals for Hyōgo tied to his obi.

They were in an open field in the middle of town. On one side, the five-story pagoda of the Kōfukuji rose above the surrounding woods; visible across the field were the houses of the Buddhist and Shinto priests. Though the day was bright and the air springlike, a thin mist hung over the lower areas, where townsmen lived. The crowd, numbering between four and five hundred people, did not seem that large because of the vastness of the field. Some of the deer, for which Nara was famous, were nosing their way among the spectators, sniffing out tasty morsels of food here and there.

"They haven't finished already, have they?" asked Hyōgo.

"No," said Sukekurō. "They seem to be taking time off for lunch."

"So even priests have to eat!"

Sukekurō laughed.

The occasion was a show of sorts. The larger cities had theaters, but in Nara and the smaller towns, shows were held in the open air. Magicians, dancers, puppeteers, as well as archers and swordsmen, all performed outdoors. Today's attraction was more than mere entertainment, though. Each year the lancer-priests of the Hōzōin held a tournament, at which they decided the order of seating at the temple. Since they were performing in public, the competitors fought hard, and the bouts were often violent and spectacular. There was a sign in front of the Kōfukuji, clearly stating that the tournament was open to all who were devoted to the martial arts, but the outsiders who dared face the lancer-priests were very, very few.

"Why don't we sit down somewhere and have our lunch?" said Hyōgo. "We seem to have plenty of time."

"Where would be a good spot?" said Sukekurō, looking around.

"Over here," called Ushinosuke. "You can sit on this." He indicated a piece of reed matting he had picked up somewhere and spread on a pleasant knoll. Hyōgo admired the boy's resourcefulness and, in general, was pleased by the way his needs were looked after, although he did not regard solicitousness as an ideal quality for a future samurai.

After they had arranged themselves, Ushinosuke passed out their simple fare: balls of unpolished rice, sour plum pickles and sweetish bean paste, all wrapped in dried bamboo to make them easier to carry.

"Ushinosuke," said Sukekurō, "run over to those priests there and get some tea. But don't tell them who it's for."

"It'd be a nuisance if they came over to pay their respects," added Hyōgo, who had a basket hat pulled down over his face. Sukekurō's features were more than half hidden by a bandanna of the type worn by priests.

As Ushinosuke got to his feet, another boy, about fifty feet away, was saying, "I can't understand it. The matting was right here."

"Forget it, Iori," said Gonnosuke. "It's no great loss."

"Somebody must have swiped it. Who do you suppose would do a thing like that?"

"Don't worry about it." Gonnosuke sat down on the grass, took out his brush and ink and began listing his expenses in a small notebook, a habit he had recently acquired from Iori.

In some ways, Iori was too serious for his years. He paid close attention to his personal finances, never wasted a thing, was meticulously neat, and felt grateful for every bowl of rice, every fair day. He was, in short, fastidious, and he looked down on people who were not.

For anyone who'd walk off with another person's

property, even if it was only a cheap piece of matting, he had only contempt.

"Oh, there it is," he cried. "Those men over there took it. Hey, you!"

He ran toward them, but stopped about ten paces short to consider what he was going to say and found himself face to face with Ushinosuke.

"What do you want?" growled Ushinosuke.

"What do you mean, what do I want?" snapped Iori.

Regarding him with the coldness country folk reserve for outsiders, Ushinosuke said, "You're the one who called to us!"

"Anybody who goes off with somebody else's things is a thief!"

"Thief? Why, you son of a bitch!"

"That matting belongs to us."

"Matting? I found it lying on the ground. Is that all you're upset about?"

"A mat's important to a traveler," said Iori rather pompously. "It protects him from the rain, provides him with something to sleep on. Lots of things. Give it back!"

"You can have it, but first take back what you said about me being a thief!"

"I don't have to apologize to get back what belongs to us. If you don't give it back, I'll take it back!"

"Just try it. I'm Ushinosuke of Araki. I have no intention of losing to a runt like you. I'm the disciple of a samurai."

"I bet you are," said Iori, standing a little straighter. "You talk big with all these people around, but you wouldn't dare fight if we were by ourselves."

"I won't forget that!"

"Come over there later."

"Where?"

"By the pagoda. Come alone."

They parted, Ushinosuke went for the tea, and by the time he came back with an earthenware teapot, the matches were under way again. Standing in a large circle with the other spectators, Ushinosuke looked pointedly at Iori, challenging him with his eyes. Iori's eyes answered. Both believed that winning was all that counted.

The noisy crowd pushed this way and that, raising yellow clouds of dust. In the center of the circle stood a priest with a lance as long as a fowling pole. One after another, rivals stepped forward and challenged him. One after another, they were struck to the ground or sent flying through the air.

"Come forward," he cried, but eventually no more came. "If there's no one else, I'm going to leave. Is there any objection to declaring me, Nankōbō, the winner?" After studying under In'ei, he had created a style of his own and was now the chief rival of Inshun, who was absent today on the pretext of illness. No one knew whether he was afraid of Nankōbō or preferred to avoid conflict.

When no one came forward, the burly priest lowered his lance, holding it horizontally, and announced, "There's no challenger."

"Wait," called a priest, running out in front of Nankōbō. "I'm Daun, a disciple of Inshun. I challenge you."

"Get ready."

After bowing to each other, the two men jumped apart. Their two lances stared at each other like living beings for such a long time that the crowd, bored, began shouting for action. Then all at once the shouting ceased. Nankōbō's lance thudded into Daun's head, and, like a scarecrow toppled by the wind, his body leaned slowly to the side, then fell suddenly to the ground. Three or four lancers ran forward, not to take revenge but merely to drag the body away.

Nankōbō arrogantly threw back his shoulders and surveyed the crowd. "There seem to be a few brave men left. If indeed there are, come ahead."

A mountain priest stepped out from behind a tent, took his traveling chest off his back and asked, "Is the tournament open only to lancers of the Hōzōin?"

"No," chorused the Hōzōin priests.

The priest bowed. "In that case, I'd like to try my hand. Can anyone lend me a wooden sword?"

Hyōgo glanced at Sukekurō and said, "This is getting interesting."

"It is, isn't it?"

"No question about the outcome."

"I don't suppose there's any chance of Nankōbō's losing."

"That's not what I meant. I don't think Nankōbō will agree to fight. If he does, he'll lose."

Sukekurō looked puzzled but didn't ask for an explanation.

Someone handed the vagabond priest a wooden sword. He walked up to Nankōbō, bowed and issued his challenge. He was a man of about forty, but his body, like spring steel, strongly suggested training not in the ascetic fashion of mountain priests but on the battlefield, a man who must have faced death many times and would be prepared to accept it philosophically. His manner of speaking was soft, his eyes placid.

Despite his arrogance, Nankōbō was no fool. "Are you an outsider?" he asked pointlessly.

"Yes," replied the challenger with another bow.

"Wait just a minute." Nankōbō saw two things clearly: His technique might be better than the priest's. He couldn't win in the long run. Quite a few celebrated warriors, defeated at Sekigahara, were still masquerading as wandering priests. There was no telling who this man was.

"I can't take on an outsider," he said, shaking his head.

"I just asked the rules and was told it was all right."

"It may be all right with others, but I prefer not to fight outsiders. When I fight, it's not for the purpose of defeating my opponent. It's a religious activity, in which I discipline my soul by means of the lance."

"I see," said the priest with a little laugh. He seemed

to have something more to say, but hesitated. After mulling it over for a moment, he retired from the ring, returned the wooden sword and disappeared.

Nankōbō chose this time to make his exit, ignoring the whispered comments that it was cowardly of him to back out. Trailed by two or three disciples, he strode away grandly, like a conquering general.

"What did I tell you?" said Hyōgo.

"You were absolutely right."

"That man is without a doubt one of those hiding out on Mount Kudo. Change his white robe and bandanna for a helmet and armor, and you'll find you're looking at one of the great swordsmen of a few years ago."

When the crowd thinned out, Sukekurō began looking around for Ushinosuke. He didn't find him. At a signal from Iori, he had gone over to the pagoda, where now they stood glaring fiercely at each other.

"Don't blame me if you get killed," said Iori.

"You talk big," said Ushinosuke, picking up a stick to use as a weapon.

Iori, sword held high, rushed to the attack. Ushinosuke jumped back. Thinking he was afraid, Iori ran straight at him. Ushinosuke leaped over him, kicking him in the side of the head. Iori's hand went to his head, and he crashed to the ground. Recovering quickly, he was on his feet again in no time. The two boys faced each other with their weapons raised.

Forgetting what Musashi and Gonnosuke had taught him, Iori charged with his eyes shut. Ushinosuke moved slightly to one side and knocked him down with his stick.

Iori lay on his stomach, moaning, sword still in hand.

"Ha! I won," shouted Ushinosuke. Then, noticing that Iori was not moving at all, he grew frightened and ran.

"No you don't!" roared Gonnosuke, his four-foot staff catching the boy on the hip.

Ushinosuke fell with a shriek of pain, but after one

look at Gonnosuke, he got to his feet and bounded off like a rabbit, only to collide head on with Sukekurō.

"Ushinosuke! What's going on here?"

Ushinosuke quickly hid behind Sukekurō, leaving the samurai face to face with Gonnosuke. For a moment, it appeared that a clash was inevitable. Sukekurō's hand went to his sword; Gonnosuke tightened his grip on the staff.

"Would you mind telling me," asked Sukekurō, "why you're chasing a mere child as though you wanted to kill him?"

"Before I answer, let me ask a question. Did you see him knock that boy down?"

"Is he with you?"

"Yes. Is this one of your attendants?"

"Not officially." Looking sternly at Ushinosuke, he asked, "Why did you hit the boy and run away? Tell the truth, now."

Before Ushinosuke could open his mouth, Iori raised his head and shouted, "It was a bout." Rising painfully to a sitting position, he said, "We had a bout and I lost."

"Did you two challenge each other in the proper way and agree to fight it out?" asked Gonnosuke. There was a trace of amusement in his eyes as he looked from one to the other.

Ushinosuke, deeply embarrassed, said, "I didn't know it was his mat when I picked it up."

The two men grinned at each other, both aware that if they had not acted with restraint themselves, a trivial, childish affair could have ended in bloodshed.

"I'm very sorry about this," said Sukekurō.

"So am I. I hope you'll forgive me."

"Don't mention it. My master's waiting for us, so I think we'd better go."

They went out the gate laughing, Gonnosuke and Iori going to the left, Sukekurō and Ushinosuke to the right.

Then Gonnosuke turned and said, "Could I ask you something? If we go straight down this road, will it take us to Koyagyū Castle?"

Sukekurō walked over to Gonnosuke and some minutes later, when Hyōgo joined them, told him who the travelers were and why they were here.

Hyōgo sighed sympathetically. "That's too bad. If only you'd come three weeks ago, before Otsū left to join Musashi in Edo."

"He's not in Edo," said Gonnosuke. "No one knows where he is, not even his friends."

"What'll she do now?" said Hyōgo, regretting he hadn't brought Otsū back to Koyagyū.

Though he held back his tears, Iori really wanted to go somewhere all alone and cry his heart out. On the way down, he'd talked incessantly of meeting Otsū, or so it had seemed to Gonnosuke. As the men's conversation shifted to events in Edo, he slowly drifted away. Hyōgo asked Gonnosuke for more information about Musashi, for news about his uncle, for details about the disappearance of Ono Tadaaki. There seemed to be no end either to his questions or to Gonnosuke's supply of information.

"Where're you going?" Ushinosuke asked Iori, coming up behind him and laying a sympathetic hand on his shoulder. "Are you crying?"

"Of course not." But as he shook his head, the tears flew.

"Hmm. . . . Do you know how to dig wild potatoes?"

"Sure."

"There are some potatoes over there. You want to see who can dig the fastest?"

Iori accepted the challenge, and they began digging.

It was getting late in the day, and since there was still much to talk about, Hyōgo urged Gonnosuke to spend a few days at the castle. Gonnosuke, however, said he preferred to continue his journey.

While they were saying their farewells, they noticed the boys were missing again. After a moment, Sukekurō pointed and said, "There they are, over there. They seem to be digging."

Iori and Ushinosuke were absorbed in their work, which because of the brittleness of the roots, involved digging carefully to a great depth. The men, amused at their concentration, walked quietly up behind them and watched for several minutes before Ushinosuke looked up and saw them. He gasped slightly, and Iori turned around and grinned. Then they redoubled their efforts.

"I've got it," cried Ushinosuke, pulling up a long potato and laying it on the ground.

Seeing Iori's arm sunk in the hole up to his shoulder, Gonnosuke said impatiently, "If you don't finish soon, I'm going on by myself."

Placing his hand on his hip like an aged farmer, Iori forced himself to a standing position and said, "I can't do it. It'd take me the rest of the day." With a look of resignation, he brushed the dirt off his kimono.

"You can't get the potato out after you've dug that far?" asked Ushinosuke. "Here, I'll pull it out for you."

"No," said Iori, pulling back Ushinosuke's hand. "It'll break." He gently pushed the dirt back in the hole and packed it down.

"Bye," called Ushinosuke, proudly shouldering his potato and accidentally revealing that the tip was broken off.

Seeing that, Hyōgo said, "You lost. You may have won the fight, but you're disqualified from the potato-digging contest."

14

Sweepers and Salesmen

The cherry blossoms were pale, past their prime, and the thistle blossoms were wilting, hinting nostalgically of the time centuries ago when Nara had been the capital. It was a little warm for walking, but neither Gonnosuke nor Iori tired of the road.

Iori tugged at Gonnosuke's sleeve and said worriedly, "That man's still following us."

Keeping his eyes straight ahead, Gonnosuke said, "Pretend you don't see him."

"He's been behind us ever since we left the Kōfukuji."

"Umm."

"And he was at the inn where we stayed, wasn't he?"

"Don't let it worry you. We don't have anything worth stealing."

"We have our lives! They're not nothing."

"Ha, ha. I keep my life locked up. Don't you?"

"I can take care of myself." Iori tightened the grip of his left hand on his scabbard.

Gonnosuke knew the man was the mountain priest who had challenged Nankōbō the previous day, but couldn't imagine why he'd be tailing them.

Iori looked around again and said, "He's not there anymore."

Gonnosuke looked back too. "He probably got tired." He took a deep breath and added, "But it does make me feel better."

They put up at a farmer's house that night and early the next morning reached Amano in Kawachi. This was a small village of low-eaved houses, behind which ran a stream of pristine mountain water. Gonnosuke had come to have the memorial tablet to his mother placed in the Kongōji, the so-called Women's Mount Kōya. But first he wanted to look up a woman named Oan, whom he had known since childhood, so there would be someone to burn incense before the tablet from time to time. If she could not be found, he intended to go on to Mount Kōya, the burial place of the rich and the mighty. He hoped he wouldn't have to; going there would make him feel like a beggar.

Asking directions from a shopkeeper's wife, he was told that Oan was the wife of a brewer named Tōroku and their house was the fourth one on the right inside the temple gate.

As he went through the gate, Gonnosuke wondered if the woman knew what she was talking about, for there was a sign saying that bringing sake and leeks into the sacred compound was prohibited. How could there be a brewery there?

This little mystery was cleared up that evening by Tōroku, who had made them feel welcome and readily agreed to talk to the abbot about the memorial tablet. Tōroku said that Toyotomi Hideyoshi had once tasted and expressed admiration for the sake made for use by the temple. The priests had then established the brewery to make sake for Hideyoshi and the other daimyō who contributed to the temple's support. Production had fallen off somewhat after Hideyoshi's death, but the temple still supplied a number of special patrons.

When Gonnosuke and Iori awoke the next morning, Tōroku was already gone. He returned a little past noon and said that arrangements had been made.

154

The Kongōji was situated in the Amano River valley, amid peaks the color of jade. Gonnosuke, Iori and Tōroku stopped for a minute on the bridge leading to the main gate. Cherry blossoms floated in the water beneath the bridge. Gonnosuke straightened his shoulders and an air of reverence seemed to settle over him. Iori rearranged his collar.

Approaching the main hall, they were greeted by the abbot, a tall, rather stout man wearing an ordinary priest's robe. A torn basket hat and a long staff would not have seemed unnatural.

"Is this the man who wants to have a service said for his mother?" he asked in a friendly voice.

"Yes, sir," replied Tōroku, prostrating himself on the ground.

Having expected a stern-visaged cleric in gold brocade, Gonnosuke was somewhat confused in his greeting. He bowed and watched as the abbot came down from the porch, slipped his big feet into dirty straw sandals and came to a halt in front of him. Prayer beads in hand, the abbot directed them to follow him and a young priest fell in behind them.

They passed the Hall of Yakushi, the refectory, the one-story treasure pagoda and the priests' living quarters. When they reached the Hall of Dainichi, the young priest came forward and spoke to the abbot. The latter nodded and the priest opened the door with an enormous key.

Entering the large hall together, Gonnosuke and Iori knelt before the priests' dais. Fully ten feet above this was a huge golden statue of Dainichi, the universal Buddha of the esoteric sects. After a few moments, the abbot appeared from behind the altar, attired in his cassock, and arranged himself on the dais. The chanting of the sutra began, and he seemed to be subtly transformed into a dignified high priest, his authority evident in the set of his shoulders.

Gonnosuke clasped his hands in front of him. A

small cloud seemed to pass before his eyes and from it emerged an image of Shiojiri Pass, where he and Musashi had tested each other. His mother was sitting to one side, straight as a board, looking worried, just as she had been when she called out the word that saved him in that fight.

"Mother," he thought, "you don't have to worry about my future. Musashi has consented to be my teacher. The day is not far off when I'll be able to establish my own school. The world may be in turmoil, but I won't stray from the Way. Nor will I neglect my duties as a son. . . ."

By the time Gonnosuke came out of his reverie, the chanting had stopped and the abbot was gone. Beside him, Iori sat transfixed, his eyes glued to the face of Dainichi, a miracle of sculptural sensitivity carved by the great Unkei in the thirteenth century.

"Why are you staring so, Iori?"

Without moving his eyes, the boy said, "It's my sister. That Buddha looks like my sister."

Gonnosuke burst out laughing. "What are you talking about? You've never even seen her. Anyway, no human could ever have the compassion and serenity of Dainichi."

Iori shook his head vigorously. "I have seen her. Near Lord Yagyū's residence in Edo. And talked to her. I didn't know she was my sister then, but just now, while the abbot was chanting, the Buddha's face turned into hers. She seemed to be saying something to me."

They went out and sat down on the porch, reluctant to break the spell of the visions they had experienced.

"The memorial service was for my mother," said Gonnosuke pensively. "But it's been a good day for the living too. Sitting here like this, it's hard to believe fighting and bloodshed exist."

The metal spire of the treasure pagoda glistened like a jeweled sword in the rays of the setting sun; all the other buildings stood in deep shadow. Stone lanterns lined the darkened path leading up the steep hill to a Muromachi-style teahouse and a small mausoleum.

Near the teahouse, an old nun, her head covered with a white silk bandanna, and a plump man of about fifty were sweeping leaves with straw brooms.

The nun sighed and said, "I guess it's better than it was." Few people came to this part of the temple, even to clear away the winter's accumulation of leaves and bird skeletons.

"You must be tired, Mother," said the man. "Why don't you sit down and rest? I'll finish up." He was dressed in a simple cotton kimono, sleeveless cloak, straw sandals, and leather socks with a cherry blossom design, and carried a short sword with an unadorned hilt made of sharkskin.

"I'm not tired," she replied with a little laugh. "But what about you? You're not used to this. Aren't your hands chapped?"

"No, not chapped, but they're covered with blisters."

The woman laughed again, saying, "Now, isn't that a nice reminder to take home with you?"

"I don't mind. I feel my heart's been purified. I hope that means our little offering of labor has pleased the gods."

"Oh, it's getting so dark. Let's leave the rest for tomorrow morning."

Gonnosuke and Iori were standing by the porch now. Kōetsu and Myōshū came down the path slowly, hand in hand. When they got near the Dainichi Hall, both started and cried, "Who's there?"

Then Myōshū said, "It's been a lovely day, hasn't it? Have you come for sightseeing?"

Gonnosuke bowed and said, "No, I've had a sutra read for my mother."

"It's nice to meet young people who are grateful to their parents." She gave Iori a maternal pat on the head. "Kōetsu, do you have any of those wheat cakes left?"

Taking a small package from his sleeve, Kōetsu offered it to Iori, saying, "Forgive me for offering you leftovers."

"Gonnosuke, may I accept it?" asked Iori.

"Yes," said Gonnosuke, thanking Kōetsu on Iori's behalf.

"From the way you talk, you seem to be from the east," said Myōshū. "May I ask where you're going?"

"It seems to be on an endless journey on a never-ending road. This boy and I are fellow disciples in the Way of the Sword."

"It's an arduous path you've chosen. Who is your teacher?"

"His name is Miyamoto Musashi."

"Musashi? You don't say!" Myōshū gazed into space, as though conjuring up a pleasant memory.

"Where is Musashi now?" asked Kōetsu. "It's been a long time since last we saw him."

Gonnosuke told them of Musashi's fortunes during the past couple of years. As he listened, Kōetsu nodded and smiled, as if to say: "That's what I'd expect of him."

When he finished, Gonnosuke asked, "May I inquire who you are?"

"Oh, forgive me for not telling you before." Kōetsu introduced himself and his mother. "Musashi stayed with us for a while, several years ago. We're very fond of him and often talk about him even now." He then told Gonnosuke about two or three incidents that had occurred when Musashi was in Kyoto.

Gonnosuke had long known of Kōetsu's reputation as a sword polisher, and more recently he had heard of Musashi's relationship with the man. But he'd never expected to run into this wealthy townsman tidying up neglected temple grounds.

"Is there a grave of someone close to you here?" he asked. "Or perhaps you've come for an outing?"

"No, nothing so frivolous as an outing," exclaimed

Kōetsu. "Not in a holy place like this. . . . Have you heard from the priests something of the history of the Kongōji?"

"No."

"In that case allow me, in the priests' stead, to tell you a little about it. Please understand, however, that I'm merely repeating what I've heard." Kōetsu paused and looked around slowly, then said, "We have just the right moon tonight," and pointed out the landmarks: above them the mausoleum, Mieidō and Kangetsutei; below, the Taishidō, Shinto shrine, treasure pagoda, refectory and two-story gate.

"Look carefully," he said, seemingly under the spell of the lonely setting. "That pine tree, those rocks, every tree, every blade of grass here, partake of the invisible constancy, the elegant tradition of our country."

He went on in this vein, solemnly telling how in the fourteenth century, during a conflict between southern and northern courts, the mountain had been a stronghold of the southern court. How Prince Morinaga, known also as Daitō no Miya, had held secret conferences to plan the overthrow of the Hōjō regents. How Kusunoki Masashige and other loyalists had fought the armies of the northern court. Later the Ashikagas had come to power, and Emperor Go-Murakami, driven from Mount Otoko, had been forced to flee from place to place. Finally he took refuge at the temple and for many years lived the same sort of life as the mountain priests, suffering the same deprivations. Using the refectory as his seat of government, he had worked tirelessly to recover the imperial prerogatives seized by the military.

At an earlier time, when samurai and courtiers had gathered around the ex-emperors Kōgon, Kōmyō and Sukō, the monk Zen'e had written poignantly: "The priests' quarters and mountain temples were all swept away. The loss is indescribable."

Gonnosuke listened humbly, respectfully. Iori, awed

by the gravity of Kōetsu's voice, could not take his eyes from the man's face.

Kōetsu took a deep breath and went on: "Everything here is a relic of that age. The mausoleum is the last resting place of the Emperor Kōgon. Since the decline of the Ashikagas, nothing's been properly taken care of. That's why my mother and I decided to do a little cleaning up, as a gesture of reverence."

Pleased by the attentiveness of his audience, Kōetsu searched diligently for words to express his heartfelt emotions.

"While we were sweeping, we found a stone with a poem carved on it, perhaps by a soldier-priest of that age. It said:

> "Though the war goes on,
> Even for a hundred years,
> Spring will return.
> Live with a song in your hearts,
> You, the Emperor's people.

"Think of the bravery, the largeness of spirit it took for a simple soldier, after fighting for years, perhaps decades, to protect the emperor, to be able to rejoice and sing. I'm sure it's because the spirit of Masashige communicated itself to him. Though a hundred years of fighting have passed, this place remains a monument to the imperial dignity. Isn't this something for which we should be very grateful?"

"I didn't know this was the site of a sacred battle," said Gonnosuke. "I hope you'll forgive my ignorance."

"I'm glad I had a chance to share with you some of my thoughts on the history of our country."

The four of them strolled down the hill together. In the moonlight, their shadows seemed thin and unsubstantial.

As they passed the refectory, Kōetsu said, "We've

been here seven days. We'll be leaving tomorrow. If you see Musashi, please tell him to come see us again."

Gonnosuke assured him that he would.

The shallow, swift-flowing stream along the outer temple wall was like a natural moat and was crossed by a dirt-floored bridge.

Gonnosuke and Iori had hardly set foot on the bridge when a large white figure armed with a staff emerged from the shadows and flew at Gonnosuke's back. Gonnosuke evaded the attack by sliding to one side, but Iori was knocked off the bridge.

The man plunged on past Gonnosuke to the road on the other side of the bridge. Turning around, he took a solid stance, his legs resembling small tree trunks. Gonnosuke saw it was the priest who had been following him the previous day.

"Who are you?" shouted Gonnosuke.

The priest said nothing.

Gonnosuke moved his staff into striking position and shouted, "Who are you? What reason do you have for attacking Musō Gonnosuke?"

The priest acted as if he hadn't heard. His eyes spat fire as his toes, protruding from heavy straw sandals, inched forward like a centipede in motion.

Gonnosuke growled and cursed under his breath. His short, heavy limbs bursting with the will to fight, he too inched forward.

The priest's staff broke in two with a resounding crack. One part flew through the air; the other the priest hurled with all his might at Gonnosuke's face. It missed, but while Gonnosuke was recovering his balance, his opponent drew his sword and stomped out onto the bridge.

"You bastard!" shouted Iori.

The priest gasped and put his hand to his face. The small stones Iori had thrown had found their mark, one hitting him squarely in the eye. He spun around and ran down the road.

THE WAY OF LIFE AND DEATH

"Stop!" shouted Iori, scrambling up the bank with a handful of stones.

"Never mind," said Gonnosuke, putting his hand on Iori's arm.

"I guess that'll show him," gloated Iori, casting the stones toward the moon.

Soon after they returned to Tōroku's house and went to bed, a squall came up. The wind roared through the trees, threatening to tear the roof off the house, but this was not the only thing that kept them from falling asleep right away.

Gonnosuke lay awake thinking about past and present, wondering if the world was really better off now than it had been in bygone ages. Nobunaga, Hideyoshi and Ieyasu had won the hearts of the people, as well as the authority to govern, but, he wondered, hadn't the true sovereign been virtually forgotten, the people led to worship false gods? The age of the Hōjōs and Ashikagas had been a hateful one, blatantly contradicting the very principle on which the country was founded. Still, even then, great warriors, like Masashige and his son, and loyalists from many provinces had followed the true warrior's code. What had become of the Way of the Samurai? Gonnosuke asked himself. Like the Way of the Townsman and the Way of the Farmer, it seemed to exist now only for the sake of the military ruler.

Gonnosuke's thoughts made his body feel warm all over. The peaks of Kawachi, the woods around the Kongōji, the howling storm, seemed to become living beings, calling to him in a dream.

Iori could not get the unknown priest out of his mind. He was still thinking of the ghostly white figure much later when the storm intensified. He pulled the covers over his eyes and fell into a deep, dreamless sleep.

When they set out the next day, the clouds above the mountains were rainbow-colored. Just outside the village, a traveling merchant materialized from the morning mist and wished them a jovial good morning.

Gonnosuke replied perfunctorily. Iori, absorbed in the thoughts that had kept him awake the night before, was no more talkative.

The man tried to strike up a conversation. "You stayed at Tōroku's house last night, didn't you? I've know him for years. Fine people, him and his wife."

This elicited only a mild grunt from Gonnosuke.

"I also call at Koyagyū Castle from time to time," said the merchant. "Kimura Sukekurō had done me a lot of favors."

This met with another grunt.

"I see you've been to the 'Women's Mount Kōya.' I suppose now you'll be going to Mount Kōya itself. It's just the right time of the year. The snow's gone, and all the roads have been repaired. You can take your time crossing Amami and Kiimi passes, spend the night at Hashimoto or Kamuro—"

The man's probing about their itinerary made Gonnosuke suspicious. "What business are you in?" he asked.

"I sell braided cord," said the man, pointing to the small bundle on his back. "The cord's made of flat-braided cotton. It was only invented recently, but it's getting popular fast."

"I see," said Gonnosuke.

"Tōroku's helped me a lot, telling worshipers at the Kongōji about my cord. As a matter of fact, I was planning to stay at his house last night, but he said he already had two guests. That was sort of a disappointment. When I stay with him, he always fills me up with good sake." He laughed.

Relaxing a bit, Gonnosuke began asking questions about places along the way, for the merchant was quite familiar with the local countryside. By the time they reached Amami plateau, the conversation had grown fairly friendly.

"Hey, Sugizō!"

A man came trotting along the road to catch up with them.

"Why did you go off and leave me? I was waiting at Amano Village. You said you'd stop by for me."

"Sorry, Gensuke," said Sugizō. "I fell in with these two and we got to talking. I forgot all about you." He laughed and scratched his head.

Gensuke, who was dressed like Sugizō, turned out to be a cord salesman too. As they walked, the two merchants fell to discussing business.

Coming to a gully about twenty feet deep, Sugizō suddenly stopped talking and pointed.

"Oh, that's dangerous," he said.

Gonnosuke stopped and looked at the gully, which might have been a gap left by an earthquake, perhaps one that happened a very long time ago.

"What seems to be the trouble?" he asked.

"Those logs, they're not safe to cross. See, there— some of the rocks supporting them have been washed away. We'll fix it so the logs are steady." Then he added, "We should do that for the sake of other travelers."

Gonnosuke watched as they squatted at the edge of the cliff and began packing rocks and dirt under the logs. While thinking that these two merchants traveled a great deal, and thus knew the difficulties of travel as well as anybody, he was a little surprised. It was unusual for men like them to care enough about others to go to the trouble of repairing a bridge.

Iori didn't give the matter any thought. Impressed by their show of concern, he contributed by gathering rocks for them.

"That should do it," said Gensuke. He took a step on the bridge, decided it was safe and said to Gonnosuke, "I'll go first." Holding his arms out for balance, he crossed quickly to the other side, then beckoned for the others to follow.

At Sugizō's urging, Gonnosuke went next, Iori just

behind him. They were not quite to the middle when they let out a shout of surprise. Ahead of them, Gensuke had a lance pointed at them. Gonnosuke looked back and saw Sugizō had also acquired a lance.

"Where did the lances come from?" thought Gonnosuke. He swore, bit his lip angrily and considered the awkwardness of his position.

"Gonnosuke, Gonnosuke . . ." Taken off guard, Iori clung to Gonnosuke's waist, while Gonnosuke, holding his arm around the boy, shut his eyes for an instant, entrusting his life to the will of heaven.

"You bastards!"

"Shut up!" shouted the priest, who stood higher up on the road, behind Gensuke, his left eye swollen and black.

"Keep calm," Gonnosuke told Iori in a soothing voice. Then he shouted. "So you're behind this! Well, watch out, you thieving bastards! You've tangled with the wrong man this time!"

The priest stared coldly at Gonnosuke. "You're not worth robbing. We know that. If you're no smarter than that, what are you doing trying to be a spy?"

"You calling me a spy?"

"Tokugawa dog! Throw that staff away. Put your hands behind your back. And don't try anything funny."

"Ah!" sighed Gonnosuke, as though the will to fight was deserting him. "Look, you're making a mistake. I did come from Edo, but I'm not a spy. My name is Musō Gonnosuke. I'm a *shūgyosha*."

"Never mind the lies."

"What makes you think I'm a spy?"

"Our friends in the east told us some time ago to be on the lookout for a man traveling with a young boy. You were sent down here by Lord Hōjō of Awa, weren't you?"

"No."

"Drop the staff and come along peacefully."

"I'm not going anywhere with you."

"Then you'll die right here."

Gensuke and Sugizō began to close in from front and back, lances ready for action.

To keep Iori out of harm's way, Gonnosuke slapped him on the back. With a loud shriek, Iori dived into the bushes covering the bottom of the gully.

Thundering "Y-a-a-h!" Gonnosuke rushed Sugizō.

The lance requires some space and good timing to be effective. Sugizō extended his arm to thrust his weapon forward but missed the exact moment. A loud croak came from his throat as the blade cut through thin air. Gonnosuke slammed into him, and he fell backward, with Gonnosuke on top of him. When Sugizō attempted to rise, Gonnosuke rammed his right fist into his face. Sugizō bared his teeth but the effect was ludicrous, for his face was already a bloody mess. Gonnosuke stood up, used Sugizō's head for a springboard and cleared the distance to the end of the bridge.

Staff poised, he shouted, "I'm here waiting, you cowards!"

Even as he shouted, three ropes came slithering across the top of the grass, one weighted with a sword guard, another with a short sword in its scabbard. One rope looped around Gonnosuke's arm, another around his legs and the third around his neck. In a moment, still another rope wound around his staff.

Gonnosuke wriggled like an insect caught in a spiderweb, but not for long. Half a dozen men ran out of the woods behind him. By the time they were finished, he lay helpless on the ground, trussed up tighter than a bundle of straw. With the exception of the surly priest, all his captors were dressed as cord salesmen.

"No horses?" asked the priest. "I don't want to walk him all the way to Mount Kudo."

"We can probably hire a horse in Amami Village."

15

A Pear Blossom

In the dark, solemn forest of cryptomerias, the voices of
the lowly shrike, mingling with those of the celestial
bulbul, sounded like the jeweled tones of the mythical
Kalavinka bird.

Two men, coming down from the top of Mount Kōya,
where they had visited the halls and pagodas of the
Kongōbuji and paid their respects at the inner shrine,
stopped on a small arched bridge between the inner and
outer temple precincts.

"Nuinosuke," said the older man pensively, "the
world is indeed fragile and impermanent, isn't it?" From
his heavy homespun cloak and utilitarian *hakama,* he
might have been taken for a country samurai, were it not
for his swords, which were of outstanding quality, and
the fact that his companion was far too suave and well-
groomed for a provincial samurai's attendant.

"You saw them, didn't you?" he continued. "The
graves of Oda Nobunaga, Akechi Mitsuhide, Ishida
Mitsunari, Kobayakawa Kingo—all brilliant, famous
generals only a few years ago. And over there, those
moss-covered stones mark the burial places of great
members of the Minamoto and Taira clans."

"Friend and foe . . . all together here, aren't they?"

"All of them nothing more than lonely stones. Were

167

names like Uesugi and Takeda really great, or were we only dreaming?"

"It gives me an odd feeling. Somehow it seems the world we live in is unreal."

"Is it that? Or is it this place that's unreal?"

"Umm. Who knows?"

"Who do you suppose thought of calling this the Bridge of Illusions?"

"It's a well-chosen name, isn't it?"

"I think illusion is truth, just as enlightenment is reality. If illusion were unreal, the world couldn't exist. A samurai who devotes his life to his master cannot—not for an instant—allow himself to be nihilistic. That's why the Zen I practice is living Zen. It's the Zen of the tainted world, the Zen of hell. A samurai who trembles at the thought of impermanence or despises the world cannot perform his duties. . . . Enough of this place. Let's go back to the other world."

He walked quickly, with a remarkably firm step for a man of his age.

Catching sight of priests from the Seiganji, he frowned and grumbled, "Why did they have to do that?" He'd stayed at the temple the night before; now about twenty young priests were lined up along the pathway, waiting to see him off, though he had said his farewells that morning with the intention of avoiding a display of this sort.

He ran the gauntlet, saying polite good-byes, and hurried on down the road overlooking the patchwork of valleys known as Kujūkutani. Only when he regained the ordinary world did he relax. Conscious as he was of his own fallible human heart, the odor of this world came as relief.

"Hello, who are you?" The question came at him like a shot as they rounded a bend in the road.

"Who are you?" asked Nuinosuke.

The well-built, light-complexioned samurai standing in the middle of the road said politely, "Forgive me if I'm mistaken, but aren't you Lord Hosokawa Tadatoshi's senior retainer, Nagaoka Sado?"

"I'm Nagaoka, to be sure. Who are you, and how did you know I was in the vicinity?"

"My name is Daisuke. I'm the only son of Gessō, who lives in retirement on Mount Kudo."

Seeing the name did not ring a bell, Daisuke said, "My father has long since discarded his former name, but until the Battle of Sekigahara he was known as Sanada Saemonnosuke."

"Do you mean Sanada Yukimura?"

"Yes, sir." With a bashfulness seemingly at odds with his appearance, Daisuke said, "A priest from the Seiganji dropped in at my father's house this morning. He said you'd come to Mount Kōya for a short visit. Though we heard you were traveling incognito, my father thought it'd be a pity not to invite you to have a cup of tea with him."

"That's very kind of him," replied Sado. He squinted for a minute, then said to Nuinosuke, "I think we ought to accept, don't you?"

"Yes, sir," replied Nuinosuke without enthusiasm.

Daisuke said, "It's still fairly early in the day, but my father would be honored if you'd spend the night with us."

Sado hesitated a moment, wondering if it was wise to accept the hospitality of a man regarded as an enemy of the Tokugawas, then nodded and said, "We can decide about that later, but I'll be delighted to join your father for a cup of tea. Don't you agree, Nuinosuke?"

"Yes, sir."

Nuinosuke seemed a bit on edge, but as they started down the road behind Daisuke, master and attendant exchanged knowing glances.

From the village of Mount Kudo, they climbed a little farther up the mountain to a residence set apart from the other houses. The enclosure, surrounded by a low stone wall topped by a fence of woven grass, resembled the semi-fortified house of a lesser provincial war-lord, but all in all one got the impression of refinement rather than military preparedness.

"My father's over there, by that thatched building," said Daisuke as they went through the gate.

There was a small vegetable garden, sufficient to provide onions and greens for the morning and evening soup. The main house stood in front of a cliff; near the side veranda was a bamboo grove, beyond which two more houses were just visible.

Nuinosuke knelt on the veranda outside the room Sado was shown to.

Sado sat down and remarked, "It's very quiet here."

A few minutes later, a young woman who appeared to be Daisuke's wife quietly served tea and left.

While Sado waited for his host, he took in the view—the garden and the valley. Below was the village, and in the distance the inn town of Kamuro. Tiny flowers bloomed on the moss clinging to the overhanging thatched roof, and there was the pleasant fragrance of a rare incense. Though he could not see it, he could hear the stream running through the bamboo grove.

The room itself evoked a feeling of quiet elegance, a gentle reminder that the owner of this unpretentious dwelling was the second son of Sanada Masayuki, lord of Ueda Castle and recipient of an income of 190,000 bush-els.

The posts and beams were thin, the ceiling low. The wall behind the small, rustic alcove was of roughly fin-ished red clay. The flower arrangement in the alcove consisted of a single sprig of pear blossoms in a slender yellow and light green ceramic vase. Sado thought of Po Chü-i's "solitary pear blossom bathed by the spring rain" and of the love that united the Chinese emperor and Yang Kuei-fei, as described in the *Chang He Ke*. He seemed to hear a voiceless sob.

His eye moved to the hanging scroll above the flower arrangement. The characters, large and naive, spelled out

"Hōkoku Daimyōjin," the name Hideyoshi was given when he was elevated to the rank of a god after his death. To one side, a notation in much smaller characters said that this was the work of Hideyoshi's son Hideyori at the age of eight. Feeling it discourteous to Hideyoshi's memory to have his back turned to the scroll, Sado shifted a little to the side. As he did so, he realized suddenly that the pleasant smell came not from incense burning right then but from the walls and shoji, which must have absorbed the fragrance when incense was placed there morning and evening to purify the room in Hideyoshi's honor. Presumably an offering of sake was also made daily, as to established Shinto deities.

"Ah," he thought, "Yukimura's as devoted to Hideyoshi as they say." What he could not fathom was why Yukimura did not hide the scroll. He had the reputation of being an unpredictable man, a man of the shadows, lurking and waiting for a propitious moment to return to the center of the country's affairs. It took no stretch of the imagination to conceive of guests later reporting his sentiments to the Tokugawa government.

Footsteps approached along the outside corridor. The small, thin man who entered the room wore a sleeveless cloak, with only a short sword in the front of his obi. There was an air of modesty about him.

Dropping to his knees and bowing to the floor, Yukimura said, "Forgive me for sending my son to bring you and for interrupting your journey."

This show of humility made Sado uncomfortable. From the legal viewpoint, Yukimura had given up his status. He was now only a rōnin who had taken the Buddhist name Denshin Gessō. Nevertheless, he was the son of Sanada Masayuki, and his older brother, Nobuyuki, was a daimyō and had close connections with the Tokugawas. Being only a retainer, Sado was of much lower rank.

"You shouldn't bow to me that way," he said, returning the greeting. "It's an unexpected honor and pleasure to meet you again. I'm glad to see you're in good health."

"You seem to be too," replied Yukimura, relaxing while Sado was still bowing. "I'm pleased to hear Lord Tadatoshi has returned to Buzen safely."

"Thank you. This is the third year since Lord Yūsai passed away, so he thought it was time."

"Has it been that long?"

"Yes. I've been in Buzen myself, though I have no idea what use Lord Tadatoshi might have for a relic like myself. I served his father and grandfather too, as you know."

When the formalities were over and they began talking of this and that, Yukimura asked, "Have you seen our Zen master recently?"

"No, I've seen or heard nothing of Gudō for some time. That reminds me, it was in his meditation room that I first saw you. You were only a boy then, and you were with your father." Sado smiled happily as he reminisced about the time he had been put in charge of constructing the Shumpoin, a building the Hosokawas had donated to the Myōshinji.

"A lot of hellions came to Gudō to get the rough edges smoothed off," said Yukimura. "He accepted them all, not caring whether they were old or young, daimyō or rōnin."

"Actually, I think he particularly liked young rōnin," mused Sado. "He used to say that a true rōnin did not seek fame or profit, did not curry favor with the powerful, did not attempt to use political power for his own ends, did not exempt himself from moral judgments. Rather he was as broad-minded as floating clouds, as quick to act as the rain and quite content in the midst of poverty. He never set himself any targets and never harbored any grudges."

"You remember that after all these years?" asked Yukimura.

Sado nodded ever so slightly. "He also maintained

that a true samurai was as hard to find as a pearl in the vast blue sea. The buried bones of the innumerable rōnin who sacrificed their lives for the good of the country he likened to pillars supporting the nation." Sado looked straight into Yukimura's eyes as he said this, but the latter did not seem to notice the allusion to men of his own adopted status.

"That reminds me," he said. "One of the rōnin who sat at Gudō's feet in those days was a young man from Mimasaka named Miyamoto . . ."

"Miyamoto Musashi?"

"That's it, Musashi. He impressed me as being a man of great depth, even though he was only about twenty at the time, and his kimono was always filthy."

"It must be the same man."

"Then you do remember him?"

"No; I didn't hear of him until recently, when I was in Edo."

"He's a man to watch. Gudō said that his approach to Zen was promising, so I kept an eye on him. Then he suddenly disappeared. A year or two later, I heard he'd won a brilliant victory against the House of Yoshioka. I remember thinking at the time that Gudō must have a very good eye for people."

"I came across him quite by accident. He was in Shimōsa and gave some villagers a lesson in how to protect themselves from bandits. Later he helped them turn a tract of wasteland into paddy."

"I think he may be the true rōnin Gudō had in mind—the pearl in the vast blue sea."

"Do you really think so? I recommended him to Lord Tadatoshi, but I'm afraid finding him is as hard as discovering a pearl. One thing you can be sure of. If a samurai like that took an official position, it wouldn't be for the sake of the income. He'd be concerned with how his work measured up to his ideals. It may be that Musashi would prefer Mount Kudo to the House of Hosokawa."

"What?"

Sado brushed off his remark with a short laugh, as if it were a slip of the tongue.

"You're joking, of course," said Yukimura. "In my present circumstances, I can hardly afford to hire a servant, let alone a well-known rōnin. I doubt whether Musashi would come even if I did invite him."

"There's no need to deny it," said Sado. "It's no secret the Hosokawas are on the side of the Tokugawas. And everybody knows you are the support on which Hideyori leans most heavily. Looking at the scroll in the alcove, I was impressed by your loyalty."

Seemingly offended, Yukimura said, "The scroll was given to me by a certain person at Osaka Castle in lieu of a memorial portrait of Hideyoshi. I try to take good care of it. But Hideyoshi is dead." He swallowed and went on. "Times change, of course. It doesn't take an expert to see that Osaka has fallen on bad days, while the power of the Tokugawas continues to grow. But I'm not able by nature to change my loyalty and serve a second lord."

"I wonder if people will believe it's that simple. If I may speak candidly, everybody says Hideyori and his mother furnish you great sums every year and at a wave of the hand you could muster five or six thousand rōnin."

Yukimura laughed deprecatingly. "Not a word of truth in it. I tell you, Sado, there's nothing worse than having people make you out to be more than you are."

"You can't blame them. You went to Hideyoshi when you were young, and he liked you better than anyone else. I understand your father's been heard to say you're the Kusunoki Masashige or the K'ung-ming of our times."

"You embarrass me."

"Isn't it true?"

"I want to spend the rest of my days here, quietly, in the shadow of the mountain where the Buddha's Law is preserved. That's all. I'm not a man of refinement. It's enough for me if I can expand my fields a little, live to see my son's child born, have freshly made buckwheat noodles in the fall, eat fresh greens in the spring. Beyond that, I'd like to live a long life, far removed from wars or rumors of war.''

"Is that really all there is to it?" Sado asked mildly.

"Laugh if you will, but I've been spending my free time reading Lao-tsu and Chuang-tsu. The conclusion I've come to is that life is enjoyment. Without enjoyment, what use is there in living?"

"Well, well," exclaimed Sado, feigning surprise.

They talked for another hour or so, over cups of fresh tea served by Daisuke's wife.

Eventually Sado said, "I fear I've stayed too long, wasting your time with my chatter. Nuinosuke, shall we be going?"

"Don't hurry off," said Yukimura. "My son and his wife have made some noodles. Poor country food, but I wish you'd have some with us. If you're planning to stop over at Kamuro, you have plenty of time.''

Daisuke appeared just then to ask his father if he was ready to have the meal served. Yukimura stood up and led the way down a corridor to the back part of the house.

When they were seated, Daisuke offered Sado a pair of chopsticks, saying, "I'm afraid the food isn't too good, but try some anyway.''

His wife, not accustomed to having strangers around, diffidently held out a sake cup, which Sado politely refused. Daisuke and his wife lingered a moment longer before excusing themselves.

"What's that noise I can hear?" asked Sado. It sounded rather like a loom, though louder and with a slightly different quality.

"Oh, that? It's a wooden wheel for making cord. I'm sorry to say, I've had to put the family and servants to work braiding cord, which we sell to help with the finances." Then he added, "We're all used to it, but I suppose it might be annoying to anyone who's not. I'll send word to have it stopped.''

"No, that's all right. It doesn't bother me. I'd hate to think I was holding up your work."

As he started to eat, Sado thought about the food, which sometimes provides insight into a man's condition. But he found nothing revealing there. Yukimura was not at all like the young samurai he had known years before, but he seemed to have shrouded his present circumstances in ambiguity.

Sado then thought about the sounds he heard—kitchen noises, people coming and going, and a couple of times the clink of money being counted. The dispossessed daimyō were not accustomed to physical labor, and sooner or later they would run out of treasures to sell. It was conceivable that Osaka Castle had ceased to be a source of funds. Still, the idea of Yukimura in tight straits was oddly disturbing.

He had been aware that his host might be trying to piece together bits of conversation to form a picture of how things were going with the House of Hosokawa, but there was no indication of this. What stood out about his recollections of their meeting was that Yukimura had not asked about his visit to Mount Kōya. Sado would have answered readily, for there was nothing mysterious about it. Many years ago, Hosokawa Yūsai had been sent by Hideyoshi to the Seiganji and had stayed for quite some time. He had left behind books, some writings and some personal effects, which had become important keepsakes. Sado had gone through them, sorted them out and arranged for the temple to turn them over to Tadatoshi.

Nuinosuke, who hadn't moved from the veranda, cast an anxious look toward the back of the house. Relations between Edo and Osaka were strained, to say the least. Why was Sado taking a risk like this? He didn't imagine Sado to be in any immediate danger, but he'd heard that the lord of Kii Province, Asano Nagaakira, had instructions to keep a strict watch on Mount Kudo. If one of Asano's men reported that Sado had paid a secret visit to Yukimura, the shogunate would become suspicious of the House of Hosokawa.

"Now's my chance," he thought, as the wind suddenly swept through the forsythia and kerria blossoms in the garden. Black clouds were forming rapidly, and it began to sprinkle.

He hurried down the corridor and announced, "It's starting to rain, sir. If we're going to leave, I think now is the time."

Grateful for the opportunity to break away, Sado stood up immediately. "Thank you, Nuinosuke," he said. "By all means, let's be on our way."

Yukimura refrained from urging Sado to stay overnight. He called Daisuke and his wife and said, "Give our guests some straw rain capes. And you, Daisuke, go with them to Kamuro."

At the gate, after expressing thanks for Yukimura's hospitality, Sado said, "I'm sure we'll meet again one of these days. Maybe it'll be another day of rain, or maybe there'll be a strong wind blowing. Until then, I wish you the best of health."

Yukimura grinned and nodded. Yes, one of these days . . . For an instant each man saw the other in his mind's eye, mounted on horseback and carrying a lance. But for the present there was only the host bowing amidst falling apricot petals and the departing guest in a straw cape streaked with rain.

As they walked slowly down the road, Daisuke said, "It won't rain much. At this time of year, we have a little shower like this every day."

Still, the clouds above Senjō Valley and the peaks of Kōya looked threatening, and they unconsciously quickened their pace.

Entering Kamuro, they were greeted by the sight of a man sharing the back of a horse with bundles of firewood and tied so tightly he couldn't move. Leading the horse was a white-robed priest, who called Daisuke's name and ran toward him. Daisuke pretended not to notice.

"Someone's calling you," said Sado, exchanging glances with Nuinosuke.

Forced to take notice of the priest, Daisuke said, "Oh, Rinshōbō. Sorry, I didn't see you."

"I've come straight from Kiimi Pass," said the priest in a loud, excited voice. "The man from Edo—the one we were told to watch for—I spotted him in Nara. He put up quite a fight, but we took him alive. Now, if we take him to Gessō and force him to talk, we'll find out—"

"What are you talking about?" broke in Daisuke.

"The man on the horse. He's a spy from Edo."

"Can't you shut up, you fool!" hissed Daisuke. "Do you know who the man with me is? Nagaoka Sado of the House of Hosokawa. We rarely have the privilege of seeing him, and I'll not have you disturbing us with your silly joke."

Rinshōbō's eyes, turning to the two travelers, betrayed his shock, and he barely caught himself before blurting out, "House of Hosokawa?"

Sado and Nuinosuke were trying to look poised and indifferent, but the wind whipped at their rain capes, making them flap out like the wings of a crane and rather spoiling their efforts.

"Why?" asked Rinshōbō in a low voice.

Daisuke drew him a little to one side and spoke in a whisper. When he returned to his guests, Sado said, "Why don't you go back now? I'd hate to put you to any more trouble."

After watching them until they were out of sight, Daisuke said to the priest, "How could you be so stupid? Don't you know enough to open your eyes before you open your mouth? My father wouldn't be pleased to hear about this."

"Yes, sir. I'm sorry. I didn't know."

Despite his robes, the man was no priest. He was Toriumi Benzō, one of Yukimura's leading retainers.

16

The Port

"Gonnosuke! . . . Gonnosuke! . . . Gonnosuke!"

Iori couldn't seem to stop himself. He called the
name over and over and over. Having found some of
Gonnosuke's belongings lying on the ground, he was
convinced the man was dead.

A day and a night had passed. He'd been in a walking
daze, oblivious of his weariness. His legs, hands and
head were spattered with blood, his kimono badly torn.

Seized by a spasm, he would look up at the sky and
cry, "I'm ready." Or stare at the ground and curse.

"Have I gone crazy?" he thought, suddenly feeling
cold. Looking into a puddle of water, he recognized his
own face and felt relieved. But he was alone, with no one
to turn to, only half believing he was still alive. When
he'd awoken at the bottom of the ravine, he couldn't
remember where he'd been the past several days. It
didn't occur to him to try to go back to the Kongōji or
Koyagyū.

An object glinting with the colors of the rainbow
caught his eye—a pheasant. He became aware of the
fragrance of wild wisteria in the air and sat down. As he
tried to make sense of his situation, thoughts of the sun
captured his mind. He imagined it as being everywhere—
beyond the clouds, among the peaks, in the valleys. He
shifted to a kneeling position, clasped his hands, shut his

179

eyes and began praying. When he opened his eyes a few minutes later, the first thing he saw was a glimpse of ocean, blue and misty, between two mountains.

"Little boy," said a motherly voice. "Are you all right?"

"Hunh?" With a start, Iori turned his hollow eyes toward the two women who were staring at him curiously.

"What do you suppose is wrong with him, Mother?" asked the younger woman, regarding Iori with distaste.

Looking puzzled, the older woman walked over to Iori, and seeing the blood on his clothes, she frowned. "Don't those cuts hurt?" she asked. Iori shook his head. She turned to her daughter and said, "He seems to understand what I say."

They asked his name, where he had come from, where he had been born, what he was doing here, and whom he had been praying to. Little by little, as he searched around for the answers, his memory came back.

More sympathetic now, the daughter, whose name was Otsuru, said, "Let's take him back to Sakai with us. Maybe he'd be useful in the shop. He's just the right age."

"That might be a good idea," said her mother, Osei. "Will he come?"

"He'll come. . . . Won't you?"

Iori nodded and said, "Uh-huh."

"Come along then, but you'll have to carry our luggage."

"Uh."

Iori acknowledged their remarks with a grunt but otherwise said nothing on the journey down the mountain, along a country road and into Kishiwada. But among people again, he became talkative.

"Where do you live?" he asked.

"In Sakai."

"Is that near here?"

"No, it's near Osaka."

"Where's Osaka?"

"We'll take a ship from here and go to Sakai. Then you'll know."

"Really! A ship?" Excited by the prospect, he rattled on for several minutes, telling them how he'd ridden any number of ferryboats on the way from Edo to Yamato, but though the ocean wasn't far from his birthplace in Shimōsa, he'd never been out to sea in a ship.

"That'll make you happy, then, won't it?" said Otsuru. "But you mustn't call my mother 'Auntie.' Say 'Madam' when you speak to her."

"Uh."

"And you mustn't answer 'Uh.' Say 'Yes, ma'am.' "

"Yes, ma'am."

"That's better. Now, if you stay with us and work hard, I'll see you're made a shop assistant."

"What does your family do?"

"My father's a shipping broker."

"What's that?"

"He's a merchant. He owns a lot of ships, and they sail all over western Japan."

"Oh, just a merchant?" sniffed Iori.

" 'Just a merchant'! Why—!" exclaimed the girl. The mother was inclined to overlook Iori's bluntness, but the daughter was indignant. Then she hesitated, saying, "I suppose he's never seen merchants other than candy sellers or clothing salesmen." The fierce pride of the Kansai merchants took over, and she informed him that her father had three warehouses, large ones, in Sakai and several tens of vessels. She gave him to understand that there were branch offices in Shimonoseki, Marukame and Shikama, and that the services performed for the House of Hosokawa in Kokura were of such great importance that her father's ships had the status of official vessels.

"And," she went on, "he's allowed to have a surname and carry two swords, like a samurai. Everyone in western Honshu and Kyushu knows the name of Kobayashi Tarōzaemon of Shimonoseki. In time of war, daimyō like Shimazu and Hosokawa never have enough ships, so my father is just as important as a general.''

"I didn't mean to make you angry," said Iori.

The two women laughed.

"We're not angry," said Otsuru. "But a boy like you, what do you know of the world?"

"I'm sorry."

Turning a corner, they were greeted by the tang of salt air. Otsuru pointed to a ship tied up at Kishiwada Pier. It had a capacity of five hundred bushels and was loaded with local produce.

"That's the ship we'll go home in," she said proudly.

The ship captain and a couple of Kobayashi agents came out of a dockside teahouse to meet them.

"Did you have a nice walk?" asked the captain. "I'm sorry to say we're very heavily loaded, so I couldn't keep much space open for you. Shall we go on board?"

He led the way to the stern of the ship, where a space had been partitioned off with curtains. A red rug had been spread, and elegant Momoyama-style lacquered utensils contained an abundance of food and sake. Iori had the feeling he was entering a small, well-appointed room in a daimyō's mansion.

The ship reached Sakai in the evening, after an uneventful voyage up Osaka Bay. The travelers went directly to the Kobayashi establishment, facing the wharf, where they were welcomed by the manager, a man named Sahei, and a large group of assistants who had gathered at the spacious entrance.

As Osei was going into the house, she turned and said, "Sahei, will you look after the child, please?"

"You mean the dirty little urchin who came off the ship?"

"Yes. He seems quick-witted, so you should be able to put him to work. . . . And do something about his clothes. He may have lice. See that he washes well and give him a new kimono. Then he can go to bed."

Iori didn't see the mistress of the house or her

daughter for the next few days. There was a half-length curtain separating the office from the living quarters in the back. It was like a wall. Without special permission, not even Sahei dared go beyond it.

Iori was given a corner of the "shop," as the office was called, in which to sleep, and though he was grateful for being rescued, he soon became dissatisfied with his new way of life.

The cosmopolitan atmosphere into which he'd been dropped had a certain fascination. He gaped at the foreign innovations he saw on the streets, at the ships in the harbor and the signs of prosperity evident in the way people lived. But it was always, "Hey, boy! Do this! . . . Do that!" From the lowest assistant to the manager, they made him chase around like a dog, not at all like their attitude when speaking to a member of the household or a customer. Then they turned into fawning sycophants. And from morning to night, they talked of money, money. If it was not that, it was work, work.

"And they call themselves human beings!" thought Iori. He longed for the blue sky and the smell of warm grass under the sun and decided any number of times to run away. The yearning was strongest when he remembered Musashi talking about ways of nourishing the spirit. He visualized how Musashi had looked, and the face of the departed Gonnosuke. And Otsū.

Matters came to a head one day when Sahei called, "Io! Io, where are you?" Getting no answer, he stood up and walked to the black-lacquered *keyaki* beam forming the threshold of the office. "You there, the new boy," he shouted. "Why don't you come when you're called?"

Iori was sweeping the walk between the office and the storehouse. He looked up and asked, "Were you calling me?"

"Were you calling me, *sir!*"

"I see."

"I see, *sir!*"

"Yes, sir."

"Don't you have ears? Why didn't you answer me?"

"I heard you say 'Io.' That couldn't be me. My name's Iori . . . sir."

"Io's enough. And another thing. I told you the other day to stop wearing that sword."

"Yes, sir."

"Give it to me."

Iori hesitated a moment, then said, "It's a keepsake from my father. I couldn't let go of it."

"Impudent brat! Give it to me."

"I don't want to be a merchant anyway."

"If it weren't for merchants, people couldn't live," Sahei said forcefully. "Who'd bring in goods from foreign countries? Nobunaga and Hideyoshi are great men, but they couldn't have built all those castles—Azuchi, Jurakudai, Fushimi—without the help of merchants. Just look at the men here in Sakai—Namban, Ruzon, Fukien, Amoi. They're all carrying on trade on a large scale."

"I know that."

"How would you know?"

"Anybody can see the big weaving houses at Ayamachi, Kinumachi and Nishikimachi, and up on the hill Ruzon'ya's establishment looks like a castle. There are rows and rows of warehouses and mansions belonging to rich merchants. This place—well, I know madam and Otsuru are proud of it, but it doesn't amount to anything by comparison."

"Why, you little son of a bitch!"

Sahei was barely out the door before Iori had dropped his broom and fled. Sahei summoned some dock workers and ordered them to catch him.

When Iori was dragged back, Sahei was fuming. "What can you do with a boy like that? He talks back and makes fun of all of us. Punish him good today." Going back into the office, he added, "Take that sword away from him."

They removed the offending weapon and tied Iori's

184

hands behind him. When they fastened the rope to a large crate of cargo, Iori looked like a monkey on a leash.

"Stay there awhile," said one of the men, smirking. "Let people make fun of you." The others guffawed and went back to their work.

There was nothing Iori hated more than this. How often Musashi and Gonnosuke had admonished him not to do things he might be ashamed of.

First he tried pleading, then promised to mend his ways. When this proved ineffective, he switched to invective.

"The manager's a fool—crazy old fart! Let me loose and give me back my sword! I won't stay in a house like this."

Sahei came out and shouted, "Quiet!" He then tried to gag Iori, but the boy bit his finger, so he gave up and had the dock workers do it.

Iori tugged at his bonds, pulling this way and that. Already under a terrible strain from being exposed to public view, he burst into tears when a horse urinated and the foamy liquid trickled toward his feet.

As he was quieting down, he saw something that almost made him faint. On the other side of a horse was a young woman, her head protected from the sweltering sun by a broad-brimmed lacquered hat. Her hemp kimono was tied up for traveling, and she carried a thin bamboo pole.

In vain, he tried to cry out her name. Stretching his neck out, he almost choked with the effort. His eyes were dry, but his shoulders shook with his sobbing. It was maddening, Otsū was so near. Where was she going? Why had she left Edo?

Later in the day, when a ship tied up at the pier, the neighborhood became even busier.

"Sahei, what's this boy doing out here, looking like a trained bear on exhibit? It's cruel to leave him like that. It's also bad for business." The man calling into the office was a cousin of Tarōzaemon. He was usually called

Namban'ya, the name of the shop where he worked. Black pockmarks added a certain sinisterness to the anger in his face. Despite his appearance, he was a friendly man and often gave sweets to Iori. "I don't care if you are punishing him," he continued. "It's not right to do it out on the street. It's bad for the Kobayashi name. Untie him."

"Yes, sir." Sahei complied immediately, all the while regaling Namban'ya with a detailed account of how useless Iori was.

"If you don't know what to do with him," said Namban'ya, "I'll take him home with me. I'll speak to Osei about it today."

The manager, fearing the consequences when the mistress of the house heard what had happened, suddenly had an urge to soothe Iori's feelings. Iori, for his part, wouldn't have anything to do with the man for the rest of the day.

On his way out that evening, Namban'ya stopped in Iori's corner of the shop. A little drunk but in high spirits, he said, "Well, you won't be going with me after all. The women wouldn't hear of it. Ha!"

His conversation with Osei and Otsuru did have one salutary effect, however. The very next day Iori entered a temple school in the neighborhood. He was allowed to wear his sword to school, and neither Sahei nor the others gave him further trouble.

But still he was unable to settle down. When he was inside, his eyes often strayed to the street. Every time a young woman even remotely like Otsū passed, his color changed. Sometimes he ran out for a closer look.

One morning toward the beginning of the ninth month, a prodigious quantity of luggage began arriving by riverboat from Kyoto. By midday, chests and baskets were piled high in front of the office. Tags identified the property as that of samurai in the House of Hosokawa. They had been in Kyoto on business similar to that which had brought Sado to Mount Kōya, looking after the posthumous affairs of Hosokawa Yūsai. Now they sat drinking barley tea and fanning themselves, some in the office, some under the eaves outside.

Coming back from school, Iori got as far as the street. He stopped and turned pale.

Kojirō, seated atop a large basket, was saying to Sahei, "It's too hot out here. Hasn't our ship docked yet?"

Sahei looked up from the manifest in his hands and pointed toward the pier. "Your ship is the *Tatsumimaru*. It's right over there. As you can see, they haven't finished loading, so your places on board aren't ready yet. I'm sorry."

"I'd much prefer to wait on board. It should be a little cooler there."

"Yes, sir. I'll go and see how things are coming along." Too rushed to wipe the sweat from his forehead, he scurried out to the street, where he caught sight of Iori.

"What're you doing there, looking as though you'd swallowed a ramrod? Go and wait on the passengers. Barley tea, cold water, hot water—give them whatever they want."

Iori went to a shed at the entrance of the alley by the storehouse, where a kettle of water was kept boiling. But instead of going about his business, he stood glaring at Kojirō.

He was usually called Ganryū now, the rather scholarly-sounding name seeming more appropriate to his present age and status. He was heavier and more solid. His face had filled out; his once piercing eyes were serene and untroubled. He no longer made frequent use of his rapier tongue, which in the past had caused so much injury. Somehow the dignity of his sword had become a part of his personality.

One result was that he had gradually been accepted by his fellow samurai. They not only spoke highly of him but actually respected him.

Pouring sweat, Sahei returned from the ship, apologized again for the long wait and announced, "The seats amidship are still not ready, but those in the prow are." This meant the foot soldiers and younger samurai could go on board. They proceeded to gather up their belongings and left in a group.

There remained only Kojirō and six or seven older men, all officials of some importance in the fief.

"Sado hasn't come yet, has he?" said Kojirō.

"No, but he should be here before long."

"We'll be getting the sun from the west soon," Sahei said to Kojirō. "It'll be cooler if you move inside."

"The flies are terrible," complained Kojirō. "And I'm thirsty. Could I have another cup of tea?"

"Right away, sir." Without getting up, Sahei shouted toward the hot-water shed. "Io, what are you doing? Bring some tea for our guests." He busily addressed himself to his manifest again, but realizing Iori had not answered, he started to repeat his order. Then he saw the boy approaching slowly with several cups of tea on a tray.

Iori offered tea to each of the samurai, bowing politely each time. Standing before Kojirō with the last two cups, he said, "Please have some tea."

Kojirō absentmindedly extended his hand but abruptly withdrew it as his eyes met Iori's. Startled, he exclaimed, "Why, it's—"

Breaking into a grin, Iori said, "The last time I had the bad luck to run into you was in Musashino."

"What's that?" rasped Kojirō, in a tone hardly appropriate to his present status.

He was about to say something else when Iori shouted, "Oh, you remember me?" and slung the tray at his face.

"Oh!" cried Kojirō, grabbing Iori by the wrist. Though the tray missed him, a bit of hot tea caught him in the left eye. The rest of the tea spilled onto his chest and lap. The tray crashed into a corner post.

"You little bastard!" shouted Kojirō. He threw Iori onto the dirt floor and planted one foot on top of him. "Manager," he called angrily. "This brat is one of your boys, isn't he? Come here and hold him down. Even if he is only a child, I won't stand for this."

Frightened out of his wits, Sahei rushed to do as he was told. But somehow Iori managed to draw his sword and take a swing at Kojirō's arm. Kojirō kicked him to the middle of the room and jumped back a pace.

Sahei turned and rushed back, screaming his lungs out. He reached Iori just as the boy jumped to his feet.

"You keep out of this!" Iori cried, then, looking Kojirō straight in the face, he spat out, "Serves you right!" and ran outside.

Kojirō picked up a carrying pole that happened to be handy and threw it at the boy, scoring a perfect hit behind his knee. Iori landed flat on his face.

At Sahei's command, several men fell on Iori and hauled him back to the hot-water shed, where a servant was wiping off Kojirō's kimono and *hakama*.

"Please forgive this outrage," pleaded Sahei.

"We don't know how to apologize," said one of the assistants.

Without looking at them, Kojirō took a damp towel from the servant and wiped off his face.

Iori had been forced to the ground, his arms bent tightly behind him. "Let me go," he begged, his body writhing in pain. "I won't run away. I'm a samurai's son. I did it on purpose and I'll take my punishment like a man."

Kojirō finished straightening his clothing and smoothed his hair. "Let him go," he said quietly.

Not knowing what to make of the placid expression on the samurai's face, Sahei stammered, "Are . . . are you sure it's all right?"

"Yes. But"—the word sounded like a nail being driven into a board—"although I have no intention of becoming involved with a mere child, if you feel he

189

should be punished, I can suggest a method. Pour a dipperful of boiling water over his head. It won't kill him."

"Boiling water!" Sahei recoiled at the suggestion.

"Yes. If you want to let him go, that's all right too."

Sahei and his men looked at each other uncertainly.

"We can't let something like that go unpunished."

"He's always up to no good."

"He's lucky he didn't get killed."

"Bring a rope."

When they started to tie him, Iori fought off their hands. "What are you doing?" he screamed. Sitting on the ground, he said, "I told you I wouldn't run away, didn't I? I'll take my punishment. I had a reason for doing what I did. A merchant might apologize. Not me. The son of a samurai is not going to cry over a little hot water."

"All right," said Sahei. "You asked for it." He rolled up his sleeve, filled a dipper with boiling water and walked slowly toward Iori.

"Shut your eyes, Iori. If you don't, you'll go blind." The voice came from across the street.

Not daring to look to see whose voice it was, Iori shut his eyes. He recalled a story Musashi had told him once in Musashino. It was about Kaisen, a Zen priest highly revered by the warriors of Kai Province. When Nobunaga and Ieyasu attacked Kaisen's temple and put it to the torch, the priest seated himself calmly in the upper floor of the gate and, while burning to death, uttered the words: "If your heart is obliterated through enlightenment, the fire is cool."

"It's only a little dipper of hot water," Iori told himself. "I mustn't think that way." He tried desperately to become a selfless void, free of delusion, without sorrows. Perhaps, if he had been younger, or much older . . . but at his age, he was too much a part of the world he lived in.

When was it coming? For a giddy moment, he

thought the sweat dripping from his forehead was boiling water. A minute seemed like a hundred years.

"Why, it's Sado," said Kojirō.

Sahei and all the others turned and stared at the old samurai.

"What's going on here?" Sado asked, coming across the street with Nuinosuke at his side.

Kojirō laughed and said lightly, "You caught us at an odd moment. They're punishing the boy."

Sado looked intently at Iori. "Punishing him? Well, if he's done something bad, he should be punished. Go right ahead. I'll watch."

Sahei glanced out of the corner of his eye at Kojirō, who sized the situation up immediately and knew he was the one who would be held responsible for the severity of the punishment. "That's enough," he said.

Iori opened his eyes. He had a little trouble focusing them, but when he recognized Sado, he said happily, "I know you. You're the samurai who came to the Tokuganji in Hōtengahara."

"You remember me?"

"Yes, sir."

"What's happened to your teacher, Musashi?"

Iori sniffled and put his hands to his eyes.

Sado's knowing the boy came as a shock to Kojirō. Thinking about it for a moment, he decided it must have something to do with Sado's search for Musashi. But he certainly didn't want Musashi's name to come up in a conversation between himself and the senior retainer. He knew that one of these days he would have to fight Musashi, but it was no longer a strictly private matter.

In fact, a split had developed in both the main line and the branches of the House of Hosokawa, one faction thinking highly of Musashi, the other partial to the former rōnin who was now the clan's chief sword instructor. Some said the real reason the fight was inevitable was behind-the-scenes rivalry between Sado and Kakubei.

To Kojirō's relief, the boatswain of the *Tatsumimaru* arrived just then with word that the ship was ready.

Sado, remaining behind, said, "The ship doesn't leave till sundown, does it?"

"That's right," replied Sahei, who was pacing about the office worrying about the consequences of today's affair.

"I have time for a little rest, then?"

"Plenty of time. Please, have some tea."

Otsuru appeared at the inner door and beckoned to the manager. After listening to her for a couple of minutes, Sahei came back to Sado and said, "The office is not really the place to receive you. It's only a step through the garden to the house. Would you mind going there?"

"That's very kind," replied Sado. "To whom am I indebted? The lady of the house?"

"Yes. She said she'd like to thank you."

"What for?"

Sahei scratched his head. "I, eh, I imagine for seeing that Iori came to no harm. Since the master isn't here . . ."

"Speaking of Iori, I'd like to talk to him. Would you call him?"

The garden was what Sado would have expected in the house of a rich Sakai merchant. Though bounded on one side by a storehouse, it was a world apart from the hot, noisy office. Rocks and plants were all freshly watered and there was a running brook.

Osei and Otsuru were kneeling in a small, elegant room facing the garden. There was a wool rug on top of the tatami and trays of cakes and tobacco. Sado noticed the spicy fragrance of mixed incense.

Sitting down at the edge of the room, he said, "I won't come in. My feet are dirty."

While serving him tea, Osei apologized for her employees and thanked him for saving Iori.

Sado said, "I had occasion some time ago to meet

that boy. I'm happy to have found him again. How does it happen he's staying in your house?"

After hearing her explanation, Sado told her about his long search for Musashi. They chatted amiably for a while, then Sado said, "I was watching Iori from across the street for several minutes. I admired his ability to remain calm. He conducted himself very well. As a matter of fact, I think it's a mistake to raise a boy with that much spirit in a merchant's establishment. I wonder if you wouldn't consent to turning him over to me. In Kokura, he could be brought up as a samurai."

Osei agreed readily, saying, "It would be the best thing that could possibly happen to him."

Otsuru got up to go look for Iori, but just then he emerged from behind a tree, where he had overheard the whole conversation.

"Do you object to going with me?" asked Sado.

Bursting with happiness, Iori begged to be taken to Kokura.

While Sado drank his tea, Otsuru got Iori ready for the trip: kimono, *hakama*, leggings, basket hat—all new. It was the first time he had ever worn a *hakama*.

That evening, as the *Tatsumimaru* spread its black wings and sailed forth under clouds turned golden by the setting sun, Iori looked back at a sea of faces—Otsuru's, her mother's, Sahei's, those of a large group of well-wishers, the face of the city of Sakai.

With a broad smile on his face, he took off his basket hat and waved at them.

17

The Writing Teacher

The sign at the entrance to a narrow alley in the fishmongers' district of Okazaki read: "Enlightenment for the Young. Lessons in Reading and Writing," and bore the name Muka, who was from all appearances one of the many impoverished but honest rōnin making a living by sharing his warrior-class education with the children of commoners.

The curiously amateurish calligraphy brought a smile to the lips of passersby, but Muka said he wasn't ashamed of it. Whenever it was mentioned, he always replied in the same way: "I'm still a child at heart. I'm practicing along with the children."

The alley ended in a bamboo grove, beyond which was the riding ground of the House of Honda. In fair weather it was always covered by a cloud of dust, since the cavalrymen often practiced from dawn to dusk. The military lineage they were so proud of was that of the famous Mikawa warriors, the tradition that had produced the Tokugawas.

Muka stirred from his midday nap, went to the well and drew water. His solid-gray unlined kimono and gray hood might well have been the dress of a man of forty, but he was in fact not yet thirty. After washing his face, he walked into the grove, where he cut down a thick bamboo with a single sword stroke.

After washing the bamboo at the well, he went back inside. Blinds hanging on one side kept out the dust from the riding ground, but since this was the direction from which light came, the one room seemed smaller and darker than it actually was. A board lay flat in one corner; above it hung an anonymous portrait of a Zen priest. Muka set the piece of bamboo on the board and tossed a bindweed flower into the hollow center.

"Not bad," he thought, as he backed away to examine his work.

Sitting down in front of his table, he took his brush and began practicing, using as models a manual on squarish, formal characters by Ch'u Sui-liang and a rubbing of the priest Kōbō Daishi's calligraphy. He had evidently been progressing steadily during the year he had lived there, for the characters he wrote now were far superior to the ones on the sign.

"May I trouble you?" asked the woman from next door, the wife of a man who sold writing brushes.

"Come in, please," said Muka.

"I only have a minute. I was just wondering. . . . A few minutes ago I heard a loud noise. It sounded like something breaking. Did you hear it?"

Muka laughed. "That was only me, cutting down a piece of bamboo."

"Oh. I was worried. I thought something might have happened to you. My husband says the samurai prowling around here are out to kill you."

"It wouldn't matter if they did. I'm not worth three coppers anyway."

"You shouldn't be so easygoing. Lots of people get killed for things they don't even remember doing. Think how sad all the girls would be if some harm came to you."

She went on her way, not asking, as she often did, "Why don't you take a wife? It isn't that you don't like women, is it?" Muka never gave a clear answer, though he'd brought it on himself by carelessly revealing enough to suggest that he would make a fine catch. His neighbors knew he was a rōnin from Mimasaka, who liked to study and had lived for a time in Kyoto and in and around Edo. He professed to want to settle down in Okazaki and run a good school. Since his youth, diligence and honesty were apparent, it wasn't surprising that a number of girls had shown an interest in marriage, as well as several parents with eligible daughters.

This small corner of society had a certain fascination for Muka. The brush seller and his wife treated him kindly, the wife teaching him how to cook and sometimes doing his washing and sewing. All in all, he enjoyed living in the neighborhood. Everybody knew everybody else, and all sought out new ways to make their lives interesting. There was always something going on, if not a festival or street dances or a religious celebration, then a funeral or a sick person to be cared for.

That evening he passed the brush seller's house as he and his wife were having dinner. With a click of her tongue, the wife said, "Where does he go? He teaches the children in the morning, takes a nap or studies in the afternoon, then in the evening he's gone. He's just like a bat."

Her husband chuckled. "What's wrong with that? He's single. You ought not to begrudge him his nightly excursions."

In the streets of Okazaki, the sounds of a bamboo flute mingled with the buzzing of captive insects in wooden cages, the rhythmical wail of blind street singers, the cries of vendors of melons and sushi. There was nothing here of the frantic bustle that characterized Edo. Lanterns flickered; people strolled about in summer kimonos. In the lingering heat of a summer day, everything seemed relaxed and in its place.

As Muka passed, the girls whispered.

"There he goes again."

"Hmph—paying no attention to anybody, as usual."

The Writing Teacher

Some of the young women bowed to him, then turned to their friends and speculated on his destination.

Muka walked straight on, past the side streets where he might have purchased the favors of the Okazaki harlots, regarded by many to be one of the chief local attractions along the Tōkaidō highroad. At the western edge of town he stopped and stretched, letting the heat out of his sleeves. Ahead of him were the rushing waters of the Yahagi River and the 208-span Yahagi Bridge, the longest on the Tōkaidō. He walked toward the thin figure waiting for him at the first post.

"Musashi?"

Musashi smiled at Matahachi, who was wearing his priest's robe. "Has the master returned?" he asked.

"No."

They walked across the bridge shoulder to shoulder. On a pine-covered hill on the opposite bank stood an old Zen temple. Since the hill was known as Hachijō, the temple had come to be called Hachijōji. They climbed up the dark slope in front of the gate.

"How are things?" asked Musashi. "Practicing Zen must be difficult."

"It is," replied Matahachi, bowing his bluish shaved head dejectedly. "I've often thought of running away. If I have to go through mental torture to become a decent human being, I might as well put my head in a noose and forget about it."

"Don't let it discourage you. You're still only at the beginning. Your real training won't come until after you've appealed to the master and persuaded him to take you as a disciple."

"It's not always impossible. I've learned to discipline myself a little. And whenever I feel low, I think of you. If you can overcome your difficulties, I should be able to overcome mine."

"That's the way it should be. There's nothing I can do that you can't do too."

197

"Remembering Takuan helps. If it hadn't been for him, I'd have been executed."

"If you can bear up under hardship, you can experience a pleasure greater than the pain," Musashi said solemnly. "Day and night, hour by hour, people are buffeted by waves of pain and pleasure, one after the other. If they try to experience only pleasure, they cease to be truly alive. Then the pleasure evaporates."

"I'm beginning to understand."

"Think of a simple yawn. The yawn of a person who's been working hard is different from the yawn of a lazy man. Lots of people die without knowing the pleasure yawning can bring."

"Umm. I hear talk like that at the temple."

"I hope the day soon comes when I turn you over to the master. I want to ask him for guidance too. I need to know more about the Way."

"When do you suppose he'll come back?"

"It's hard to say. Zen masters sometimes float around the country like a cloud for two or three years at a time. Now that you're here, you should resolve to wait four or five years for him, if it comes to that."

"You, too?"

"Yes. Living in that back alley, among poor and honest people, is good training—part of my education. It's not time wasted."

After leaving Edo, Musashi had passed through Atsugi. Then, driven by doubts about his future, he had disappeared into the Tanzawa Mountains, to emerge two months later more worried and haggard than ever. Solving one problem only led him to another. At times he was so tortured his sword seemed like a weapon turned against him.

Among the possibilities he had considered was choosing the easy way. If he could bring himself to live in a comfortable, ordinary way with Otsū, life would be simple. Almost any fief would be willing to pay him enough to live on, perhaps five hundred to a thousand bushels. But when he put it to himself in the form of a question, the answer was always no. An easy existence imposed restrictions; he could not submit to them.

At other times he felt as lost in base, craven illusions as the hungry demons in hell; then, for a time, his mind would clear, and he would bask in the pleasure of his proud isolation. In his heart there was a continual struggle between light and dark. Night and day, he wavered between exuberance and melancholy. He'd think of his swordsmanship and be dissatisfied. Thinking of how long the Way was, how far he was from maturity, a sickness came over his heart. Other days, the mountain life cheered him and his thoughts strayed to Otsū.

Coming down from the mountains, he'd gone to the Yugyōji in Fujisawa for a few days, then on to Kamakura. It was here that he'd met Matahachi. Determined not to return to a life of indolence, Matahachi was in Kamakura because of the many Zen temples there, but he was suffering from an even deeper sense of malaise than Musashi.

Musashi reassured him, "It's not too late. If you learn self-discipline, you can make a fresh start. It's fatal to tell yourself that it's all over, that you're no good."

He felt constrained to add, "To tell the truth, I myself have run up against a wall. There are times when I wonder if I have any future. I feel completely empty. It's like being confined in a shell. I hate myself. I tell myself I'm no good. But by chastising myself and forcing myself to go on, I manage to kick through the shell. Then a new path opens up before me.

"Believe me, it's a real struggle this time. I'm floundering around inside the shell, unable to do a thing. I came down from the mountains because I remembered a person who I think can help me."

The person was the priest Gudō.

Matahachi said, "He's the one who helped you when

you were first seeking the Way, isn't he? Couldn't you introduce me and ask him to accept me as his disciple?"

At first, Musashi was skeptical about Matahachi's sincerity, but after hearing of the trouble he'd been in in Edo, he decided that he really meant it. The two of them made inquiries about Gudō at a number of Zen temples, but learned little. Musashi knew the priest was no longer at the Myōshinji in Kyoto. He had left several years earlier and traveled for some time in the east and northeast. He also knew he was a most erratic man, who might be in Kyoto giving lectures on Zen to the Emperor one day and out wandering the countryside the next. Gudō had been known to stop several times at the Hachijōji in Okazaki, and one priest suggested that might be the best place to wait for him.

Musashi and Matahachi sat in the little shed where Matahachi slept. Musashi often visited him here and they talked late into the night. Matahachi wasn't allowed to sleep in the dormitory, which, like the other buildings of the Hachijōji, was a rustic, thatched-roof affair, since he had not yet been officially accepted as a priest.

"Oh, these mosquitoes!" said Matahachi, waving away smoke from the insect repellent, then rubbing his irritated eyes. "Let's go outside."

They walked to the main hall and sat down on the porch. The grounds were deserted and there was a cool breeze.

"Reminds me of the Shippōji," said Matahachi, his voice barely audible.

"It does, doesn't it," said Musashi.

They fell silent. They always did at times like this, thoughts of home invariably bringing back memories of Otsū or Osugi or events neither of them wanted to talk about for fear of upsetting their present relationship.

But after a few moments, Matahachi said, "The hill the Shippōji was on was higher, wasn't it? There isn't any ancient cryptomeria here, though." He paused, stared for a time at Musashi's profile, then said diffidently, "There's a request I've been wanting to make, but . . ."

"What is it?"

"Otsū—" Matahachi began, but immediately choked up. When he thought he could manage it, he went on: "I wonder what Otsū's doing right now, and what will happen to her. I think of her often these days, apologizing in my heart for what I did. I'm ashamed to admit it, but in Edo I made her live with me. Nothing happened, though. She refused to let me touch her. I guess after I went to Sekigahara, Otsū must have been like a fallen blossom. Now she's a flower blooming on a different tree, in different soil." His face showed his earnestness and his voice was grave.

"Takezō—no . . . Musashi: I beg you, marry Otsū. You're the only person who can save her. I've never been able to bring myself to say that, but now that I've decided to become a disciple of Gudō, I'm resigned to the fact that Otsū is not mine. Even so I worry about her. Won't you look for her and give her the happiness she longs for?"

It was about three o'clock in the morning when Musashi started down the dark mountain path. His arms were folded, his head was bowed; Matahachi's words rang in his ears. Anguish seemed to tug at his legs. He wondered how many nights of torment Matahachi must have spent mustering up the courage to speak. Yet it seemed to Musashi that his own dilemma was uglier and more painful.

Matahachi, he thought, was hoping to flee from the flames of the past to the cool salvation of enlightenment— trying, like a baby being born, to find in the twofold mysterious pain of sadness and ecstasy a life worth living.

Musashi had not been able to say, "I can't do that," much less, "I don't want to marry Otsū. She's your fiancée. Repent, purify your heart and win her back." In the end, he had said nothing, for anything he might have said would have been a lie.

Matahachi had pleaded fervently, "Unless I'm sure Otsū will be cared for, it'll do me no good to become a disciple. You're the one who urged me to train and discipline myself. If you're my friend, save Otsū. That's the only way to save me."

Musashi had been surprised when Matahachi had broken down and wept. He hadn't suspected he was capable of such depth of feeling. And when he'd stood up to leave, Matahachi clutched his sleeve and begged for an answer. "Let me think about it," was all Musashi could say. Now he cursed himself for being a coward and lamented his inability to overcome his inertia.

Musashi thought sadly that those who have not suffered from this malady cannot know its agony. It was not a matter merely of being idle, which is often a pleasant state, but of wanting desperately to do something and not being able to. Musashi's mind and eyes seemed dull and empty. Having gone as far as he could in one direction, he found himself powerless either to retreat or to embark on a new path. It was like being imprisoned in a place with no exit. His frustration bred self-doubt, recrimination, tears.

Getting angry with himself, recalling all the things he had done wrong, did not help. It was because he was experiencing early symptoms of his ailment that he had parted with Iori and Gonnosuke and severed ties with his friends in Edo. But his intention to kick through the shell before it was well formed had failed. The shell was still there, enclosing his empty self like the abandoned skin of a cicada.

He walked on irresolutely. The wide expanse of the Yahagi River came into view, and the wind coming off the river felt cool on his face.

Suddenly, warned by a piercing whistle, he leapt to one side. The shot passed within five feet of him, and the report of a musket reverberated across the river. Counting two breaths between the bullet and the sound, Musashi concluded the gun had been fired from quite a distance. He jumped under the bridge and clung batlike to a post.

Several minutes passed before three men came running down Hachijō Hill like pine cones driven by the wind. Near the end of the bridge, they stopped and began searching for the body. Convinced he'd scored a hit, the musketeer threw away the fuse. He was dressed in darker clothes than the other two and masked, only his eyes visible.

The sky had lightened a little and brass ornaments on the gun butt gave off a soft glow.

Musashi couldn't imagine who in Okazaki wanted him dead. Not that there was any shortage of candidates. In the course of his battles, he had defeated many men who might still burn with the desire for revenge. He had killed many others whose families or friends might wish to pursue a vendetta.

Any person who followed the Way of the Sword was constantly in danger of being killed. If he survived one close call, chances were that by that very act he made new enemies or created a new peril. Danger was the grindstone on which the swordsman whetted his spirit. Enemies were teachers in disguise.

To be taught by danger to be alert even when asleep, to learn from enemies at all times, to use the sword as a means of letting people live; governing the realm, achieving enlightenment, sharing one's joys in life with others— they were all inherent in the Way of the Sword.

As Musashi crouched under the bridge, the cold reality of the situation stimulated him and his lassitude evaporated. Breathing very shallowly, noiselessly, he let his attackers approach. Failing to find the corpse, they searched the deserted road and the space under the end of the bridge.

Musashi's eyes widened. Though dressed in black, like bandits, the men carried samurai swords and were well shod. The only samurai in the district were those serving the House of Honda in Okazaki and the Owari House of Tokugawa in Nagoya. He was not aware of having enemies in either fief.

One man dived into the shadows and recovered the fuse, then lit it and waved it, leading Musashi to think there were more men across the bridge. He couldn't move, not now anyway. If he showed himself, he would invite more musket fire. Even if he gained the opposite bank, danger, perhaps greater danger, lay waiting. But he couldn't stay where he was much longer, either. Knowing he had not crossed the bridge, they would move in on him and possibly discover his hiding place.

His plan came to him like a flash of light. It was not reasoned out by the theories of the Art of War, which constituted the fiber of the trained warrior's intuition. To reason out a mode of attack was a dilatory process, often resulting in defeat in situations where speed was of the essence. The warrior's instinct was not to be confused with animal instinct. Like a visceral reaction, it came from a combination of wisdom and discipline. It was an ultimate reasoning that went beyond reason, the ability to make the right move in a split second without going through the actual process of thinking.

"There's no point in your trying to hide," he shouted. "If you're looking for me, I'm right here." The wind was fairly strong now; he wasn't sure whether his voice carried or not.

The question was answered by another shot. Musashi, of course, was no longer there. While the bullet was still in the air, he jumped nine feet nearer the end of the bridge.

He rushed into their midst. They separated slightly, facing him from three directions but totally lacking in coordination. He struck downward at the man in the middle with his long sword, simultaneously slicing laterally with his short sword at the man on his left. The third man fled across the bridge, running, stumbling and bouncing off the railing.

Musashi followed at a walk, keeping to one side and stopping from time to time to listen. When nothing more happened, he went home and to bed.

The next morning two samurai appeared at his house. Finding the entranceway full of children's sandals, they went around to the side.

"Are you Muka *Sensei?*" asked one. "We're from the House of Honda."

Musashi looked up from his writing and said, "Yes, I'm Muka."

"Is your real name Miyamota Musashi? If it is, don't try to conceal it."

"I'm Musashi."

"I believe you're acquainted with Watari Shima."

"I don't think I know him."

"He says he's been at two or three haiku parties when you were present."

"Now that you mention it, I do remember him. We met at the house of a mutual friend."

"He was wondering if you wouldn't come and spend an evening with him."

"If he's looking for someone to compose haiku with, he has the wrong man. Though it's true I've been invited to a few such parties, I'm a simple man with little experience in such matters."

"I think what he has in mind is discussing the martial arts with you."

Musashi's pupils were staring worriedly at the two samurai. For a few moments, Musashi gazed at them too, then said, "In that case, I shall be delighted to call on him. When?"

"Could you come this evening?"

"Fine."

"He'll send a palanquin for you."

"That's very kind of him. I'll be waiting."

After they'd gone, he turned back to his pupils. "Come, now," he said. "You mustn't let yourselves be distracted. Get back to work. Look at me. I'm practicing too. You have to learn to concentrate so completely that you don't even hear people talking or cicadas singing. If you're lazy when you're young, you'll turn out like me and have to practice after you're grown." He laughed and looked around at the ink-smeared faces and hands.

By twilight, he had donned a *hakama* and was ready to go. Just as he was reassuring the brush seller's wife, who looked ready to cry, that he would be safe, the palanquin arrived—not the simple basket type seen around town but a lacquered sedan chair, which was accompanied by two samurai and three attendants.

Neighbors, dazzled by the sight, crowded around and whispered. Children called their friends and chattered excitedly.

"Only great people ride in palanquins like that."

"Our teacher must be somebody."

"Where's he going?"

"Will he ever come back?"

The samurai closed the door of the palanquin, cleared the people out of the way, and they set off.

While not knowing what to expect, Musashi suspected there was a connection between the invitation and the incident at Yahagi Bridge. Perhaps Shima was going to take him to task for killing two Honda samurai. Then again, maybe Shima was the person behind the spying and the surprise attack and was now ready to confront Musashi openly. Not believing any good could come from tonight's meeting, Musashi resigned himself to facing a difficult situation. Speculation wouldn't get him very far. The Art of War demanded that he find out where he stood and act accordingly.

The palanquin rocked gently, like a boat at sea. Hearing the wind soughing through the pines, he thought they must be in the forest near the north castle wall. He did not look like a man bracing himself for an unpredictable onslaught. Eyes half shut, he appeared to be dozing.

After the castle gate grated open, the pace of the bearers was slower, the samurai's tones more subdued. They passed flickering lanterns and came to the castle buildings. When Musashi alighted, servants ushered him silently but politely to an open pavilion. Since the blinds were rolled up on all four sides, the breeze wafted through in pleasant waves. The lamps dimmed and flared riotously. It did not seem like the sweltering summer night it was.

"I am Watari Shima," said his host. He was a typical Mikawa samurai—sturdy, virile, alert but not ostensibly so, betraying no signs of weakness.

"I am Miyamoto Musashi." The equally simple reply was accompanied by a bow.

Shima returned the bow, said, "Make yourself comfortable," and proceeded to the point without further formalities. "I'm told you killed two of our samurai last night. Is that true?"

"Yes, it is." Musashi stared at Shima's eyes.

"I owe you an apology," said Shima gravely. "I heard about the incident today when the deaths were reported. There was an investigation, of course. Though I've known your name for a long time, I did not know until now that you were living in Okazaki.

"As for the attack, I was told you were fired on by a group of our men, one of whom is a disciple of Miyake Gumbei, a martial expert of the Tōgun Style."

Musashi, sensing no subterfuge, accepted Shima's words at face value, and the story unfolded gradually. Gumbei's disciple was one of several Honda samurai who had studied at the Yoshioka School. The firebrands among them got together and decided to kill the man who had put an end to the glory of the Yoshioka School.

Musashi knew Yoshioka Kempō's name was still revered throughout the country. In western Japan, particularly, it would have been difficult to find a fief in which there were no samurai who had not studied under him. Musashi told Shima he understood their hatred of him but regarded it as a personal grudge rather than a legitimate reason for revenge in accordance with the Art of War.

Shima apparently agreed. "I called the survivors in and reprimanded them. I hope you'll forgive us and forget the matter. Gumbei, too, was very displeased. If you don't mind, I'd like to introduce him to you. He would like to offer his apologies."

"That's not necessary. What happened was a common occurrence for any man committed to the martial arts."

"Even so—"

"Well, let's dispense with the apologies. But if he'd like to talk about the Way, I'd be delighted to meet him. The name is familiar."

A man was sent for Gumbei, and when the introductions were over, the talk turned to swords and swordsmanship.

Musashi said, "I'd like to hear about the Tōgun Style. Did you create it?"

"No," replied Gumbei. "I learned it from my teacher, Kawasaki Kaginosuke, from Echizen Province. According to the manual he gave me, he developed it while living as a hermit on Mount Hakuun in Kōzuke. He seems to have learned many of his techniques from a Tendai monk named Tōgumbo. . . . But tell me about yourself. I've heard your name mentioned a number of times. I had the impression you were older. And since you're here, I wonder if you'd favor me with a lesson." The tone was friendly. Nevertheless, this was an invitation to battle.

"Some other time," Musashi replied lightly. "I should be going now. I don't really know the way home."

"When you go," said Shima, "I'll send someone with you."

"When I heard two men had been cut down," Gumbei went on, "I went over to take a look. I found I couldn't reconcile the positions of the bodies with the wounds, so I questioned the man who escaped. His impression was that you were using two swords at once. Could that be true?"

With a smile, Musashi said he had never done so consciously. He regarded what he was doing as fighting with one body and one sword.

"You shouldn't be so modest," said Gumbei. "Tell us about it. How do you practice? What do the weights have to be for you to use two swords freely?"

Seeing he wasn't going to be able to leave before he gave some sort of explanation, he directed his eyes around the room. They came to rest on two muskets in the alcove and he asked to borrow them. Shima consented, and Musashi went to the middle of the room holding the two weapons by the barrels, one in each hand.

Musashi raised one knee and said, "Two swords are as one sword. One sword is as two swords. One's arms are separate; they both belong to the same body. In all things, the ultimate reasoning is not dual but single. All styles and all factions are alike in this respect. I will show you."

The words came out spontaneously and when they stopped, he raised his arm and said, "By your leave." Then he began twirling the muskets. They spun around like reels, creating a small whirlwind. The other men blanched.

Musashi stopped and drew his elbows to his sides. He walked over to the alcove and put the muskets back. With a slight laugh, he said, "Perhaps that will help you to understand." Offering no further explanation, he bowed to his host and took his leave. Astounded, Shima forgot all about sending someone with him.

Outside the gate, Musashi turned for a final look, relieved to be out of Watari Shima's grasp. He still did not know the man's real intentions, but one thing was clear. Not only was his identity known; he had become involved in an incident. The wisest thing would be to leave Okazaki this very night.

He was thinking about his promise to Matahachi to wait for Gudō's return when the lights of Okazaki came into view and a voice called to him from a small roadside shrine.

"Musashi, it's me, Matahachi. We were worried about you, so we came out here to wait."

"Worried?" said Musashi.

"We went to your house. The woman next door said people had been spying on you recently."

"We?"

"The master came back today."

Gudō was seated on the veranda of the shrine. He was a man of unusual mien, his skin as black as a giant cicada's, his deep-set eyes shining brilliantly under high eyebrows. He looked to be somewhere between forty and fifty, but it was impossible to tell with a man like this. Thin and wiry, he had a booming voice.

Musashi went over, knelt and lowered his forehead to the ground. Gudō regarded him silently for a minute or two. "It's been a long time," he said.

Lifting his head, Musashi said quietly, "A very long time." Gudō or Takuan—Musashi had long been convinced that only one or the other of these two men could deliver him from his present impasse. Here, at last, after a wait of a whole year, was Gudō. He gazed at the priest's face as he might at the moon on a dark night.

Suddenly and forcefully, he cried out, *"Sensei!"*

"What is it?" Gudō had no need to ask; he knew what Musashi wanted, anticipated it as a mother divines a child's needs.

Musashi, head to the ground again, said, "It's been nearly ten years since I studied under you."

"Is it that long?"

"Yes. But even after all those years, I doubt my progress along the Way is measurable."

"You still talk like a child, don't you? You couldn't have come very far."

"I'm full of regrets."

"Are you?"

"My training and self-discipline have accomplished so little."

"You're always talking about such things. So long as you do that, it's futile."

"What would happen if I gave up?"

"You'd be tied up in knots again. You'd be human rubbish, worse off than before, when you were merely an ignorant fool."

"If I desert the Way, I fall into the depths. Yet when I try to pursue it to the peak, I find I'm not up to the task. I'm twisting in the wind halfway up, neither the swordsman nor the human being I want to be."

"That seems to sum it up."

"You can't know how desperate I've been. What should I do? Tell me! How can I free myself from inaction and confusion?"

"Why ask me? You can only rely on yourself."

"Let me sit at your feet again and receive your chastisement. Me and Matahachi. Or give me a blow with your staff to awaken me from this dark emptiness. I beg you, *Sensei*, help me." Musashi had not lifted his head. He shed no tears, but his voice choked up.

Completely unmoved, Gudō said, "Come, Matahachi," and together they walked away from the shrine.

Musashi ran after the priest, grabbed his sleeve, pleaded and begged.

The priest shook his head silently. When Musashi persisted, he said, "Not one thing!" Then, angrily: "What have I to tell you? What more have I to give you? There is only a blow on the head." He waved his fist in the air but did not strike.

Musashi, letting go of his sleeve, was about to say something else. The priest walked rapidly away, not pausing to look back.

At Musashi's side, Matahachi said, "When I saw him at the temple and explained our feelings and why we wanted to become his disciples, he barely listened. When I finished, he said, 'Oh?' and told me I could follow along and wait on him. Maybe if you just follow us, whenever he seems to be in a good mood you can ask him what you want to ask."

Gudō turned and called Matahachi.

"Coming," said Matahachi. "Do what I told you," he advised Musashi as he rushed off to catch up with the priest.

Thinking that letting Gudō out of his sight again would be fatal, Musashi decided to follow Matahachi's advice. In the flow of universal time, a man's life of sixty or seventy years was only a lightning flash. If in that brief span he was privileged to meet a man like Gudō, it would be foolish to let the chance slip by.

"It's a sacred opportunity," he thought. Warm tears gathered at the corners of his eyes. He had to follow Gudō, to the end of the earth if need be, pursue him until he heard the word he longed for.

Gudō walked away from Hachijō Hill, apparently no longer interested in the temple there. His heart had already begun to flow with the water and the clouds. When he reached the Tōkaidō, he turned west, toward Kyoto.

18

The Circle

The Zen master's approach to travel was whimsically eccentric. One day when it rained he stayed inside the inn all day and had Matahachi give him a moxa treatment. In Mino Province, he stopped over at the Daisenji for seven days and then spent a few days at a Zen temple in Hikone, so it was only gradually that they approached Kyoto.

Musashi slept wherever he could find a place. When Gudō stayed at an inn he spent the night either outdoors or at another inn. If the priest and Matahachi were stopping at a temple, Musashi took shelter under the gate. Privations were as nothing compared to his need for a word from Gudō.

One night outside a temple by Lake Biwa, suddenly aware of the coming of autumn, he took a look at himself and saw that he resembled nothing so much as a beggar. His hair, of course, was a rat's nest, since he'd resolved not to comb it until the priest relented. It was weeks since he'd had a bath and a shave. His clothes were quickly being reduced to tatters; they felt like pine bark rubbing against his skin.

The stars seemed ready to fall from the sky. He looked at his reed mat and thought: "What a fool I am!" All at once, his attitude appeared insane. He laughed bitterly. He'd stuck to his goal doggedly, silently, but what was it he was seeking from the Zen master? Was it impossible to go through life without torturing himself so? He even began to feel sorry for the lice inhabiting his body.

Gudō had stated unequivocally that he had "not one thing" to offer. It was unreasonable to press him for something he did not possess, wrong to resent him, even though he showed less consideration than he might have for a stray dog along the wayside.

Musashi gazed upward through the hair hanging over his eyes. No doubt about it—it was an autumn moon. But the mosquitoes. His skin, already peppered with red welts, was no longer sensitive to their bites.

He was quite prepared to admit to himself that there was something he did not understand, but he thought of it as being one thing. If only he could figure out what it was, his sword would be released from its bonds. Everything else would be solved in an instant. Then just as he felt on the verge of grasping it, it always eluded him.

If his pursuit of the Way was to end here, he would prefer to die, for he saw nothing else to live for. He stretched out under the roof of the gate. When sleep would not come, he asked what it could be. A sword technique? No; not only that. A secret for getting on in the world? No; more than that. A solution to the problem of Otsū? No; no man could be this miserable over the love of a woman. It had to be one all-encompassing answer, yet for all its magnitude, it could, at the same time, be no larger than a poppy seed.

Wrapped in his matting, he looked like a caterpillar. He wondered if Matahachi was sleeping well. Comparing himself with his friend, he felt envious. Matahachi's problems did not seem to disable him. Musashi always seemed to be searching out new problems with which to torture himself.

His eyes fell on a plaque hanging on a gatepost. He got up and went up to it for a closer look. By the light of the moon, he read:

I beg you, try to find the fundamental source.
Pai-yün was moved by the merits of Pai-ch'ang;
Hu-ch'iu sighed over the teachings left by Pai-yün.
Like our great predecessors,
Do not merely pinch off the leaves
Or concern yourselves only with the branches.

It appeared to be a quotation from the *Testament* of Daitō Kokushi, the founder of the Daitokuji.

Musashi reread the last two lines. Leaves and branches . . . How many people were thrown off course by irrelevant matters? Was he himself not an example? While the thought seemed to lighten his burden, his doubts would not go away. Why would his sword not obey him? Why did his eyes wander from his goal? What prevented him from achieving serenity?

Somehow it all seemed so unnecessary. He knew that it was when one had pursued the Way as far as possible that vacillation set in and one was attacked by fretfulness—leaves and branches. How did one break through the cycle? How did one get at the core and destroy it?

I laugh at my ten-year pilgrimage—
Wilted robe, tattered hat, knocking at Zen gates.
In reality, the Buddha's Law is simple:
Eat your rice, drink your tea, wear your clothes.

Musashi recalled this verse written by Gudō in self-mockery. Gudō had been about the same age Musashi was now when he composed it.

On Musashi's first visit to the Myōshinji, the priest had all but kicked him away from the door. "What strange line of thinking leads you to my house?" he had shouted. But Musashi persisted, and later, after he'd gained admittance, Gudō regaled him with this ironic verse. And he laughed at him, saying the same thing he had said a few weeks ago: "You're always talking. . . . It's futile."

Thoroughly disheartened, Musashi gave up the idea of sleep and walked around the gate, just in time to see two men emerge from the temple.

Gudō and Matahachi were walking at an unusually rapid pace. Perhaps an urgent summons had come from the Myōshinji, the head temple of Gudō's sect. In any event, he brushed past the monks gathered to see him off and headed straight for the Kara Bridge in Seta.

Musashi followed, through the town of Sakamoto, which was asleep, the woodblock print shops, the greengrocer's, even the bustling inns, all tightly shuttered. The only presence was the ghostly moon.

Leaving the town, they climbed Mount Hiei, past the Miidera and the Sekiji in their veils of mist. They met almost no one. When they reached the pass, Gudō stopped and said something to Matahachi. Below them lay Kyoto, in the other direction the tranquil expanse of Lake Biwa. Aside from the moon itself, everything was like mica, a sea of soft silvery mist.

Reaching the pass a few moments later, Musashi was startled to find himself only a few feet from the master. Their eyes met for the first time in weeks.

Gudō said nothing.

Musashi said nothing.

"Now . . . it has to be now," thought Musashi. If the priest got as far as the Myōshinji, it might be necessary to wait many weeks for the opportunity to see him again.

"Please, sir," he said. His chest swelled and his neck twisted. His voice sounded like that of a frightened child, attempting to tell his mother something he really did not want to say. He edged forward timidly.

The priest did not condescend to ask what he wanted. His face might have belonged to a dry-lacquer statue. The eyes alone stood out whitely, glaring angrily at Musashi.

"Please, sir." Musashi, oblivious of everything save

the flaming impulse propelling him forward, fell to his knees and bowed his head. "One word of wisdom. Just one word . . ."

He waited for what seemed like hours. When he was unable to restrain himself any longer, he started to renew his plea.

"I've heard all that," Gudō interrupted. "Matahachi talks about you every night. I know all there is to know, even about the woman."

The words were like slivers of ice. Musashi could not have lifted his head if he had wanted to.

"Matahachi, a stick!"

Musashi shut his eyes, steeling himself for the blow, but instead of striking, Gudō drew a circle around him. Without another word, he threw the stick away and said, "Let's go, Matahachi." They walked away quickly.

Musashi was incensed. After the weeks of cruel mortification he'd undergone in a sincere effort to receive a teaching, Gudō's refusal was far more than a lack of compassion. It was heartless, brutal. He was toying with a man's life.

"Swine of a priest!"

Musashi glared viciously at the departing pair, his lips set tightly in an angry scowl.

"Not one thing." Reflecting on Gudō's words, he decided they were deceitful, suggesting the man had something to offer when in fact there was "not one thing" in his foolish head.

"Wait and see," thought Musashi. "I don't need you!" He would rely on no one. In the final analysis, there *was* no one to rely on but himself. He was a man, just as Gudō was a man and all the earlier masters had been men.

He stood up, half lifted by his own rage. For several minutes, he stared at the moon, but as his anger cooled, his eyes fell to the circle. Still inside it, he turned all the way around. As he did so, he remembered the stick that had not struck him.

"A circle? What could it mean?" He let his thoughts flow.

A perfectly round line, no beginning, no end, no deviation. If expanded infinitely, it would become the universe. If contracted, it would become coequal with the infinitesimal dot in which his soul resided. His soul was round. The universe was round. Not two. One. One entity—himself and the universe.

With a click, he drew his sword and held it out diagonally. His shadow resembled the symbol for "o" [才]. The universal circle remained the same. By the same token, he himself was unchanged. Only the shadow had changed.

"Only a shadow," he thought. "The shadow is not my real self." The wall against which he had been beating his head was a mere shadow, the shadow of his confused mind.

He raised his head and a fierce shout broke from his lips.

With his left hand, he held out his short sword. The shadow changed again, but the image of the universe—not by one whit. The two swords were but one. And they were part of the circle.

He sighed deeply; his eyes had been opened. Looking up at the moon again, he saw that its great circle could be regarded as identical with the sword or with the soul of one who treads the earth.

"*Sensei!*" he cried, bounding off after Gudō. He sought nothing more from the priest, but he owed him an apology for having hated him with such vehemence.

After a dozen steps, he halted. "It's only leaves and branches," he thought.

19

Shikama Blue

"Is Otsū here?"

"Yes, here I am."

A face appeared above the top of the hedge.

"You're the hemp dealer Mambei, aren't you?" said Otsū.

"That's right. Sorry to bother you when you're busy, but I heard some news that might interest you."

"Come in." She gestured toward the wooden door in the fence.

As was evident from the cloth hanging from branches and poles, the house belonged to one of the dyers who made the sturdy fabric known throughout the country as "Shikama Blue." This involved immersing the cloth in indigo dye several times and pounding it in a large mortar after each immersion. The thread became so saturated with dye that it wore out long before it faded.

Otsū was not yet used to handling the mallet, but she worked hard and her fingers were stained blue. In Edo, after learning Musashi was gone, she had called at the Hōjō and Yagyū residences, then immediately set out on her search again. In Sakai the previous summer, she boarded one of Kobayashi Tarōzaemon's ships and came to Shikama, a fishing village situated on the triangular estuary where the Shikama River flows into the Inland Sea.

Remembering that her wet nurse was married to a dyer from Shikama, Otsū had looked her up and was living with her. Since the family was poor, Otsū felt obliged to help with the dyeing, which was the work of the young unmarried women. They often sang as they worked, and villagers said they could tell from the sound of a girl's voice whether she was in love with one of the young fishermen.

Having washed her hands and wiped the sweat from her forehead, Otsū invited Mambei to sit down and rest on the veranda.

He declined with a wave of his hand and said, "You came from the village of Miyamoto, didn't you?"

"Yes."

"I go up that way on business, to buy hemp, and the other day I heard a rumor. . . ."

"Yes?"

"About you."

"Me?"

"I also heard something about a man named Musashi."

"Musashi?" Otsū's heart was in her throat and her cheeks flushed.

Mambei gave a little laugh. Though it was autumn, the sun was still fairly strong. He folded a hand towel, put it on his head and squatted on his heels. "Do you know a woman named Ogin?" he asked.

"You mean Musashi's sister?"

Mambei nodded vigorously. "I ran into her at Mikazuki Village in Sayo. I happened to mention your name. She looked very surprised."

"Did you tell her where I was?"

"Yes. I didn't see any harm in that."

"Where's she living now?"

"She's staying with a samurai named Hirata—a relative of hers, I think. She said she'd like very much to see you. She said several times how much she missed

220

you, how much she had to tell you. Some of it was secret, she said. I thought she was going to start crying."

Otsū's eyes reddened.

"There in the middle of the road was no place to write a letter, of course, so she asked me to tell you to come to Mikazuki. She said she'd like to come here, but couldn't just now." Mambei paused. "She didn't go into details, but she said she'd had word from Musashi." He added that he was going to Mikazuki the next day and suggested she go with him.

Though Otsū's mind was made up right then, she felt she should talk it over with the dyer's wife. "I'll let you know this evening," she said.

"Fine. If you decide to go, we should get an early start." With the sea murmuring in the background, his voice sounded particularly loud, and even Otsū's soft reply seemed rather shrill.

As Mambei went out the gate, a young samurai who had been sitting on the beach rubbing a handful of sand stood up and watched him with piercing eyes, as if to verify his thoughts about the man. Handsomely attired and wearing a straw basket hat shaped like a ginkgo leaf, he appeared to be eighteen or nineteen years old. When the hemp dealer was out of sight, he turned and stared at the dyer's house.

Despite the excitement caused by Mambei's news, Otsū picked up her mallet and resumed her work. The sounds of other mallets, accompanied by singing, floated through the air. No sound came from Otsū's lips when she worked, but in her heart was a song of her love for Musashi. Now she silently whispered a poem from an ancient collection:

> Since our first meeting,
> My love has been more profound
> Than that of others,
> Though it matches not the hues
> Of the cloth from Shikama.

She felt sure that if she visited Ogin, she would learn where Musashi was. And Ogin was a woman too. It would be easy to tell her her feelings.

The beats of her mallet slowed to an almost languid pace. Otsū was happier than she had been for a long time. She understood the feelings of the poet. Often the sea seemed melancholy and alien; today it was dazzling, and the waves, though gentle, appeared to be bursting with hope.

She hung the cloth on a high drying pole and, heart still singing, wandered out through the open gate. Out of the corner of her eyes, she caught sight of the young samurai strolling unhurriedly along the water's edge. She had no idea who he was, but somehow he held her attention, and she noticed nothing else, not so much as a bird riding the salty breeze.

Their destination was not very far; even a woman could walk the distance with little difficulty, stopping over once on the way. It was nearly noon now.

"I'm sorry to put you to all this trouble," said Otsū.

"No trouble. You seem to have good walking legs," said Mambei.

"I'm used to traveling."

"I heard you've been to Edo. That's quite a journey for a woman traveling alone."

"Did the dyer's wife tell you that?"

"Yes. I've heard everything. The people in Miyamoto talk about it too."

"Oh, they would," said Otsū with a little frown. "It's so embarrassing."

"You shouldn't feel embarrassed. If you love a person that much, who's to say whether you're to be pitied or congratulated. But it seems to me this Musashi is a little coldhearted."

"Oh, he's not—not at all."

"You don't resent the way he's acted?"

"I'm the one to blame. His training and discipline

are his only interest in life, and I can't resign myself to that."

"I don't see anything wrong with the way you feel."

"But it seems to me I've caused him a lot of trouble."

"Hmph. My wife should hear that. That's the way women ought to be."

"Is Ogin married?" asked Otsū.

"Ogin? Oh, I'm not quite sure," said Mambei, and changed the subject. "There's a teahouse. Let's rest awhile."

They went inside and ordered tea to go with their box lunches. As they were finishing, some passing grooms and porters called out in familiar tones to Mambei.

"Hey, you, why don't you drop in on the game in Handa today? Everybody's complaining—you left with all our money the other day."

In some confusion, he shouted back, as though he hadn't understood them, "I don't have any use for your horses today." Then quickly, to Otsū, "Shall we be going?"

As they hurried out of the shop, one of the grooms said, "No wonder he's giving us the brush-off. Take a look at the girl!"

"I'm going to tell your old woman on you, Mambei."

They heard more comments of this sort as they walked quickly on ahead. Asaya Mambei's shop in Shikama was certainly not among the more prominent business establishments there. He bought hemp in the nearby villages and parceled it out to the fishermen's wives and daughters to make into sails, nets and other things. But he was the proprietor of his own enterprise, and his being on such friendly terms with common porters struck Otsū as strange.

As if to dispel her unspoken doubts, Mambei said, "What can you do with riffraff like that? Just because I do them the favor of asking them to carry stuff from the mountains, that's no reason for them to get familiar!''

They spent the night in Tatsuno, and when they left the next morning, Mambei was as kind and solicitous as ever. By the time they reached Mikazuki, it was getting dark in the foothills.

"Mambei," asked Otsū anxiously, "isn't this Mikazuki? If we cross the mountain we'll be in Miyamoto." She had heard that Osugi was in Miyamoto again.

Mambei halted. "Why, yes, it's just on the other side. Does it make you homesick?"

Otsū lifted her eyes to the black, wavy crest of the mountains and the evening sky. The area seemed very desolate, as if somehow the people who should be there were missing.

"It's only a little farther," said Mambei, walking on ahead. "Are you tired?"

"Oh, no. Are you?"

"No. I'm used to this road. I come this way all the time."

"Just where is Ogin's house?"

"Over that way," he replied, pointing. "She's sure to be waiting for us."

They walked a little faster. When they reached the place where the slope became steeper, there was a scattering of houses. This was a stopover on the Tatsuno highroad. It was hardly large enough to be described as a town, but it boasted a cheap "one-tray" eating place, where grooms hung out, and a few low-priced inns strung out on both sides of the road.

Once they were past the village, Mambei declared, "We have to climb a little now." Turning off the road, he started up a steep flight of stone stairs leading to the local shrine.

Like a small bird chirping because of a sudden drop in the temperature, Otsū sensed something out of the ordinary. "Are you sure we haven't come the wrong way? There're no houses around here," she said.

"Don't worry. It's a lonely place, but you just sit down and rest on the shrine porch. I'll go and fetch Ogin."

"Why should you do that?"

"Have you forgotten? I'm sure I mentioned it. Ogin said there might be guests it would be inconvenient for you to run into. Her house is on the other side of this grove. I'll be back very soon." He hurried off along a narrow path through the dark cryptomerias.

As the evening sky grew darker, Otsū began to feel distinctly ill at ease. Dead leaves stirred by the wind came to rest in her lap. Idly she picked one up and turned it around in her fingers. Foolishness or purity—something made her the perfect picture of virginity.

A loud cackling came suddenly from behind the shrine. Otsū jumped to the ground.

"Don't move, Otsū!" commanded a hoarse, scary voice.

Otsū gasped and put her hands over her ears.

Several shadowy shapes came from behind the shrine and surrounded her quaking form. Though her eyes were shut, she could clearly see one of them, more frightening and seemingly larger than the others, the white-haired hag she had so often seen in nightmares.

"Thank you, Mambei," said Osugi. "Now gag her before she starts screaming and take her to Shimonoshō. Be quick about it!" She spoke with the fearsome authority of the King of Hell condemning a sinner to the inferno.

The four or five men were apparently village toughs having some connection with Osugi's clan. Shouting their assent, they went at Otsū like wolves fighting over prey and tied her up so that only her legs were free.

"Take the shortcut."

"Move!"

Osugi remained behind to settle with Mambei. As she fished the money from her obi, she said, "Good of you to bring her. I was afraid you might not be able to manage it.'' Then she added, ''Don't say a word to anybody.''

With a satisfied look, Mambei tucked the money into his sleeve. ''Oh, it wasn't so hard,'' he said. ''Your plan worked just fine.''

''Ah, that was something to see. Frightened, wasn't she?''

''She couldn't even run. Just stood there. Ha, ha. But maybe . . . it was rather wicked of us.''

''What's wicked about it? If you only knew what I've been through.''

''Yes, yes; you told me all about it.''

''Well, I can't be wasting time here. I'll see you again one of these days. Come visit us in Shimonoshō.''

''Be careful. That path's not easy walking,'' he called over his shoulder as he started back down the long, dark steps.

Hearing a gasp, Osugi whirled and shouted, ''Mambei! Was that you? What's wrong?''

There was no answer.

Osugi ran to the top of the steps. She let out a little cry, then swallowed her breath as she squinted at the shadow standing beside the fallen body and the sword, dripping blood, slanting downward from the shadow's hand.

''Wh-who's there?''

There was no reply.

''Who are you?'' Her voice was dry and strained, but the years had not diminished her blustering bravado.

The man's shoulders shook slightly with laughter. ''It's me, you old hag.''

''Who are you?''

''Don't you recognize me?''

''I never heard your voice before. A robber, I suppose.''

''No robber'd bother with an old woman as poor as you.''

"But you've been keeping an eye on me, haven't you?"

"I have."

"On me?"

"Why ask twice? I wouldn't come all the way to Mikazuki to kill Mambei. I come to teach you a lesson."

"Ech?" It sounded as though Osugi's windpipe had burst. "You've got the wrong person. Who are you anyway? My name is Osugi. I'm the dowager of the Hon'iden family."

"Oh, how good to hear you say that! It brings back all my hatred. Witch! Have you forgotten Jōtarō?"

"Jō-jō-tarō?"

"In three years, a newborn babe ceases to be a baby and becomes a three-year-old. You're an old tree; I'm a sapling. Sorry to say, you can't treat me like a sniveling brat anymore."

"Surely it can't be true. Are you really Jōtarō?"

"You ought to have to pay for all the grief you've caused my teacher over the years. He avoided you only because you're old and he didn't want to harm you. You took advantage of that, traveling around everywhere, even to Edo, spreading malicious rumors about him and acting as though you had a legitimate reason to take revenge on him. You even went so far as to prevent his appointment to a good post."

Osugi was silent.

"Your spite didn't end there, either. You bedeviled Otsū and tried to injure her. I thought at last you'd given up and retired to Miyamoto. But you're still at it, using that Mambei to carry out some scheme against Otsū."

Still Osugi did not speak.

"Don't you ever tire of hating? It'd be easy to slice you in two, but fortunately for you, I'm no longer the son of a wayward samurai. My father, Aoki Tanzaemon, has returned to Himeji and, since last spring, is serving the House of Ikeda. To avoid bringing dishonor on him, I shall refrain from killing you."

Jōtarō took a couple of steps toward her. Not knowing whether to believe him or not, Osugi moved back and cast about for a way to escape. Thinking she saw one, she bolted toward the path the men had taken. Jōtarō caught up with her in one leap and grabbed her by the neck.

She opened her mouth wide and cried, "What do you think you're doing?" She turned around and drew her sword in the same motion, struck at him and missed.

While dodging, Jōtarō pushed her violently forward. Her head struck hard against the ground.

"So you've learned a thing or two, have you?" she moaned, her face half buried in the grass. She seemed unable to dislodge from her mind the idea that Jōtarō was still a child.

With a growl, he placed his foot on her spine, which seemed very fragile, and pitilessly wrenched her arm around her back.

Dragging her in front of the shrine, he pinned her down with his foot, but couldn't decide what to do with her.

There was Otsū to think about. Where was she? He had come to know of her presence in Shikama largely by accident, though it may have been because their karmas were intertwined. Along with his father's reinstatement, Jōtarō had been given an appointment. It was while he was on one of his errands that he had caught a glimpse through a gap in the fence of a woman who looked like Otsū. Returning to the beach two days ago, he had verified his impression.

While he was grateful to the gods for leading him to Otsū, his long-dormant hatred of Osugi for the way she had persecuted Otsū had been rekindled. If the old woman was not disposed of, it would be impossible for Otsū to live in peace. The temptation was there. But killing her would embroil his father in a dispute with a family of country samurai. They were troublesome people at the best of times; if offended by a daimyō's direct vassal, they were certain to cause trouble.

Finally, he decided the best way was to punish Osugi quickly and then turn his attention to rescuing Otsū.

"I know the place for you," he said. "Come along."

Osugi clung fiercely to the ground, despite his attempts to yank her along. Seizing her by the waist, he carried her under his arm around to the back of the shrine. The hillside had been shaved off when the shrine was built, and there was a small cave there, the entrance to which was just big enough for a person to crawl through.

Otsū could see a single light in the distance. Otherwise, everything was pitch black—mountains, fields, streams, Mikazuki Pass, which they had just crossed by a rocky path. The two men in front were leading her by a rope, as they would a criminal.

When they neared the Sayo River, the man behind her said, "Stop a minute. What do you suppose happened to the old woman? She said she'd be right along."

"Yeah; she should have caught up by now."

"We could stop here a few minutes. Or go on to Sayo and wait at the teahouse. They're probably all in bed, but we could wake them up."

"Let's go there and wait. We can have a cup or two of sake."

They searched along the river for a shallow place and had started to cross when they heard a voice hailing them from a distance. It came again a minute or two later, from much nearer.

"The old woman?"

"No; it sounds like a man's voice."

"It can't have anything to do with us."

The water was as chillingly cold as a sword blade, especially for Otsū. By the time they heard the sound of running feet, their pursuer was almost upon them. With great splashes, he beat them to the other bank and confronted them.

"Otsū?" called Jōtarō.

Shivering from the spray of water that had fallen on them, the three men closed in around Otsū and stood where they were.

"Don't move," shouted Jōtarō, arms outstretched.

"Who are you?"

"Never mind. Release Otsū!"

"You crazy? Don't you know you can get killed meddling in other people's business?"

"Osugi said you're to hand Otsū over to me."

"You're lying through your teeth." All three men laughed.

"I'm not. Look at this." He held out a piece of tissue paper with Osugi's handwriting on it. The message was short: "Things went wrong. There's nothing you can do. Give Otsū to Jōtarō, then come back for me."

The men, brows wrinkled, looked up at Jōtarō and moved onto the bank.

"Can't you read?" taunted Jōtarō.

"Shut up. I suppose you're Jōtarō."

"That's right. My name is Aoki Jōtarō."

Otsū had been staring fixedly at him, trembling slightly from fear and doubt. Now, scarcely knowing what she was doing, she screamed, gasped and stumbled forward.

The man closest to Jōtarō shouted, "Her gag's come loose. Tighten it!" Then menacingly to Jōtarō: "This is the old woman's handwriting, no doubt about it. But what happened to her? What does she mean, 'come back for me'?"

"She's my hostage," Jōtarō said loftily. "You give me Otsū, I tell you where she is."

The three men looked at each other. "Are you trying to be funny?" asked one man. "Do you know who we are? Any samurai in Himeji, if that's where you're from, should be familiar with the House of Hon'iden in Shimo-noshō.''

"Yes or no—answer! If you don't surrender Otsū, I'll leave the old woman where she is until she starves to death."

"You little bastard!"

One man grabbed Jōtarō and another unsheathed his sword and took a stance. The first growled, "You keep talking nonsense like that and I'll break your neck. Where's Osugi?"

"Will you give me Otsū?"

"No!"

"Then you won't find out. Hand over Otsū, and we can put an end to this without anybody getting hurt."

The man who had grabbed Jōtarō's arm pulled him forward and tried to trip him.

Using his adversary's strength, Jōtarō threw him over his own shoulder. But the next second, he was sitting on his behind, clutching at his right thigh. The man had whipped out his sword and struck in a mowing motion. Fortunately, the wound was not deep. Jōtarō jumped to his feet at the same time as his attacker. The other two men moved in on him.

"Don't kill him. We have to take him alive if we're to get Osugi back."

Jōtarō quickly lost his reluctance to become involved in bloodshed. In the ensuing melee, the three men managed at one point to throw him to the ground. He uttered a roar and used the same tactic that moments before had been used against him. Ripping out his short sword, he jabbed straight through the belly of the man about to fall on him. Jōtarō's hand and arm, halfway up to the shoulder, came away as red as if he'd stuck them into a barrel of plum vinegar, but his head was cleared of everything save the instinct for self-preservation.

On his feet·again, he shouted and struck downward at the man in front of him. The blade hit a shoulder bone, and glancing sideways, tore off a slice of meat the size of a fish fillet. Screaming, the man grabbed for his sword, but it was too late.

"Sons of bitches! Sons of bitches!" Shouting with each stroke of his sword, Jōtarō held off the other two, then managed to seriously wound one of them.

They had taken their superiority for granted, but now they lost self-control and started swinging their arms with utter abandon.

Beside herself, Otsū ran around in circles, wriggling her bound hands frantically. "Somebody come! Save him!" But her words were soon lost, drowned by the sound of the river and the voice of the wind.

Suddenly she realized that instead of calling for help, she should be relying on her own strength. With a little cry of desperation, she sank to the ground and began rubbing the rope against the sharp edge of a rock. It was only loosely woven straw rope picked up by the wayside and she was soon able to free herself.

She picked up some rocks and ran straight toward the action. "Jōtarō," she called, as she threw a rock at the face of one man. "I'm here too. It's going to be all right!" Another rock. "Keep it up!" Still another rock, but like the first two, it missed its target. She rushed back to get more.

"That bitch!" In two leaps, one man disengaged himself from Jōtarō and took after Otsū. He was about to bring the blunt edge of his sword down on her back when Jōtarō reached him. Jōtarō drove his sword so deep into the small of the man's back that the blade pointed straight out from the man's navel.

The other man, wounded and dazed, started to slink away, then broke into an unsteady run.

Jōtarō planted his feet firmly on either side of the corpse, withdrew the sword and screamed, "Stop!"

As he started to give chase, Otsū pounced forcefully on him and screamed, "Don't do it! You mustn't attack a badly wounded man when he's fleeing." The fervency of her plea astonished him. He could not imagine what psychological quirk would move her to sympathize with a man who had so recently been tormenting her.

Otsū said, "I want to hear what you've been doing all these years. I have things to tell you too. And we should get out of here as fast as we can."

Jōtarō agreed quickly, knowing that if word of the incident reached Shimonoshō, the Hon'idens would round up the whole village to come after them.

"Can you run, Otsū?"

"Yes. Don't worry about me."

And run they did, on and on through the darkness until their breath gave out. To both, it seemed like the old days when they had been a young girl and a mere boy, making their way together.

At Mikazuki, the only lights visible were at the inn. One shone in the main building, where only a little earlier a group of travelers—a metal merchant whose business took him to the local mines, a thread salesman from Tajima, an itinerant priest—had been sitting around, talking and laughing. They had all drifted off to bed.

Jōtarō and Otsū sat talking by the other light, in a small detached room where the innkeeper's mother lived with her spinning wheel and the pots in which she boiled silkworms. The innkeeper suspected the couple he was taking in were eloping, but he had the room straightened up for them anyway.

Otsū was saying, "So you didn't see Musashi in Edo either." She gave him an account of the last few years.

Saddened to hear that she had not seen Musashi since that day on the Kiso highroad, Jōtarō found it difficult to speak. Yet he thought he was able to offer a ray of hope.

"It's not much to go on," he said, "but I heard a

rumor in Himeji that Musashi would be coming there soon.''

"To Himeji? Could it be true?'' she asked, eager to latch on to even the flimsiest straw.

"It's only what people say, but the men in our fief are talking as though it's already decided. They say he'll pass through on his way to Kokura, where he's promised to meet a challenge from Sasaki Kojirō. That's one of Lord Hosokawa's retainers.''

"I heard something like that too, but I couldn't find anybody who had heard from Musashi or even knew where he was.''

"Well, the word going around Himeji Castle is probably reliable. It seems the Hanazono Myōshinji in Kyoto, which has close connections with the House of Hosokawa, informed Lord Hosokawa of Musashi's whereabouts, and Nagaoka Sado—he's a senior retainer—delivered the letter of challenge to Musashi.''

"Is it supposed to happen soon?''

"I don't know. Nobody seems to know exactly. But if it's to be in Kokura, and if Musashi's in Kyoto, he'll pass through Himeji on the way.''

"He might go by boat.''

Jōtarō shook his head. "I don't think so. The daimyō at Himeji and Okayama and other fiefs along the Inland Sea will ask him to stop over for a night or so. They want to see what kind of man he really is and sound him out about whether he's interested in a position. Lord Ikeda wrote to Takuan. Then he made inquiries at the Myōshinji and instructed the wholesalers in his area to report if they see anyone answering Musashi's description.''

"That's all the more reason to suppose he won't go by land. There's nothing he hates worse than a lot of fuss. If he knows about it, he'll do his best to avoid it.'' Otsū seemed depressed, as if she'd suddenly lost all hope. "What do you think, Jōtarō?'' she asked pleadingly. "If I went to the Myōshinji, do you think I'd be able to find out anything?''

"Well, maybe, but you have to remember it's only gossip."

"But there must be something to it, don't you think?"

"Do you feel like going to Kyoto?"

"Oh, yes. I'd like to leave right away. . . . Well, tomorrow."

"Don't be in such a hurry. That's why you're always missing Musashi. The minute you hear a rumor, you accept it as fact and go flying off. If you want to spot a nightingale, you have to look at a point in front of where its voice comes from. It seems to me you're always trailing along behind Musashi, rather than anticipating where he might be next."

"Well, maybe, but love's not logical." Not having stopped to think of what she was saying, she was surprised to see his face go crimson at the mention of the word "love." Recovering quickly, she said, "Thank you for the advice. I'll think it over."

"Do that, but in the meantime, come back to Himeji with me."

"All right."

"I want you to come to our house."

Otsū was silent.

"From the way my father talks, I guess he knew you fairly well until you left the Shippōji. . . . I don't know what he has in mind, but he said he'd like to see you once more and talk with you."

The candle was threatening to go out. Otsū turned and looked out under the tattered eaves at the sky. "Rain," she said.

"Rain? And we have to walk to Himeji tomorrow."

"What's an autumn shower? We'll wear rain hats."

"I'd like it better if it was fair."

They closed the wooden rain shutters, and the room soon became very warm and humid. Jōtarō was acutely conscious of Otsū's feminine fragrance.

"Go to bed," he said. "I'll sleep over here." Placing

a wooden pillow under the window, he lay down on his side, facing the wall.

"Aren't you asleep yet?" grumbled Jōtarō. "You should go to bed." He pulled the thin covers over his head, but tossed and turned awhile longer before falling into a deep slumber.

20

The Mercy of Kannon

Otsū sat listening to the water dripping from a leak in the roof. Driven by the wind, the rain whipped in under the eaves and splashed against the shutters. But it was autumn, and there was no way of telling: morning might dawn bright and clear.

Then Osugi came into her thoughts. "I wonder if she's out in this storm, all wet and cold. She's old. She might not last till morning. Even if she does, it could be days before she's found. She could die of starvation."

"Jōtarō," she called softly. "Wake up." She was afraid he'd done something cruel, since she'd heard him tell the old woman's henchmen he was punishing her and had casually made a similar remark on the way to the inn.

"She's not really bad at heart," she thought. "If I'm honest with her, one of these days she'll understand me. . . . I must go to her."

Thinking: "If Jōtarō gets angry, it can't be helped," she opened a shutter. Against the blackness of the sky, the rain showed whitely. After tucking up her skirts, she took from the wall a basket hat made out of bamboo bark and tied it on her head. Then she threw a bulky straw rain cape around her shoulders, put on a pair of straw sandals and dashed through the sheet of rain pouring off the roof.

On approaching the shrine where Mambei had taken

her, she saw that the stone steps leading up to it had become a many-tiered waterfall. At the top, the wind was much stronger, howling through the cryptomerias like a pack of angry dogs.

"Where can she be?" she thought, as she peered into the shrine. She called into the dark space underneath it, but no answer came.

She went around to the back of the building and stood there for a few minutes. The wailing wind swept over her like breakers on a raging sea. Gradually she became aware of another sound, almost indistinguishable from the storm. It stopped and started again.

"Oh-h-h. Hear me, somebody. . . . Isn't somebody out there? . . . Oh-h-h."

"Granny!" shouted Otsū. "Granny, where are you?" Since she was literally crying into the wind, the sound did not carry far.

But somehow the feeling communicated itself. "Oh! There's someone there. I know it. . . . Save me. Here! Save me!"

In the snatches of sound that reached her ears, Otsū heard the cry of desperation.

"Where are you?" she screamed hoarsely. "Granny, where are you?" She ran all the way around the shrine, stopped a moment, then ran around it again. Almost by accident, she noticed what looked like a bear's cave, about twenty paces away, near the bottom of the steep path leading up to the inner shrine.

As she drew closer, she knew for certain the old woman's voice was coming from within. Arriving at the entrance, she stopped and stared at the large rocks blocking it.

"Who is it? Who's there? Are you a manifestation of Kannon? I worship her every day. Have pity on me. Save a poor old woman who's been trapped by a fiend." Osugi's pleas took on a hysterical tone. Half crying, half begging, in the dark interval between life and death, she formed a vision of the compassionate Kannon and hurled toward it her fervent prayer for continued life.

"How happy I am!" she cried deliriously. "Kannon the all-merciful has seen the goodness of my heart and taken pity on me. She's come to rescue me! Great compassion! Great mercy! Hail to the Bodhisattva Kannon, hail to the Bodhisattva Kannon, hail to—"

Her voice broke off abruptly. Perhaps she was thinking that was sufficient, for it was only natural that in her extremity Kannon would come in some form or other to her aid. She was the head of a fine family, a good mother, and believed herself to be an upright and flawless human being. And whatever she did was, of course, morally just.

But then, sensing that whoever was outside the cave was not an apparition but a real, living person, she relaxed, and when she relaxed, she passed out.

Not knowing what the sudden cessation of Osugi's cries meant, Otsū was beside herself. Somehow, the opening to the cave had to be cleared. As she doubled her efforts, the band holding her basket hat came loose, and the hat and her black tresses tossed wildly in the wind.

Wondering how Jōtarō had been able to put the rocks in place by himself, she pushed and pulled with the strength of her whole body, but nothing budged. Exhausted by the effort, she felt a pang of hatred for Jōtarō, and the initial relief she had felt on locating Osugi turned to gnawing anxiety.

"Hold on, Granny. Just a little longer. I'll get you out," she shouted. Though she pressed her lips to a crack in the rocks, she failed to elicit a response.

By and by, she made out a low, feeble chant:

"Or if, meeting man-eating devils,
Venomous dragons, and demons,
He thinks of Kannon's power,
At once none will dare harm him.
If, surrounded by vicious beasts,

> With sharp tusks and frightening claws,
> He thinks of Kannon's power . . .''

Osugi was intoning the *Sutra on Kannon*. Only the voice of the bodhisattva was perceptible to her. With her hands clasped together, she was at ease now, tears flowing down her cheeks, lips quivering as the sacred words poured from them.

Struck by an odd feeling, Osugi left off her chanting and put her eye to a crack between the rocks. "Who's there?" she shouted. "I ask you who's there?"

The wind had ripped off Otsū's rain cape. Bewildered, exhausted, covered with mud, she bent down and cried, "Are you all right, Granny? It's Otsū."

"Who did you say?" came the suspicious question.

"I said it's Otsū."

"I see." There was a long, dead pause before the next incredulous question. "What do you mean, you're Otsū?"

It was at this point that the first shock wave hit Osugi, rudely scattering her religious thoughts. "Wh-why have you come here? Oh, I know. You're looking for that devil Jōtarō!"

"No. I've come to rescue you, Granny. Please, forget the past. I remember how good you were to me when I was a little girl. Then you turned against me and tried to hurt me. I don't hold it against you. I admit I was very willful."

"Oh, so your eyes are open now and you can see the evil of your ways. Is that it? Are you saying you'd like to come back to the Hon'iden family as Matahachi's wife?"

"Oh, no, not that," Otsū said quickly.

"Well, why are you here?"

"I felt so sorry for you I couldn't stand it."

"And now you want to put me under obligation to you. That's what you're trying to do, isn't it?"

Otsū was too shocked to say a word.

"Who asked you to come to my rescue? Not me!

And I don't need your help now. If you think by doing me a favor you can stop me from hating you, you're mistaken. I don't care how badly off I am; I'd rather die than lose my pride."

"But, Granny, how can you expect me to leave a person your age in a terrible place like this?"

"There you go, talking nice and sweet. Do you think I don't know what you and Jōtarō are up to? You two plotted to put me in this cave to make fun of me, and when I get out, I'm going to get even. You can be sure of that."

"I'm sure the day will come very soon when you'll understand how I really feel. Anyway, you can't stay in there. You'll get sick."

"Hmph. I'm tired of this nonsense."

Otsū stood up, and the obstacle that she had been unable to budge by force was dislodged as if by her tears. After the topmost rock rolled to the ground, she had surprisingly little difficulty rolling the one below it aside.

But it hadn't been Otsū's tears alone that had opened the cave. Osugi had been pushing from inside. She burst forth, her face a fiery red.

Still staggering from the exertion, Otsū uttered a cry of joy, but no sooner was Osugi in the open than she seized Otsū by the collar. From the fierceness of the attack, it looked as though her sole purpose in wanting to stay alive was to attack her benefactor.

"Oh! What are you doing? Ow!"

"Shut up!"

"Wh-wh-why—"

"What did you expect?" cried Osugi, forcing Otsū to the ground with the fury of a wild woman. Otsū was horrified beyond belief.

"Now let's go," snorted Osugi, as she started to drag the girl across the sodden ground.

Clasping her hands together, Otsū said, "Please, please. Punish me if you want, but you mustn't stay out in this rain."

"What idiocy! Have you no shame? Do you think you can make me feel sorry for you?"

"I won't run away. I won't— Oh! That hurts!"

"Of course it hurts."

"Let me—" In a sudden burst of strength, Otsū wrenched herself free and sprang to her feet.

"Oh, no you don't!" Instantly renewing the attack, Osugi clutched a fistful of Otsū's hair. Otsū's white face turned skyward; rain poured down it. She closed her eyes.

"You tramp! How I've suffered all these years because of you!"

Each time Otsū opened her mouth to speak or made an effort to wriggle free, the old woman gave a vicious tug at her hair. Without letting go of it, she threw Otsū to the ground, trampled on her and kicked her.

Then a startled look flashed across Osugi's face and she let go of the hair.

"Oh, what have I done?" she gasped in consternation. "Otsū?" she called anxiously as she looked at the limp form lying at her feet.

"Otsū!" Bending down, she stared intently at the rain-soaked face, as cold to the touch as a dead fish. As far as she could tell, the girl wasn't breathing.

"She's . . . she's dead."

Osugi was aghast. Though unwilling to forgive Otsū, she had not intended to kill her. She straightened up, moaning and backing away.

Gradually she quieted down, and it was not long before she was saying, "Well, I suppose there's nothing to be done but go for help." She started to walk away, hesitated, turned and came back. Taking Otsū's cold body in her arms, she carried it into the cave.

Though the entrance was small, the inside was roomy. Near one wall was a place where, in the distant past, religious pilgrims seeking the Way had sat for long hours in meditation.

When the rain let up, she went to the entrance and was about to crawl out, when the clouds opened again. From the stream sluicing over the mouth, water splashed nearly to the innermost part of the cave.

"It won't be long until morning," she thought. Nonchalantly she squatted and waited for the storm to die down again.

Being in total darkness with Otsū's body slowly began to work on her mind. She had the feeling that the chilly ashen face was staring accusingly at her. At first she reassured herself by saying, "Everything that happens is destined to happen. Take your place in paradise as a newborn Buddha. Don't hold a grudge against me." But before long fear and the sense of her awful responsibility prompted her to seek refuge in piety. Closing her eyes, she began to chant a sutra. Several hours passed.

When at last her lips were silent and she opened her eyes, she could hear birds chirping. The air was still; the rain had stopped. Through the mouth of the cave, a golden sun glared at her, shedding fresh white rays on the rough ground inside.

"What's that, I wonder?" she said aloud as she got to her feet and her eyes fell on an inscription carved by some unknown hand on the wall of the cave.

She stood before it and read: "In the year 1544, I sent my sixteen-year-old son, whose name was Mori Kinsaku, to fight at the battle of Tenjinzan Castle on the side of Lord Uragami. I have never seen him since. Because of my grief, I wander to various places sacred to the Buddha. Now I am placing in this cave an image of the Bodhisattva Kannon. I pray that this, and a mother's tears, will protect Kinsaku in his future life. If in later times anyone should pass here, I beg that he invoke the name of the Buddha. This is the twenty-first year since Kinsaku's death. Donor: The Mother of Kinsaku, Aita Village."

The eroded characters were difficult to read in places. It had been nearly seventy years since the villages nearby—Sanumo, Aita, Katsuta—had been attacked by the Amako family and Lord Uragami had been driven from his castle. One childhood memory that would never be erased from Osugi's memory was the burning of this fortress. She could still see the black smoke billowing up in the sky, the corpses of men and horses littering the fields and byways for days afterward. The fighting had reached almost to the houses of the farmers.

Thinking of the boy's mother, of her sorrow, her wanderings, her prayers and offerings, Osugi felt a stab of pain. "It must have been terrible for her," she said. She knelt and joined her hands together.

"Hail to the Buddha Amida. Hail to the Buddha Amida . . ."

She was sobbing, and tears fell on her hands, but not until she had cried herself out did her mind again become conscious of Otsū's face, cold and insensitive to the morning light, by the side of her knee.

"Forgive me, Otsū. It was wicked of me, terrible! Please forgive me, please." Her face twisted with remorse, she lifted Otsū's body in a gentle embrace. "Frightening . . . frightening. Blinded by motherly love. Out of devotion to my own child, I became a devil to another woman's. You had a mother too. If she had known me, she would have seen me as . . . as a vile demon. . . . I was sure I was right, but to others I'm a vicious monster."

The words seemed to fill the cave and bound back to her own ears. There was no one there, no eyes to watch, no ears to hear. The darkness of night had become the light of the Buddha's wisdom.

"How good you were, Otsū. To be tormented so many long years by this horrible old fool, yet never returning my hatred. To come in spite of everything to try to save me. . . . I see it all now. I misunderstood. All the goodness in your heart I saw as evil. Your kindness I rewarded with hatred. My mind was warped, distorted. Oh, forgive me, Otsū.''

She pressed her damp face against Otsū's. ''If only my son were as sweet and good as you. . . . Open your eyes again, see me begging for forgiveness. Open your mouth, revile me. I deserve it. Otsū . . . forgive me.''

While she stared at the face and shed bitter tears, there passed before her eyes a vision of herself as she must have appeared in all those ugly past encounters with Otsū. The realization of how thoroughly wicked she had been gripped at her heart. Over and over she murmured, ''Forgive me . . . forgive me.'' She even wondered if it wouldn't be right to sit there until she joined the girl in death.

''No!'' she exclaimed decisively. ''No more weeping and moaning. Maybe . . . maybe she's not dead. If I try, maybe I can nurse her back to life. She's still young. Her life is still ahead of her.''

Gently she laid Otsū back on the ground and crawled out of the cave into the blinding sunlight. She shut her eyes and cupped her hands to her mouth. ''Where is everybody? You people from the village, come here! Help!'' Opening her eyes, she ran forward a few steps, still shouting.

There was some movement in the cryptomeria grove, then a shout: ''She's here. She's all right after all!''

About ten members of the Hon'iden clan came out of the grove. After hearing the story told by the blood-smeared survivor of the fight with Jōtarō the night before, they had organized a search party and set out immediately, despite the blinding rain. Still wearing their rain capes, they had a bedraggled look about them.

''Ah, you're safe,'' exulted the first man to reach Osugi. They gathered around her, their faces reflecting their immense relief.

''Don't worry about me,'' Osugi commanded. ''Quick, go and see if you can do something for that girl in the cave. She's been unconscious for hours. If we don't give her some medicine right away . . ." Her voice was thick. Almost in a trance, she pointed toward the cave. Perhaps not since Uncle Gon's death had the tears she'd shed been those of grief.

THE WAY OF LIFE AND DEATH

beauty. Flowers bloomed and flowers fell. In the floating world of the licensed quarter, time passed rapidly.

Yoshino Dayū. The name would have evoked memories of snowy nights, of a fire made of peony wood, of a broken lute.

"It's been eight years now since we first met," remarked Kōetsu.

"Yes, eight years," echoed Musashi, wondering where the years could have gone. He had the feeling his boarding the ship today marked the close of one phase of his life.

Matahachi was among the well-wishers, as were several samurai from the Hosokawa residence in Kyoto. Other samurai conveyed best wishes from Lord Karasumaru Mitsuhiro, and there was a group of between twenty and thirty swordsmen who, despite Musashi's protest, had been led by their acquaintance with him in Kyoto to regard themselves as his followers.

He was going to Kokura in the province of Buzen, where he would face Sasaki Kojirō in a test of skill and maturity. Due to the efforts of Nagaoka Sado, the fateful confrontation, so long in the making, was finally to take place. Negotiations had been long and difficult, necessitating the dispatch of many couriers and letters. Even after Sado had ascertained the previous autumn that Musashi was at Hon'ami Kōetsu's house, completion of the arrangements had required another half year.

Though he knew it was coming, Musashi had not in his wildest dreams been able to imagine what it would be like to set forth as the champion of a huge number of followers and admirers. The size of the crowd was an embarrassment. It also made it impossible for him to talk as he would have liked to with certain people.

What struck him most forcefully about this great send-off was its absurdity. He had no desire to be anybody's idol. Still, they were here to express their goodwill. There was no way to stop them.

Some, he felt, understood him. For their good wishes

he was grateful; their admiration infused him with a sense of reverence. At the same time, he was being swept up on a wave of that frivolous sentiment called popularity. His reaction was almost one of fear, that the adulation might go to his head. He was, after all, only an ordinary man.

Another thing that upset him was the long prelude. If it could be said that both he and Kojirō saw where their relationship was leading them, it could also be said that the world had pitted them one against the other and decreed that they must decide once and for all who was the better man.

It had started with people saying, "I hear they're going to have it out."

Later, it was: "Yes, they're definitely going to face each other."

Still later: "When is the bout?"

Finally, the very day and hour were being bruited about before the principals themselves had formally decided them.

Musashi resented being a public hero. In view of his exploits, it was inevitable that he would be made one, but he did not seek this. What he really wanted was more time to himself for meditation. He needed to develop harmony, to make sure his ideas did not outpace his ability to act. Through his most recent experience with Gudō, he had advanced a step on the path toward enlightenment. And he had come to sense more keenly the difficulty of following the Way—the long Way through life.

"And yet . . ." he thought. Where would he be if it were not for the goodness of the people who supported him? Would he be alive? Would he have the clothes on his back? He was dressed in a black short-sleeved kimono sewn for him by Kōetsu's mother. His new sandals, the new basket hat in his hand, all the belongings he carried now, had been given to him by someone who valued him. The rice he ate—grown by other people. He lived on the bounties of labor not his own. How could he repay people for all they had done for him?

When his thoughts turned in this direction, his resentment at the demands made on him by his legion of supporters lessened. Nevertheless, the fear of letting them down lingered.

It was time to set sail. There were prayers for a safe voyage, final words of farewell, invisible time already flowing between the men and women on the pier and their departing hero.

The moorings were cast off, the ship drifted toward the open sea, and the great sail spread like wings against the azure sky.

A man ran out to the end of the pier, stopped and stamped his foot in disgust. "Too late!" he growled. "I shouldn't have taken a nap."

Kōetsu approached him and asked, "Aren't you Musō Gonnosuke?"

"Yes," he replied, tucking his staff under his arm.

"I met you once at the Kongōji in Kawachi."

"Yes, of course. You're Hon'ami Kōetsu."

"I'm glad to see you're well. From what I heard, I wasn't sure you were still alive."

"Heard from who?"

"Musashi."

"Musashi?"

"Yes; he was staying with me until yesterday. He had several letters from Kokura. In one, Nagaoka Sado said you'd been taken prisoner on Mount Kudo. He thought you might have been injured or killed."

"It was all a mistake."

"We learned, too, that Iori is living at Sado's house."

"Then he's safe!" he exclaimed, relief flooding his face.

"Yes. Let's sit down somewhere and talk."

He steered the burly staff expert to a nearby shop. Over tea, Gonnosuke told his story. Luckily for him, after one look Sanada Yukimura had come to the conclusion he was not a spy. Gonnosuke was released, and the two men became friendly. Yukimura not only apologized for his subordinates' error, but sent a group of men to search for Iori.

When they failed to find the boy's body, Gonnosuke assumed he was still alive. He had spent his time since then searching the neighboring provinces. When he heard that Musashi was in Kyoto and a bout between him and Kojirō was imminent, he had intensified his efforts. Then, returning to Mount Kudo yesterday, he had learned from Yukimura that Musashi was to sail for Kokura today. He had dreaded facing Musashi without Iori at his side, or any news of him. But not knowing whether he would ever again see his teacher alive, he came anyway. He apologized to Kōetsu as though the latter were a victim of his negligence.

"Don't let it worry you," said Kōetsu. "There'll be another ship in a few days."

"I really wanted to travel with Musashi." He paused, then went on earnestly. "I think this trip may be the decisive point in Musashi's life. He disciplines himself constantly. He isn't likely to lose to Kojirō. Still, in a fight like that, you never know. There's a superhuman element involved. All warriors have to face it; winning or losing is partly a matter of luck."

"I don't think you need to worry. Musashi's composure was perfect. He seemed completely confident."

"I'm sure he did, but Kojirō has a high reputation too. And they say since he went into Lord Tadatoshi's service, he's been practicing and keeping himself fit."

"It'll be a test of strength between a man who's a genius, but really somewhat conceited, and an ordinary man who's polished his talents to the utmost, won't it?"

"I wouldn't call Musashi ordinary."

"But he is. That's what's extraordinary about him. He's not content with relying on whatever natural gifts he may have. Knowing he's ordinary, he's always trying to improve himself. No one appreciates the agonizing effort he's had to make. Now that his years of training have yielded such spectacular results, everybody's talking about his 'god-given talent.' That's how men who don't try very hard comfort themselves.''

"Thank you for saying that," said Gonnosuke. He felt Kōetsu might have been referring to him, as well as to Musashi. Looking at the older man's broad, placid profile, he thought: "It's the same with him too."

Kōetsu looked like what he was, a man of leisure who had deliberately set himself apart from the rest of the world. At the moment, his eyes lacked that gleam that emanated from them when he concentrated on artistic creation. Now they were like a smooth sea, calm and unruffled, under a clear, bright sky.

A young man stuck his head in the door and said to Kōetsu, "Shall we go back now?"

"Ah, Matahachi," Kōetsu replied amiably. Turning to Gonnosuke, he said, "I suppose I'll have to leave you. My companions seem to be waiting."

"Are you going back by way of Osaka?"

"Yes. If we get there in time, I'd like to take the evening boat to Kyoto."

"Well, then, I'll walk that far with you." Rather than wait here for the next boat, Gonnosuke had decided to travel overland.

The three of them walked side by side, their talk rarely straying from Musashi, his present status and past exploits. At one point, Matahachi expressed concern, saying, "I hope Musashi wins, but Kojirō's sharp. His technique is terrific, you know." But his voice lacked enthusiasm; the memory of his own encounter with Kojirō was too vivid.

By twilight, they were on the crowded streets of Osaka. Simultaneously Kōetsu and Gonnosuke noticed Matahachi was no longer with them.

"Where could he have gone?" asked Kōetsu.

Retracing their steps, they found him standing by the end of the bridge. He was looking spellbound out over the riverbank, where wives from nearby dwellings, a row of broken-down shacks covered by a single roof, were washing cooking utensils, unhulled rice and vegetables.

"That's an odd expression on his face," said Gonnosuke. He and Kōetsu stood a little apart and watched.

"It is her," cried Matahachi. "Akemi!"

In the first flash of recognition, he was struck by the capriciousness of fate. But immediately it began to seem otherwise. Destiny was not playing tricks—merely confronting him with his past. She had been his common-law wife. Their karmas, too, were entwined. So long as they inhabited the same earth, they were fated to come together again, sooner or later.

He'd had trouble recognizing her. The charm and coquettishness of even two years ago had vanished. Her face was incredibly thin; her hair was unwashed and tied in a bun. She wore a tubular-sleeved cotton kimono reaching slightly below her knees, the utilitarian garment of all lower-class urban housewives. It was a far cry from the colorful silks she had donned as a prostitute.

She was crouching down in the position expected of peddlers and had in her arms a heavy-looking basket, from which she was selling clams, abalone and kelp. The things still left unsold suggested business was not very good.

Tied to her back with a soiled strip of cloth was a baby about a year old.

More than anything else, it was the child that made Matahachi's heart beat faster. Pressing his palms against his cheeks, he counted up the months. If the baby was in its second year, it had been conceived while they were in Edo . . . and Akemi had been pregnant when they were publicly whipped.

The light of the evening sun, reflected from the river, danced on Matahachi's face, making it seem bathed in tears. He was deaf to the bustle of traffic moving along the street. Akemi was walking slowly down by the river. He started after her, waving his arms and shouting. Kōetsu and Gonnosuke followed.

"Matahachi, where are you going?"

He had forgotten all about the two men. He stopped and waited for them to catch up. "I'm sorry," he mumbled. "To tell the truth . . ." Truth? How could he explain to them what he was going to do when he couldn't explain it to himself? Sorting out his emotions was beyond him at the moment, but finally he blurted out, "I've decided not to be a priest—to return to ordinary life. I haven't been ordained yet."

"Returning to ordinary life?" exclaimed Kōetsu. "So suddenly? Hmm. You look strange."

"I can't explain it now. Even if I did, it'd probably sound crazy. I just saw the woman I used to live with. And she's carrying a baby on her back. I think it must be mine."

"Are you sure?"

"Yes, well . . ."

"Now calm down and think. Is it really your child?"

"Yes! I'm a father! . . . I'm sorry. I didn't know . . . I'm ashamed. I can't let her go through life like that— selling things out of a basket like a common tramp. I've got to go to work and help my child."

Kōetsu and Gonnosuke looked at each other in dismay. Though not quite sure whether Matahachi was still in his right mind, Kōetsu said, "I suppose you know what you're doing."

Matahachi took off the priest's robe covering his ordinary kimono and handed it to Kōetsu, together with his prayer beads. "I'm sorry to trouble you, but will you give these to Gudō at the Myōshinji? I'd appreciate it if you'd tell him I'm going to stay here in Osaka, get a job and be a good father."

"Are you sure you want to do this? Give up the priesthood, just like that?"

"Yes. Anyway, the master told me I could go back to ordinary life anytime I wanted to."

"Hmm."

"He said you don't have to be in a temple to practice religious discipline. It's more difficult, but he said it's more praiseworthy to be able to control yourself and keep your faith in the midst of lies and filth and conflict—all the ugly things in the outside world—than in the clean, pure surroundings of a temple."

"I'm sure he's right."

"I've been with him more than a year now, but he hasn't given me a priestly name. Always just calls me Matahachi. Maybe something'll come up in the future I don't understand. Then I'll go to him immediately. Tell him that for me, won't you?"

And with that, Matahachi was gone.

22

The Evening Boat

A single red cloud, looking like a great streamer, hung low over the horizon. Near the bottom of the glassy waveless sea was an octopus.

Around noon a small boat had tied up in the estuary of the Shikama River, discreetly out of sight. Now, as twilight deepened, a thin column of smoke rose from a clay brazier on the deck. An old woman was breaking sticks and feeding the fire.

"Are you cold?" she asked.

"No," answered the girl lying in the bottom of the boat behind some red matting. She shook her head weakly, then lifted it and looked at the old woman. "Don't worry about me, Granny. You should be careful yourself. Your voice sounds a bit husky."

Osugi put a pot of rice on the brazier to make gruel. "It's nothing," she said. "But you're sick. You have to eat properly, so you'll feel strong when the boat comes in."

Otsū held back a tear and looked out to sea. There were some boats fishing for octopus and a couple of cargo vessels. The ship from Sakai was nowhere to be seen.

"It's getting late," said Osugi. "They said the ship would be here before evening." There was a hint of complaint in her voice.

News of the departure of Musashi's ship had spread

rapidly. When it reached Jōtarō in Himeji, he sent a messenger to tell Osugi. She, in turn, had hurried straight to the Shippōji, where Otsū lay ill, suffering from the effects of the beating the old woman had given her.

Since that night, Osugi had begged forgiveness so often and tearfully that listening to her had come to be rather a burden for Otsū. Otsū did not hold her responsible for her sickness; she thought it was a recurrence of the malady that had kept her confined for several months at Lord Karasumaru's house in Kyoto. In the mornings and evenings, she coughed a lot and had a slight fever. And she lost weight, which made her face more beautiful than ever, but it was an excessively delicate beauty and saddened those who met and talked with her.

Still, her eyes shone. For one thing, she was happy about the change that had come over Osugi. Having finally understood that she had been mistaken about Otsū and Musashi, the Hon'iden dowager was like a woman reborn. And Otsū had hope, springing from the certainty that the day was near when she would see Musashi again.

Osugi had said, "To atone for all the unhappiness I've caused you, I'm going to get down on my hands and knees and beg Musashi to set things right. I'll bow. I'll apologize. I'll persuade him." After announcing to her own family and the whole village that Matahachi's betrothal to Otsū was nullified, she destroyed the document recording the promise to marry. From then on, she made it her business to tell one and all that the only person who would be a proper and fitting husband for Otsū was Musashi.

Since the village had changed, the person Otsū knew best in Miyamoto was Osugi, who took it upon herself to nurse the girl back to health, calling each morning and evening at the Shippōji with the same solicitous questions: "Have you eaten? Did you take your medicine? How do you feel?"

One day, she said with tears in her eyes, "If you

hadn't come back to life that night in the cave, I would have wanted to die there too."

The old woman had never before hesitated to bend the truth or tell outright lies, one of the last of which turned out to be about Ogin's being in Sayo. In fact no one had seen or heard from Ogin for years. All that was known was that she had married and gone to another province.

So at first Otsū found Osugi's protestations unbelievable. Even if she was sincere, it seemed likely her remorse would wear off after a time. But as days turned into weeks, she grew more devoted and more attentive to Otsū.

"I never dreamed she was such a good person at heart," was how Otsū came to think of her. And since Osugi's newfound warmth and kindness extended to everyone around her, this sentiment was widely shared by both the family and the villagers, though many expressed their astonishment less delicately, saying things like, "What do you suppose got into the old hag?"

Even Osugi marveled at how kind everyone was to her now. It used to be that even those people closest to her were inclined to cringe at the very sight of her; now they all smiled and spoke cordially. At last, at an age when simply being alive was something to be thankful for, she was learning for the first time what it was like to be loved and respected by others.

One acquaintance asked frankly, "What happened to you? Your face looks more attractive every time I see you."

"Maybe so," thought Osugi later that same day, looking at herself in her mirror. The past had left its mark. When she went away from the village, there had still been black hair mixed with gray. Now it was all white. She didn't mind, for she believed that her heart, at least, was free of blackness now.

* * *

The Evening Boat

The ship Musashi was on made a regular overnight stop at Shikama to discharge and take on cargo.

Yesterday, after telling Otsū this, Osugi had asked, "What are you going to do?"

"I'm going to be there, of course."

"In that case, I'll go too."

Otsū got up from her sickbed, and they were on their way within the hour. It took them until late afternoon to walk to Himeji; all the while, Osugi hovered over Otsū as though she were a child.

At Aoki Tanzaemon's house that night, plans were laid to hold a congratulatory dinner at Himeji Castle for Musashi. It was assumed that because of his previous experience at the castle, he would now deem it an honor to be feted in this fashion. Even Jōtarō thought so.

It was also decided, in consultation with Tanzaemon's fellow samurai, that it wouldn't do for Otsū to be seen openly with Musashi. People might get the idea she was his secret lover. Tanzaemon told Otsū and Osugi the gist of this and suggested the boat as a way for Otsū to be present but at the same time not be a source of embarrassing gossip.

The sea darkened, and the color faded from the sky. Stars began to twinkle. Near the dyer's house where Otsū lived, a contingent of some twenty samurai from Himeji had been waiting since midafternoon to welcome Musashi.

"Maybe this is the wrong day," remarked one of them.

"No, don't worry," said another. "I sent a man to Kobayashi's local agent to make sure."

"Hey, isn't that it?"

"It looks like the right kind of sail."

Noisily they moved closer to the water's edge.

Jōtarō left them and ran off to the small boat in the estuary.

"Otsū! Granny! The ship's in sight—Musashi's ship!" he shouted to the excited women.

259

"Did you really see it? Where?" asked Otsū. She nearly fell overboard as she got to her feet.

"Be careful," warned Osugi, grabbing her from behind. They stood side by side, eyes searching the darkness. Gradually a tiny distant spot grew into a large sail, black in the starlight and seemingly gliding right into their eyes.

"That's it," cried Jōtarō.

"Hurry, grab the scull," said Otsū. "Take us out to the ship."

"There's no need to rush. One of the samurai on the beach will row out and get Musashi."

"Then we have to go now! Once he's with that bunch, there won't be a chance for Otsū to talk to him."

"We can't do that. They'll all see her."

"You spend too much time worrying about what other samurai will think. And that's the reason we're stuck away in this little boat. If you ask me, we should have waited at the dyer's house."

"No, you're wrong. You don't realize how people talk. Relax. My father and I'll find a way to bring him here." He stopped to think for a fraction of a minute. "When he gets to shore, he'll go to the dyer's house for a short rest. I'll get to him then and see to it that he comes here to you. Just wait here. I'll be back soon." He rushed off toward the beach.

"Try to get a little rest," said Osugi.

Though Otsū lay down obediently, she seemed to have trouble catching her breath.

"Cough bothering you again?" asked Osugi gently. She knelt and rubbed the girl's back. "Don't worry. Musashi'll be here before long."

"Thank you. I'm all right now." Once her coughing had subsided, she patted and smoothed her hair, trying to make herself a little more presentable.

As time passed and Musashi failed to appear, Osugi grew fidgety. Leaving Otsū in the boat, she went up on the bank.

The Evening Boat

When she was out of sight, Otsū pushed her pallet and pillow behind some matting, retied her obi and straightened her kimono. The palpitations of her heart seemed in no way different from what she had experienced as a girl of seventeen or eighteen. The red light of the small beacon fire, suspended near the prow, pierced her heart with warmth. Stretching her delicate white arm over the gunwale, she moistened her comb and ran it through her hair again. Then she applied some powder to her cheeks, but so lightly that it was nearly undetectable. After all, she thought, even samurai, when suddenly summoned from a deep sleep into their lordship's presence, would sometimes sneak into a dressing room and cover up their pallor with a little rouge.

What really troubled her was the question of what she would say to him. Fearfully she thought of becoming tongue-tied, as she had when she had seen him at other times. She didn't want to say anything that would upset him, so she had to be particularly careful about that. He was on his way to a bout. The whole country was talking about it.

At this important moment in her life, Otsū did not believe he would lose to Kojirō, yet it was not absolutely certain he would win. Accidents could happen. If she did something wrong today, and if Musashi was killed later, she would regret it for the rest of her life. Nothing would be left for her but to cry herself to death, hoping, like the ancient Chinese emperor, to be joined with her loved one in the next life.

She must say what she had to say, no matter what he himself might say or do. She had mustered the strength to come this far. Now the meeting was near at hand and her pulse raced wildly. With so many things on her mind, the words she wanted to say would not take form.

Osugi had no such problem. She was choosing the words she would use to apologize for misunderstanding and hatred, to unburden her heart and beg forgiveness.

261

As proof of her sincerity, she would see that Otsū's life was entrusted to Musashi.

The darkness was broken only by an occasional reflection from the water. And it was quiet until Jōtarō's running footsteps became audible.

"You've finally come, have you?" said Osugi, who was still standing on the bank. "Where's Musashi?"

"Granny, I'm sorry."

"You're *sorry?* What does that mean?"

"Just listen. I'll explain everything."

"I don't want explanations. Is Musashi coming, or isn't he?"

"He's not coming."

"Not coming?" Her voice was empty and full of disappointment.

Jōtarō, looking very awkward, related what had happened, namely that when a samurai had rowed out to the ship, he was told that it wasn't stopping there. There were no passengers wanting to get off at Shikama; the cargo had been taken off by lighter. The samurai had asked to see Musashi, who came to the side of the ship and talked with the man but said disembarking was out of the question. Both he and the captain wanted to reach Kokura as quickly as possible.

By the time the samurai returned to the beach with this message, the ship was already heading out to the open sea again.

"You can't even see it anymore," said Jōtarō dejectedly. "It's already rounded the pine woods at the other end of the beach. I'm sorry. Nobody's to blame."

"Why didn't you go out in the boat with the samurai?"

"I didn't think. . . . Anyway, there's nothing we can do, no use talking about it now."

"I suppose you're right, but what a shame! What are we going to tell Otsū? You'll have to do it, Jōtarō; I haven't the heart. You can tell her exactly what happened

. . . but try to calm her first, or her sickness might get worse."

But there was no need for Jōtarō to explain. Otsū, seated behind a piece of matting, had heard everything. The lapping of the water against the side of the boat seemed to resign her heart to suffering.

"If I missed him tonight," she thought, "I'll see him another day, on another beach."

She thought she understood why Musashi was set against leaving the ship. Throughout western Honshu and Kyushu, Sasaki Kojirō was acknowledged to be the greatest of all swordsmen. In challenging his primacy, Musashi would be burning with determination to win. His mind would be on that—only that.

"To think that he was so near," she sighed. Tears streaming down her cheeks, she gazed after the invisible sail, making its way slowly westward. She leaned disconsolately against the boat rail.

Then, for the first time, she became conscious of an enormous force, swelling up with her tears. Despite her frailness, somewhere deep in her being was a font of superhuman strength. Though she had not realized it, her willpower was indomitable and had enabled her to persevere through the long years of illness and anguish. Fresh blood infused her cheeks, giving them new life.

"Granny! Jōtarō!"

They came down the bank slowly, Jōtarō asking, "What is it, Otsū?"

"I heard you talking."

"Oh?"

"Yes. But I'm not going to cry about it anymore. I'll go to Kokura. I'll see the bout for myself. . . . We can't take it for granted Musashi will win. If he doesn't, I intend to receive his ashes and bring them back with me."

"But you're sick."

"Sick?" She'd pushed the very idea from her mind; she seemed filled with a vitality transcending the weakness of her body. "Don't think about it. I'm perfectly all right. Well, maybe I'm still a little sick, but until I see how the bout turns out—"

"I'm determined not to die" were the words that nearly escaped her lips. She stifled them and busied herself making preparations for her journey. When she was ready, she got out of the boat all by herself, though she had to cling tightly to the rail in order to do so.

23

A Falcon and a Woman

At the time of the Battle of Sekigahara, Kokura had been the site of a fortress commanded by Lord Mōri Katsunobu of Iki. Since then the castle had been rebuilt and enlarged and acquired a new lord. Its towers and glistening white walls bespoke the great power and dignity of the House of Hosokawa, headed now by Tadatoshi, who had succeeded his father, Tadaoki.

In the short time since Kojirō's arrival, the Ganryū Style, developed on the foundation he had learned from Toda Seigen and Kanemaki Jisai, had swept over all Kyushu. Men even came from Shikoku to study under him, hoping that after a year or two of training they would be awarded a certificate and receive sanction to return home as teachers of this new style.

Kojirō enjoyed the esteem of those around him, including Tadatoshi, who had been heard to remark with satisfaction, "I found myself a very good swordsman." In every quarter of the extensive Hosokawa household, it was agreed that Kojirō was a person of "outstanding character." And when he traveled between his home and the castle, he did so in style, attended by seven lancers. People went out of their way to approach him and pay their respects.

Until his coming, Ujiie Magoshirō, a practitioner of the Shinkage Style, had been the clan's chief sword

265

instructor, but his star dimmed rapidly as Kojirō's grew more brilliant. Kojirō treated him magniloquently. To Lord Tadatoshi, he had said, "You mustn't let Ujiie go. While his style is not flashy, it does have a certain maturity we younger men lack." He suggested that he and Magoshirō give lessons in the castle's dōjō on alternate days, and this was put into practice.

At one point, Tadatoshi said, "Kojirō says Magoshirō's method is not flashy, but mature. Magoshirō says Kojirō is a genius with whom he cannot match swords. Who is right? I'd like to see a demonstration."

The two men agreed to subsequently face each other with wooden swords in his lordship's presence. At the first opportunity, Kojirō discarded his weapon, and seating himself at his opponent's feet, announced, "I'm no match for you. Forgive my presumption."

"Don't be modest," replied Magoshirō. "I'm the one who's not a worthy opponent."

Witnesses were divided as to whether Kojirō acted out of compassion or self-interest. In any case, his reputation rose still higher.

Kojirō's attitude toward Magoshirō remained charitable, but whenever someone made favorable mention of Musashi's growing fame in Edo and Kyoto, he was quick to set him straight.

"Musashi?" he would say with disdain. "Oh, he's been crafty enough to make something of a name for himself. He talks about his Two-Sword Style, I'm told. He's always had a certain natural ability. I doubt whether there's anybody in Kyoto or Osaka who could defeat him." He always made it appear that he was restraining himself from saying more.

An experienced warrior visiting Kojirō's house one day said, "I've never met the man, but people say this Miyamoto Musashi is the greatest swordsman since Kōizumi and Tsukahara, with the exception of Yagyū Sekishūsai, of course. Everybody seems to think that if he's not the greatest swordsman, he's at least reached the level of a master.''

Kojirō laughed and the color rose in his face. ''Well, people are blind,'' he said bitingly. ''So I suppose some consider him a great man or an expert swordsman. That just goes to show you how far the Art of War has declined, with regard to both style and personal conduct. We live in an age when a clever publicity seeker can rule the roost, at least as far as ordinary people are concerned.

''Needless to say, I look at it differently. I saw Musashi trying to sell himself in Kyoto some years ago. He gave an exhibition of his brutality and cravenness in his bout with the Yoshioka School at Ichijōji. Cravenness is not a low enough word for the likes of him. All right, so he was outnumbered, but what did he do? He showed his back at the earliest possible moment. Considering his past and his overweening ambition, I see him as a man not worth spitting on. . . . Ha, ha—if a man who spends his life trying to learn the Art of War is an expert, then I suppose Musashi's an expert. But a master of the sword—no, not that.''

He obviously took praise of Musashi as a personal affront, but his insistence on winning anyone and everyone over to his point of view was so vehement that even his staunchest admirers began to wonder. Eventually the word got around that there was a long-standing enmity between Musashi and Kojirō. Before long, rumors of a match were flying.

It was at Lord Tadatoshi's order that Kojirō had finally issued a challenge. In the several months since then, the entire Hosokawa fief had buzzed with speculation as to when the fight would be held and how it would turn out.

Iwama Kakubei, now well along in years, called on Kojirō morning and evening, whenever he could find the slightest excuse. On an evening early in the fourth month, when even the pink double-petal cherry blossoms had fallen, Kakubei walked through Kojirō's front garden, past bright red azaleas blooming in the shadows of ornamental rocks. He was shown to an inner room lit only by the failing light of the evening sun.

"Ah, Master Iwama, good to see you," said Kojirō, who was standing just outside, feeding the falcon on his fist.

"I have news for you," said Kakubei, still standing. "The clan council discussed the pace for the bout today in his lordship's presence and reached a decision."

"Have a seat," said an attendant from the adjacent room.

With no more than a grunt of thanks, Kakubei sat down and continued: "A number of sites were suggested, among them Kikunonagahama and the bank of the Murasaki River, but they were all rejected because they were too small or too accessible to the public. We could put up bamboo fencing, of course, but even that wouldn't prevent the riverbank from being overrun by swarms of people looking for thrills."

"I see," replied Kojirō, still intently watching the falcon's eyes and beak.

Kakubei, expecting his report to be received more or less with bated breath, was crestfallen. A guest would not normally do such a thing, but Kakubei said, "Come inside. This is nothing to be talking about while you're standing out there."

"In a minute," Kojirō said casually. "I want to finish feeding the bird."

"Is that the falcon Lord Tadatoshi gave you after you went hunting together last fall?"

"Yes. Its name is Amayumi. The more I get used to it, the better I like it." He threw away the rest of the food and, winding up the red-tasseled cord attached to the bird's neck, said to the young attendant behind him, "Here, Tatsunosuke—put it back in its cage."

The bird was passed from fist to fist, and Tatsunosuke started across the spacious garden. Beyond the customary man-made hillock was a grove of pines, bordered on the other side by a fence. The compound lay along the Itatsu River; many other Hosokawa vassals lived in the vicinity.

"Forgive me for making you wait," said Kojirō.

"Think nothing of it. I'm not exactly an outsider. When I come here, it's almost like being at my son's house."

A maid of twenty or so came in and gracefully poured tea. With a glance at the guest, she invited him to have a cup.

Kakubei shook his head admiringly. "It's good to see you, Omitsu. You're always so pretty."

She blushed down to the collar of her kimono. "And you're always making fun of me," she replied before quickly slipping out of the room.

Kakubei said, "You say the more you get used to your falcon, the better you like it. What about Omitsu? Wouldn't it be better to have her at your side, rather than a bird of prey? I've been meaning to ask you about your intentions regarding her."

"Has she by any chance secretly visited your house at one time or another?"

"I'll admit she did come to talk to me."

"Stupid woman! She hasn't said a word about it to me." He shot an angry glance at the white shoji.

"Don't let it upset you. There's no reason why she shouldn't come." He waited until he thought Kojirō's eyes had softened a little, then went on: "It's only natural for a woman to worry. I don't think she doubts your affection for her, but anybody in her position would worry about the future. I mean, what's to become of her?"

"I suppose she told you everything?"

"Why shouldn't she? It's the most ordinary thing in the world to happen between a man and a woman. One of these days you'll want to get married. You have this big house and lots of servants. Why not?"

"Can't you imagine what people would say if I married a girl I'd previously had in my house as a maid?"

"Does it really make any difference? You certainly can't throw her aside now. If she weren't a suitable bride for you, it might be awkward, but she's of good blood, isn't she? I'm told she's the niece of Ōno Tadaaki."

"That's correct."

"And you met her when you went to Tadaaki's dōjō and opened his eyes to the sad state his school of swordsmanship was in."

"Yes. I'm not proud of it, but I can't keep it from someone as close to me as you are. I'd planned to tell you the whole story sooner or later. . . . As you say, it happened after my bout with Tadaaki. It was already dark when I started for home, and Omitsu—she was living with her uncle at the time—brought a small lantern and walked down Saikachi Slope with me. Without giving it a thought, I flirted with her a bit along the way, but she took me seriously. After Tadaaki disappeared, she came to see me and—"

Now it was Kakubei's turn to be embarrassed. He waved his hand to let his protégé know he had heard enough. Actually, he had not known until very recently that Kojirō had taken the girl in before leaving Edo for Kokura. He was surprised not only at his own naiveté but also at Kojirō's ability to attract a woman, have an affair with her and keep the whole thing secret.

"Leave everything to me," he said. "At the moment, it would be rather inappropriate for you to announce your marriage. First things first. It can be done after your bout." Like so many others, he was confident that final justification for Kojirō's fame and position would be forthcoming within a few days.

Remembering why he'd come, he went on: "As I said, the council has decided the location for the bout. Since one requirement was that it be within Lord Tadatoshi's domain, but somewhere that crowds can't get to easily, it was agreed that an island would be ideal. The island chosen is a small one called Funashima, between Shimonoseki and Moji.''

He looked thoughtful for a minute, then said, ''I wonder if it wouldn't be wise to look the terrain over before Musashi arrives. It might give you a certain advantage.'' His reasoning was that from a knowledge of the lay of the land, a swordsman would have an idea of how the fighting would proceed, how tightly to tie his sandals, how to make use of the terrain and the position of the sun. At the very least, Kojirō would have a sense of security, which would be impossible if he were entering the place for the first time.

He suggested they hire a fishing boat and go out to look at Funashima the next day.

Kojirō disagreed. ''The whole point of the Art of War is to be quick to seize an opening. Even when a man takes precautions, it often happens that his opponent will have anticipated them and devised means of offsetting them. It's much better to approach the situation with an open mind and move with perfect freedom.''

Seeing the logic of this argument, Kakubei made no more mention of going to Funashima.

Summoned by Kojirō, Omitsu served them sake, and the two men drank and chatted until late in the evening. From the relaxed way in which Kakubei sipped his sake, it was evident that he was pleased with life and felt that his efforts to assist Kojirō had been rewarded.

Rather like a proud father, he said, ''I think it's all right to tell Omitsu. When this is over, we can invite her relatives and friends here for the marriage ceremony. It's a fine thing for you to be devoted to your sword, but you must also have a family if your name is to be carried on. When you're married, I'll feel I've done my duty by you.''

Unlike the happy old retainer with many years of service, Kojirō showed no signs of drunkenness. But then he was prone to silence these days anyway. Once the bout had been decided on, Kakubei had suggested and

Tadatoshi had agreed to release Kojirō from his duties. He had enjoyed the unaccustomed leisure at first, but as the day approached and more and more people came to call, he found himself forced to entertain them. Recently, times when he could rest had become few. Still, he was reluctant to shut himself away and have people turned back at the gate. If he did that, people would think he'd lost his composure.

The idea that came to him was to go out into the country every day, his falcon on his fist. In nice weather, hiking over field and mountain with only the bird for a companion did his spirit good.

When the falcon's alert azure eyes spotted a victim in the sky, Kojirō would release it. Then his own eyes, equally alert, would follow it as it rose and swooped down on its quarry. Until the feathers began to drift to earth, he remained breathless, transfixed, as though he himself were the falcon.

"Good! That's the way!" he exclaimed when the falcon made the kill. He had learned much from this bird of prey, and as a result of these hunting excursions, his face showed more confidence with the passage of each day.

Returning home in the evening, he was met by Omitsu's eyes, swollen from crying. It hurt him to observe her efforts to disguise this. To him, losing to Musashi was inconceivable. Nevertheless, the question of what would happen to her if he was killed crept into his mind.

So did the image of his dead mother, to whom he had given scarcely a thought for years. And each night as he was falling asleep, a vision of the falcon's azure eyes and the swollen eyes of Omitsu came to visit him, jumbled in an odd way with a fleeting memory of his mother's face.

24

Before the Thirteenth Day

Shimonoseki, Moji, the castle town of Kokura—during the past several days many travelers had come but few had left. The inns were all full, and horses were lined up side by side at the hitching posts outside.

The command issued by the castle said:

> On the thirteenth day of this month, at eight o'clock in the morning, on Funashima in the Nagato Straits of Buzen, Sasaki Kojirō Ganryū, a samurai of this fief, will at his lordship's bidding fight a bout with Miyamoto Musashi Masana, a rōnin from the province of Mimasaka.
>
> It is strictly forbidden for supporters of either swordsman to go to his aid or set forth on the water between the mainland and Funashima. Until ten o'clock on the morning of the thirteenth, no sightseeing vessels, passenger ships and fishing boats will be permitted to enter the straits. Fourth month [1612].

The announcement was posted conspicuously on bulletin boards at all major intersections, piers and gathering places.

"The thirteenth? That's the day after tomorrow, isn't it?"

"People from all over will want to see the bout, so they can go home and talk about it."

"Of course they will, but how's anybody going to see a fight taking place on an island two miles from shore?"

"Well, if you go to the top of Mount Kazashi, you can see the pine trees on Funashima. People'll come anyway, just to gawk at the boats and crowds in Buzen and Nagato."

"I hope the weather stays good."

Because of the restriction of shipping activities, boatmen who might otherwise have been turning a tidy profit were doing poorly. Travelers and townsmen, however, took it in their stride, busily searching out vantage points from which they might catch a glimpse of the excitement on Funashima.

About noon on the eleventh, a woman giving breast to her baby was pacing back and forth in front of a "one-tray" eatery where the road from Moji entered Kokura.

The baby, tired from traveling, would not stop crying. "Sleepy? Take a little nap now. There, there. Sleep, sleep." Akemi patted her foot rhythmically on the ground. She wore no makeup. With a baby to nurse, her life had changed considerably, but there was nothing in her present circumstances that she regretted.

Matahachi came out of the shop, wearing a sleeveless kimono of subdued color. The only hint of the days when he had aspired to becoming a priest was the bandanna on his head, hiding the once shaven head.

"Oh, my, what's this?" he said. "Still crying? You should be sleeping. Go on, Akemi. I'll take him while you eat. Eat a lot, so you'll have plenty of milk." Taking the child in his arms, he began crooning a soft lullaby.

"Well, this is a surprise!" came a voice from behind him.

"Huh?" Matahachi stared at the man, unable to place him.

"I'm Ichinomiya Gempachi. We met several years

ago at the pine forest near Gojō Avenue in Kyoto. I guess you don't remember me." When Matahachi continued to stare blankly at him, Gempachi said, "You were going around calling yourself Sasaki Kojirō."

"Oh!" Matahachi gasped loudly. "The monk with the staff . . ."

"That's right. Good to see you again."

Matahachi hastened to bow, which awakened the baby. "Now, let's not start crying again," he pleaded.

"I wonder," said Gempachi, "if you could tell me where Kojirō's house is. I understand he lives here in Kokura."

"Sorry, I have no idea. I just got here myself."

Two samurais' attendants emerged from the shop, and one said to Gempachi, "If you're looking for Kojirō's house, it's right by the Itatsu River. We'll show you the way, if you like."

"Very kind of you. Good-bye, Matahachi. See you again." The samurai walked off, and Gempachi fell in step with them.

Matahachi, noticing the dirt and grime clinging to the man's clothes, thought: "I wonder if he's come all the way from Kōzuke." He was deeply impressed that news of the bout had spread to such faraway places. Then the memory of the encounter with Gempachi flowed through his mind, and he shuddered. How worthless, how shallow, how shameless he'd been in those days! To think he had actually been brazen enough to try to pass off the certificate from the Chūjō School as his own, to impersonate . . . Still, that he could see how churlish he had been was a hopeful sign. At least he'd changed since then. "I suppose," he thought, "even a stupid fool like me can improve if he stays awake and tries."

Hearing the baby crying again, Akemi bolted her meal and rushed outdoors. "Sorry," she said. "I'll take him now."

Having placed the baby on Akemi's back, Matahachi hung a candy peddler's box from his shoulder and prepared to forge on. A number of passersby looked enviously at this poor, but apparently happy, couple.

An elderly, genteel-looking woman approached and said, "What a lovely baby! How old is he? Oh, look, he's laughing." As if on command, the manservant accompanying her stooped and peered at the baby's face.

They all walked together for a way. Then, as Matahachi and Akemi started to turn into a side street to look for an inn, the woman said, "Oh, are you going that way?" She bade them good-bye, and almost as an afterthought, asked, "You seem to be travelers, too, but would you happen to know where Sasaki Kojirō's house is?"

Matahachi imparted the information he had just heard from the two attendants. As he watched her go off, he mumbled gloomily, "I wonder what my mother's doing these days." Now that he had a child of his own, he had begun to appreciate her feelings.

"Come on, let's go," said Akemi.

Matahachi stood and stared vacantly at the old woman. She was about the same age as Osugi.

Kojirō's house was full of guests.

"It's a great opportunity for him."

"Yes, this'll make his reputation, once and for all."

"He'll be known everywhere."

"True enough, but we mustn't forget who his opponent is. Ganryū will have to be very careful."

Many had arrived the previous night, and callers spilled out into the great entrance hall, the side entrances, the outside corridors. Some hailed from Kyoto or Osaka, others from western Honshu, one from the village of Jōkyōji in distant Echizen. Since there weren't enough servants in the household, Kakubei had sent some of his to help out. Samurai who were studying under Kojirō came and went, their faces eager with anticipation.

All these friends, all these disciples, had one thing in common: whether they knew Musashi or not, he was the enemy. Particularly virulent in their hatred were the provincial samurai who had at one time or another studied the methods of the Yoshioka School. The humiliation of the defeat at Ichijōji gnawed at their minds and hearts. Moreover, the single-minded determination with which Musashi had pursued his career was such that he had made himself many enemies. Kojirō's students despised him as a matter of course.

A young samurai led a recent arrival from the entrance hall into the crowded parlor and announced, "This man has made the trip from Kōzuke."

The man said, "My name is Ichinomiya Gempachi," and modestly took his place among them.

A murmur of admiration and respect went around the room, for Kōzuke lay a thousand miles to the northeast. Gempachi asked that a talisman he had brought from Mount Hakuun be placed on the household altar, and there were more murmurs of approval.

"The weather will be good on the thirteenth," remarked one man, glancing out under the eaves at the flaming evening sun. "Today's the eleventh, tomorrow the twelfth, the next day . . ."

Addressing Gempachi, one guest said, "I think your coming so far to say a prayer for Kojirō's success is quite remarkable. Do you have some connection with him?"

"I'm a retainer of the House of Kusanagi in Shimonida. My late master, Kusanagi Tenki, was the nephew of Kanemaki Jisai. Tenki knew Kojirō when Kojirō was still a young boy."

"I'd heard Kojirō studied under Jisai."

"That's true. Kojirō came from the same school as Itō Ittōsai. I've heard Ittōsai say many times that Kojirō was a brilliant fighter." He went on to recount how Kojirō had chosen to reject Jisai's certificate and create a style of his own. He told, too, of how tenacious Kojirō had been, even as a child. Meeting eager questions with detailed answers, Gempachi talked on and on.

"Isn't Ganryū *Sensei* here?" asked a young attendant, picking his way through the crowd. Not seeing him, he went from room to room. He was grumbling to himself by the time he came upon Omitsu, who was cleaning Kojirō's room. "If you're looking for the master," she said, "you'll find him at the falcon cage."

Kojirō was inside the cage, looking intently into Amayumi's eyes. He had fed the bird, brushed off loose feathers, held it for a time on his fist and was now patting it affectionately.

"*Sensei*."

"Yes?"

"There's a woman who says she's come from Iwa-kuni to visit you. She said you'd know her when you see her."

"Hmm. It may be my mother's younger sister."

"Which room should I show her to?"

"I don't want to see her. I don't want to see any-body. . . . Oh, I suppose I have to. She is my aunt. Take her to my room."

The man left and Kojirō called out the door, "Tatsu-nosuke."

"Yes, sir." Tatsunosuke came inside the cage and knelt on one knee behind Kojirō. A student who lived at his house, he was seldom far from his master's side.

"Not long to wait now, is there?" said Kojirō.

"No, sir."

"Tomorrow I'll go to the castle and pay my respects to Lord Tadatoshi. I haven't seen him recently. After that, I want to spend a quiet night."

"There are all those guests. Why don't you refuse to see them, so you can have a good rest?"

"That's what I intend to do."

"There are so many people around here, you could be defeated by your own supporters."

"Don't talk like that. They've come from near and far. . . . Whether I win or not depends on what happens at the appointed time. It's not entirely a matter of fate, but then again . . . That's the way with warriors—

sometimes win, sometimes lose. If Ganryū dies, you'll find two last testaments in my writing cabinet. Give one of them to Kakubei and the other to Omitsu."

"You've written a will?"

"Yes. It's only proper for a samurai to take that precaution. One other thing. On the day of the fight, I'm allowed one attendant. I want you to go with me. Will you come?"

"It's an honor I don't deserve."

"Amayumi too." He looked at the falcon. "It'll be a comfort to me on the boat trip."

"I understand perfectly."

"Good. I'll see my aunt now."

He found her sitting in his room. Outside, the evening clouds had blackened, like newly forged steel that has just cooled off. The white light of a candle brightened the room.

"Thank you for coming," he said as he seated himself with a great show of reverence. After his mother's death, his aunt had reared him. Unlike his mother, she had not spoiled him in the least. Conscious of her duty to her elder sister, she had striven single-mindedly to make him a worthy successor to the Sasaki name and an outstanding man in his own right. Of all his kinsmen, she was the one who had paid closest attention to his career and his future.

"Kojirō," she began solemnly, "I understand you're about to face one of the decisive moments of your life. Everybody back home is talking about it, and I felt I had to see you, one more time at least. I'm happy to see you've come as far as you have." She was silently comparing the dignified, well-to-do samurai in front of her with the youth who had left home with nothing but a sword.

Head still lowered, Kojirō replied, "It's been ten years. I hope you'll forgive me for not keeping in touch with you. I don't know whether people consider me a

success or not, but I have by no means achieved all I am
determined to achieve. That's why I haven't written."

"It doesn't matter. I hear news of you all the time."

"Even in Iwakuni?"

"Oh, indeed. Everyone there is for you. If you were
to lose to Musashi, the whole Sasaki family—the whole
province—would be disgraced. Lord Katayama Hisayasu
of Hōki, who's staying as a guest in the Kikkawa fief, is
planning to bring a large group of Iwakuni samurai to see
the bout."

"Is he?"

"Yes. They'll be terribly disappointed, I suppose,
since no boats will be allowed out. . . . Oh, I'm forgetting.
Here, I brought this for you." She opened a small bundle
and took out a folded underrobe. It was made of white
cotton; on it were written the names of the god of war
and a protective goddess worshiped by warriors. A Sanskrit good-luck charm had been embroidered on both
sleeves by a hundred of Kojirō's female supporters.

He thanked her and reverently held the garment up
before his forehead. Then he said, "You must be tired
from your trip. You can stay here in this room and go to
bed whenever you wish. Now, if you'll excuse me."

He left her and went to sit in another room, to which
guests soon came offering him a variety of gifts—a sacred
charm from the Hachiman Shrine on Mount Otoko, a
coat of mail, an enormous sea bream, a barrel of sake.
Before long, there was hardly a place to sit down.

While these well-wishers were sincere in their
prayers for his victory, it was also true that eight out of
ten of them, not doubting that he would win, were curry-
ing favor in the hope of advancing their own ambitions
later on.

"What if I were a rōnin?" thought Kojirō. Though
the sycophancy depressed him, he took satisfaction from
the fact that it was he and no one else who had caused
his supporters to trust him and believe in him.

"I must win. I must, I must."

Thinking of winning placed a psychological burden on him. He realized this but could not help himself. "Win, win, win." Like a wind-driven wave, the word kept on repeating itself somewhere in his mind. Not even Kojirō was able to grasp why the primitive urge to conquer buffeted his brain with such persistence.

The night wore on, but quite a number of guests stayed up, drinking and talking. It was quite late when the word came.

"Musashi arrived today. He was seen getting off a boat in Moji and later walking down a street in Kokura."

The response was electric, though uttered furtively, in excited whispers.

"It stands to reason."

"Shouldn't some of us go over there and take a look around?"

25

At Daybreak

Musashi arrived in Shimonoseki several days early. Since he knew no one there, and no one knew him, he passed his time quietly, unbothered by sycophants and busybodies.

On the morning of the eleventh, he crossed the Kammon Strait to Moji to call on Nagaoka Sado and confirm his acceptance of the time and place of the bout.

A samurai received him at the entrance hall, staring unabashedly, one thought going through his mind: "So this is the famous Miyamoto Musashi!" All the young man said aloud, however, was: "My master is still at the castle but should be back shortly. Please come in and wait."

"No, thank you; I have no other business with him. If you'd just be so kind as to give him my message . . ."

"But you've come so far. He'll be very disappointed to have missed you. If you really have to go, please let me at least tell the others that you're here."

He'd hardly disappeared into the house when Iori came rushing out and into Musashi's arms.

"*Sensei!*"

Musashi patted him on the head. "Have you been studying, like a good boy?"

"Yes, sir."

"You've grown so tall!"

"Did you know I was here?"

"Yes; Sado told me in a letter. I also heard about you at Kobayashi Tarōzaemon's in Sakai. I'm glad you're here. Living in a house like this will be good for you."

Looking disappointed, Iori said nothing.

"What's the matter?" asked Musashi. "You mustn't forget that Sado's been very good to you."

"Yes, sir."

"You have to do more than just practice martial arts, you know. You have to learn from books. And although you should be the first to help when help is needed, you should try to be more modest than the other boys."

"Yes, sir."

"And don't fall into the trap of feeling sorry for yourself. Many boys like you, who've lost a father or mother, do that. You can't repay the warmheartedness of others unless you're warm and kind in return."

"Yes, sir."

"You're bright, Iori, but be careful. Don't let your rough upbringing get the best of you. Keep yourself under tight rein. You're still a child; you have a long life ahead of you. Guard it carefully. Save it until you can give it for a really good cause—for your country, your honor, the Way of the Samurai. Hold on to your life and make it honest and brave."

Iori had the sinking feeling that this was a parting, a final farewell. His intuition probably would have told him this even if Musashi hadn't spoken of such serious matters, but the mention of the word "life" left little doubt. No sooner had Musashi said it than Iori's head was buried in his chest. The child sobbed uncontrollably.

Musashi, noting that Iori was very well groomed—his hair nicely combed and tied and his white socks immaculate—now regretted his sermon. "Don't cry," he said.

"But what if you . . . ."

"Stop your bawling. People will see you."

"You . . . you're going to Funashima the day after tomorrow?"

"Yes, I have to."

"Win, please win. I can't bear to think of not seeing you again."

"Ha, ha. You're crying about that?"

"Some people say you can't beat Kojirō—you shouldn't have agreed to fight him in the first place."

"I'm not surprised. People always talk like that."

"You can win, though, can't you, *Sensei?*"

"I wouldn't even waste my time thinking about it."

"You mean you're sure you won't lose?"

"Even if I do lose, I promise to do it bravely."

"But if you think you might, couldn't you just go away somewhere for a while?"

"There's always a germ of truth in the worst of gossip, Iori. I may have made a mistake, but now that it's gone this far, to run away would be to forsake the Way of the Samurai. That would bring dishonor not only on me but on many others as well."

"But didn't you say I should hang on to my life and guard it carefully?"

"Yes, I did, and if they bury me on Funashima, let that be a lesson to you and avoid getting into fights that may end in your throwing your life away." Sensing that he was overdoing it, he changed the subject. "I've already asked that my respects be conveyed to Nagaoka Sado. I want you to convey them too, and tell him that I'll see him on Funashima."

Musashi gently shook himself free of the boy. As he walked toward the gate, Iori clung to the basket hat in his hand. "Don't . . . Wait . . ." was all he could say. He put his other hand to his face. His shoulders were shaking.

Nuinosuke came through a door beside the gate and introduced himself to Musashi. "Iori seems reluctant to let you go, and I'm inclined to sympathize with him. I'm sure you have other things to do, but couldn't you just stay over here one night?"

Musashi, returning his bow, said, "It's good of you to ask, but I don't think I should. In a couple of days I may be asleep for good. I don't think it'd be right for me to burden others now. It might prove to be an embarrassment later on."

"That's very considerate of you, but I'm afraid the master will be furious with us for letting you go."

"I'll send him a note explaining everything. I only came today to pay my respects. I think I should be leaving now."

Outside the gate, he turned toward the beach, but before he'd got halfway there, he heard voices calling from behind. Looking back, he saw a handful of elderly-looking samurai from the House of Hosokawa, two of whom had gray hair. Not recognizing any of them, he assumed they were shouting to someone else and walked on.

Upon reaching the shore, he stood and gazed out over the water. A number of fishing boats rested at anchor in the offing, their furled sails ashen in the misty light of early evening. Beyond the larger mass of Hikojima, the outline of Funashima was barely visible.

"Musashi!"

"You are Miyamoto Musashi, aren't you?"

Musashi turned to face them, wondering what business these aged warriors could have with him.

"You don't remember us, do you? Didn't think you would. It's been too long. My name's Utsumi Magobeinojō. All six of us are from Mimasaka. We used to be in the service of the House of Shimmen at Takeyama Castle."

"And I'm Koyama Handayū. Magobeinojō and I were close friends of your father's."

Musashi smiled broadly. "Well, this is a surprise!" Their drawl, unmistakably that of his native village, stirred up many childhood memories. After bowing to each of them, he said, "It's good to see you. But tell me,

285

how does it happen you're all here together, so far from home?"

"Well, as you know, the House of Shimmen was disbanded after the Battle of Sekigahara. We became rōnin and fled to Kyushu, came here to Buzen Province. For a while, to keep body and soul together, we wove straw horseshoes. Later, we had a stroke of good luck."

"Is that so? Well, I must say, I never expected to meet friends of my father's in Kokura."

"It's an unexpected pleasure for us too. You're a fine-looking samurai, Musashi. Too bad your father isn't here to see you now."

For a few minutes they commented to one another on Musashi's fine appearance. Then Magobeinojō said, "Stupid of me; I'm forgetting what we came after you for. We just missed you at Sado's house. Our plan was to spend an evening with you. It's all been arranged with Sado."

Handayū chimed in, "That's right. It was very rude of you to come as far as the front door and leave without seeing Sado; you're the son of Shimmen Munisai. You should know better. Now come back with us." Apparently he felt that having been a friend of Musashi's father authorized him to issue orders to the son. Without waiting for an answer, he started walking away, expecting Musashi to follow.

Musashi, on the point of accompanying them, stopped himself.

"I'm sorry," he said. "I don't think I should go. I apologize for being so rude, but I think it'd be wrong for me to join you."

Everyone came to a halt, and Magobeinojō said, "Wrong? What's wrong about it? We want to give you a proper welcome—same village and all that, you know."

"Sado's looking forward to it too. You don't want to offend him, do you?"

Magobeinojō, sounding resentful, added, "What's the matter? Angry about something?"

"I'd like to go," Musashi said politely, "but there are other things to consider. Though it's probably just a rumor, I've heard that my bout with Kojirō is a source of friction between the two oldest retainers in the House of Hosokawa, Nagaoka Sado and Iwama Kakubei. They say Iwama's side has the approval of Lord Tadatoshi, and Nagaoka is trying to strengthen his own faction by opposing Kojirō."

This was met with murmurs of surprise.

"I feel sure," Musashi continued, "that it's no more than idle speculation, but still, public talk is a dangerous thing. What happens to a rōnin like myself doesn't matter much, but I wouldn't want to do anything to fan the rumors and raise suspicions about either Sado or Kakubei. They're both valuable men in the fief."

"I see," said Magobeinojō.

Musashi smiled. "Well, at least that's my excuse. To tell the truth, being a country boy, it's difficult for me to have to sit around and be polite all evening. I'd just like to relax."

Impressed with Musashi's consideration for others but still reluctant to part with him, they put their heads together and discussed the situation.

"This is the eleventh day of the fourth month," said Handayū. "For the past ten years, the six of us have been getting together on this date. We have an ironclad rule against inviting outsiders, but you're from the same village, you're Munisai's son, so we'd like to ask you to join us. It may not be the sort of entertainment we should provide, but you won't have to worry about having to be polite, or being seen or talked about."

"If you put it that way," said Musashi, "I don't see how I can refuse."

The answer pleased the old samurai immensely. After another short huddle, it was arranged that Musashi would meet one of them, a man named Kinami Kagashirō, a couple of hours later in front of a tea shop, and they went their separate ways.

THE WAY OF LIFE AND DEATH

Musashi met Kagashirō at the appointed hour, and they walked about a mile and a half from the center of town to a place near Itatsu Bridge. Musashi saw no samurai houses or restaurants, nothing but the lights of a solitary drinking shop and a cheap inn, both some distance away. Ever on the alert, he began turning possibilities over in his mind. There was nothing suspicious about their story; they looked the right age and their dialect fit in with their story. But why an out-of-the-way place like this?

Kagashirō left him and went toward the riverbank. Then he called Musashi, saying, "They're all here. Come on down," and led the way along the narrow path on the dike.

"Maybe the party's on a boat," thought Musashi, smiling at his own excessive cautiousness. But there was no boat. He found them sitting on reed mats in formal style.

"Forgive us for bringing you to a place like this," said Magobeinojō. "This is where we hold our meeting. We feel some special good fortune has brought you to be with us. Sit down and rest awhile." His manner grave enough to be welcoming an honored guest into a fine parlor with silver-covered shoji, he pushed a strip of matting forward for Musashi.

Musashi wondered if this was their idea of elegant restraint or if there was some particular reason for not meeting in a more public place. But as a guest, he felt constrained to act as one. Bowing, he seated himself formally on the mat.

"Make yourself comfortable," urged Magobeinojō. "We'll have a little party later, but first we have to perform our ceremony. It won't take long."

The six men rearranged themselves more informally, each man taking a sheaf of the straw they'd brought with them, and they proceeded to weave straw horseshoes. Mouths tightly closed, eyes never leaving their work, they appeared solemn, even pious. Musashi watched respectfully, sensing strength and fervor in their movements as they spat on their hands, ran the straw through their fingers and plaited it between their palms.

"I guess this'll do," said Handayū, laying down a finished pair of horseshoes and looking around at the others.

"I'm finished too."

They placed their horseshoes in front of Handayū, brushed themselves off and straightened their clothes. Handayū piled the horseshoes on a small table in the middle of the circle of samurai, and Magobeinojō, the oldest, stood up.

"It's now the twelfth year since the Battle of Sekigahara, since that day of defeat that will never be erased from our memories," he began. "We've all lived longer than we had any right to expect. This we owe to the protection and bounty of Lord Hosokawa. We must see that our sons and grandsons remember his lordship's goodness to us."

Murmurs of assent went around the group. They sat in a reverent attitude, their eyes lowered.

"We must also remember forever the largesse of successive heads of the House of Shimmen, even though that great house no longer exists. Nor should we ever forget the misery and hopelessness that were ours when we came here. It is to remind us of these three things that we hold this meeting each year. Now let us pray as one man for one another's health and welfare."

In chorus, the men replied, "The goodness of Lord Hosokawa, the largesse of the House of Shimmen, the bounty of heaven that has delivered us from distress—we will not forget for a day."

"Now make the obeisance," said Magobeinojō.

They turned toward the white walls of Kokura Castle, seen dimly against the dark sky, and bowed to the ground. Then they turned in the direction of Mimasaka Province and bowed again. Finally, they faced the horseshoes and bowed a third time. Each movement was carried out with the utmost gravity and sincerity.

To Musashi, Magobeinojō said, "Now we're going to the shrine above here and make an offering of the horseshoes. After that we can get on with the party. If you'll just wait here."

The man who led the way carried the table with the horseshoes at forehead level, the others following single file. They tied their handiwork to the branches of a tree beside the shrine entrance. Then, after clapping their hands once before the deity, they rejoined Musashi.

The fare was simple—a stew with taros, bamboo shoots with bean paste, and dried fish—the sort of meal served in local farmhouses. But there was much sake, and much laughter and talk.

When the mood became convivial, Musashi said, "It's a great honor to be asked to join you, but I've been wondering about your little ceremony. It must have some very special meaning for you."

"It does," said Magobeinojō. "When we came here as defeated warriors, we had no one to turn to. We would rather have died than steal, but we had to eat. Finally, we hit on the idea of setting up shop over there by the bridge and making horseshoes. Our hands were calloused from training with lances, so it took some effort to teach them to weave straw. We did that for three years, selling our work to passing grooms and somehow making enough to stay alive.

"The grooms came to suspect that weaving straw wasn't our usual occupation, and eventually someone told Lord Hosokawa Sansai about us. Learning we were former vassals of Lord Shimmen, he sent a man to offer us positions."

He told how Lord Sansai had offered a collective stipend of five thousand bushels, which they refused. They were willing to serve him in good faith, but they felt the lord-to-vassal relationship should be on a man-to-man basis. Sansai understood their feelings and came back with an offer of individual stipends. He had also been understanding when his retainers expressed fears that the six rōnin would not be able to attire themselves in a suitable manner to be presented to his lordship. But when a special allowance for clothes was suggested, Sansai said no, it would only cause embarrassment. Actually the fears were unwarranted, for as low as they had sunk, they were still able to dress in starched clothes and wear their two swords when they went to receive their appointments.

"It wouldn't have been difficult to forget how hard our lives were doing menial work. If we hadn't stuck together, we wouldn't have been alive for Lord Sansai to engage us. We mustn't let ourselves forget that providence took care of us during those difficult years."

Ending his recital, he held up a cup, saying, "Forgive me for talking so long about us. I just wanted you to know we're men of goodwill, even if our sake's not first class and the food not very plentiful. We want you to put up a brave fight the day after tomorrow. If you lose, we'll bury your bones for you, don't worry."

Accepting the cup, Musashi replied, "I'm honored to be here among you. It's better than drinking the very best sake in the finest mansion. I only hope I'll be as lucky as you've been."

"Don't hope that! You'll have to learn to weave horseshoes."

The sound of sliding dirt cut short their laughter. Their eyes went to the dike, where they saw the crouching batlike figure of a man.

"Who's there?" cried Kagashirō, on his feet at once. Another man rose, drawing his sword, and the two climbed the dike and peered through the mist.

Laughing, Kagashirō called down, "It seems to have been one of Kojirō's followers. He probably thinks we're Musashi's seconds and we're having a secret strategy session. He got away before we got a good look at him."

"I can see Kojirō's supporters doing that," remarked one man.

The atmosphere remained lighthearted, but Musashi decided not to linger any longer. The last thing he wanted was to do anything that might bring harm to these men later. He thanked them profusely for their kindness and left them to their party, walking casually into the darkness.

At least, he seemed casual.

Nagaoka's cold wrath for letting Musashi leave his house fell on several people, but he waited until the morning of the twelfth to dispatch men to look for him.

When the men reported they couldn't find Musashi—had no idea where he was—Sado's white eyebrows shot up anxiously. "What could have happened to him? Is it possible—" He did not want to finish the thought.

Also on the twelfth, Kojirō called at the castle and was warmly received by Lord Tadatoshi. They had some sake together, and Kojirō left in high spirits, riding his favorite pony.

By evening, the town was humming with rumors.

"Musashi probably got scared and ran away."

"No doubt about it. He's gone."

That night was a sleepless one for Sado. He tried to convince himself that it simply wasn't possible—Musashi wasn't the type to run away. . . . Still, it was not unknown for a seemingly reliable person to break down under stress. Fearing the worst, Sado foresaw having to commit seppuku, the only honorable solution if Musashi, whom he had recommended, failed to show up.

The bright, clear dawn of the thirteenth found him walking in the garden with Iori, asking himself over and over: "Was I mistaken? Did I misjudge the man?"

"Good morning, sir." Nuinosuke's tired face appeared at the side gate.

"Did you find him?"

"No, sir. None of the innkeepers have seen anyone even resembling him."

"Did you ask at the temples?"

"The temples, the dōjō, all the other places students of the martial arts go to. Magobeinojō and his group have been out all night and—"

"They haven't come back yet." Sado's brow furrowed. Through the fresh leaves of the plum trees, he could see the blue sea; the waves seemed to be beating against his very chest. "I don't understand it."

"He's nowhere to be found, sir."

One by one the searchers returned, tired and disappointed. Assembling near the veranda, they talked the situation over in a mood of anger and desperation.

According to Kinami Kagashirō, who had passed by Sasaki Kojirō's house, several hundred supporters had gathered outside the gate. The entrance was bedecked with bunting bearing a festive gentian crest, and a gold screen had been placed directly before the door from which Kojirō was to emerge. At dawn, contingents of his followers had gone to the three main shrines to pray for his victory.

Unrelieved gloom prevailed at Sado's house, the burden being especially heavy for the men who had known Musashi's father. They felt betrayed. If Musashi reneged, it would be impossible for them to face their fellow samurai or the world at large.

When Sado dismissed them, Kagashirō vowed, "We'll find the bastard. If not today, some other day. And when we do, we'll kill him."

Returning to his own room, Sado lit the incense in the incense burner, as he did every day, but Nuinosuke detected a special gravity in the deliberateness of his movements. "He's preparing himself," he thought, grieved to think that it had come to this.

Just then Iori, standing at the edge of the garden gazing at the sea, turned and asked, "Did you try the house of Kobayashi Tarōzaemon?"

Nuinosuke realized instinctively that Iori had hit on something. No one had gone to the shipping broker's establishment, but it was exactly the sort of place Musashi would choose so as to keep out of sight.

"The boy's right," exclaimed Sado, his face brightening. "How stupid of us! Get over there right away!"

"I'm going too," said Iori.

"Is it all right for him to go along?"

"Yes, he can go too. Now hurry. . . . No, wait a minute."

He dashed off a note and informed Nuinosuke of its contents: "Sasaki Kojirō will cross to Funashima in a boat provided by Lord Tadatoshi. He will arrive by eight o'clock. You can still make it by then. I suggest you come here and make your preparations. I'll provide a boat to take you to your glorious victory."

In Sado's name, Nuinosuke and Iori procured a fast craft from the fief's boatmaster. They made it to Shimonoseki in record time, then proceeded directly to Tarōzaemon's shop.

In response to their inquiry, a clerk said, "I don't know any details, but it appears there's a young samurai staying at the master's house."

"That's it! We've found him." Nuinosuke and Iori grinned at each other and rapidly covered the short distance between shop and house.

Confronting Tarōzaemon directly, Nuinosuke said, "This is fief business, and it's urgent. Is Miyamoto Musashi staying here?"

"Yes."

"Thank heaven. My master's been worried sick. Quick now, tell Musashi I'm here."

Tarōzaemon went into the house and reappeared a minute later, saying, "He's still in his room. He's sleeping."

"Sleeping?" Nuinosuke was appalled.

"He was up late last night, talking with me over some sake."

"This is no time to be sleeping. Wake him up. Right now!"

The merchant, refusing to be pressured, showed Nuinosuke and Iori into a guest room before going to awaken Musashi.

When Musashi joined them, he appeared well rested, eyes as clear as a baby's.

"Good morning," he said cheerfully as he seated himself. "Is there something I can do for you?"

Nuinosuke, deflated by the nonchalant greeting, silently handed him Sado's letter.

"How good of him to write," said Musashi, raising the letter to his forehead before breaking the seal and opening it. Iori was staring a hole through Musashi, who acted as if he wasn't even there. After reading the letter, he rolled it up and said, "I'm grateful for Sado's thoughtfulness." Only then did he glance at Iori, causing the boy to lower his head to hide his tears.

Musashi wrote a reply and handed it to Nuinosuke. "I've explained everything in the letter," he said, "but be sure to convey my thanks and my best wishes." He added that they were not to worry. He would go to Funashima in his own good time.

There was nothing they could do, so they left. Iori hadn't said a word to Musashi, nor Musashi to him. Yet the two had communicated to each other the mutual devotion of teacher and pupil.

As Sado read Musashi's reply, a look of relief spread across his face. The letter said:

> My deepest thanks for your offer of a boat to take me to Funashima. I do not deem myself worthy of such an honor. Moreover, I do not feel that I should accept. Please take into consideration that Kojirō and I are facing each other as opponents, and that he is using a boat provided by Lord Tadatoshi. If I were to go in your

boat, it would appear that you were opposing his lordship. I do not think you should do anything on my behalf.

Although I should have told you this earlier, I refrained because I knew you would insist upon helping me. Rather than involve you, I came and stayed at Tarōzaemon's house. I shall also have the use of one of his boats to go to Funashima, at the hour I think appropriate. Of that you may rest assured.

Deeply impressed, Sado stared silently at the writing for a time. It was a good letter, modest, thoughtful, considerate, and he was now ashamed of his agitation of the day before.

"Nuinosuke."

"Yes, sir."

"Take this letter and show it to Magobeinojō and his comrades, as well as the others concerned."

Nuinosuke had just left, when a servant came in and said, "If your business is finished, sir, you should get ready to leave now."

"Yes, of course, but there's still plenty of time," Sado replied quietly.

"It's not early. Kakubei's already left."

"That's his business. Iori, come here a minute."

"Sir?"

"Are you a man, Iori?"

"I think so."

"Do you think you can keep from crying, whatever happens?"

"Yes, sir."

"All right then, you can go to Funashima with me as my attendant. But remember one thing: we may have to pick up Musashi's corpse and bring it back with us. Could you still keep from crying?"

"Yes, sir. I will, I swear I will."

Nuinosuke had no sooner hurried through the gate

than a shabbily dressed woman called to him. "Pardon me, sir, but are you a retainer in this house?"

Nuinosuke stopped and looked at her suspiciously. "What do you want?"

"Forgive me. Looking the way I do, I shouldn't be standing in front of your gate."

"Well, why are you doing it, then?"

"I wanted to ask . . . it's about the fight today. People are saying Musashi's run away. Is that true?"

"You stupid wench! How dare you! You're talking about Miyamoto Musashi. Do you think he'd do a thing like that? Just wait until eight o'clock and you'll see. I've just been to see Musashi."

"You saw him?"

"Who are you?"

She dropped her eyes. "I'm an acquaintance of Musashi."

"Hmph. But still you worry about groundless rumors? All right—I'm in a hurry, but I'll show you a letter from Musashi." He read it aloud for her, not noticing the man with tearful eyes looking over his shoulder. When he did notice, he jerked his shoulder back and said, "Who are you? What do you think you're doing?"

Wiping the tears from his eyes, the man bowed sheepishly. "Sorry. I'm with this woman."

"Her husband?"

"Yes, sir. Thank you for showing us the letter. I feel like I've actually seen Musashi. Don't you, Akemi?"

"Yes; I feel so much better. Let's go find a place to watch."

Nuinosuke's anger evaporated. "If you go to the top of that hill over there by the shore, you should be able to see Funashima. As clear as it is today, you might even be able to make out the sandbar."

"We're sorry to have made a nuisance of ourselves when you're in a hurry. Please forgive us."

As they started to walk away, Nuinosuke said, "Just

a minute—what are your names? If you don't mind, I'd like to know."

They turned and bowed. "My name's Matahachi. I was born in the same village as Musashi."

"My name's Akemi."

Nuinosuke nodded and ran off.

They watched him for a few moments, exchanged glances and hurried on to the hill. From there, they could see Funashima jutting up among a number of other islands, the mountains of Nagato in the distance beyond. They spread some reed matting on the ground and sat down. The waves rumbled below them, and a pine needle or two floated down. Akemi took the baby from her back and began nursing it. Matahachi, his hands on his knees, stared fixedly out over the water.

26

The Marriage

Nuinosuke went first to Magobeinojō's house, showed him the letter and explained the circumstances. He left immediately, not even taking time for a cup of tea, and made quick stops at the other five houses.

Up the beach from the shore commissioner's office, he positioned himself behind a tree and watched the bustle that had been going on since early morning. Several teams of samurai had already left for Funashima—the ground cleaners, the witnesses, the guards—each group in a separate boat. On the beach another small boat stood ready for Kojirō. Tadatoshi had had it built especially for this occasion, of new timber, with new water brooms and new hemp-palm ropes.

The people seeing Kojirō off numbered about a hundred. Nuinosuke recognized some as friends of the swordsman; many others he did not know.

Kojirō finished his tea and came out of the commissioner's office, accompanied by the officials. Having entrusted his favorite pony to friends, he walked across the sand toward the boat. Tatsunosuke followed close behind. The crowd silently arranged itself into two rows and made way for their champion. Seeing the way Kojirō was dressed made many imagine that they themselves were about to go into battle.

He had on a narrow-sleeved silk kimono, solid white

with a raised figured pattern; over this, a sleeveless cloak of brilliant red. His purple leather *hakama* was of the type that is gathered just below the knees and is tight, like leggings, on the calf. His straw sandals appeared to have been dampened slightly to keep them from slipping. Besides the short sword he always carried, he had the Drying Pole, which he had not used since becoming an official in the House of Hosokawa. His white, full-cheeked face was a study in calm above the flaming red of his cloak. There was something grand, something almost beautiful, about Kojirō today.

Nuinosuke could see that Kojirō's smile was quiet and confident. Flashing his grin in all directions, he looked happy and perfectly at ease.

Kojirō stepped into the boat. Tatsunosuke got in after him. There were two crewmen, one in the prow and the other manning the scull. Amayumi perched on Tatsunosuke's fist.

Once clear of the shore, the sculler moved his arms with great languid strokes, and the little vessel glided gently forward.

Startled by the cries of the well-wishers, the falcon flapped its wings.

The crowd broke up into small groups and slowly dispersed, marveling over Kojirō's calm demeanor and praying that he would win this fight of all fights.

"I must get back," thought Nuinosuke, remembering his responsibility to see that Sado departed on time. As he turned away, he caught sight of a girl. Omitsu's body was pressed tightly against the trunk of a tree, and she was crying.

Feeling it indecent to stare, Nuinosuke averted his eyes and slipped away noiselessly. Out in the street again, he took a parting look at Kojirō's boat, then at Omitsu. "Everyone has a public and private life," he thought. "Behind all that fanfare, a woman stands weeping her heart out."

On the boat, Kojirō asked Tatsunosuke for the falcon and held out his left arm. Tatsunosuke transferred Amayumi to his fist and respectfully moved away.

The tide was flowing swiftly. The day was perfect—clear sky, crystal water—but the waves were rather high. Each time water splashed over the gunwale, the falcon, in a fighting mood, ruffled its feathers.

When they were about halfway to the island. Kojirō removed the band from its leg and threw the bird into the air, saying, "Go back to the castle."

As though hunting as usual, Amayumi attacked a fleeing seabird, sending down a flurry of white feathers. But when its master did not call it back, it swooped down low over the islands, then soared into the sky and disappeared.

After releasing the falcon, Kojirō began stripping himself of the Buddhist and Shinto good-luck charms and writings showered on him by his supporters, casting them overboard, one by one—even the cotton underrobe with the embroidered Sanskrit charm given him by his aunt.

"Now," he said softly, "I can relax." Faced with a life-or-death situation, he did not want to be bothered with memories or personalities. Being reminded of all those people who were praying for his victory was a burden. Their good wishes, no matter how sincere, were now more of a hindrance than a help. What mattered now was himself, his naked self.

The salty breeze caressed his silent face. His eyes were fixed on the green pines of Funashima.

In Shimonoseki, Tarōzaemon walked past a row of beach sheds and entered his shop. "Sasuke," he called. "Hasn't anybody seen Sasuke?" Sasuke was among the youngest of his many employees, but also one of the brightest. Treasured as a household servant, he also helped out in the shop from time to time.

"Good morning," said Tarōzaemon's manager, emerging from his station in the accounting office. "Sasuke was here just a few minutes ago." Turning to a young assistant, he said, "Go find Sasuke. Hurry."

The manager started to bring Tarōzaemon up to date on business matters, but the merchant cut him off, shaking his head as though a mosquito were after him. "What I want to know is whether anybody's been here looking for Musashi."

"As a matter of fact, there was someone here already this morning."

"The messenger from Nagaoka Sado? I know about him. Anybody else?"

The manager rubbed his chin. "Well, I didn't see him myself, but I'm told that a dirty-looking man with sharp eyes came last night. He was carrying a long oak staff and asked to see 'Musashi *Sensei*.' They had a hard time getting rid of him."

"Somebody blabbed. And after I told them how important it was to keep quiet about Musashi's being here."

"I know. I told them too, in no uncertain terms. But you can't do anything with the young ones. Having Musashi here makes them feel important."

"How did you get rid of the man?"

"Sōbei told him he was mistaken, Musashi's never been here. He finally left, whether he believed it or not. Sōbei noticed there were two or three people waiting outside for him, one a woman."

Sasuke came running up from the pier. "Do you want me, sir?"

"Yes. I wanted to make sure you're ready. It's very important, you know."

"I realize that, sir. I've been up since before sunrise. I washed in cold water and put on a new white cotton loincloth."

"Good. The boat's all ready, the way I told you last night?"

'Well, there wasn't much to do. I picked out the fastest and cleanest of the boats, sprinkled salt around to purify it and swabbed it down inside and out. I'm ready to leave whenever Musashi is."

"Where's the boat?"

"On the shore with the other boats."

After thinking a moment, Tarōzaemon said, "We'd better move it. Too many people will notice when Musashi leaves. He doesn't want that. Take it up by the big pine, the one called the Heike Pine. Hardly anyone goes by there."

"Yes, sir."

The shop, usually quite busy, was nearly deserted. Nervously upset, Tarōzaemon went out into the street. Here and in Moji, on the opposite shore, people were taking the day off—men who appeared to be samurai from neighboring fiefs, rōnin, Confucian scholars, blacksmiths, armorers, lacquer-makers, priests, townsmen of all descriptions, some farmers from the surrounding countryside. Scented women in veils and broad traveling hats. Fishermen's wives with children on their backs or clinging to their hands. They were all moving in the same general direction, trying vainly to get closer to the island, though there was no vantage point from which anything smaller than a tree could be seen.

"I see what Musashi means," thought Tarōzaemon. To be set upon by this mob of sightseers, to whom the fight was merely a spectacle, would be unendurable.

Returning to his house, he found the whole place fastidiously clean. In the room open to the beach, wave patterns flickered on the ceiling.

"Where have you been, Father? I've been looking for you." Otsuru came in with tea.

"Nowhere in particular." He lifted his teacup and gazed pensively into it.

Otsuru had come to spend some time with her beloved father. By chance, traveling from Sakai on the same vessel with Musashi, she had discovered they both had ties with Iori. When Musashi came to pay his respects to Tarōzaemon and thank him for taking care of the boy, the merchant had insisted Musashi stay at his house and had instructed Otsuru to look after him.

The night before, while Musashi talked to his host, Otsuru sat in the next room sewing the new loincloth and stomach wrapper he'd said he wanted on the day of the bout. She had already prepared a new black kimono, from which at a moment's notice she could remove the basting used to keep the sleeves and skirt properly folded until time for use.

It crossed Tarōzaemon's mind that Otsuru just might be falling in love with Musashi. There was a worried look on her face; something serious was on her mind.

"Otsuru, where's Musashi? Have you given him his breakfast?"

"Oh, yes. Long ago. After that, he shut the door to his room."

"Getting ready, I suppose."

"No, not yet."

"What's he doing?"

"He seems to be painting a picture."

"Now?"

"Yes."

"Hmm. We were talking about painting, and I asked him if he'd paint a picture for me. I guess I shouldn't have done that."

"He said he'd finish it before he left. He's painting one for Sasuke too."

"Sasuke?" Tarōzaemon echoed incredulously. He was growing more and more nervous. "Doesn't he know it's getting late? You should see all the people milling about the streets."

"From the look on Musashi's face, you'd think he'd forgotten the bout."

"Well, it's no time to be painting. Go tell him that. Be polite, but let him know that can wait till later."

"Why me? I couldn't . . ."

"And why not?" His suspicion that she was in love was confirmed. Father and daughter communicated silently but perfectly. Grumbling good-naturedly, "Silly child. Why are you crying?" he got up and went toward Musashi's room.

Musashi was kneeling silently, as though in meditation, his brush, ink box and brush pot beside him. He had already finished one painting—a heron beneath a willow tree. The paper before him now was still blank. He was considering what to draw. Or more exactly, quietly trying to put himself into the right frame of mind, for that was necessary before he could visualize the picture or know the technique he would employ.

He saw the white paper as the great universe of nonexistence. A single stroke would give rise to existence within it. He could evoke rain or wind at will, but whatever he drew, his heart would remain in the painting forever. If his heart was tainted, the picture would be tainted; if his heart was listless, so would the picture be. If he attempted to make a show of his craftsmanship, it could not be concealed. Men's bodies fade away, but ink lives on. The image of his heart would continue to breathe after he himself was gone.

He realized that his thoughts were holding him back. He was on the brink of entering the world of nonexistence, of letting his heart speak for itself, independent of his ego, free from the personal touch of his hand. He tried to be empty, waiting for that sublime state in which his heart could speak in unison with the universe, selfless and unhampered.

The sounds from the street did not reach his room. Today's bout seemed completely apart from himself. He was conscious merely of the tremulous movements of the bamboo in the inner garden.

"May I intrude?" The shoji behind him opened noiselessly, and Tarōzaemon peered in. It seemed wrong, almost evil, to barge in, but he braced himself and said, "I'm sorry to distract you when you seem to be enjoying your work so."

"Ah, please come in."

"It's nearly time to leave."

"I know."

"Everything's ready. All the things you'll need are in the next room."

"That's very kind of you."

"Please don't worry about the paintings. You can finish them when you come back from Funashima."

"Oh, it's nothing. I feel very fresh this morning. It's a good time to paint."

"But you have to think of the time."

"Yes, I know."

"Whenever you want to make your preparations, just call. We're waiting to help you."

"Thank you very much." Tarōzaemon started to leave, but Musashi said, "What time is high tide?"

"At this season, the tide's lowest between six and eight in the morning. It should be on the rise again about now."

"Thank you," Musashi said absently, again addressing his attention to the white paper.

Tarōzaemon quietly closed the shoji and went back to the parlor. He intended to sit down and wait quietly, but before long his nerves got the better of him. He rose and strode out to the veranda, from where he could see the current running through the strait. The water was already advancing on the beach.

"Father."

"What is it?"

"It's time for him to leave. I put his sandals out at the garden entrance."

"He's not ready yet."

"Still painting?"

"Yes."

"I thought you were going to make him stop and get ready."

"He knows what time it is."

A small boat pulled up on the beach nearby, and Tarōzaemon heard his name called. It was Nuinosuke, asking, "Has Musashi left yet?" When Tarōzaemon said no, Nuinosuke said rapidly, "Please tell him to get ready and start as quickly as possible. Kojirō's already left, and so has Lord Hosokawa. My master's leaving from Kokura right now."

"I'll do my best."

"Please! Maybe I sound like an old woman, but we want to be sure he's not late. It'd be a shame to bring dishonor on himself at this point." He rowed away hurriedly, leaving the shipping broker and his daughter to fret by themselves on the veranda. They counted the seconds, glancing from time to time toward the little room in the back, from which came not the slightest sound.

Soon a second boat arrived with a messenger from Funashima, sent to hurry Musashi along.

Musashi opened his eyes at the sound of shoji opening. There was no need for Otsuru to announce her presence. When she told him about the boat from Funashima, he nodded and smiled affably. "I see," he said, and left the room.

Otsuru glanced at the floor where he had been sitting. The piece of paper was now heavily blotched with ink. At first the picture looked like an indistinct cloud, but she soon saw that it was a landscape of the "broken ink" variety. It was still wet.

"Please give that picture to your father," Musashi called above the sound of splashing water. "And the other one to Sasuke."

"Thank you. You really shouldn't have done it."

"I'm sorry I don't have anything better to offer, after all the trouble you've gone to, but I hope your father will accept it as a keepsake."

Otsuru replied thoughtfully, "Tonight, by all means, come back and sit by the fire with my father, as you did last night."

Hearing the rustling of clothes in the next room, Otsuru felt pleased. At last he was getting dressed. Then there was silence again, and the next thing she knew, he was talking to her father. The conversation was very brief, only a few succinct words. As she passed through the next room, she noticed he had neatly folded his old clothes and placed them in a box in the corner. An indescribable loneliness seized her. She bent over and nestled her face against the still warm kimono.

"Otsuru!" called her father. "What are you doing? He's leaving!"

"Yes, Father." She brushed her fingers over her cheeks and eyelids and ran to join him.

Musashi was already at the garden gate, which he had chosen to avoid being seen. Father, daughter and four or five others from the house and shop came as far as the gate. Otsuru was too overwrought to utter a word. When Musashi's eyes turned toward her, she bowed like the others.

"Farewell," said Musashi. He went through the low gate of woven grass, closed it behind him and said, "Take good care of yourselves." By the time they raised their heads, he was walking rapidly away.

They stared after him, but Musashi's head did not turn.

"I guess that's the way it's supposed to be with samurai," someone mumbled. "He leaves—just like that: no speech, no elaborate good-byes, nothing."

Otsuru disappeared immediately. A few seconds later, her father retreated into the house.

The Heike Pine stood in solitude about two hundred yards up the beach. Musashi walked toward it, his mind completely at rest. He had put all his thoughts into the black ink of the landscape painting. It had felt good to be painting, and he considered his effort a success.

Now for Funashima. He was setting forth calmly, as though this were any other journey. He had no way of knowing whether he would ever return, but he had stopped thinking about it. Years ago, when at the age of twenty-two he had approached the spreading pine at Ichijōji, he had been very keyed up, shadowed by a sense of impending tragedy. He had gripped his lonely sword with intense determination. Now he felt nothing.

It was not that the enemy today was less to be feared than the hundred men he had confronted then. Far from it. Kojirō, fighting alone, was a more formidable opponent than any army the Yoshioka School could have mounted against him. There was not the least doubt in Musashi's mind but that he was going into the fight of his life.

"*Sensei!*"

"Musashi!"

Musashi's mind did a turn at the sound of the voices and the sight of two people running toward him. For an instant he was dazed.

"Gonnosuke!" he exclaimed. "And Granny! How did you two get here?"

Both, grimy from travel, knelt in the sand in front of him.

"We had to come," said Gonnosuke.

"We came to see you off," said Osugi. "And I came to apologize to you."

"Apologize? To me?"

"Yes. For everything. I must ask you to forgive me."

He looked inquiringly at her face. The words sounded unreal. "Why do you say that, Granny? Has something happened?"

She stood with her hands clasped pleadingly. "What can I say? I've done so many evil things, I can't hope to apologize for all of them. It was all . . . all a horrible mistake. I was blinded by my love for my son, but now I know the truth. Please forgive me."

He stared at her for a moment, then knelt and took her hand. He dared not raise his eyes, for fear there might be tears in them. Seeing the old woman so contrite made him feel guilty. But he felt gratitude too. Her hand trembled; even his was quivering slightly.

It took him a moment to pull himself together. "I believe you, Granny. I'm grateful to you for coming.

Now I can face death without regrets, go into the bout with my spirit free and my heart untroubled."

"Then you'll forgive me?"

"Of course I will, if you'll forgive me for all the trouble I've caused you since I was a boy."

"Of course; but enough of me. There's another person who needs your help. Someone who's very, very sad." She turned, inviting him to look.

Under the Heike Pine, looking shyly at them, her face pale and dewy with anticipation, stood Otsū.

"Otsū!" he shouted. In a second, he was before her, not knowing himself how his feet had transported him there. Gonnosuke and Osugi stood where they were, wishing they could disappear into thin air and leave the shore to the couple alone.

"Otsū, you've come."

Words did not exist to bridge the chasm of years, to convey the world of feeling brimming inside him.

"You don't look well. Are you ill?" He mumbled the words, like an isolated line from a long poem.

"A little." Eyes lowered, she struggled to remain cool, to keep her wits about her. This moment—perhaps the last—must not be spoiled, nor wasted.

"Is it just a cold?" he asked. "Or something serious? What's wrong? Where have you been these past few months?"

"I went back to the Shippōji last fall."

"Back home?"

"Yes." She looked straight at him, her eyes becoming as limpid as the ocean depths, struggling to hold back the tears. "But there's no real home for an orphan like me. Only the home inside me."

"Don't talk like that. Why, even Osugi seems to have opened her heart to you. That makes me very happy. You must recover your health and learn to be happy. For me."

"I'm happy now."

"Are you? If that's true, I'm happy too. . . ."

310

Otsū . . ." He bent toward her. She stood stiffly, conscious of Osugi and Gonnosuke. Musashi, who had forgotten them, put his arm around her and brushed his cheek against hers.

"You're so thin . . . so thin." He was acutely conscious of her fevered breathing. "Otsū, please forgive me. I may seem heartless, but I'm not, not where you're concerned."

"I . . . I know that."

"Do you? Truly?"

"Yes, but I beg you, say one word for me. Just one word. Tell me that I'm your wife."

"It would spoil it if I told you what you know already."

"But . . . but . . ." She was sobbing with her whole body, but with a burst of strength, she seized his hand and cried, "Say it. Say I'm your wife throughout this life."

He nodded, slowly, silently. Then one by one he pulled her delicate fingers from his arm and stood erect. "A samurai's wife must not weep and go to pieces when he goes off to war. Laugh for me, Otsū. Send me away with a smile. This may be your husband's last departure."

Both knew the time had come. For a brief moment, he looked at her and smiled. Then he said, "Until then."

"Yes. Until then." She wanted to return his smile but only managed to hold back the tears.

"Farewell." He turned and walked with firm strides toward the water's edge. A parting word rose to her throat but refused to be uttered. The tears welled up irrepressibly. She could no longer see him.

The strong, salty wind ruffled Musashi's sideburns. His kimono flapped briskly.

"Sasuke! Bring the boat a little closer."

Though he had been waiting for over two hours and knew Musashi was on the beach, Sasuke had carefully kept his eyes averted. Now he looked at Musashi and said, "Right away, sir."

With a few strong, rapid movements, he poled the boat in. When it touched shore, Musashi jumped lightly into the prow, and they moved out to sea.

"Otsū! Stop!" The shout was Jōtarō's.

Otsū was running straight toward the water. He raced after her. Startled, Gonnosuke and Osugi joined in the chase.

"Otsū, stop! What are you doing?"

"Don't be foolish!"

Reaching her simultaneously, they threw their arms around her and held her back.

"No, no," she protested, shaking her head slowly. "You don't understand."

"Wh-what are you trying to do?"

"Let me sit down, by myself." Her voice was calm.

They released her, and she walked with dignity to a spot a few yards away, where she knelt on the sand, seemingly exhausted. But she had found her strength. She straightened her collar, smoothed her hair, and bowed toward Musashi's little craft.

"Go without regrets," she said.

Osugi knelt and bowed. Then Gonnosuke. And Jōtarō. After coming all the way from Himeji, Jōtarō had missed his chance to speak to Musashi, despite his intense yearning to say a parting word. His disappointment was softened by the knowledge that he had given his share of Musashi's time to Otsū.

27

The Soul of the Deep

With the tide at its peak, the water coursed through the strait like a swollen torrent in a narrow ravine. The wind was to their rear, and the boat moved swiftly across the waves. Sasuke looked proud; he intended to be praised for his work with the scull today.

Musashi was seated in the middle of the boat, his knees spread wide. "Does it take long to get there?" he asked.

"Not very long with this tide, but we're late."

"Mm."

"It's well after eight o'clock."

"Yes, it is, isn't it? What time do you think we'll get there?"

"It'll probably be ten or a little after."

"That's just right."

The sky Musashi looked at that day—the sky Ganryū looked at—was a deep azure. Snow covering the ridge of the Nagato Mountains looked like a white streamer fluttering across a cloudless sky. The houses of the city of Mojigasaki and the wrinkles and crevices of Mount Kazashi were clearly discernible. On the mountainsides, droves of people were straining their eyes toward the islands.

"Sasuke, may I have this?"

"What is it?"

"This broken oar in the bottom of the boat."

"I don't need it. Why do you want it?"

"It's about the right size," Musashi said cryptically. He held the slightly waterlogged oar out with one hand and squinted down it to see if it was straight. One edge of the blade was split off.

He placed the oar on his knee and, totally absorbed, began carving with his short sword. Sasuke cast backward glances toward Shimonoseki several times, but Musashi seemed oblivious of the people he had left behind. Was this the way a samurai approached a life-and-death battle? To a townsman like Sasuke, it seemed cold and heartless.

Musashi finished his carving and brushed the chips from his *hakama*. "Do you have something I could put around me?" he asked.

"Are you cold?"

"No, but the water's splashing in."

"There should be a quilted coat under the seat."

Musashi picked up the garment and threw it over his shoulders. Then he took some paper from his kimono and began rolling and twisting each sheet into a string. When he had accumulated more than twenty of these, he twisted them together end to end to make two cords, which he then braided to make a *tasuki,* the band used to tie sleeves back when fighting. Sasuke had heard that making *tasuki* from paper was a secret art, passed down from generation to generation, but Musashi made the process look easy. Sasuke watched with admiration the deftness of his fingers and the grace with which he slipped the *tasuki* over his arms.

"Is that Funashima?" asked Musashi, pointing.

"No. That's Hikojima, part of the Hahajima group. Funashima's a thousand yards or so to the northeast. It's easy to recognize because it's flat and looks like a long sandbar. There between Hikojima and Izaki is the Strait of Ondo. You've probably heard of it."

"To the west, then, that must be Dairinoura in Buzen Province."

"That's right."

"I remember now. The inlets and islands around here were where Yoshitsune won the last battle against the Heike."

Sasuke was growing more nervous with each stroke of the scull. He had broken out in a cold sweat; his heart was palpitating. It seemed eerie to be talking about inconsequential matters. How could a man going into battle be so calm?

It would be a fight to the death; no question about that. Would he be taking a passenger back to the mainland later? Or a cruelly maimed corpse? There was no way of knowing. Musashi, thought Sasuke, was like a white cloud floating across the sky.

This was not a pose on Musashi's part, for in fact he was thinking of nothing at all. He was, if anything, a little bored.

He looked over the side of the boat at the swirling blue water. It was deep here, infinitely deep, and alive with what seemed to be eternal life. But water had no fixed, determined form. Was it not because man had a fixed, determined form that he cannot possess eternal life? Does not true life begin only when tangible form has been lost?

To Musashi's eyes, life and death seemed like so much froth. He felt goose pimples on his skin, not from the cold water but because his body felt a premonition. Though his mind had risen above life and death, body and mind were not in accord. When every pore of his body, as well as his mind, forgot, there would remain nothing inside his being but the water and the clouds.

They were passing Teshimachi Inlet on Hikojima. Unseen by them were some forty samurai standing watch on the shore. All were supporters of Ganryū, and most were in the service of the House of Hosokawa. In violation of Tadatoshi's orders, they had crossed over to

Funashima two days earlier. In the event that Ganryū was beaten, they were ready to take revenge.

This morning, when Nagaoka Sado, Iwama Kakubei and the men assigned to stand guard arrived on Funashima, they discovered this band of samurai, upbraided them severely and ordered them to go to Hikojima. But since most of the officials were in sympathy with them, they went unpunished. Once they were off Funashima, it was not the officials' responsibility what they did.

"Are you sure it's Musashi?" one of them was saying.

"It has to be."

"Is he alone?"

"He seems to be. He's got a cloak or something around his shoulders."

"He probably has on light armor and wants to hide it."

"Let's go."

Tensely eager for battle, they piled into their boats and lay in readiness. All were armed with swords, but in the bottom of each boat lay a long lance.

"Musashi's coming!"

The cry was heard around Funashima only moments later.

The sound of the waves, the voices of the pines and the rustling of the bamboo grass blended softly. Since early morning the little island had had a desolate air, despite the presence of the officials. A white cloud rising from the direction of Nagato grazed past the sun, darkening the tree and bamboo leaves. The cloud passed, and brightness returned.

It was a very small island. At the north end was a low hill, covered with pine trees. To the south the ground was level at a height about half that of the hill until the island dropped off into the shoals.

A canopy had been hung between some trees at a considerable distance from the shore. The officials and their attendants waited quietly and inconspicuously, not wishing to give Musashi the impression that they were trying to add to the dignity of the local champion.

Now, two hours past the appointed time, they were beginning to show their anxiety and resentment. Twice they had sent fast boats out to hurry Musashi on.

The lookout from the reef ran up to the officials and said, "It's him! No doubt about it."

"Has he really come?" asked Kakubei, rising involuntarily, and by doing so committing a serious breach of etiquette. As an official witness, he was expected to remain coolly reserved. His excitement was only natural, however, and was shared by others in his party, who also stood up.

Realizing his gaffe, Kakubei brought himself under control and motioned to the others to sit down again. It was essential that they not allow their personal preference for Ganryū to color their actions or their decision. Kakubei glanced toward Ganryū's waiting area. Tatsunosuke had hung a curtain with a gentian crest from several wild peach trees. Next to the curtain was a new wooden bucket with a bamboo-handled ladle. Ganryū, impatient after his long wait, had asked for a drink of water and was now resting in the shade of the curtain.

Nagaoka Sado's position was beyond Ganryū's and slightly higher. He was surrounded by guards and attendants, Iori at his side. When the lookout arrived with his news, the boy's face—even his lips—turned pale. Sado was seated in formal fashion, straight and motionless. His helmet shifted slightly to his right, as though he were looking at the sleeve of his kimono. In a low voice, he called Iori's name.

"Yes, sir." Iori bowed to the ground before looking up under Sado's helmet. Unable to control his excitement, he was trembling from head to feet.

"Iori," said Sado, looking straight into the boy's eyes. "Watch everything that happens. Don't miss a single thing. Keep in mind that Musashi has laid his life on the line to teach you what you are about to see.''

Iori nodded. His eyes sparkled like flames as he fixed his gaze on the reef. The white spray of the waves breaking against it dazzled his eyes. It was about two hundred yards away, so it would be impossible for him to see the small movements and the breathing of the fighters. But it was not the technical aspects Sado wanted him to watch. It was the dramatic moment when a samurai enters a life-and-death struggle. This was what would live on in his mind and influence him throughout his life.

The waves of grass rose and fell. Greenish insects darted hither and thither. A small, delicate butterfly moved from one blade of grass to another, then was seen no more.

"He's nearly here," gasped Iori.

Musashi's boat approached the reef slowly. It was almost exactly ten o'clock.

Ganryū stood up and walked unhurriedly down the hillock behind the waiting stations. He bowed to the officials on his right and left and walked quietly through the grass to the shore.

The approach to the island was an inlet of sorts, where waves became wavelets, then mere ripples. Musashi could see the bottom through the clear blue water.

"Where should I land?" asked Sasuke, who had tempered his stroke and was scanning the shore with his eyes.

"Go straight in." Musashi threw off the quilted coat.

The bow advanced at a very restrained pace. Sasuke could not bring himself to stroke with vigor; his arms moved only slightly, exerting little force. The sound of bulbuls was in the air.

"Sasuke."

"Yes, sir."

"It's shallow enough here. There's no need to get too close. You don't want to damage your boat. Besides, it's about time for the tide to turn."

Silently, Sasuke fixed his eyes on a tall, thin pine tree, standing alone. Underneath it, the wind was playing with a brilliant red cloak.

Sasuke started to point but realized that Musashi had already seen his opponent. Keeping his eyes on Ganryū, Musashi took a russet hand towel from his obi, folded it in four lengthwise, and tied it around his windblown hair. Then he shifted his short sword to the front of his obi. Taking off his long sword, he laid it in the bottom of the boat and covered it with a reed mat. In his right hand, he held the wooden sword he had made from the broken oar.

"This is far enough," he said to Sasuke.

Ahead of them was nearly two hundred feet of water. Sasuke took a couple of long strokes with the scull. The boat lurched forward and grounded on a shoal, the keel shuddering as it rose.

At that moment, Musashi, his *hakama* hitched high on both sides, jumped lightly into the sea, landing so lightly he made barely a splash. He strode rapidly toward the waterline, his wooden sword cutting through the spray.

Five steps. Ten steps. Sasuke, abandoning his scull, watched in wonderment, unconscious of where he was, what he was doing.

As Ganryū streaked away from the pine like a red streamer, his polished scabbard caught the glint of the sun.

Sasuke was reminded of a silver fox tail. "Hurry!" The word flashed through his mind, but Ganryū was already at the water's edge. Sasuke, sure that Musashi was done for, couldn't bear to watch. He fell face down in the boat, chilled and trembling, hiding his face as if he were the one who might at any moment be split in two.

"Musashi!"

Ganryū planted his feet resolutely in the sand, unwilling to give up an inch.

Musashi stopped and stood still, exposed to the water and the wind. A hint of a grin appeared on his face.

"Kojirō," he said quietly. There was an unearthly fierceness in his eyes, a force pulling so irresistibly it threatened to draw Kojirō inexorably into peril and destruction. The waves washed his wooden sword.

Ganryū's were the eyes that shot fire. A bloodthirsty flame burned in his pupils, like rainbows of fierce intensity, seeking to terrify and debilitate.

"Musashi!"

No answer.

"Musashi!"

The sea rumbled ominously in the distance; the tide lapped and murmured at the two men's feet.

"You're late again, aren't you? Is that your strategy? As far as I'm concerned, it's a cowardly ploy. It's two hours past the appointed time. I was here at eight, just as I promised. I've been waiting."

Musashi did not reply.

"You did this at Ichijōji, and before that at the Rengeōin. Your method seems to be to throw your opponent off by deliberately making him wait. That trick will get you nowhere with Ganryū. Now prepare your spirit and come forward bravely, so future generations won't laugh at you. Come ahead and fight, Musashi!" The end of his scabbard rose high behind him as he drew the great Drying Pole. With his left hand, he slid the scabbard off and threw it into the water.

Waiting just long enough for a wave to strike the reef and retreat, Musashi suddenly said in a quiet voice, "You've lost, Kojirō."

"What?" Ganryū was shaken to the core.

"The fight's been fought. I say you've been defeated."

"What are you talking about?"

"If you were going to win, you wouldn't throw your scabbard away. You've cast away your future, your life."

"Words! Nonsense!"

"Too bad, Kojirō. Ready to fall? Do you want to get it over with fast?"

"Come . . . come forward, you bastard!"

"H-o-o-o!" Musashi's cry and the sound of the water rose to a crescendo together.

Stepping into the water, the Drying Pole positioned high above his head, Ganryū faced Musashi squarely. A line of white foam streaked across the surface as Musashi ran up on shore to Ganryū's left. Ganryū pursued.

Musashi's feet left the water and touched the sand at almost the same instant that Ganryū's sword—his whole body—hurtled at him like a flying fish. When Musashi sensed that the Drying Pole was coming toward him, his body was still at the end of the motion that had taken him out of the water, leaning slightly forward.

He held the wooden sword with both hands, extended out to the right behind him and partially hidden. Satisfied with his position, he half grunted, an almost noiseless sound that wafted before Ganryū's face. The Drying Pole had appeared to be on the verge of a downward slice, but it wavered slightly, then stopped. Nine feet away from Musashi, Ganryū changed direction by leaping nimbly to the right.

The two men stared at each other. Musashi, two or three paces from the water, had the sea to his back. Ganryū was facing him, his sword held high with both hands.

Their lives were totally absorbed in deadly combat, and both were free from conscious thought.

The scene of the battle was a perfect vacuum. But in the waiting stations and beyond the sound of the waves, countless people held their breath.

Above Ganryū hovered the prayers and the hopes of those who believed in him and wanted him to live, above Musashi the prayers and hopes of others.

Of Sado and Iori, on the island.

Of Otsū and Osugi and Gonnosuke, on the beach at Shimonoseki.

THE WAY OF LIFE AND DEATH

Of Akemi and Matahachi, on their hill in Kokura.

All their prayers were directed to heaven.

Here, hopes, prayers and the gods were of no assistance, nor was chance. There was only a vacuum, impersonal and perfectly impartial.

Is this vacuum, so difficult of achievement by one who has life, the perfect expression of the mind that has risen above thought and transcended ideas?

The two men spoke without speaking. Then to each came the unconscious realization of the other. The pores of their bodies stood out like needles directed at the adversary.

Muscles, flesh, nails, hair, even eyebrows—all bodily elements that partake of life—were united into a single force against the enemy, defending the living organism of which they were a part. The mind alone was one with the universe, clear and untroubled, like the reflection of the moon in a pond amidst the ragings of a typhoon. To reach this sublime immobility is the supreme achievement.

It seemed like eons, but the interval was in fact short—the time required for the waves to come in and recede half a dozen times.

Then a great shout—more than vocal, coming from the depths of being—shattered the instant. It came from Ganryū, and was followed immediately by Musashi's shout.

The two cries, like angry waves lashing a rocky shore, sent their spirits skyward. The challenger's sword, raised so high that it seemed to threaten the sun, streaked through the air like a rainbow.

Musashi threw his left shoulder forward, drew his right foot back and shifted his upper body into a position half-facing his opponent. His wooden sword, held in both hands, swept through the air at the same moment that the tip of the Drying Pole came down directly before his nose.

The breathing of the two combatants grew louder than the sound of the waves. Now the wooden sword was extended at eye level, the Drying Pole high above its bearer's head. Ganryū had bounded about ten paces away, where he had the sea to one side. Though he had not succeeded in injuring Musashi in his first attack, he had put himself in a much better position. Had he remained where he was, with the sun reflecting from the water into his eyes, his vision would soon have faltered, then his spirit, and he would have been at Musashi's mercy.

With renewed confidence, Ganryū began inching forward, keeping a sharp eye out for a chink in Musashi's defense and steeling his own spirit for a decisive move.

Musashi did the unexpected. Instead of proceeding slowly and cautiously, he strode boldly toward Ganryū, his sword projecting before him, ready to thrust into Ganryū's eyes. The artlessness of this approach brought Ganryū to a halt. He almost lost sight of Musashi.

The wooden sword rose straight in the air. With one great kick, Musashi leapt high, and folding his legs, reduced his six-foot frame to four feet or less.

"Y-a-a-ah!" Ganryū's sword screamed through the space above him. The stroke missed, but the tip of the Drying Pole cut through Musashi's headband, which went flying through the air.

Ganryū mistook it for his opponent's head, and a smile flitted briefly across his face. The next instant his skull broke like gravel under the blow of Musashi's sword.

As Ganryū lay where the sand met the grass, his face betrayed no consciousness of defeat. Blood streamed from his mouth, but his lips formed a smile of triumph.

"Oh, no!"

"Ganryū!"

Forgetting himself, Iwama Kakubei jumped up, and with him all his retinue, their faces distorted with shock. They they saw Nagaoka Sado and Iori, sitting calmly and sedately on their benches. Shamed, they somehow managed to keep from running forward. They tried to regain a degree of composure, but there was no concealing their grief and disillusion. Some swallowed hard, refusing to believe what they had seen, and their minds went blank.

In an instant, the island was as quiet and still as it had ever been. Only the rustle of the pines and the swaying grasses mocked the frailty and impermanence of mankind.

Musashi was watching a small cloud in the sky. As he did, his soul returned to his body, and it became possible for him to distinguish between the cloud and himself, between his body and the universe.

Sasaki Kojirō Ganryū did not return to the world of the living. Lying face down, he still had a grip on his sword. His tenacity was still visible. There was no sign of anguish on his face. Nothing but satisfaction at having fought a good fight, not the faintest shadow of regret.

The sight of his own headband lying on the ground sent shivers up and down Musashi's spine. Never in this life, he thought, would he meet another opponent like this. A wave of admiration and respect flowed over him. He was grateful to Kojirō for what the man had given him. In strength, in the will to fight, he ranked higher than Musashi, and it was because of this that Musashi had been able to excel himself.

What was it that had enabled Musashi to defeat Kojirō? Skill? The help of the gods? While knowing it was neither of these, Musashi was never able to express a reason in words. Certainly it was something more important than either strength or godly providence.

Kojirō had put his confidence in the sword of strength and skill. Musashi trusted in the sword of the spirit. That was the only difference between them.

Silently, Musashi walked the ten paces to Kojirō and knelt beside him. He put his left hand near Kojirō's nostrils and found there was still a trace of breath. "With the right treatment, he may recover," Musashi told himself. And he wanted to believe this, wanted to believe that this most valiant of all adversaries would be spared.

But the battle was over. It was time to go.

"Farewell," he said—to Kojirō, then to the officials on their benches.

Having bowed once to the ground, he ran to the reef and jumped into the boat. There was not a drop of blood on his wooden sword.

The tiny craft moved out to sea. Who is to say where? There is no record as to whether Ganryū's supporters on Hikojima attempted to take revenge.

People do not give up their loves and hates as long as life lasts. Waves of feeling come and go with the passage of time. Throughout Musashi's lifetime, there were those who resented his victory and criticized his conduct on that day. He rushed away, it was said, because he feared reprisal. He was confused. He even neglected to administer the coup de grace.

The world is always full of the sound of waves.

The little fishes, abandoning themselves to the waves, dance and sing and play, but who knows the heart of the sea, a hundred feet down? Who knows its depth?